U0057088

新制多益

NEW TOEIC

擬真試題600問

＋超詳解

宮野智靖　監修

入江 泉　著

葉紋芳　譯

CONTENTS

TEST 1 模擬試題 解答＋完全解析

正確答案一覽表

題號	答案	題號	答案	題號	答案	題號	答案	題號	答案
1	D	41	A	81	C	121	A	161	D
2	C	42	C	82	D	122	C	162	B
3	C	43	A	83	D	123	C	163	D
4	A	44	D	84	A	124	A	164	A
5	B	45	A	85	A	125	B	165	B
6	A	46	D	86	A	126	A	166	B
7	C	47	D	87	D	127	B	167	D
8	B	48	A	88	A	128	B	168	D
9	C	49	B	89	B	129	C	169	C
10	B	50	C	90	A	130	D	170	D
11	A	51	C	91	D	131	B	171	A
12	C	52	B	92	C	132	B	172	D
13	C	53	B	93	B	133	A	173	C
14	B	54	C	94	B	134	C	174	A
15	A	55	B	95	C	135	C	175	C
16	A	56	B	96	D	136	D	176	C
17	B	57	D	97	A	137	A	177	D
18	C	58	A	98	C	138	B	178	B
19	A	59	D	99	A	139	D	179	B
20	B	60	B	100	B	140	C	180	A
21	C	61	C	101	D	141	B	181	C
22	B	62	C	102	A	142	A	182	D
23	A	63	A	103	D	143	C	183	D
24	B	64	A	104	B	144	B	184	B
25	A	65	D	105	D	145	C	185	A
26	C	66	B	106	D	146	D	186	C
27	B	67	C	107	C	147	D	187	C
28	C	68	C	108	D	148	B	188	A
29	A	69	B	109	B	149	A	189	D
30	B	70	D	110	A	150	B	190	D
31	B	71	B	111	B	151	C	191	A
32	D	72	D	112	C	152	B	192	B
33	B	73	C	113	B	153	C	193	A
34	C	74	A	114	C	154	D	194	C
35	C	75	D	115	D	155	A	195	D
36	A	76	B	116	A	156	B	196	A
37	D	77	C	117	C	157	C	197	B
38	C	78	B	118	A	158	C	198	C
39	D	79	A	119	D	159	A	199	A
40	A	80	A	120	C	160	C	200	C

PART 1

錄音原文與翻譯	解答與解析

 1

(A) She's looking at her watch.
(B) She's waving to someone.
(C) She's holding up a tool.
(D) She's talking on a phone.

(A) 她正在看手錶。
(B) 她正在向某人揮手。
(C) 她正把工具拿起來。
(D) 她正在講電話。

答案 (D) 〔人物（1人）〕

(D)適當表達女子的動作。(B)wave to～（向～揮手）是錯誤描述。(C)hold up～（拿起～）。hold有「手上拿著」之意，與fold（收折～、折疊、（手臂或腳）交叉）發音相似，須仔細分辨。

□ tool [tul] 名 工具

 2

(A) They're giving a presentation.
(B) They're setting up the stage.
(C) They're playing musical instruments.
(D) They're marching outside the theater.

(A) 他們正在發表演說。
(B) 他們正在架設舞台。
(C) 他們正在演奏樂器。
(D) 他們正在劇院外面遊行示威。

答案 (C) 〔人物（2人以上）〕

(C)適當表達正在演奏樂器的男子們的動作。(musical) instrument（樂器）。

□ give a presentation 發表演說
□ march [mɑrtʃ] 動 遊行示威

 3

(A) There are two pictures hung above the bed.
(B) Some pillows are piled on the floor.
(C) The bedcover has been straightened.
(D) Reading material has been placed on the couch.

(A) 床上方掛有 2 張畫。
(B) 有些枕頭被堆在地上。
(C) 床罩已經被拉直了。
(D) 閱讀刊物已經被放在長沙發上。

答案 (C) 〔無人物〕

(C)適當表達床的狀態。straighten為動詞，有「把皺褶的東西拉直」、「整理～」之意。(A)的hung是hang（掛～）的過去分詞，修飾前面的名詞，圖示僅掛一幅畫，所以描述錯誤。(C)與(D)為現在完成式被動語態〈have [has] been ＋過去分詞〉，若能聽懂動詞意思（本題是指straightened和placed），就算不理解文法結構，也不影響答題。

□ pillow [`pɪlo] 名 枕頭
□ pile [paɪl] 動 堆～
□ reading material 閱讀刊物
□ place [ples] 動 放～

錄音原文與翻譯	解答與解析

4 🇺🇸

(A) The dock overlooks the waterfront.
(B) The ferry has docked at the platform.
(C) Some people are moving toward the pier.
(D) Passengers are standing in line at the ticket booth.

(A) 碼頭俯瞰著水邊。
(B) 渡輪已停靠在登船處。
(C) 一些人正往碼頭移動。
(D) 乘客們正在票亭前排隊。

答案 (A) 〔人物（2人以上）〕

適當表達碼頭狀態的(A)是正確答案。overlook 指的是「主詞（某地點）俯瞰～」。因為船正在行進，所以(B)描述錯誤。platform一般是指「（車站的）月台」，這裡是指登船處。(C)描述的moving（移動）是錯的，因為人們並無移動至某處的動作。(D)雖難以判斷有無line（排隊），但ticket booth（票亭）是錯的。

□ dock [dɑk] 名動 碼頭、（船）駛入碼頭

5 🇨🇦

(A) The chairs have been stacked on the floor.
(B) The umbrellas have been folded up.
(C) The umbrellas are sheltering people from the sun.
(D) A covered yard is being swept.

(A) 椅子已經被堆在地上。
(B) 傘已經被收折起來。
(C) 傘正保護人們免受陽光照射。
(D) 有頂棚的庭院正被打掃著。

答案 (B) 〔無人物〕

(B)適當表達傘的狀態。fold up（收折～）和(A)的stack（堆積～）在Part 1是常用字。(D)因為圖片中沒有人物，所以是錯誤描述。swept是sweep（打掃～）的過去分詞。現在進行式被動語態〈is [are] being＋過去分詞〉（正被～）省略了〈by＋施予動作者〉

□ shelter A from B 保護A免受B影響

6 🇬🇧

(A) A man is seated by the rear of the vehicle.
(B) A woman is standing with her arms folded.
(C) There are two chairs facing away from each other.
(D) Some refreshments are being served.

(A) 一名男子坐在車後方。
(B) 一名女子正雙手交叉站著。
(C) 有兩張椅子互相背對著。
(D) 這裡有供應茶點。

答案 (A) 〔人物（2人以上）〕

(A)適當表達男子的狀態。rear（後面、後方）為名詞。記住car、vehicle、automobile等都是與「車」相關的類類單字。(B)with（和、保持～的狀態）後面的形容是錯的。從fold one's arms（雙手交叉）可知，with her arms folded是「保持雙手交叉的狀態」之意。(C)face（面對）後面是錯誤描述。(D)的refreshment用複數表達時，為「茶點」的意思。桌上雖可見飲料，但卻不是提供的點心。

□ vehicle ['viɪk!] 名 車

PART 2 CD 1 8-13

☑ 7 W 🇺🇸 W 🇬🇧

W: How often do you work overtime?
W: (A) For a week or so.
　　(B) We're extremely busy.
　　(C) Hardly ever.

W：你經常加班嗎？
W：(A) 大約一週左右。
　　(B) 我們非常忙。
　　(C) 幾乎沒有。

答案 (C) 〔疑問詞〕

How often～（多常）是問頻率，How many times～（多少次）是問次數，兩者有別。hardly ever是「幾乎沒有」之意，用在頻率或次數上，所以(C)是正確的。seldom（很少）也是同樣的意思及用法。只有hardly是表達「幾乎沒有」的程度。因為不是問有多久的時間，所以(A)是錯的。注意不要因work overtime（加班）聯想到busy而選(B)喔！

□ extremely [ɪk`strimlɪ] 副 非常

☑ 8 M 🇨🇦 M 🇦🇺

M: Why don't we have a working lunch tomorrow?
M: (A) Yes, I enjoy walking.
　　(B) Sounds good.
　　(C) It would take time.

M：我們明天何不來個午餐會議？
M：(A) 是的，我喜歡走路。
　　(B) 聽起來不錯。
　　(C) 它需要時間。

答案 (B) 〔特殊疑問句及對話表達〕

Why don't we～?（我們何不～）是在表達邀請對方。(B)即是接受邀請之意。可配合Why don't you～?（你（你們）何不～）這類的提議句型一起學習。這類句型常會搭配with me [us]（和我（們）一起）來邀約對方。(A)walking與問句的working發音類似，注意不要混淆。

☑ 9 W 🇬🇧 M 🇦🇺

W: When will the art gallery reopen?
M: (A) Through the entrance.
　　(B) He's a talented artist.
　　(C) Sometime next week.

W：藝術畫廊何時重新開放？
M：(A) 通過入口。
　　(B) 他是一位有天賦的藝術家。
　　(C) 下星期的某個時候。

答案 (C) 〔疑問詞〕

聽到When（何時），選擇提到「時間」的(C)才正確。sometime是「某天、某個時候」之意。(A)回答場所，所以不符合。(B)會誘使我們把問句中的art（藝術）與artist（藝術家）做連結，要注意。

□ reopen [ri`opən] 動 重新開放
□ entrance [`ɛntrəns] 名 入口
□ talented [`tæləntɪd] 形 有天賦的

☑ 10 M 🇦🇺 M 🇨🇦

M: Are you going to work at home tomorrow?
M: (A) I usually drive my car here.
　　(B) I'll be in the office in the morning.
　　(C) The traffic was very heavy.

M：你明天在家工作嗎？
M：(A) 我通常開車來這裡。
　　(B) 我明天早上會在辦公室。
　　(C) 交通非常繁忙。

答案 (B) 〔Yes / No〕

Are you going to～?（你將會～嗎？）是詢問對方的預定安排及想法。聽到「明天在家工作嗎？」，選擇(B)「明天早上會在辦公室（不在家）」才正確。(A)回答的是移動方式，與問題不符。

□ traffic [`træfɪk] 名 交通、通行

☑ 11 W 🇺🇸 M 🇨🇦

W: How's the project coming along?
M: (A) It'll be finished shortly.
　　(B) It's been a long time.
　　(C) He's coming, too.

W：計畫進展如何？
M：(A) 很快即將完成。
　　(B) 過很久時間了。
　　(C) 他也要來。

答案 (A) 〔疑問詞〕

come along有「（工作之類）進展」之意，用How（如何）來詢問計畫進展的狀況。針對問句，(A)回答「（計畫）很快即將完成」才是符合現狀。形容詞short（短的）字尾加上ly成為副詞，意即「不久，馬上」。問句的along（與come搭配，come along意為進展）和(B)a long（很長）可別混淆。(C)雖然跟問句一樣提及coming，但是He是誰並不清楚。

CD 1 14-18

錄音原文與翻譯	解答與解析

☑ **12** M 🇦🇺 W 🇬🇧

M：Who's recording the meeting minutes today?
W：(A) It belongs to Ms. Benson.
　　(B) I haven't listened to them.
　　(C) Our secretary will.

M：今天誰做會議紀錄？
W：(A) 它是班森 （Benson） 女士的東西。
　　(B) 我還沒有拿來聽過。
　　(C) 我們的祕書會做。

答案 (C) 　　　　　　疑問詞

Who's [Who is]～?是問「誰」，(C)具體說出「祕書」，所以是正確答案。is recording（將記錄～、正在記錄～）表示即將發生的現在進行式。Who's與Whose（關係代名詞所有格）同音，(A)有說出是誰的，如果誤把recording（記錄）視為名詞，就會選錯。(B)要注意的是，listen（聽）容易從問句的recording做聯想而選錯。

□ record [rɪˋkɔrd] 動 記錄
□ minute [ˋmɪnɪt] 名（慣用複數形）會議紀錄
□ belong to～　屬於～的物品

☑ **13** W 🇺🇸 M 🇨🇦

W：We've run out of envelopes.
M：(A) That's good exercise.
　　(B) I'll get some more letters.
　　(C) Have you checked the stationery cabinet?

W：我們已經把信封用完了。
M：(A) 那是很好的運動。
　　(B) 我去拿更多信紙來。
　　(C) 你去文具櫃看過了嗎？

答案 (C) 　　　　　　陳述句

run out of～意即「將～用完」。最常用現在完成式，表示「已經用到沒有了」。(C)「你去文具櫃看過了嗎？（＝文具櫃沒有信封嗎？）」最正確。如果把run（跑）當重點字可能就會誤選(A)exercise（運動）。(B)誘使我們將envelope（信封）與letter（信）做連結。

□ stationery [ˋsteʃən͵ɛrɪ] 名 文具

☑ **14** M 🇦🇺 W 🇬🇧

M：How far is it from the hotel to the ferry terminal?
W：(A) Not so fast.
　　(B) About a ten-minute walk.
　　(C) One-way or return?

M：從飯店到渡輪碼頭有多遠？
W：(A) 先別那麼快動作。
　　(B) 走路大約 10 分鐘。
　　(C) 單趟還是往返？

答案 (B) 　　　　　　疑問詞

How far～意指「多少距離或是有多遠」。可以回答具體的距離，如「大約2公里」，也可以回答如(B)「走路大約10分鐘」，用花費的時間來表現「距離遠近」。(A)要注意分辨far（遠）和fast（快）的發音。(C)描述內容會讓人從ferry（渡輪）聯想，但答案不符合問句。return在英式英文中是「來回的」意思。

☑ **15** W 🇺🇸 M 🇦🇺

W：Isn't this the new list of prices?
M：(A) No, it's from last month.
　　(B) Oh, we're far behind.
　　(C) It cost more than expected.

W：這不是新的價格清單嗎？
M：(A) 不是，它是上個月的。
　　(B) 喔，我們遠遠落後。
　　(C) 它的價格高於預期。

答案 (A) 　　　　特殊疑問句及對話表達

問句是否定疑問句。聽到「這不是新的價格清單嗎？」時，如果回答是肯定的，就答Yes，否定則答No，(A)回答No，表「不是新的價格清單」，接著說「是上個月的」，所以是正確答案。不過有些國家的肯定、否定表達不以前面的Yes / No為準，所以否定疑問句的回答出現Yes / No時，要以後面的內容為主。這裡的(A)回答它是上個月的（it's from last month），更能清楚理解。

☑ **16** M 🇨🇦 W 🇺🇸

M：When was George transferred to the Seattle office?
W：(A) At least five years ago.
　　(B) It opened before he started working.
　　(C) Even I've never been there.

M：喬治（George）是何時被調往西雅圖辦公室的？
W：(A) 至少 5 年前。
　　(B) 他開始上班之前某地就已營業了。
　　(C) 甚至連我都未曾去過那裡。

答案 (A) 　　　　　　疑問詞

當問到When（何時），回答「時間」的(A)最正確。這題是transfer A to B（將A調往B）的被動疑問句。at least意為「至少」，five years ago（5年前）是(A)的重要關鍵字。(B)before（在～之前）雖然是代表「時間」，但回答與問題不符。

□ at least　至少

錄音原文與翻譯	解答與解析

☑ **17** M 🇨🇦 W 🇬🇧

M: Did the camera you bought include batteries?
W: (A) I'll take them, thank you.
　　(B) No, they were extra.
　　(C) Yes, because they were flat.

M：你買的相機包括電池嗎？
W：(A) 我要他們，謝謝。
　　(B) 不是，是外加的。
　　(C) 是的，因為它們沒電了。

答案 (B)　　　　　Yes / No

the camera you bought意思是「你買的相機」，但是關鍵在於必須掌握Did the camera include batteries?（相機包括電池嗎？）這個提問。(B)回答No，表「沒有附電池」，後面補充「外加的」，所以是正確答案。(A)似乎是客人對店員說的話。(C)的flat在英式英文中有「（電池）電用完」之意，所以答不對題。

☑ **18** W 🇺🇸 M 🇨🇦

W: Could you please get me a copy of the annual report?
M: (A) There's a copier down the hall.
　　(B) It needs to be repaired.
　　(C) I'll print one out right now.

W：可以請你給我一份年度報告副本嗎？
M：(A) 走廊走到底有一台影印機。
　　(B) 它需要被修理。
　　(C) 我馬上印一份。

答案 (C)　　特殊疑問句及對話表達

Could you please～?（能不能請你～）是禮貌性的請求表達法。問句中〈get＋人＋物〉表「拿（物）給（人）」，常用於會話。注意問句的copy是「（相同書籍與雜誌等的）份、冊」之意，並非「想影印」的請求。(C)呼應請求回答「我馬上印一份」最正確。print～ out（將～印出來）。

□ copier [ˋkɑpɪɚ] 名 影印機
□ right now 立刻

☑ **19** W 🇬🇧 W 🇺🇸

W: How much paper will we need for the newsletters?
W: (A) We'll need quite a bit.
　　(B) One hundred eighty dollars.
　　(C) That's really good news.

W：我們即將需要多少紙張做消息刊物？
W：(A) 我們會需要很多。
　　(B) 180 元。
　　(C) 那真是個好消息。

答案 (A)　　　　　　疑問詞

How much～?（多少～）是問數量及程度。paper（紙張）雖是不可數名詞，但皆可與many和much搭配使用。(A)回答含糊的quite a bit（很多）而非具體的紙張數量最正確。注意不要誤解How much是問金額而選(B)。(C)news（新聞、消息）讓我們誤認與問句的newsletters（消息刊物）相似。

☑ **20** W 🇺🇸 M 🇨🇦

W: I'm not sure if Janet will be coming to the conference today.
M: (A) As far as I know, it did.
　　(B) She said she'll be too busy.
　　(C) Let's meet at the lobby then.

W：我不太確定潔妮（Janet）今天是否會來參加會議。
M：(A) 據我所知，是這樣的。
　　(B) 她說她那時會太忙。
　　(C) 那我們在大廳見面吧！

答案 (B)　　　　　　陳述句

I'm not sure if～（不太確定～）是對事情不太確定時的固定句型。(B)的回答呼應「潔妮來嗎？」→「那時會非常忙（因此無法來）」，所以最正確。too busy後面若補加to come就更明確，如句型〈too～ to do〉（因為太～而無法）。(A)前面的As far as I know符合問句，但下一句it did不對。

□ conference [ˋkɑnfərəns] 名 會議
□ as far as I know 據我所知

☑ **21** W 🇬🇧 W 🇺🇸

W: What should I do if I'm running late for the appointment?
W: (A) Please remove your shoes first.
　　(B) I haven't been feeling well lately.
　　(C) Call me immediately.

W：如果我約會遲到了該怎麼辦？
W：(A) 請先脫鞋。
　　(B) 我最近不舒服。
　　(C) 馬上打電話給我。

答案 (C)　　　　　　疑問詞

What should I do～?（我該怎麼做～？）是有求於對方意見或建議時的句型。回應run late for～（～遲到），指示馬上打電話的(C)最正確。(A)也是向對方指示的命令句，但與問題不符。

□ remove [rɪˋmuv] 動 脫掉（衣服）
□ lately [ˋletlɪ] 副 最近
□ immediately [ɪˋmidɪɪtlɪ] 副 馬上

CD 1 24-28

| 錄音原文與翻譯 | 解答與解析 |

☑ **22** M 🇨🇦 W 🇬🇧

M: Why wasn't Jennifer at the seminar last week?
W: (A) It was very informative for her.
  (B) I guess she'd taken it before.
  (C) I think it was somewhere in Europe.

M：為何珍妮佛（Jennifer）上週沒參加研討會？
W：(A) 這對她來說是資訊豐富而有用的。
  (B) 我猜她之前參加過了。
  (C) 我認為是在歐洲的某個地方。

答案 (B) ┃特殊疑問句及對話表達┃

疑問詞與否定疑問句的組合型態。Why wasn't 意思是「為何沒～」。針對題目問到珍妮佛沒參加研討會的理由，(B)回答「之前參加過了」最正確。(A)內容雖聽似跟研討會有關，但卻沒有說出缺席的理由。問句沒有提及場所，所以(C)是錯的。

□ informative [ɪnˋfɔrmətɪv] 形 資訊豐富而有用的

☑ **23** W 🇬🇧 W 🇺🇸

W: Should I order more office supplies, or wait until next week?
W: (A) Let's get some more now, just in case.
  (B) Yes, we need more office space.
  (C) I was surprised to hear that.

W：我該訂更多的文書用品，或是等到下週再說？
W：(A) 那就現在買多一些，以防萬一。
  (B) 是的，我們需要更多辦公空間。
  (C) 我很驚訝聽到那消息。

答案 (A) ┃特殊疑問句及對話表達┃

選擇性疑問句。這題是在詢問「該訂更多的文書用品」或是「等到下週」。正確答案(A)是指同意前面選項而提議「那就現在買多一些」。(B)已將話題從文書用品變成空間了，與問題不符。(C)要注意surprised（驚訝）與問句的supplies（用品）發音不要混淆。

□ supply [səˋplaɪ] 名 （慣用複數形）生活用品
□ just in case 以防萬一

☑ **24** M 🇨🇦 M 🇦🇺

M: What percentage of sales comes from advertising on the Internet?
M: (A) I got several e-mails.
  (B) Around a third.
  (C) They sell a lot of computers.

M：現在多少百分比的營業額來自網路廣告？
M：(A) 我收到幾封電子郵件。
  (B) 約 3 分之 1。
  (C) 他們賣很多電腦。

答案 (B) ┃疑問詞┃

What percentage of～是問百分比。正確答案(B)用「約3分之1」取代具體回答百分比。只要有聽懂What percentage of，應該就會選(B)。注意(A)誘使我們將Internet（網路）與e-mails（電子郵件）做連結。

□ sales [selz] 名 營業額
□ advertising [ˋædvɚˌtaɪzɪŋ] 名 廣告

☑ **25** W 🇺🇸 M 🇨🇦

W: Is it too late to change the reservation time?
M: (A) No, it shouldn't be a problem.
  (B) I'll be there at noon.
  (C) You'll find the tools inside.

W：現在更改預約時間是否為時已晚？
M：(A) 不會，應該不成問題。
  (B) 中午我會在那裡。
  (C) 你會在裡面找到工具。

答案 (A) ┃Yes / No┃

too～ to do（太～無法做～）。針對問句「現在更改預約時間是否為時已晚？」，(A)回答No（不會太晚），後面接著說「不成問題」，符合題意。因為不是在問「時間」，所以(B)不對。(C)tools（工具）跟問句的too（也是）不要混淆。

☑ **26** M 🇦🇺 M 🇨🇦

M: I'd like this file to go to the processing department.
M: (A) Yes, it's already been a while.
  (B) I seldom go to the department store.
  (C) I can take it there this afternoon.

M：我想把這個檔案送到資訊運算部門。
M：(A) 是的，已經過一段時間了。
  (B) 我很少去百貨公司。
  (C) 我今天下午可以拿去那裡。

答案 (C) ┃陳述句┃

I'd like～ to do（想讓～做～、希望～做～）。這題問句是「想讓～做～」的委婉相求之意。所以配合委託而回答I can～（我可以）的(C)是正確的。it是指this file（這個檔案），there是指the processing department（資訊運算部門）。注意(A)while（一段時間）與問句的file（檔案）發音相似，不要混淆。

□ department [dɪˋpartmənt] 名 部、事業部；（百貨公司的）賣場

9

| 錄音原文與翻譯 | 解答與解析 |

☑ **27** W 🇺🇸 M 🇦🇺

W: You'll be attending the opening ceremony, won't you?
M: (A) It's definitely enjoyable.
　　(B) Sorry, I have another engagement.
　　(C) Yes, we're open twenty-four hours.

W：你會出席開幕儀式，對吧？
M：(A) 它肯定很有趣。
　　(B) 抱歉，我已另外有約了。
　　(C) 是的，我們 24 小時營業。

答案 (B)　　　　特殊疑問句及對話表達

附加疑問句最後的語詞只是為了跟對方確認而附加的，所以僅需理解逗點前面的內容就沒問題。這題問句是要確認對方是否出席開幕儀式「你要出席開幕儀式＋對吧？」。(B)回答 Sorry，接著說不出席的理由「已另外有約」最正確。(A)的 It 即使是指開幕儀式，但卻沒有對是否出席做回應，所以是錯的。

□ definitely [ˈdɛfənɪtlɪ] 副 明確地、肯定
□ engagement [ɪnˈgedʒmənt] 名 約會、預定的事

☑ **28** W 🇬🇧 W 🇺🇸

W: Don't leave without introducing yourself to the new supervisor.
W: (A) OK, I'll tell him about it.
　　(B) No, I did it myself.
　　(C) Thanks for reminding me.

W：在沒向新上司自我介紹之前不要離開。
W：(A) 好的，我會告訴他。
　　(B) 不，我自己做的。
　　(C) 感謝提醒。

答案 (C)　　　　　　　　陳述句

Don't～是否定命令句。直譯就是「在沒向新上司自我介紹之前不要離開」，指示對方在離開之前要向新上司自我介紹。正確答案(C)說出謝意「感謝提醒」。(A)回答 OK 雖然是接受指示的意思，但後面的 it 所指為何不明確。(B)要注意 yourself 與 myself 不要混淆。

□ supervisor [ˌsupɚˈvaɪzɚ] 名 上司
□ remind [rɪˈmaɪnd] 動 提醒

☑ **29** W 🇬🇧 M 🇦🇺

W: Was Mr. Stevens the one who signed these sales receipts?
M: (A) Yes, that's right.
　　(B) There are enough seats for everyone.
　　(C) He signed more than one.

W：在這些銷售收據上簽名的是史蒂芬斯（Stevens）先生嗎？
M：(A) 是的，沒錯。
　　(B) 有足夠的座位給每個人。
　　(C) 他簽了不止一份。

答案 (A)　　　　　　　　Yes / No

讓我們按照前後順序，用關係代名詞練習理解句子：「史蒂芬斯先生是～的人？＋在這些銷售收據簽名」。一邊聽，一邊同步解讀「在這些銷售收據上簽名的是史蒂芬斯先生嗎？」。(A)回答「沒錯（＝是史蒂芬斯先生）」來表示同意，所以是正確答案。

□ sign [saɪn] 動 簽名於～

☑ **30** W 🇺🇸 M 🇦🇺

W: We should have heard from management by now, shouldn't we?
M: (A) No, it's probably not very easy.
　　(B) They've been experiencing some delays.
　　(C) Yes, we had better not stay here.

W：我們到現在應該得到管理部門的回覆了，不是嗎？
M：(A) 不，可能不是很容易。
　　(B) 他們有些耽擱。
　　(C) 是的，我們最好別待在這裡。

答案 (B)　　　　特殊疑問句及對話表達

此題為附加疑問句。〈should have＋過去分詞〉有「應該～（卻沒有）」及「估計應該」的意思。從 by now（現在為止）得知「我們到現在應該得到管理部門的回覆了＋不是嗎？」這層意思。(B)回答還沒得到回覆的理由，所以正確。(C)had better not do（最好別做～）。

□ management [ˈmænɪdʒmənt] 名 管理部門
□ delay [dɪˈle] 名 延誤

☑ **31** M 🇦🇺 M 🇨🇦

M: Where did Ms. Smith say today's meeting would be held?
M: (A) Anytime would be fine with me.
　　(B) Hasn't it been postponed until tomorrow?
　　(C) Honestly, it's better than nothing.

M：史密斯（Smith）女士說今天的會議在哪裡召開？
M：(A) 任何時間我都可以。
　　(B) 不是延到明天了嗎？
　　(C) 老實說，總比沒有好。

答案 (B)　　　　　　　　疑問詞

這是在疑問詞和疑問句中插入〈did＋主詞＋say〉的句型。插入部分不重要，重點在是否能理解 Where... today's meeting would be held?（今天的會議在哪裡召開？）。正確答案(B)是反問「不是延期了嗎？」而非回答具體的「場所」。(A)回答的是「時間」，所以錯誤。

□ postpone [postˈpon] 動 使～延期
□ honestly [ˈɑnɪstlɪ] 副 老實說

PART 3 CD 1 34-35 M 🍁 W 🇺🇸

錄音原文	錄音原文翻譯
Questions 32 through 34 refer to the following conversation.	試題 32-34 請參考以下會話。

M: Hi, Marie. Just to remind you that I'm off to Sydney tomorrow to attend a medical convention next Monday. I won't be back until Friday.

W: Yes, that'll be no problem at all. I contacted Dr. Andrews from Lynfield Medical Center last week, and he agreed to come in while you're away. Have you arranged your accommodation?

M: Well, I'm planning to stay with a friend of mine for the whole week. He's lived there for more than ten years, and he's going to show me around for a day or two once the convention is over.

W: Sounds great. There's so much to see and do there.

M：嗨，瑪莉（Marie）。我只是要提醒你，明天我要出發到雪梨（Sydney）參加下週一的醫學會議。我要到週五才會回來。

W：好的，完全沒問題。我上週已聯絡林菲爾德（Lynfield）醫學中心的安德魯斯（Andrews）醫師，你不在時，他答應來這裡代班。你已經安排好住宿了嗎？

M：嗯，我計畫整個星期住在我朋友住處。他在當地住超過 10 年了，等會議結束後，他會帶我四處走走一兩天。

W：聽起來真不錯。那裡有很多值得看跟做的事情。

Vocabulary

□ remind～ that... 對～提醒…… □ convention [kənˋvɛnʃən] 名 會議 □ arrange [əˋrendʒ] 動 安排～
□ accommodation [əˌkɑməˋdeʃən] 名 住宿 □ whole [hol] 形 整個的

試題	試題翻譯	解答與解析
☑ **32** Who most likely is the woman? (A) A conference planner (B) A patient (C) A tour conductor (D) A secretary	誰最有可能是女性的角色？ (A) 會議策劃人 (B) 病患 (C) 導遊 (D) 祕書	**答案 (D)** 概述 從會話中的medical（醫學的）及Dr. Andrews（安德魯斯醫師）、Medical Center（醫療中心）等語詞，可知2人的工作與醫療相關。男性對女性叮囑明天開始出差，而女性回答「沒問題」後，從I contacted Dr. Andrews...的內容可知她還安排其他醫師來代班不在的男性。因此，以女性的角色來說，可能性最高的就是(D)祕書。
☑ **33** What will the man do next Monday? (A) Take a day off (B) Attend a convention (C) See a client (D) Go sightseeing in Sydney	男性下週要做什麼？ (A) 休假 (B) 參加會議 (C) 見一位客戶 (D) 在雪梨觀光	**答案 (B)** 下一步動作 男性第1句就提到attend a medical convention next Monday，所以正確答案是(B)。從男性第2句可知(D)是週一會議結束之後的活動。 □ client [ˋklaɪənt] 名 客戶
☑ **34** How long will the man be away? (A) One day (B) Two days (C) About a week (D) More than two weeks	男性要離開多久？ (A) 1 天 (B) 2 天 (C) 大約 1 週 (D) 2 週以上	**答案 (C)** 其他細節 男性第1句就提到明天出發參加週一的會議，週五回來。雖然這個訊息沒有特別指名出發日是星期幾，但是從第2次發言提到stay with a friend of mine for the whole week，可以得知週一會議進行，那週會一直在雪梨，因此(C)是正確答案。可別因為會話中提到for a day or two 而誤選(A)和(B)。

錄音原文	錄音原文翻譯

Questions 35 through 37 refer to the following conversation.

W: Roger! It's been a while. How have you been?

M: Hi, Barbara. I'm great, thanks. I just heard at the general meeting yesterday that we're opening a branch office in Baltimore next year. I'm curious about what kind of jobs are going to be available there. Do you know anything?

W: Have you checked the bulletin board in the main hall? I noticed several internal postings for the Marketing and Sales departments just this morning.

M: Wow, thanks. I'll check them out. By the way, if you have time, would you mind looking over my résumé and cover letter?

試題 35-37 請參考以下會話。

W：羅傑（Roger）！好久不見。近來如何？

M：嗨，芭芭拉（Barbara）。我很好，謝謝妳。只是昨天我在全體大會上聽到明年我們要在巴爾的摩（Baltimore）開分公司，我很好奇那裡會有什麼樣的職缺。妳知道什麼嗎？

W：你看過主大廳的公告欄了嗎？今早我才注意到市場行銷和營業部門開了幾個在公司內部徵人的職缺。

M：哇，謝謝妳。我會去看看。對了，如果妳有時間，可否過目一下我的履歷及求職信呢？

Vocabulary

- □ bulletin board　公告欄　　□ internal [ɪn'tɝn!] 形 內部的、公司內部的　　□ look over~　瀏覽、過目　　□ résumé [ˌrɛzjʊ'me] 名 履歷表
- □ cover letter　求職信、附加在上面的信

試題	試題翻譯	解答與解析

35

What does the man want to know about?
(A) A general meeting
(B) A client's contact information
(C) Other positions in the company
(D) The location of the main hall

男性想知道什麼？

(A) 全體大會
(B) 一名顧客的聯絡資料
(C) 公司內部其他職位
(D) 主大廳的位置

答案 (C)　　其他細節

男性第1句說I'm curious about what kind of jobs are going to be available there。curious about即是「好奇想知道」之意，與本題相符。there是指在巴爾的摩分公司。所以(C)是正確答案。

□ location [lo'keʃən] 名 位置、地點

36

What does the woman suggest the man do?
(A) Look at the bulletin board
(B) Apply to another company
(C) Complete a required form
(D) Speak with a sales manager

女性建議男性做什麼？

(A) 看公告欄
(B) 應徵其他公司
(C) 完成必要的表格
(D) 跟行銷經理談

答案 (A)　　請求、建議、提出

女性被男性問及有關新分公司的職缺，回答了Have you checked the bulletin board in the main hall?，由此可知女性對男性的建議，所以正確答案是(A)。

□ apply to~　向~應徵
□ required [rɪ'kwaɪrd] 形 必要的
□ form [fɔrm] 名 表格

37

What does the man ask the woman to do?
(A) Find a new job for him
(B) Contact his department
(C) Fill out some paperwork
(D) Review his application documents

男性請求女性做什麼？

(A) 幫他找一份新工作
(B) 跟他的部門聯絡
(C) 填寫一些文書工作
(D) 瀏覽他的申請文件

答案 (D)　　請求、建議、提出

注意聽男性的對話有無表示要求之意，最後他提到..., would you mind looking over my résumé and cover letter?，而Would you mind ~ing?（可否幫我做~嗎？）就是請求的句型，因此(D)是正確答案。look over（瀏覽）和résumé and cover letter（履歷及求職信）也可以分別改用答案中的review（瀏覽）和application documents（申請文件）來表達。

□ fill out~　填寫~
□ paperwork ['pepɚˌwɝk] 名 文書工作
□ application [ˌæplə'keʃən] 名 申請

CD 1 37 [M 🇦🇺] [W 🇺🇸]

錄音原文	錄音原文翻譯

Questions 38 through 40 refer to the following conversation.

M: Hi, I'm calling from room 608. I checked in earlier today, and when I came back I noticed that the bathtub tap is leaking considerably. I tried, but I can't seem to get it to stop. It's making quite a bit of noise.

W: I'm terribly sorry about that, Mr. Whitehall. Our maintenance staff are gone for the day, but what I will gladly do is move you to another room. We have several rooms open down on the third floor.

M: I'd appreciate that. But, that's three floors down, and I have some heavy bags. Could you send someone to help me move them?

W: Sure. I'll send someone right away.

試題 38-40 請參考以下會話。

M：嗨，我這邊是 608 號房。我今天稍早辦理入房登記，但是當我外出回來時，發現浴缸水龍頭嚴重漏水。我試著處理，可是似乎無法讓它停止。它發出了相當大的噪音。

W：懷特沃（Whitehall）先生，對此我深感抱歉。我們的維修人員今日下班了，但是我很樂意為您換另一個房間。3 樓有數間空房。

M：我很感激。不過那要往下 3 個樓層，但我有些很重的提袋，可否請妳派人來幫我搬呢？

W：當然。我馬上派人過去。

Vocabulary

- □ considerably [kən`sɪdərəblɪ] 副 相當地　　□ seem to *do* 似乎～　　□ get～ to *do* 使～做～
- □ quite a bit of～ 相當大的～　　□ be gone for the day 下班回家　　□ gladly [`glædlɪ] 副 樂意地
- □ appreciate [ə`priʃɪˌet] 動 感激　　□ right away 馬上

試題	試題翻譯	解答與解析

☑ **38**

What is the man's problem?

(A) He is missing some bags.
(B) The room next door is noisy.
(C) The plumbing is broken.
(D) His room needs cleaning.

男性遇到什麼問題？

(A) 他遺失一些行李。
(B) 隔壁房間很吵。
(C) 管線壞了。
(D) 他的房間需要打掃。

答案 (C) 〔概述〕

男性的問題是the bathtub tap is leaking considerably（浴缸水龍頭嚴重漏水），(C)回答「管線壞了」最正確。plumbing（管線）。注意不要聽到題目中的quite a bit of noise（很大的聲音）就誤選(B)。

☑ **39**

What floor is the man currently on?

(A) The third floor
(B) The fourth floor
(C) The fifth floor
(D) The sixth floor

男性目前住幾樓？

(A) 3 樓
(B) 4 樓
(C) 5 樓
(D) 6 樓

答案 (D) 〔其他細節〕

有關數字的問題，大部分的會話中會出現2個以上的數字。先看到題目問什麼，並注意聽有關樓層的單字。從開頭句I'm calling from room 608似乎可以判斷在6樓，但是慎重起見再繼續聽，3樓（the third floor）有空房，是再往下3個樓層（that's three floors down），所以可知現在在6樓無誤。

□ currently [`kɝəntlɪ] 副 現在

☑ **40**

What does the man ask the woman to do?
(A) Provide assistance with luggage
(B) Offer him an upgraded room
(C) Stop the noise in an adjacent room
(D) Call a maintenance worker

男性請求女性做什麼？

(A) 提供行李協助
(B) 提供房間升等
(C) 停止隔壁的噪音
(D) 打電話給維修工人

答案 (A) 〔請求、建議、提出〕

這題使用〈ask＋O＋to *do*〉句型來問請求內容。會話中的Could you～?句型大多是請求表現法。男性客人最後要求女性Could you send someone to help me move them?，them是指前面說的some heavy bags，所以答案是(A)。bags改用選項中的luggage來替代，luggage表示整個行李，是不可數名詞，不論幾件行李，都寫成luggage。

□ assistance [ə`sɪstəns] 名 協助
□ adjacent [ə`dʒesənt] 形 鄰接的

錄音原文	錄音原文翻譯

Questions 41 through 43 refer to the following conversation.

W: John, do you know if the new projector in Meeting Room 1 is functioning yet? We're scheduled to do a presentation there next week.

M: Oh. Maintenance said they'll have it ready by Monday, including the new overhead screen. Is that too late?

W: Well, I'm just worried I won't have time to try out the new projector beforehand. The presentation's on Tuesday morning, and I'd like to make sure I can operate it smoothly.

M: Well, I suppose we still have enough time to reschedule the presentation to Meeting Room 3. It has an older projector and it's on the 3rd floor, but on the other hand, the room is bigger and it's near the cafeteria.

試題 41-43 請參考以下會話。

W：約翰（John），你知道第1會議室新的投影機是否可以運作了？我們預定下週要在那間做簡報。

M：喔。維修人員說包括在上頭的新螢幕，他們最遲會在週一處理好。會不會太晚？

W：嗯，我只是擔心沒有時間事先試用新的投影機。簡報是在週二早上，而且我想確認我可以順利操作它。

M：嗯，我認為我們有充裕的時間把簡報重新安排在第3會議室。那間會議室在 3 樓，有一台舊投影機，但另一方面，那間空間較大，而且靠近自助餐廳。

Vocabulary

- projector [prə`dʒɛktə] 名 投影機
- maintenance [`mentənəns] 名 維修（人員）
- have～ ready 使～完成、準備好
- including [ɪn`kludɪŋ] 介 包括～
- overhead [`ovə`hɛd] 形 在上頭的
- make sure (that)～ 確認～
- reschedule [ri`skɛdʒʊl] 動 重新安排～的時間
- on the other hand 另一方面

試題	試題翻譯	解答與解析

☑ 41

What are maintenance workers going to do by next Monday?
(A) Install new equipment
(B) Remove furniture
(C) Replace a floor
(D) Repair a wall

維修人員最遲下週一要做什麼？
(A) 安裝新設備
(B) 丟掉家具
(C) 更換地板
(D) 修牆壁

答案 (A)　其他細節

一開頭女性就詢問... the new projector in Meeting Room 1 is functioning yet？，function 是「運作」之意。男性針對問話回答 Maintenance said... by Monday，所以正確答案是(A)。選項內的new equipment（新設備）是把the new projector（新投影機）這項具體的東西抽象化。

- install [ɪn`stɔl] 動 安裝～
- equipment [ɪ`kwɪpmənt] 名 設備
- remove [rɪ`muv] 動 丟掉、搬開～

☑ 42

What is the woman worried about?

(A) Using old equipment
(B) Postponing a meeting
(C) Testing a new projector
(D) Rescheduling a presentation

女性擔心什麼？

(A) 使用舊設備
(B) 將會議延期
(C) 試用新的投影機
(D) 重新安排簡報的時間

答案 (C)　概述

女性第2次說話時提到I'm just worried...，接著後面就可聽出「擔心」的內容。beforehand是「事先」之意，因為做簡報是在週二早上，所以可使用新投影機的時間是週一，因而擔心沒有試用的時間，所以(C)是正確答案。try out～（試用～）可以改用選項內的test（測試）做替換。

☑ 43

What does the man suggest the woman do?
(A) Use another room
(B) Try a bigger screen
(C) Go to the cafeteria
(D) Cancel the meeting

男性建議女性什麼？

(A) 用另一個房間
(B) 嘗試更大的螢幕
(C) 去自助餐廳
(D) 取消會議

答案 (A)　請求、建議、提出

男性第2次說話時提到I suppose we still have...，建議（不要Meeting Room 1）要不要改到Meeting Room 3。(A)的another room（另一個房間）意指Meeting Room 3，所以是正確答案。

錄音原文	錄音原文翻譯
Questions 44 through 46 refer to the following conversation. **M**: How is the new 7th Street property coming along? **W**: It's going pretty well. The electricians should finish updating the wiring in four of the apartments by Friday. After that, they'll need painting. You talked to the painters, right? **M**: Yes. They're coming next week on Monday. I have the carpet layers scheduled to come in on the following Thursday. That should be enough time for the paint to dry. Have all of the units been rented? **W**: Tenants have signed leases for six of them. The other two are still listed on our Web site, but I'm also going to run an ad all next week in the *Daily Times*.	試題 44-46 請參考以下會話。 M：第 7 街的新房產進行得如何？ W：很順利。電工在週五前應該可以更新完大樓 4 間公寓的配線。之後需要粉刷，你跟油漆工談了，對吧？ M：是的。他們下週一來。接著我安排工人在再下一週的週四來鋪地毯。那應該有足夠的時間讓油漆變乾。所有的房間都出租了嗎？ W：已有 6 間有房客簽了租約。其他 2 間仍刊登在我們的網站，不過我下週會在每日時報（*Daily Times*）刊登一整週的廣告。

Vocabulary

☐ property [`prɑpɚtɪ] 名 房產　　☐ come along　（工作等）進展、進行　　☐ wiring [`waɪrɪŋ] 名 線路
☐ layer [`leɚ] 名 鋪設者　　☐ lease [lis] 名 租約　　☐ list A on B　將A刊登於B

試題	試題翻譯	解答與解析
☑ **44** What work will be finished by Friday? (A) Carpet installation (B) A Web site design (C) A promotional campaign (D) Electrical construction	哪個工程會在週五前完成？ (A) 鋪地毯 (B) 網站設計 (C) 促銷活動 (D) 電氣施工	**答案 (D)**　其他細節 注意聽關鍵字Friday（週五），女性第1次發言提到The electricians should finish updating the wiring in four of the apartments by Friday，所以答案是(D)。electrician是「電工」，electrical是「電氣的」。選項(A)指的是再下一週的星期四預計的工程。
☑ **45** What does the man say about the painting? (A) The work will begin next Monday. (B) The work has been finished. (C) The painters are behind schedule. (D) The cost is reasonable.	關於油漆工程，男性說了什麼？ (A) 工程將於下週一開始。 (B) 工程已完成。 (C) 油漆工的進度延遲了。 (D) 價錢合理。	**答案 (A)**　其他細節 被女性問及是否已跟油漆工接洽，男性回答了Yes. They're coming next week on Monday.，所以答案是(A)。油漆工程是日後才要開始，所以(B)和(C)都錯。 ☐ reasonable [`riznəbl] 形 適當的
☑ **46** How does the woman say she will find more renters? (A) By passing out brochures (B) By talking to other tenants (C) By creating a Web site (D) By advertising in a newspaper	女性表示要如何找更多房客？ (A) 發宣傳冊子 (B) 跟其他房客談 (C) 製作網站 (D) 在報紙登廣告	**答案 (D)**　其他細節 問句的renter意為「承租人」，與會話中的tenant（房客）相同意思。女性第2次回應時，針對尚未出租的房間有說I'm also going to run an ad all next week in the *Daily Times*，所以答案是(D)。run an ad是在報章雜誌「登廣告」的意思，可以改用選項內的advertise（廣告）表達。~*Times*是報紙名稱。

錄音原文	錄音原文翻譯

Questions 47 through 49 refer to the following conversation.

W: Oh, hi, James. Did you have lunch yet? I didn't see you in the cafeteria.

M: Right. I was just on my way there now. Mr. Lee from Shanghai came by earlier this morning. We ended up talking for longer than I'd expected. By the way, did you hear that Alan got the marketing manager position?

W: I did! Isn't that great? I thought he might not have enough managerial experience for the position, but he's enthusiastic and talented, and he gets along well with his coworkers.

M: Yeah, definitely. Also, he often has fresh and original ideas, which is something they were definitely looking for.

試題 47-49 請參考以下會話。

W：嗨，傑姆斯（James），吃午餐了嗎？在自助餐廳沒看到你。

M：是的。我現在正要去那裡。來自上海的李（Lee）先生今天上午來訪。結果我們聊得比我預期的還久。對了順帶一提，你有聽說艾倫（Alan）要擔任市場行銷經理嗎？

W：聽說了！很棒對吧？我認為他在這個職位上雖然沒有足夠的管理經驗，但是他熱情、有天分，而且與他的同事們和睦相處。

M：是的，沒錯。而且，他經常有新穎及獨到的創意，這肯定是公司看中的。

Vocabulary

- on one's way (to)～　往～途中
- end up ～ing　結果～、最終變得
- marketing [`mɑrkɪtɪŋ] 名 市場行銷
- managerial [ˌmænə`dʒɪrɪəl] 形 管理（人）的
- enthusiastic [ɪn͵θjuzɪ`æstɪk] 形 熱心的、熱情的
- talented [`tæləntɪd] 形 有天分的
- get along (well) with～　與～相處和睦
- coworker [`ko͵wɝkə] 名 同事
- definitely [`dɛfənɪtlɪ] 副 肯定地、沒錯（用於感嘆詞上的）
- original [ə`rɪdʒən!] 形 有獨創性的

試題	試題翻譯	解答與解析

☑ 47

What are the speakers mainly discussing?
(A) A coworker's transfer
(B) A lunch engagement
(C) A job opening in Shanghai
(D) A colleague's promotion

2 位主要在討論什麼？
(A) 一位同事的調職
(B) 午餐之約
(C) 上海的工作職缺
(D) 同事的升遷

答案 (D)　概述

一般對話的主題大多放在一開頭，但是這段「主要的」話題是放在男性第1次回應時，在表達話題轉換的By the way（順帶一提）之後。對於Alan got the marketing manager position，女性回應說很棒，所以對男女雙方來說，這是個好話題。接下來的對話是在談艾倫（同事）成為經理的原因，因此(D)同事（擔任經理職）的升遷是正確答案。

- colleague [`kɑlig] 名 同事
- promotion [prə`moʃən] 名 升遷

☑ 48

What does the woman say about Alan?
(A) He has a positive attitude.
(B) He has gained considerable experience.
(C) He is a confident public speaker.
(D) He has not worked long enough at the company.

關於艾倫，女性說了什麼？
(A) 他有積極的態度。
(B) 他已取得相當多的經驗。
(C) 他是一位有自信的公開演說家。
(D) 他在公司工作的時間不夠長。

答案 (A)　其他細節

關於艾倫，女性第2次的回應提到he's enthusiastic and talented, and he gets along well with his coworkers，正確答案(A)positive attitude（積極的態度）表達的即是該意。另外女性有提到艾倫任管理職的經驗不足，所以(B)是錯的。注意對話中雖然有出現not～ enough（不夠～）的用法，但是別誤選為(D)。

☑ 49

What quality was desirable for the position?
(A) Being bilingual
(B) Being creative
(C) Having marketing experience
(D) Having knowledge of the global market

這個職位的期望資質是什麼？
(A) 能流利地說 2 國語言
(B) 有創意的
(C) 有市場行銷經驗
(D) 有全球行銷的知識

答案 (B)　其他細節

這題的desirable是指「期望的、有吸引力的」。the position是指艾倫要擔任的經理職。男性第2次的回應就提到he often has fresh and original ideas，這正是公司看中的特點，因此(B)creative（有創意的）是正確答案。

- bilingual [baɪ`lɪŋgwəl] 形 能流利地說2國語言的

CD 1 41　W  M

錄音原文	錄音原文翻譯
Questions 50 through 52 refer to the following conversation.	試題 50-52 請參考以下會話。

W: Excuse me. I'm looking for magazines on women's fashion. Could you tell me where they are?

M: Ah ... Sure. They're in aisle 3, next to the sale items display. Unfortunately, our selection is quite small at the moment—the publisher has been having trouble with shipping.

W: I see. I suppose that could be a result of the terrible weather in the Midwest.

M: That's probably the case. Anyway, we hope to be getting more magazines next week. If you'd like to leave me your name and number, I can give you a call as soon as they come in.

W：打擾一下，我正在找女性流行雜誌，可以請你告訴我，它們放在哪兒嗎？

M：嗯……當然。它們位在走道 3，陳列在銷售商品旁。很可惜，目前我們店裡提供的選擇有限──出版社在運送方面遇到麻煩。

W：了解。我猜是中西部惡劣天候造成的。

M：應該是。總之，希望下週會有更多雜誌。如果妳願意留下大名及電話，等他們一送來，我可以打電話給你。

Vocabulary

□ aisle [aɪl] 名 走道　　□ display [dɪˋsple] 名 陳列　　□ publisher [ˋpʌblɪʃɚ] 名 出版社　　□ the Midwest　中西部
□ give~ a call　打電話給~

試題	試題翻譯	解答與解析
☑ **50** What is the problem? (A) The store is closing. (B) A sale has just ended. (C) Only a few items are available. (D) Some equipment is not working.	他們面臨什麼問題？ (A) 店家正在打烊。 (B) 剛結束銷售。 (C) 只能買到一些品項。 (D) 一些設備無法運作。	**答案 (C)**　　概述 這題的重點提示就在會話中的否定表現法。面對客人詢問女性流行雜誌的位置，男性店員回答在走道3，接著說Unfortunately（很可惜）等否定的內容，而(C)的說法等同our selection is quite small，所以是正確答案。only a few的意思是「只有一些」。items（品項、物品）在這裡是指「女性流行雜誌」。 □ available [əˋveləb!] 形 （東西）可用的、可買到的
☑ **51** Why does the man say, "That's probably the case"? (A) He has a better idea. (B) He is offering his opinion. (C) He agrees with the woman. (D) He hopes the weather will clear up.	男性為何說 「That's probably the case」？ (A) 他有更好的主意。 (B) 他在提供自己的意見。 (C) 他同意女性所言。 (D) 他希望天氣變好。	**答案 (C)**　　說話者的目的 聽這段對話之前，如果有瞥見這是要問說話者的目的，就先確認選項，再將該語句放在腦海中繼續聽對話。That's the case（就是這樣、應該是）係用於同意對方意見時，所以正確答案是(C)。男性店員認同出版社在運送方面遇到的麻煩是中西部惡劣天候所致。
☑ **52** Why does the man request the woman's telephone number? (A) To get an update on her details (B) To notify her when more stock arrives (C) To tell her about an upcoming sale (D) To give her details of another location	男性為何要女性的電話號碼？ (A) 得到關於她的最新資料。 (B) 有更多進貨時要通知她。 (C) 告訴她即將舉辦的拍賣。 (D) 給她另一家店所在地的資料。	**答案 (B)**　　其他細節 男性第2次的回應中If you'd like to leave me your name and number符合這題的提問，所以要充分聽懂後述內容。I can give you a call as soon as they come in的they是指女性流行雜誌。針對目前商品不全，表示要等到more stock arrives，所以(B)是正確答案。 □ request [rɪˋkwɛst] 動 請求、要求 □ update [ʌpˋdet] 名 最新資料 □ notify [ˋnotəˏfaɪ] 動 通知~ □ upcoming [ˋʌpˏkʌmɪŋ] 形 即將到來的~、下一個的

錄音原文	錄音原文翻譯

Questions 53 through 55 refer to the following conversation with three speakers.

W : Steve? Ben? Did either of you talk to the window washers?
M-1 : I did. What about it?
W : When did they say they could come?
M-1 : Ahh, as early as nine on Friday, but I scheduled them to come on Saturday morning.
M-2 : Oh, thanks, Ben. Do you think they'll be able to clean all the windows in just a few hours, including the ones in the kitchen?
M-1 : I'm pretty sure. They're professionals. It's what they do.
M-2 : Well, if they can do that, I'll be impressed. The windows by the booths are particularly filthy.
W : Me, too. To be honest, I know the owner's wanted them cleaned for a while now, but I was worried that it would interfere with our customers. I wonder, Ben ... could you come in early on Saturday to let the workers in?
M-1 : Sure, no problem. I'll be here by 8:30.

試題 53-55 請參考以下 3 人的會話。

W ：史蒂文（Steve）？還是班（Ben）？你們兩位有誰跟洗窗業者談了？
M-1：我談過了，怎麼了？
W ：他們有說什麼時候來嗎？
M-1：嗯，快的話週五 9 點，不過我是安排他們週六早上來。
M-2：喔，謝謝班。包括廚房在內，你覺得他們可以在幾小時內清潔所有的窗戶嗎？
M-1：我滿確定的。他們是專家，那就是他們的工作。
M-2：好吧，如果他們可以做到，我會覺得他們很厲害。因為餐廳雅座旁的窗戶特別髒。
W ：我也這麼認為。老實說，我知道老闆想清潔它們已有一段時間了，但我擔心會影響我們的客人。我在想，班……你週六可以早點來，幫洗窗工人開門嗎？
M-1：當然，沒問題。我會在 8 點 30 分前到。

Vocabulary

- [ ] schedule~ to *do*　對～安排預定計畫
- [ ] particularly [pə`tɪkjələ-lɪ] 副 特別地
- [ ] filthy [`fɪlθɪ] 形 不乾淨的
- [ ] interfere with~　妨礙~

試題	試題翻譯	解答與解析

53

Where most likely does the conversation take place?
(A) In a dry-cleaning shop
(B) In a restaurant
(C) In a hospital
(D) In a repair shop

你認為這段對話地點最有可能在哪裡？

(A) 在乾洗店
(B) 在餐廳
(C) 在醫院
(D) 在修理店

答案 (B) 概述

這是 3 個人之間的對話。從一開頭的內容就知道是 3 個人在談有關洗窗業者。由對話中 in the kitchen（在廚房）及 interfere with our customers（影響我們的客人）等資訊就可知 (B) 是正確答案。

54

When will the work be done?

(A) On Friday morning
(B) On Friday afternoon
(C) On Saturday morning
(D) On Saturday afternoon

這項工作何時完成？

(A) 週五早上
(B) 週五下午
(C) 週六早上
(D) 週六下午

答案 (C) 其他細節

這題的 the work 是指店裡的洗窗工作。從對話的前半段可知，業者週六早上來，在幾小時內清潔完窗戶。而且根據最後那句，男性（M-1）在週六早上 8 點 30 分會開門讓業者進來，所以工作完成的時間是 (C) On Saturday morning。注意別聽到 as early as nine on Friday（快的話週五 9 點）就誤選 (A)。連接詞 but 後面的內容才是要把握的重點。

55

Who does the woman ask Ben to let in on Saturday?
(A) The owner
(B) Cleaning staff
(C) Cooks
(D) Customers

女性要求班週六早上讓誰進來？

(A) 老闆
(B) 清潔人員
(C) 廚師
(D) 客人

答案 (B) 請求、建議、提出

這篇 3 人會話有 2 名同為男性，因為是對特定人名（這題是指班）的相關問題，所以要注意聽對話內容有提及符合名字的部分。女性最後拜託班時說，I wonder, Ben... could you come in early on Saturday to let the workers in?，the workers 是指洗窗業者，正確答案 (B) cleaning staff 即是代表該意。let~ in 意思是「讓~進入」。

W 🇬🇧 M 🇦🇺

錄音原文	錄音原文翻譯
Questions 56 through 58 refer to the following conversation.	試題 56-58 請參考以下會話。

W: I'm thinking we should update our brochures before spring. They don't include our latest discounts on advance summer reservations.

M: You're right. We should do that. Speaking of which, our Web site could use an overhaul, too. It should have separate pages for each of our travel packages.

W: That's true, but Web sites take some time to design, and I think it would be a good idea if we hired a specialist. Do you think we'll have time to focus on both the Web site and the brochure?

M: Hmm .... It might be a little tough, but I think it's worth the effort if it means more bookings.

W：我認為我們應該在春季之前更新宣傳冊子。因為它們不含夏季預訂折扣的最新資訊。

M：你說的沒錯。我們應該那麼做。說到這個，我們的網站也該全面檢修。我們每一種套裝旅遊應該做不同的分頁。

W：確實如此，但是網站設計需要花一些時間，如果我們聘請一位專家，我認為那會是個好主意。你覺得我們有時間同時專注於網站跟宣傳冊子這 2 件事嗎？

M：嗯……可能有點棘手，但如果能得到更多預約，我認為這是值得努力的。

Vocabulary

☐ brochure [broˋʃʊr] 名 小冊子　　☐ advance [ədˋvæns] 形 事先的　　☐ speaking of which　說到這個
☐ separate [ˋsɛprɪt] 形 個別的　　☐ travel package　套裝旅遊行程　　☐ specialist [ˋspɛʃəlɪst] 名 專家　　☐ focus on～　焦點集中於～
☐ tough [tʌf] 形（解決問題等）棘手的　　☐ worth the effort　值得努力　　☐ booking [ˋbʊkɪŋ] 名 預約

試題	試題翻譯	解答與解析
☑ **56** What type of business do the speakers work for? (A) A mailing service (B) A travel agency (C) A design company (D) A newspaper	對話的 2 人從事哪種工作？ (A) 郵寄服務 (B) 旅行社 (C) 設計公司 (D) 報業	**答案 (B)** 〔概述〕 從會話中的our brochures（我們的宣傳冊子）及summer reservations（夏季預訂）、our travel packages（我們的套裝旅遊）、more bookings（更多預約）等語詞，可得知(B)是正確答案。不要因會話中提到design（設計）誤導而選(C)。 ☐ agency [ˋedʒənsɪ] 名 代辦機構
☑ **57** What is the woman concerned about? (A) The cost of advertising (B) The location of the company (C) The travel destination (D) The time required for the work	女性擔心什麼事？ (A) 廣告費用 (B) 公司所在地 (C) 旅行目的地 (D) 工作所需的時間	**答案 (D)** 〔概述〕 女性所擔心的事，就在第2次回應時提到That's true, but...之後的內容。從Web sites take some time to design及Do you think we'll have time to focus on both the Web site and the brochure?，這些語句可知女性擔心工作需要時間，所以正確答案是(D)。(A)雖然宣傳冊子及網站檢修是可能要擔心的項目，但是整個會話沒有提及費用問題。
☑ **58** What does the man imply when he says, "I think it's worth the effort"? (A) Hard work will pay off in the future. (B) Travel packages should be worth more. (C) Efficient design requires effort. (D) A specialist has provided valuable feedback.	男性說 「I think it's worth the effort」 時，表示什麼？ (A) 努力工作未來會有回報。 (B) 套裝旅遊應該更有價值。 (C) 有效率的設計需要投注大量精力。 (D) 專家已提供寶貴的意見。	**答案 (A)** 〔說話者的目的〕 對於女性擔心是否可騰出時間做宣傳冊子跟網站檢修一事，男性說it's worth the effort（這是值得努力的）。(A)是正確答案，effort（精力、努力）可以替換成hard work（努力、勤奮）。pay off是「（努力等）帶來好結果（效果）」之意。注意不要因會話中提到worth（有價值的）和effort而誤選(B)和(C)。 ☐ efficient [ɪˋfɪʃənt] 形 有效率的 ☐ feedback [ˋfid͵bæk] 名 意見、回饋

錄音原文	錄音原文翻譯

Questions 59 through 61 refer to the following conversation.

W: Hello, I'd like to order one of your new water-saving shower heads that you're advertising on TV.

M: Certainly. May I ask which model you'd like—standard or deluxe—and in what color?

W: Silver, and ... deluxe, please. And ... just curious, how soon do you usually ship your products? I live in Oklahoma.

M: If you place the order right now, it'll ship tomorrow from our warehouse in Chicago.

W: So, when will it be delivered here?

M: It should arrive in the evening the following day.

試題 59-61 請參考以下會話。

W：哈囉，我想訂你們在電視上廣告的新型省水蓮蓬頭。

M：沒問題。可否請教您要的型號——標準的或豪華的——還有什麼顏色？

W：麻煩給我銀色，還有……豪華型的。還有……好奇問一下，你們通常多快會運送產品？我住在奧克拉荷馬（Oklahoma）。

M：如果您現在下訂單，明天會從我們芝加哥（Chicago）的倉庫配送。

W：所以，何時會送到這兒？

M：應該再隔一天傍晚會抵達。

Vocabulary

□ water-saving [`wɔtɚ `sevɪŋ] 形 省水的　□ shower head 蓮蓬頭　□ advertise [`ædvɚˌtaɪz] 動 廣告、做～宣傳
□ ship [ʃɪp] 動 運送、發送～　□ place an order 下訂單　□ warehouse [`wɛrˌhaʊs] 名 倉庫
□ following [`fɑləwɪŋ] 形 接著的

試題	試題翻譯	解答與解析

59

What is the purpose of the telephone call?
(A) To purchase a television
(B) To open an account
(C) To schedule an appointment
(D) To place an order

這通電話的目的是什麼？
(A) 購買電視
(B) 開帳戶
(C) 安排約會
(D) 下訂單

答案 (D) 概述

一來一往的對話次數多時，要全神貫注從頭到尾不漏聽是不容易的，盡可能先大略瞄一下3道問題，再聽對話內容掌握聽懂的重點。打電話的目的，通常就在對話一開始。對話中一開始就說I'd like to order...，所以(D)是正確答案。I'd like to do（我想～）是表達「電話目的」的一種表現法。要購買的東西是蓮蓬頭而不是電視，所以(A)是錯的。不要被對話中提到的on TV誤導了。

60

What does the man ask the woman for?
(A) Her telephone number
(B) Her preferred model
(C) Her delivery address
(D) Her credit card number

男性向女性問什麼？
(A) 她的電話號碼
(B) 她喜歡的型號
(C) 她的投遞地址
(D) 她的信用卡卡號

答案 (B) 請求、建議、提出

問題的ask O for～是「向某人問～」。從男性第1次的回應說May I ask which model you'd like...?，可知他在詢問對方想買標準的或豪華的型號，所以正確答案是(B)。

□ preferred [prɪ`fɚd] 形 喜歡的
□ delivery [dɪ`lɪvɚɪ] 名 投遞

61

When will the item probably arrive?
(A) This evening
(B) Tomorrow evening
(C) In two days
(D) In a week

產品可能何時到達？
(A) 今晚
(B) 隔天傍晚
(C) 2 日後
(D) 1 週後

答案 (C) 其他細節

問題的the item是指女性現在用電話訂購的商品（省水蓮蓬頭）。根據男性第2次的回應內容可知，如果現在下訂單，翌日配送，送達女性住處是再隔一天的傍晚，也就是後天（2日後），所以(C)是正確答案。

錄音原文	錄音原文翻譯

Questions 62 through 64 refer to the following conversation.

M: Seena, you're aware there's a film festival being held downtown this weekend, right?

W: Yes. Friday through Sunday. Why?

M: Well, last year it drew some 3,000 people. <u>Accommodations could be hard to come by</u>. Do you think it'll be a problem for our attendees?

W: Ah, right. Our district meeting on Saturday and Sunday. I took the liberty of reserving rooms for at least 50 people at the Westwood about a month ago. That's about how many people we had last year.

M: Oh, what a relief. The Westwood? That's right across the street from the venue.

試題 62-64 請參考以下會話。

M：西恩娜（Seena），妳知道市中心這週末會舉辦電影節，對吧？

W：是的，週五到週日。為何講這個？

M：嗯，去年它吸引了約 3,000 人。應該很難訂到住房。對我們的出席者來說，你認為那將是個問題嗎？

W：喔，沒錯。我們的區會議是週六跟週日。約一個月前，我就擅自在威斯特伍德飯店（Westwood）取得至少 50 人的訂房了。去年大約是那樣的出席人數。

M：哇，鬆了一口氣。是威斯特伍德飯店嗎？剛好就在會場的對街。

Vocabulary

☐ attendee [ə`tɛndi] 名 出席者　　☐ district [`dɪstrɪkt] 名 地區　　☐ take the liberty of ～ing　擅自（雖失禮）做～

☐ relief [rɪ`lif] 名 輕鬆（的感覺）　　☐ venue [`vɛnju] 名 場地

試題	試題翻譯	解答與解析

62

What are the speakers mainly discussing?
(A) Last year's sales
(B) A film review
(C) An upcoming meeting
(D) A conference location

2 人主要在談論什麼？
(A) 去年的銷售
(B) 影評
(C) 即將到來的會議
(D) 會議的地點

答案 (C)　〔概述〕

一開始男性就提到這週末的電影節，話題接著就是有關電影節對他們區會議的影響，所以(C)是正確答案。雖然談到最後有觸及會議地點，但不是主要話題，不適合選(D)。

☐ review [rɪ`vju] 名 評論、回顧

63

What does the man imply when he says, "<u>Accommodations could be hard to come by</u>"?
(A) Local hotels may not have vacancies.
(B) Access to a venue may be difficult.
(C) A festival may need to be cancelled.
(D) Too many people may come to the meeting.

男性說「Accommodations could be hard to come by」時，表示什麼？

(A) 當地飯店可能沒有空房。
(B) 進入會場可能很困難。
(C) 可能需要取消節日活動。
(D) 會議可能來太多人。

答案 (A)　〔說話者的目的〕

accommodation是指「住宿」，come by在這裡為「取得」之意。因為週末電影節會有很多人來市中心，男性擔心他們的會議出席者是否有地方住，所以(A)是正確答案。

64

What does the woman say she has done?
(A) Booked hotel rooms in advance
(B) Contacted a specialist
(C) Arranged for adequate seating
(D) Inquired about attendance

女性說她做了什麼？

(A) 事先訂房
(B) 聯絡了專家
(C) 安排了足夠的座位
(D) 詢問了出席人數

答案 (A)　〔其他細節〕

由女性第2次的回應就知道(A)是正確答案，只是把reserving rooms和about a month ago分別換為Booked hotel rooms和in advance的說法而已。(C)的seating（座位）如果換成hotel rooms（飯店房間）就是正確選項。使用現在完成式的問題會常出現，大家要多加熟悉。

☐ in advance　事先
☐ adequate [`ædəkwɪt] 形 適當的、足夠的
☐ inquire [ɪn`kwaɪr] 動 詢問

錄音原文	錄音原文翻譯

Questions 65 through 67 refer to the following conversation and chart.

W: Jonathan, do you know where I should shelve the books in this box?

M: Ah. That's our new shipment of foreign novels in translation.

W: So ... that means they go on the 1st floor, not the 2nd.

M: You got it. Novels is our biggest section, which is why it's at the front of the store. Oh, and one other thing. The upcoming book fair. That'll be on the same floor, but in the other section. It would help if you could clear off some of the tables by the door by Friday.

W: Sure. I'll do that right after I put these books on the shelves.

Section	Location
Novels & Poetry	1F West
Business & Travel	1F East
Non-Fiction	2F West
Foreign Books	2F East

試題 65-67 請參考以下會話及圖表。

W：強納森（Jonathan），你知道我應該把箱子裡的書放在哪個架上嗎？

M：喔。那是我們新到貨的外國小說譯本。

W：嗯……所以那表示它們要放在 1 樓，不是 2 樓。

M：沒錯。小說類是我們最大的區，這就是為何我們要把這區放在店裡最前面的原因。喔，另外還有件事。再不久就是書展了，將辦在同一樓層，但會在不同區。如果週五前妳可以門邊的幾張桌子移走，那會幫我很大的忙。

W：了解。待我把這些書放在架上後，我會立刻去做。

區域	位置
小說與詩	1 樓　西
商業類與旅遊書	1 樓　東
非小說類	2 樓　西
外國書籍	2 樓　東

Vocabulary

☐ shelve [ʃɛlv] 動 將～放在架上　　☐ in translation　譯本　　☐ clear off～　移開、除去　　☐ shelves [ʃɛlvz] 名 shelf（書架）的複數

試題	試題翻譯	解答與解析

☑ 65

Where is the conversation most likely taking place?
(A) At a school
(B) At a real estate agency
(C) At a publishing company
(D) At a bookstore

這篇對話地點可能在哪裡？

(A) 在學校
(B) 在房地產仲介公司
(C) 在出版社
(D) 在書店

答案 (D) 　　概述

關於問對話地點的題目，我們要掌握對話中的關鍵字來做判斷。從shelve the books（將書放在架上）、foreign novels（外國小說）、upcoming book fair（即將到來的書展）等語詞來判斷，(D)是正確答案。

☐ real estate　不動

☑ 66

Look at the graphic. Where will the book fair be held?
(A) 1F West
(B) 1F East
(C) 2F West
(D) 2F East

依圖表所示，書展將在哪裡舉辦？

(A) 1 樓　西
(B) 1 樓　東
(C) 2 樓　西
(D) 2 樓　東

答案 (B) 　　圖表問題

遇到圖表問題，要在聽錄音原文之前，先大略確認圖表與問題。看到選項，就知道是問圖表Location（位置），接著再從問題，掌握book fair（書展）一詞。關於book fair，男性說That'll be on the same floor, but in the other section.。其中the same floor（同一樓層）就是前面提及1樓西區小說所在的1樓。至於「同一樓層的另一區」，根據圖表，就是指1樓東區。the other～意思是「所在區域的另一邊」。

☑ 67

What will the woman do next?

(A) Clean some tables
(B) Move some shelves
(C) Put some books on display
(D) Go to the second floor

女性接下來要做什麼？

(A) 清潔一些桌子
(B) 移動一些架子
(C) 把一些書陳列展出
(D) 去 2 樓

答案 (C) 　　下一步動作

會話之後要做的動作，大部分是由最後回應的人說的。女性最後說I'll do that right after I put these books on the shelves.，而正確答案(C)只是將put these books on the shelves換成另一種說法而已。注意對話中提到的clear off（移開、除去），和(A)的clean（使～乾淨、清除～的髒汙）意思不同。

☐ on display　陳列

 CD 1 47 W 🇺🇸 M 🇨🇦

錄音原文	錄音原文翻譯

Questions 68 through 70 refer to the following conversation and label.

W: Excuse me. This label says September 10, but does that mean this pizza is only good for three more days?

M: Oh, that's only if you buy them before they're frozen.

W: They're sold unfrozen, too?

M: Yes. Many of our customers buy them that way, but we do freeze some of them right after we make them. As long as they stay frozen, our pizzas last for at least two weeks past the marked date. We pride ourselves on freshness, however, which is why we discount our frozen items.

試題 68-70 請參考以下會話及標籤。

W：請問，這標籤上印 9 月 10 日，意思是這份披薩只能再放3天嗎？

M：不，那是指如果妳買的時候，披薩是未冷凍的。

W：你們也賣未冷凍的？

M：是的，很多客人都是購買那種，但是我們會做好之後，馬上拿一些冷凍起來。只要是保持冷凍，我們的披薩至少可以持續放到標記日期後 2 週。然而，因為我們以新鮮自豪，所以這就是為何冷凍產品有打折。

```
Pete's 披薩
隨時新鮮　隨時美味
莫札瑞拉起司與培根
8.99 美元
製造日期：9 月 5 日
有效日期：9 月 10 日
```

Vocabulary

☐ unfrozen [ʌn`frozn] 形 不冷凍的　　☐ freeze [friz] 動 將～冷凍　　☐ as long as～　只要　　☐ last [læst] 動 持續、長久

☐ past [pæst] 介 經過～　　☐ mark [mɑrk] 動 打印、標記（物品上的號碼等）　　☐ pride *oneself* on～　以～自豪

☐ freshness [`frɛʃnɪs] 名 新鮮

試題	試題翻譯	解答與解析

☐ 68

Look at the graphic. When does the conversation take place?
(A) September 2
(B) September 5
(C) September 7
(D) September 10

依圖所示，這篇對話是發生在什麼時候？
(A) 9 月 2 日
(B) 9 月 5 日
(C) 9 月 7 日
(D) 9 月 10 日

答案 (C) 　圖表問題

圖表是商品標籤。從問題與選項來看，我們可以推測是問會話當天的日期，或是有關標籤上的製造與有效日期等等。女性看到標籤上的有效日期9月10日而詢問does that mean this pizza is only good for three more days?，由此可知對話的時間是9月10日的前3天，也就是9月7日。

☐ 69

What does the man emphasize?

(A) The price of an item
(B) The quality of an item
(C) The ingredients of an item
(D) The location of an item

男性強調什麼？

(A) 產品價格
(B) 產品品質
(C) 產品原料
(D) 產品位置

答案 (B) 　其他細節

這是店內的女性客人與男性店員的對話。女性詢問貼在冷凍披薩上的標籤載明的有效日期，男性店員詳細地回答。從他說「以新鮮自豪」的話裡，可知正確答案是(B)。

☐ ingredient [ɪn`gridɪənt] 名 材料、原料

☐ 70

What does the man say about the pizzas?
(A) They are only available frozen.
(B) There are many different sizes.
(C) The price goes down after two weeks.
(D) A discount is applicable to frozen ones.

關於披薩，男性說了什麼？

(A) 只有賣冷凍的。
(B) 有很多不同尺寸。
(C) 2 週後降價。
(D) 打折適用於冷凍產品。

答案 (D) 　其他細節

這題重點在男性最後說，which is why we discount our frozen items（這就是為何要對冷凍產品打折之故）。items是指披薩，所以(D)是正確答案。(A)與文中所說的Many of our customers buy them that way(＝unfrozen)不符。

☐ be applicable to～　適用於～

PART 4

錄音原文	錄音原文翻譯
Questions 71 through 73 refer to the following talk.	試題 71-73 請參考以下演說。

I'd like to announce that this year's Annual Company Charity Fun Run will be held on May 2nd. It starts from Windsor Park, and participants can take part in one of three options: a two, five, or ten kilometer run. There will be thirty-minute intervals between the start time of each run. Only some roads will be closed to traffic, so remember that you might be sharing the road with vehicles in some places. Last year we raised more than 8,000 dollars for the construction of a new community pool. This year, all money raised will be donated to the children's hospital. See you on the 2nd!

我在此宣布，今年公司年度慈善公益歡樂路跑活動 （Annual Company Charity Fun Run） 將於 5 月 2 日舉行。 從溫莎公園 （Windsor Park） 出發，參加者可從 3 種路程中擇一參加：2 公里、5 公里及 10 公里。 每種路程的起跑時間有 30 分鐘的間隔。 僅有一些道路會實施交通封閉，所以請記得你在一些路段會人車共行。 去年我們為新社區游泳池的建設工程募得超過 8,000 元的款項。 而今年所有的募款將會捐給兒童醫院。 期待我們 5 月 2 日相見了！

Vocabulary

☐ participant [pɑrˋtɪsəpənt] 名 參加者　　☐ interval [ˋɪntəvɪ] 名 間隔　　☐ share A with B　和B共有A
☐ raise [rez] 動 募（款）　　☐ construction [kənˋstrʌkʃən] 名 建設　　☐ donate A to B　把A捐給B

試題	試題翻譯	解答與解析
☑ **71** How many kinds of races are there? (A) Two (B) Three (C) Five (D) Ten	路跑有幾種？ (A) 2 種 (B) 3 種 (C) 5 種 (D) 10 種	**答案 (B)**　　[其他細節] 關於路跑的種類，內容有提到participants can take part in one of three options: a two, five, or ten kilometer run。participant是「參加者」，take part in～是「參加～」。因為有2公里、5公里、10公里等3種路程，所以正確答案是(B)。雖然從three options（3種選項）這個字彙可知答案，但a two, five, or ten kilometer run的說明更能確定無誤。
☑ **72** What should participants be aware of? (A) Start times are different from last year. (B) The course will be very challenging. (C) Some parts of the course may be closed. (D) Some roads may have normal traffic flow.	參加者應該注意什麼？ (A) 起跑時間與去年不同。 (B) 路線頗具挑戰。 (C) 部分路線會被封閉。 (D) 一些道路可能有正常的車流量。	**答案 (D)**　　[其他細節] 正確答案(D)是把呼籲參加者（聽眾）要注意的部分remember that you might be sharing the road with vehicles in some places改成另一種說法而已。traffic flow是「車流量」。因為封閉的不是部分路線，而是部分道路，所以(C)錯誤。注意不要被演說中的some roads will be closed to traffic誤導。
☑ **73** What was the money from last year's event used for? (A) A children's hospital (B) A local school (C) A swimming pool (D) Road construction	去年活動的募款用來做什麼？ (A) 兒童醫院 (B) 地方學校 (C) 游泳池 (D) 道路建設	**答案 (C)**　　[其他細節] 問句一旦長就容易焦慮，但是通常不需要完全聽懂整句話的含意。像這題即使只有聽到money（錢）、last year（去年）、used（用），應該可以推測到「去年的錢用於哪裡（捐到哪裡）？」這類提問。再從Last year we raised... a new community pool.可知正確答案是(C)。注意(A)提到的「兒童醫院」是今年的捐贈對象。

錄音原文	錄音原文翻譯
Questions 74 through 76 refer to the following telephone message. Dr. Jones, this is Alex Frasier calling from Metro Estate about a location for your office in Petersville. We've just listed a commercial space on the first floor of the Bixby Building, on 3rd Street and Wenton Avenue. The building's about a hundred years old, but it's been well maintained. Also, its plumbing and wiring were updated about four years ago, which is something I'm aware you'd wanted. It's fairly spacious at around two thousand square feet, and there's ample parking nearby. This property will probably rent quickly, so if you're interested in viewing it, please give us a call as soon as possible. Thank you.	試題 74-76 請參考以下電話留言。 瓊斯（Jones）醫師，我是大都會（Metro）不動產的艾力克斯·佛雷澤（Alex Frasier），我想要提供您有關在彼得斯維爾（Petersville）的辦公室地點。我們剛刊登一個商業空間物件，在溫頓（Wenton）大道和第三街交叉口的比克斯比（Bixby）大廈一樓。這幢老建築約百年歷史，但維護得很好。而且，它的配管和線路在 4 年前已換新，我知道這是您想要的。場地相當寬敞，約有 2,000 平方呎，附近還有足夠的停車位。這個不動產物件可能很快就會被出租，如果您有興趣看看，請盡快撥電話給我們。謝謝您。

Vocabulary

- □ commercial [kə`mɝʃəl] 形 商業的
- □ plumbing [`plʌmɪŋ] 名 （水管）配管
- □ wiring [`waɪrɪŋ] 名 （電線）線路
- □ be aware (that)～ 知道～
- □ fairly [`fɛrlɪ] 副 相當
- □ spacious [`speʃəs] 形 寬敞的
- □ square feet 平方呎
- □ ample [`æmpl̩] 形 足夠的
- □ nearby [`nɪr͵baɪ] 副 在附近
- □ property [`prɑpɚtɪ] 名 不動產物件
- □ rent [rɛnt] 動 出租

試題	試題翻譯	解答與解析
74 What does the speaker say about the building? (A) It is very old. (B) It is residential. (C) It needs some updating. (D) It is on a major bus route.	留言者對於建築物有什麼看法？ (A) 很舊。 (B) 是住宅用途的。 (C) 需要一些翻新。 (D) 位於主要巴士路線上。	**答案 (A)** 　其他細節 整個留言是在說明物件（建築物），而這道題是問全面性的。從The building's about a hundred years old這段話就知道(A)是正確答案。a location for your office意指客人要找的是租賃辦公室，留言者推薦a commercial space（商業空間），也沒有提到住宅建築，所以(B)不對。留言中只說配管和線路已換新的訊息，所以選(C)不合適。(D)的巴士資訊，留言中並沒有提到。
75 According to the message, what feature is Dr. Jones looking for? (A) A second-floor location (B) A low rental price (C) Adequate parking (D) Modern plumbing	根據留言，瓊斯醫師要尋找什麼特色的物件？ (A) 2 樓的位置 (B) 低租金 (C) 足夠的停車位 (D) 新式的配管	**答案 (D)** 　其他細節 瓊斯醫師是留言的收聽人。物件說明中有提到換新的部分是its plumbing and wiring were updated about four years ago，而從which is something I'm aware you'd wanted這句可以得知瓊斯醫師希望的條件，(D)只是將「換新」（were updated）改說為「新式的」（modern），所以是正確答案。 □ according to～ 根據～
76 Why does the speaker suggest viewing the property as quickly as possible? (A) Its price will increase soon. (B) Others will be interested in it. (C) The listing is about to end. (D) The office will be closed soon.	留言者為何建議要盡快看這個物件？ (A) 它的價格很快就會升高。 (B) 其他人會有興趣。 (C) 刊登即將結束。 (D) 辦公室將很快關閉。	**答案 (B)** 　請求、建議、下一步動作 問句的view the property是「看物件」，as quickly as possible是「盡快」之意。留言者急於帶看物件的理由就是This property will probably rent quickly，因此(B)是正確答案。別的租客要是有興趣，可能馬上就會出租了。

錄音原文	錄音原文翻譯
Questions 77 through 79 refer to the following telephone message. Hello, Mr. Fraser. This is Anne James from Unlimited Vacations. I'm calling to confirm your reservation for the seven-day Italian bus tour. We have made the itinerary changes you requested for Rome on the fifth day. Your tour now includes an excursion to several ancient Roman landmarks. The tour will begin after lunch. I will e-mail you the itinerary and details of your tour accommodation later. If you need any further assistance, please feel free to contact me at 555-2400.	試題 77-79 請參考以下電話留言。 哈囉！菲沙（Fraser）先生，我是無限假期（Unlimited Vacations）的安妮·傑姆斯（Anne James）。打電話給您是要確認您預約的義大利7日巴士遊。我們已經依您的要求變更第 5 天在羅馬的旅程。現在您的行程已包含一趟短途旅行，途中走訪幾個古羅馬史跡地標。行程會在午餐後開始。稍後我會把行程表和旅遊住宿的詳細資料傳至您的電子信箱。如果您還需要任何協助，請別客氣並撥打電話 555-2400 給我。

Vocabulary

- □ confirm [kən`fɝm] 動 確認（預約）
- □ itinerary [aɪ`tɪnəˌrɛrɪ] 名 行程（表）
- □ excursion [ɪk`skɝʒən] 名 短途（遊覽）旅行
- □ landmark [`lændˌmɑrk] 名 受保護的文物（史跡）地標建築
- □ feel free to *do* 別客氣、儘管做～

試題	試題翻譯	解答與解析
77 What is the purpose of the call? (A) To advertise a new tour (B) To change a departure date (C) To respond to a customer's request (D) To cancel a customer's accommodations	這通電話的目的是什麼？ (A) 廣告新的旅遊行程 (B) 變更出發日 (C) 回應客戶的需求 (D) 取消客戶的住宿	**答案 (C)** 〔概述〕 打電話的目的，通常是由一開始講話的那方闡述。這篇的關鍵是在 We have made the itinerary changes you requested...。(C)是將「依您的要求做變更」改說為「回應客戶的需求」，所以是正確答案。respond to～是「回應～」。(B)是錯在變更第5日而非出發日。注意不要看到選項有change（變更）就誤選。
78 What will Mr. Fraser do in Rome? (A) Go out on a boat excursion (B) Explore historic places (C) Visit a historical museum (D) Attend a theater performance	菲沙先生打算在羅馬做什麼？ (A) 乘船遊覽 (B) 探索具有歷史意義的地方 (C) 參觀歷史博物館 (D) 觀賞戲劇表演	**答案 (B)** 〔請求、建議、下一步動作〕 在Part 4部分，I或we是代表講話的人，you是代表聽者。若留言中有出現第3人，作答關鍵就在要把人物關係記在腦中並認真聽內容。這題的菲沙先生就是這篇留言的接收方，意即預約義大利巴士旅遊的人。在羅馬的行程就是Your tour now includes an excursion to several ancient Roman landmarks.。(B)是將ancient Roman landmarks（古羅馬史跡地標）改說為historic places（具有歷史意義的地方），所以是正確答案。
79 How will Mr. Fraser receive the itinerary? (A) By e-mail (B) By fax (C) By phone (D) By post	菲沙先生將如何收到行程表？ (A) 用電子郵件 (B) 用傳真 (C) 用電話 (D) 用郵寄	**答案 (A)** 〔其他細節〕 從I will e-mail you the itinerary可知正確答案是(A)。(C)的「電話」是在If you need any further assistance的條件下才使用的方式。

錄音原文	錄音原文翻譯

Questions 80 through 82 refer to the following announcement.

Welcome to Save More, where we always save you more. Today's green-label specials include our dairy department—get three liters of farm-fresh milk for only four dollars! Our meat and fish department is featuring grade-A beef for just a dollar nineteen per 100 grams. <u>Look for a host of green-tag items throughout the store.</u> And don't forget our delicatessen—our soups and made-to-order sandwiches are perfect for a fresh, hot lunch on the go. This week, our chicken sandwich and minestrone soup set is half off, at just three-fifty. Remember, savings are always in store, here at Save More.

試題 80-82 請參考以下公告。

歡迎來到省更多（Save More）商場，在這裡我們讓您省更多。今天的綠標特價商品包括乳製品區——僅需 4 美元的 3 公升農場直送鮮奶！肉品及魚類區則是以每 100 公克 1 美元 19 分錢的 A 級牛肉為主打商品。眾多綠標商品遍布整個賣場。還有別忘了我們的熟食區——我們的湯品及客製化的三明治非常適合來個新鮮、熱騰騰的午餐帶著走。本週，我們的雞肉三明治和義大利蔬菜濃湯組合 5 折優惠，只要 3 美元 50 分錢。請記得，在店裡隨時都能省到錢，就在省更多商場。

Vocabulary

☐ dairy [ˋdɛrɪ] 形 乳製品的　　☐ feature [ˋfitʃɚ] 動 以～為（主打）特色　　☐ a host of～　很多的～　　☐ throughout [θruˋaʊt] 介 遍及～
☐ made-to-order [ˋmedtʊˋɔrdɚ] 形 客製化的　　☐ on the go　帶著走　　☐ minestrone soup　義大利蔬菜濃湯

試題	試題翻譯	解答與解析

☑ 80

What does the speaker imply when she says, "<u>Look for a host of green-tag items throughout the store</u>"?
(A) There are many bargain items.
(B) The store was newly opened.
(C) Departments are organized by color.
(D) Customers must search for salespeople.

播報者說 「Look for a host of green-tag items throughout the store」 時，表示什麼？
(A) 有很多特價商品。
(B) 店家新開幕。
(C) 賣場各區用顏色區分。
(D) 客人必須找銷售人員。

答案 (A)　　說話者的目的

把本篇是公告文放在心上再聽本文，從開頭首句的Welcome to Save More，就可推測是店內播報。Today's green-label specials（今天的綠標特價商品）及only four dollars（僅需4美元）、just a dollar nineteen（僅需1美元19分錢）、half off（5折優惠）、at just three-fifty（只要3美元50分錢）等，整個播報內容聽到的都是有關特賣的語句。畫底線句中的green-tag items就是指開頭第2句的Today's green-label specials，意即綠標商品是特價品，所以(A)是正確答案。

☐ search for～　尋找～

☑ 81

Where can shoppers get lunch?

(A) In the dairy department
(B) In the meat and fish section
(C) In the deli department
(D) In the vegetables and fruit section

購物客人可以在哪裡買午餐？

(A) 在乳製品區
(B) 在肉品及魚類區
(C) 在熟食區
(D) 在蔬果區

答案 (C)　　其他細節

文中說了幾個賣區，所以要專心聽有關lunch（午餐）的部分。從And don't forget our delicatessen... a fresh, hot lunch on the go.這段話就可知(C)是正確答案。delicatessen (section)就是所謂的「已煮熟的家常菜區」，簡寫為deli (section)。選項的department有「賣區」之意，用在這邊與section（部分、分區）意思相同。

☑ 82

What item is fifty percent off?

(A) Milk
(B) Today's fish
(C) Grade-A beef
(D) A sandwich and soup set

什麼商品打 5 折？

(A) 牛奶
(B) 今日魚類
(C) A 級牛肉
(D) 三明治和湯品組合

答案 (D)　　其他細節

文中說了很多商品的折扣價格，有提到5折商品。從our chicken sandwich and minestrone soup set is half off這句可知，(D)是正確答案。文中說的half off（半價）就是本題問的fifty percent off（打5折）。

錄音原文	錄音原文翻譯

Questions 83 through 85 refer to the following radio broadcast.

This is Mike Ryan with the Evening News at six o'clock, for Thursday, March 5th. Tonight's top story: engineers are working to repair a roadside wall that gave way along Highway 34 just east of the Ford River Bridge around 3 A.M., amid this week's unseasonably heavy rains. No injuries have been reported in the landslide, however, a portion of Highway 34 including the bridge remains closed. Motorists should expect increasing traffic delays on the detour route. Engineers hope to reopen Highway 34 by Friday afternoon, however, the National Weather Service has reported that unstable weather may continue, which could cause further delays. Motorists are advised to seek alternate routes.

試題83-85 請參考以下的廣播。

我是麥克·雷恩（Mike Ryan），為大家播報 3 月 5 日週四的 6 點晚間新聞。今夜頭條：本週非季節性豪雨，造成沿著福特河大橋（Ford River Bridge）東邊的 34 號公路路邊牆面於凌晨 3 點崩塌，工程師正沿線全力修復中。目前尚無任何因山坡崩滑而受傷的消息，不過包括這橋樑在內的部分 34 號公路仍然封閉。駕駛人應預期繞道路線上的交通延誤狀況將愈加嚴重。工程師希望在週五下午前能再度開通 34 號公路，不過由於國立氣象局已預報天氣將會持續不穩定，因此可能會延遲開通。建議駕駛人尋求替代路線。

Vocabulary

- □ highway [`haɪ͵we] 名 公路幹道　　□ amid [ə`mɪd] 介 在～之中　　□ unseasonably [ʌn`siznəbl̩ɪ] 副 非季節性、不合季節地
- □ injury [`ɪndʒərɪ] 名 傷害　　□ a portion of～　～的一部分　　□ motorist [`motərɪst] 名 駕駛人　　□ detour route　繞道
- □ unstable [ʌn`steb!] 形 不穩定的　　□ alternate [`ɔltə·nɪt] 形 供替換的、替代的

試題	試題翻譯	解答與解析

☑ 83

Why has Highway 34 been closed?

(A) A bridge has collapsed.
(B) A traffic accident has occurred.
(C) A river has flooded.
(D) Part of the road is being repaired.

為何封閉 34 號公路？

(A) 有座橋崩塌。
(B) 發生交通事故。
(C) 河川氾濫。
(D) 部分道路正在修復。

答案 (D) 〔其他細節〕

從engineers are working to repair a roadside wall that gave way along Highway 34這句可知，沿著34號公路的路邊牆面正在進行修復。接著後面提到a portion of Highway 34...remains closed，這邊就可判斷修復工作就是部分道路禁止通行的原因，所以(D)是正確答案。

- □ collapse [kə`læps] 動 崩塌
- □ occur [ə`kɝ] 動 發生
- □ flood [flʌd] 動 氾濫

☑ 84

What time did the incident happen?

(A) Around 3 A.M.
(B) Around 4 A.M.
(C) Around 5 P.M.
(D) Around 6 P.M.

這起事件何時發生？

(A) 約凌晨 3 點
(B) 約凌晨 4 點
(C) 約下午 5 點
(D) 約下午 6 點

答案 (A) 〔其他細節〕

題目說的the incident就是指崩塌事件。從a roadside wall that gave way along Highway 34... around 3 A.M.這段話可知凌晨3點沿著34號公路的路邊牆面崩塌（gave way），所以正確答案是(A)。而(D)的下午6點是這則新聞播放的時間。

- □ incident [`ɪnsədnt] 名 （伴隨而來的）事件、小插曲

☑ 85

What does the speaker imply when he says, "Motorists should expect increasing traffic delays on the detour route"?
(A) The detour route is no longer the best way.
(B) The detour route was provided later than expected.
(C) Motorists should follow the detour signs.
(D) Motorists should watch out for falling debris.

播報者說 「Motorists should expect increasing traffic delays on the detour route」 時，表示什麼？

(A) 繞道路線不再是最好的方式。
(B) 繞道路線提供的時間晚於預期。
(C) 駕駛人應依繞道路線標示行駛。
(D) 駕駛人應注意落石。

答案 (A) 〔說話者的目的〕

針對traffic delays on the detour route（繞道路線上的交通延誤），駕駛人該如何因應呢？這篇報導最後說了Motorists are advised to seek alternate route.（建議利用替代道路），所以正確答案是(A)。這邊畫底線句中的expect（預期）並不是指「期待」之意，請仔細分辨。

錄音原文	錄音原文翻譯
Questions 86 through 88 refer to the following advertisement. Are you passionate about fashion? Taylor Kingdom offers the latest clothing fashions and top brands, as well as the highest quality of service. We are looking for a talented and motivated person to become a Store Manager at our brand-new Westgate store, opening in the second week of March. The successful applicant will have one to two years' experience in a similar role within the fashion industry, and have the ability to inspire and manage a sales team. If this sounds like the position for you, get your application in today by applying online at our Web site, TaylorKingdom.com.	試題 86-88 請參考以下廣告。 你對流行充滿熱情嗎？泰勒王國（Taylor Kingdom）不但提供最新的服裝時尚和頂尖品牌，還有最高級的服務品質。我們正在尋找一位有才能且積極的人來擔任 3 月第 2 週即將全新開幕的西門（Westgate）店的店經理。符合成功條件的申請人，要有 1 至 2 年在流行業界內類似職務的相關經驗，以及有能力激勵和管理一個銷售團隊。如果這聽起來像適合你的職位，今天就上我們的網站 TaylorKingdom.com 提出應徵申請吧。

Vocabulary

□ passionate [`pæʃənɪt] 形 熱情的　　□ latest [`letɪst] 形 最新的　　□ clothing [`kloðɪŋ] 名 衣服　　□ brand [brænd] 名 品牌
□ as well as～ 　而且、以及　　□ quality [`kwɑlətɪ] 名 品質　　□ motivated [`motɪvetɪd] 形 積極的　　□ brand-new [`brænd`nu] 形 全新的
□ similar [`sɪmələ] 形 類似的　　□ within [wɪ`ðɪn] 介 在～內　　□ industry [`ɪndəstrɪ] 名 行業　　□ ability to do 　做～的能力
□ inspire [ɪn`spaɪr] 動 激勵、啟發　　□ manage [`mænɪdʒ] 動 管理

試題	試題翻譯	解答與解析
☑ **86** What position is being advertised? (A) Shop manager (B) Retail assistant (C) Fashion show coordinator (D) Sales consultant	這則廣告在徵求什麼職務？ (A) 店經理 (B) 零售助理 (C) 時裝秀統籌者 (D) 銷售顧問	**答案 (A)**　概述 如果有機會先看這道題，就可以猜測並聽懂這篇是有關招募的內容。開頭的部分，似乎是跟服裝時尚（clothing fashions）相關的公司。接下來，要招募哪種職務，從We are looking for... person to become a Store Manager這句，就可知道(A)是正確答案。只是將store manager改說為shop manager。 □ coordinator [ko`ɔrdn͵etə] 名 統籌、協調者
☑ **87** What is a requirement for the position? (A) To be able to work on weekends (B) To have at least two years of work experience (C) To have a university degree (D) To have a background in fashion	這項職務要求什麼條件？ (A) 可在週末上班 (B) 至少要有 2 年工作經驗 (C) 有大學學歷 (D) 有流行方面相關背景	**答案 (D)**　其他細節 這項工作要求的條件在The successful applicant will have...這句有提到。所謂「符合成功條件的申請人」，意即「成功符合當店經理條件的應徵者」。而從後續的have one to two years' experience in a similar role within the fashion industry這段，就可知道(D)是正確答案。one to two years' experience是指就算1年經驗也符合，所以(B)至少2年的說法是錯的。
☑ **88** What should listeners do to apply for the position? (A) Go to the company Web site (B) Visit the store in person (C) Talk to the store manager (D) Send a résumé by mail	聽眾該如何應徵這項職務？ (A) 進入公司網站 (B) 親自到店面 (C) 跟店經理談 (D) 用電子郵件傳履歷表	**答案 (A)**　其他細節 應徵的方式在廣告最後有提到，就是If this sounds like the position for you, get your application in today by applying online at our Web site, TaylorKingdom.com這句。從by applying online（以上網申請的方式）即可知(A)是正確答案。選項只是把online（上網）換成Web site（網站）。 □ apply for～ 　應徵～

錄音原文	錄音原文翻譯
Questions 89 through 91 refer to the following speech.	試題 89-91 請參考以下演說。

Good morning, everyone. Today, I'm pleased to introduce to you the new head of our marketing department, Ms. Jessica Adams. Jessica comes to us from Crover Communications with a wealth of experience. She has worked on many high-profile accounts, including the "One Mind" campaign, which set new standards in computer marketing strategies. That campaign earned Jessica the "Innovative Marketer of the Year" award from the Foundation of Marketing Excellence. I'm sure she'd like to say a few words, so let's give her our applause.

大家早安。今天很高興為大家介紹我們的行銷部新任長官，潔西卡·亞當斯（Jessica Adams）女士。潔西卡帶著豐富的經驗從克羅佛通訊（Crover Communications）公司來我們這裡。她做過許多備受矚目的案子，包括訂定電腦行銷策略新標準的「一條心」（One Mind）行銷活動。該行銷活動讓潔西卡獲得行銷卓越基金會（Foundation of Marketing Excellence）「年度創新行銷人」的殊榮。我想她一定想跟大家說一些話，讓我們一起鼓掌歡迎她。

Vocabulary

- □ introduce to *someone*～　向（人）介紹～
- □ head [hɛd] 图（集團的）首長
- □ a wealth of～　豐富的～
- □ high-profile [haɪ ˋprofaɪl] 圈 備受矚目的
- □ account [əˋkaʊnt] 图 案子、客戶
- □ set a standard　制定標準
- □ strategy [ˋstrætədʒɪ] 图 策略
- □ innovative [ˋɪnoˏvetɪv] 圈 創新的
- □ marketer [ˋmɑrkɪtə] 图 市場行銷人員
- □ applause [əˋplɔz] 图 鼓掌歡迎

試題	試題翻譯	解答與解析

☑ 89

What is the main topic of the speech?

(A) To present an award
(B) To welcome a new employee
(C) To describe a new work schedule
(D) To plan a retirement party

演說的主題是什麼？

(A) 頒獎
(B) 歡迎新員工
(C) 敘述新的工作時程
(D) 計畫退休派對

答案 (B)　　概述

先記住本文是場演說，然後再繼續聽。從 I'm pleased to introduce to you the new head of our marketing department, Ms. Jessica Adams 這句可知，演說者在介紹今天來公司的新人潔西卡·亞當斯。所以(B)是正確答案。至於選項(A)說的獎（award）在本文後半部有提到，但不是授予（present）的場面。

☑ 90

What does the speaker say about Jessica Adams?
(A) She has received an award.
(B) She has worked abroad.
(C) She has appeared on television.
(D) She has been an accountant for years.

演說者說了什麼有關潔西卡·亞當斯的話？

(A) 她有獲獎過。
(B) 她在國外工作過。
(C) 她曾參與電視演出。
(D) 她當會計師已多年。

答案 (A)　　其他細節

演說者說了很多關於潔西卡·亞當斯的內容，其中(A)最符合 That campaign earned Jessica the "Innovative Marketer of the Year" award... 這句。earn [receive] an award 是「獲獎」之意。

- □ appear [əˋpɪr] 勔 演出
- □ accountant [əˋkaʊntənt] 图 會計師

☑ 91

What will most likely happen next?

(A) The meeting will end.
(B) A demonstration will take place.
(C) Refreshments will be served.
(D) A speech will be made.

接下來最有可能發生什麼事？

(A) 會議結束。
(B) 舉行實地示範。
(C) 提供茶點。
(D) 進行一場演說。

答案 (D)　　請求、建議、下一步動作

演說後的「下一步動作」，一般會在最後提到。I'm sure she'd like to say a few words, so... 這句的 she 就是潔西卡·亞當斯，所以(D)是正確答案。選項只是把 say a few words（簡短演說）換成 speech（演說）。

- □ demonstration [ˏdɛmənˋstreʃən] 图 實地示範
- □ take place　舉行

CD 1 · 56 · 🇬🇧

錄音原文	錄音原文翻譯

Questions 92 through 94 refer to the following telephone message and receipt.

Hi, I know your store is closed now, so I'm leaving this message for customer service. I bought some items earlier today out at the Falkland Mall store, including a set of eight mugs. I haven't used them at all, and although I love the design, I just didn't happen to pay attention to the little label that says they're not microwaveable. And using mugs in the microwave oven is something I often do. The saucepan and bowl are microwaveable, so I'd like to keep those, but I'm wondering if you allow returns on sale items. I live kind of far away from Falkland, so if you could give me a call back tomorrow as to whether this is possible, I'd appreciate it. My name is Angie, and I'm at 641-555-7172. Oh, and I do have the receipt. Thanks so much. Bye.

```
Receipt
Bowl ················· $8
Mug Set ··············· $25
Saucepan ··············· $60
Microwave oven ······· $120

** cash payment, thank you**
```

試題 92-94 請參考以下的電話留言與收據。

嗨,我知道現在店已打烊,所以我留言給客服。今天稍早我在福克蘭購物中心(Falkland Mall)分店買了一些商品,包括一組 8 個馬克杯。我都還沒使用,而且雖然我很喜歡它的設計,但是卻剛好沒有注意小標籤說它們是不能微波的。而我經常用馬克杯來微波。平底深鍋和碗可以微波,所以我想留著,但是不知你們是否可接受特價商品退貨。我住得離福克蘭有點遠,要是你們明天回電告知關於可否退貨,我會非常感激。我的名字叫安及(Angie),電話是 641-555-7172。對了,我有保留收據。非常感謝。再見。

```
收據
碗 ---------------------- 8 元
馬克杯組 ------------ 25 元
平底深鍋 ------------ 60 元
微波爐 -------------- 120 元
** 請以現金支付,謝謝您 **
```

Vocabulary

□ happen to *do* 碰巧~　　□ pay attention to~ 注意~　　□ microwaveable [ˋmaɪkrəweɪvəbl] 圈 可微波的
□ kind of 有一點　　□ as to~ 關於~　　□ whether [ˋhwɛðɚ] 連 是否

試題	試題翻譯	解答與解析

☑ 92

What problem does the woman describe?
(A) She did not care for a product's design.
(B) She was given an incorrect item.
(C) She missed some information on an item.
(D) She was overcharged for a purchase.

女性描述了什麼問題?

(A) 她不喜歡商品的設計。
(B) 她收到不對的商品。
(C) 她沒看到商品上的一些資訊。
(D) 她被要求付過高的價錢。

答案 (C) 　概述

女性針對在店裡買的馬克杯說明了although I love the design, I just didn't happen to pay attention to the little label...,也提到I'm wondering if you allow returns on sale items,希望退還馬克杯。(C)用「沒看到資訊」來表示「沒有注意到標籤」,所以是正確答案。〈although A, B〉(雖然A但是B)這樣的句型,B的部分(這篇是指I just...)才是要表達的重點。

□ care for~　(通常用於否定、疑問、條件句) 喜歡~
□ incorrect [ˌɪnkəˋrɛkt] 圈 錯誤的
□ overcharge [ˋovɚˋtʃɑrdʒ] 動 對~要價過高

☑ 93

Look at the graphic. How much was the item the woman wants to return?
(A) $8
(B) $25
(C) $60
(D) $120

請看圖。 女性想退回的商品是多少元?

(A) 8 元
(B) 25 元
(C) 60 元
(D) 120 元

答案 (B) 　圖表問題

這張圖,是載明4種商品和價格的收據。先確定這題問的是價格,再從講句中推斷出女性有想要退還的商品。a set of eight mugs(一組8個馬克杯)正是她想退還的,從收據上的Mug Set(馬克杯組)→25元就可知正確答案是(B)。

☑ 94

When should the listener return the call?
(A) Later today
(B) Tomorrow
(C) Early next week
(D) In a few days

聽到電話留言的人該於何時回電?

(A) 今天晚些時候
(B) 明天
(C) 下週初
(D) 在這幾天內

答案 (B) 　其他細節

對聽話者的指示或請求內容,通常會在最後表達出來,從if you could give me a call back tomorrow as to...這句可知,正確答案是(B)。

錄音原文	錄音原文翻譯

Questions 95 through 97 refer to the following excerpt from a meeting and schedule.

Hi, everyone. Could I have your attention, please? We're just about to begin our monthly meeting here. Could I have you all take a look at the schedule on the paper in front of you? As you can see, we have four speakers lined up. However, just 10 minutes ago I got a call from Eric. He said he got a flat tire on the highway, so what I've done is ... Eric will switch places with Helen ... which, now that I think about it, might be a good thing. We'll start with what happened in the past, and end with a talk about the future. I hope that makes sense. OK then. Helen, do you need a minute to get ready?

試題 95-97 請參考以下的會議部分內容及時間表。

嗨,各位好。請注意聽我說。現在我們即將開始每月的例行會議。請大家看一下你們面前紙上的時間表。如同各位看到的,我們已安排 4 位演講人。不過,就在 10 分鐘前我接到艾瑞克（Eric）的電話,說他的車在公路上爆胎,所以我所做的就是……將艾瑞克與海倫（Helen）的順序調換……而現在我覺得,這樣可能也是好的。我們從過去發生的事情開始,最後談及未來。我想那樣比較合理。好!那麼海倫,你需要一點時間準備嗎?

Speakers	Topics	Time
Eric Freeman	Discussion: future goals	9:00 A.M.
Ai Hye-suk	Last Month's Sales figures	9:30 A.M.
Mark Feddle	Marketing strategies for this month	10:00 A.M.
Helen Clark	Last quarter's lessons	10:30 A.M.

演講人	議題	時間
艾瑞克·弗雷曼（Eric Freeman）	討論:未來的目標	9:00 A.M.
艾·慧素（Ai Hye-suk）	上個月的銷售數字	9:30 A.M.
馬克·費德（Mark Feddle）	本月的行銷策略	10:00 A.M.
海倫·克拉克（Helen Clark）	上一季的省思	10:30 A.M.

Vocabulary

□ have [get]～ lined up　已安排～　　□ get a flat tire　爆胎　　□ switch [swɪtʃ] 動 調換

試題	試題翻譯	解答與解析

☑ 95

What problem does the speaker describe?
(A) A conference must be delayed.
(B) A meeting space is not available.
(C) A participant will be late.
(D) A schedule is incomplete.

發言者描述了什麼問題?

(A) 必須延遲會議。
(B) 沒有可使用的會議空間。
(C) 有位參與者會遲到。
(D) 時間表是不完整的。

答案 (C)　概述

However, ...（然而）或是but（但是）後面提到的,大多是重要的問題點。本文中間However, ...往下繼續聽,從「10分鐘前接到艾瑞克電話」、「車在公路上爆胎」、「艾瑞克改第4順位」這些過程,可推斷艾瑞克會遲到,所以(C)是正確答案。

☑ 96

Look at the graphic. At what time will Eric speak after the change?
(A) 9:00 A.M.
(B) 9:30 A.M.
(C) 10:00 A.M.
(D) 10:30 A.M.

請看圖表。經過互換,艾瑞克改成幾點演說?

(A) 9:00 A.M.
(B) 9:30 A.M.
(C) 10:00 A.M.
(D) 10:30 A.M.

答案 (D)　圖表問題

快速瀏覽圖表,先記住4位演講人和主題、時間之後再聽這段話。針對遲到的艾瑞克,內容提到Eric will switch places with Helen,意即艾瑞克和海倫互換成為第4順位。所以艾瑞克演說的時間是10:30 A.M.。

☑ 97

According to the speaker, what might be good about the change?
(A) The topics will be in chronological order.
(B) The meeting time will be shorter.
(C) The discussion will begin earlier.
(D) There will be more speakers.

根據發言者的說法,為何改變可能是好的?

(A) 主題會依時間順序排列。
(B) 能縮短會議時間。
(C) 能提早開始討論。
(D) 能增加演講人。

答案 (A)　其他細節

問句的the change（改變）就是指艾瑞克改為第4順位一事。對此,發言者說...might be a good thing（可能也是好的),具體的說明就在下一句We'll start with what happened in the past, and end with a talk about the future.。(A)只是將「從過去發生的事情開始,最後談及未來」換成「主題會依時間順序排列」的說法來表達,所以是正確答案。

□ chronological [ˌkrɑnəˈladʒɪk!] 形 依年代排列的、依時間順序排列的
□ order [ˈɔrdə] 名 順序

錄音原文	錄音原文翻譯

Questions 98 through 100 refer to the following excerpt from a meeting and chart.

So, here are the results for last quarter's travel magazine sales. Now, what I'd like to do—I mean, to discuss—is, how can we improve sales to our least selling groups? For example, I was thinking we could run a special issue especially geared toward twenty-somethings. Since people in this age group have the least money and time to spend on vacations, we could focus on short-term getaways at bargain prices. These could be arranged through our travel coordinators. As marketing director, I can probably convey your opinions directly to them. And next, that's what I'd like you to give me: your opinions. Would anyone like to start?

試題 98-100 請參考以下的會議部分內容及圖表。

所以,這是上一季的旅遊雜誌銷售的結果。現在,我想做的——我是說,我想討論的——是如何才能改善銷售最少的族群的銷售量?例如,我在想我們可以發行特別號,專門以 20 幾歲的年輕人為對象。因為這個年齡層的人最沒有錢和時間度假,所以我們可以把焦點放在特價的短期假期。這可以透過我們的旅遊策畫人員來安排。身為行銷總監,我或許可以向他們直接傳達你們的意見。接下來,我希望你們能給我:你們的意見。有誰要先開始?

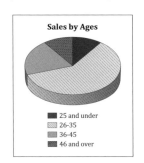

Sales by Ages
■ 25 and under
▨ 26-35
▨ 36-45
■ 46 and over

依年齡區分的銷售量
■ 25 歲(含)以下
▨ 26～35 歲
■ 36～45 歲
■ 46 歲(含)以上

Vocabulary

- quarter [`kwɔrtə] 名 季
- issue [`ɪʃjʊ] 名 發行物、(雜誌等的)期數
- gear [gɪr] 動 使適合～
- short-term getaway 短期假期
- convey [kən`ve] 動 傳達

試題	試題翻譯	解答與解析

98

Who most likely are the listeners?

(A) Travel agents
(B) Magazine subscribers
(C) Marketing representatives
(D) Airline coordinators

誰最有可能是聽眾?

(A) 旅行社職員
(B) 雜誌訂戶
(C) 行銷代表
(D) 航空公司協調人員

答案 (C)　聽眾與發言者

這是詢問聽眾是誰的問題。從一開始的 travel magazine sales(旅遊雜誌銷售),可知男性說的是有關雜誌的銷售結果。而且在最後階段的 As marketing director, ...這句,男性表示他身為行銷總監,要求聽眾們說出意見,所以(C)是正確答案。

- subscriber [səb`skraɪbə] 名 訂戶
- representative [rɛprɪ`zɛntətɪv] 名 代表人、負責人

99

Look at the graphic. Which age group does the speaker suggest focusing on?
(A) 25 years old and under
(B) 26 to 35 years old
(C) 36 to 45 years old
(D) 46 years old and over

請看圖。 發言者建議要把焦點放在哪一個年齡層?

(A) 25 歲 (含) 以下
(B) 26～35 歲
(C) 36～45 歲
(D) 46 歲 (含) 以上

答案 (A)　圖表問題

由圖可知這是依年齡區分的商品銷售圖表。問題的重點就是發言者想要專攻的年齡層。從 how can we improve sales to our least selling groups 這句來看,發言者想討論的是有關銷售量最少的25歲(含)以下和46歲(含)以上族群。接著又提到,we could run... toward twenty-somethings,因此他要說的是有關25歲(含)以下的具體方案。

100

What does the speaker say he will do next?
(A) Arrange a meeting time
(B) Gather people's ideas
(C) Contact a marketing director
(D) Increase funding for advertising

發言者說接下來他要做什麼?

(A) 安排會議時間
(B) 蒐集大家的意見
(C) 聯絡行銷總監
(D) 增加廣告資金

答案 (B)　請求、建議、下一步動作

問發言者下一步動作的題目,通常在最後會有提示。從最後的句子 that's what I'd like you to give me: your opinions. Would anyone like to start?,可知(B)是正確答案。

- funding [`fʌndɪŋ] 名 資金

PART 5

☑ 101

Although Leroy Dysangco could have asked his colleague to send out the estimates to his clients, he decided to deliver ------- himself.

(A) ones
(B) it
(C) their
(D) them

雖然雷洛伊·戴桑格（Leroy Dysangco）可以要求同事把估價單發給客戶，但是他決定自己遞送。

答案 (D) [文法]

這是人稱代名詞問題。空格後面的himself是指「他自己」。填空處是deliver（遞送）的受詞。作答時先思考要遞送什麼，再看前半句有提到the estimates（估價單），所以要讓客戶收到的是這個，因此(D)的them是正確答案。(A)的ones也可當前述the estimates的可數代名詞，但它是表示不特定的東西，所以語意不符。(B)的it也可當受詞，但這題用單數形不對。

☐ send out～　發出～
☐ estimate [`ɛstə,met] 名 估價（單）

☑ 102

According to a national survey conducted by Interland Travels, Spain was the most ------- destination for vacationers this year.

(A) popular
(B) popularly
(C) popularity
(D) popularize

根據英特蘭德旅行社（Interland Travels）進行的全國性調查，西班牙（Spain）是今年最受歡迎的旅遊度假目的地。

答案 (A) [詞性]

整句文脈就是「西班牙是最～的目的地」。空格被夾在the most和名詞（destination）之間，用形容詞最適當。所以(A)的popular（受歡迎）是正確答案。這題若只看the most ------- destination的部分也能作答。

☐ according to～　根據～
☐ conduct a survey　進行調查
☐ popularly [`pɑpjələlɪ] 副 一般地
☐ popularity [,pɑpjə`lærətɪ] 名 受歡迎
☐ popularize [`pɑpjələ,raɪz] 動 使～普及

☑ 103

Additional measures ------- to be implemented in the plant quarantine section at Houston Airport in order to prevent the spread of the new crop disease.

(A) having
(B) has
(C) not have
(D) will have

為了預防新作物的疾病擴散，休士頓 （Houston） 機場農作物檢疫區必須要實施額外的措施才行。

答案 (D) [文法]

Additional measures（額外的措施）是主詞，------- to be implemented（-------被實施）是述語動詞。選項中可當述語動詞的是(B)或(D)，不過主詞是複數，所以不可選(B)。(C)為否定形式，用在整句文法上不適當，必須改成Additional measures do not have to be～，前面還要再追加助動詞do。

☐ measure [`mɛʒɚ] 名 （慣用複數形）措施
☐ implement [`ɪmpləmənt] 動 實施～
☐ quarantine [`kwɔrən,tin] 名 檢疫
☐ in order to do　為了～

☑ 104

Smoking is prohibited both inside and outside the building ------- in designated areas.

(A) alone
(B) except
(C) through
(D) alongside

這棟建築物除了指定區域外，室內外都禁菸。

答案 (B) [選項混和型]

空格後是接「指定的場所」。整句「建築物內外都禁菸」＋「指定的場所除外」才會語意貫通，因此(B)是正確答案。except（除外）雖是介系詞，也可以像這題後面接副詞句（子句）。(A)的alone是形容詞或副詞，意為「獨自」。(C)的through是介系詞或副詞時，意為「通過～」；當形容詞時，意為「結束的」。(D)的alongside是介系詞或副詞，意為「（～的）旁邊，（與～）一起」。

☐ prohibit [prə`hɪbɪt] 動 禁止

☑ 105

Dr. Fergusson will be the new industrial ------- for Autocross Industries starting from next year.

(A) physical
(B) physically
(C) physics
(D) physician

佛格森（Fergusson）醫師從明年開始將成為越野（Autocross）實業公司新的（企業）特約醫師。

答案 (D) [詞性]

前面的industrial（產業的）是形容詞，所以空格要填名詞。(C)的physics（物理學）和(D)的physician（醫師）雖然都是名詞，但是要配合主詞Dr. Fergusson做補語用，所以是physician。

☐ physical [`fɪzɪk!] 形 身體的
☐ physically [`fɪzɪk!ɪ] 副 身體上

試題與翻譯	解答與解析

☑ **106**

Philadelphia Telecom help-desk staff are required to ------- to customers' inquiries on the spot unless they need to pass the issue on to technical representatives.

(A) deal
(B) answer
(C) manage
(D) reply

費城（Philadelphia）電信客服櫃台人員必須當場回答客戶的詢問，除非該問題須交由技術人員處理。

答案 (D)　　　字彙

這是有關不及物動詞和及物動詞的問題。be required to *do* 是「被要求做～」，雖然從接下來的語句可推斷是「對客戶的詢問做回答」之意，但由空格後面接介系詞 to 更可確定 (D) 的 reply to～（對～做回答）是正確答案。(A) 要改為 deal with（處理～）才正確。(B) 的 answer（回答），用在「問題」或「信件」這類的受詞之前，不需要接 to。(C) 的 manage 當及物動詞寫成 manage to *do* 時，是指「設法做～」。

☐ unless　除非～
☐ pass～ on to...　將～交給……

☑ **107**

The corporate medical insurance policy covers the medical expenses of ------- the employees but also their spouses and children.

(A) up to
(B) apart from
(C) not only
(D) as soon as

公司的醫療保險契約涵蓋的醫療費用不僅包括員工，還有他們的配偶及子女。

答案 (C)　　　慣用語

這句重點在後面的 but also，not only A but (also) B 是指「不僅 A 還有 B 也是」，所以 (C) 是正確答案。即使不懂句子或選項的意思，看到 but also 當下馬上就知道選 (C)。

☐ corporate [`kɔrpərɪt] 形 公司的
☐ expense [ɪk`spɛns] 名 費用
☐ spouse [spaʊz] 名 配偶
☐ up to～　直到～、至多～
☐ apart from～　除了～以外
☐ as soon as～　一～立即

☑ **108**

The upgraded printing system that has been released by Yaletown Solutions features greater maintenance efficiency ------- to previous models.

(A) dedicated
(B) accustomed
(C) referred
(D) compared

由耶魯鎮（Yaletown Solutions）公司發表的升級版印刷系統，其特色是比先前的型號有更高的維護效率。

答案 (D)　　　慣用語

重點在 greater（更好）是比較級。注意空格後面是介系詞 to，所以最適合表達比較的句型是 (D) 的 compared to～（和～比較）。(A) 的 dedicate to～是「奉獻給～」。(B) 的 be accustomed to～是「習慣於～」。(C) 的 refer to～是「提到～、參考～」。

☐ feature [fitʃə] 動 以～為特色
☐ efficiency [ɪ`fɪʃənsɪ] 名 效率
☐ previous [`priviəs] 形 先前的、以前的

☑ **109**

Researchers at the Allahabad Institute are experimenting to find out how two individually developed mechanisms interact with ------- other.

(A) some
(B) each
(C) one after
(D) even

阿拉哈巴德（Allahabad）研究機構的研究員正在實驗，以理解 2 個各別發展的結構如何彼此相互作用。

答案 (B)　　　慣用語

用 how 開頭的子句主詞是 two individually developed mechanisms，動詞是 interact。interact with～是「與～相互作用」。注意空格後面接 other，所以 each other（互相）是正確答案。each other 是用 2 個單字來合做 1 個名詞。interact 是不及物動詞，所以要注意不能寫成 interact each other。

☐ experiment [ɪk`spɛrəmənt] 名 實驗
☐ individually [ˌɪndə`vɪdʒʊəlɪ] 副 各別地
☐ mechanism [`mɛkəˌnɪzəm] 名 結構

☑ **110**

Thanks to our engineering team's quick response, the impact of the system failure was -------.

(A) minimized
(B) examined
(C) enhanced
(D) appeared

感謝我們公司技術團隊的快速回應，使系統故障的影響減至最小。

答案 (A)　　　字彙

空格前面是 was，所以這是被動句。由於技術團隊快速地回應，所以系統故障的影響會如何，從這種疑問來思考，(A) 最正確。minimize（將～減至最小），是在 minim(um)（最小的）字尾加上 ize（使成為～），變成動詞。

☐ impact [`ɪmpækt] 名 影響
☐ failure [`feljə] 名 （機器等的）故障
☐ examine [ɪg`zæmɪn] 動 檢查
☐ enhance [ɪn`hæns] 動 提高
☐ appear [ə`pɪr] 動 出現

35

☑ 111

All employees ------- security passwords have not been changed for over a month are reminded via e-mail to change them.

(A) why
(B) whose
(C) who
(D) whomever

超過 1 個月沒有變更安全密碼的所有員工，都由電子郵件提醒要變更。

答案 (B)　　文法

這是關係代名詞的問題。主詞是All employees（所有員工），動詞是are reminded（被提醒），從空格到month（月）為止是主詞All employees的修飾語。從All employees和security passwords（安全密碼）的關係可知，這是指「員工的安全密碼」，所以(B)的所有格whose是正確答案。(C)的who作為主格時，是接〈S＋V〉的句型，而security passwords have not been changed是被動式，不需要受詞，所以who(m)是錯的。

☑ 112

The labor union's ------- on better benefits and higher salaries was eventually rewarded.

(A) command
(B) summary
(C) insistence
(D) applause

工會對更好福利和更高工資的堅持，最終獲得回報。

答案 (C)　　字彙

The labor union's（工會的）------- 是主詞，was eventually rewarded（最終獲得回報）是述語動詞。根據空格後面的on，再思考是什麼事獲得回報，(C)的insistence on～是「對～的堅持」之意，所以是正確答案。
☐ benefit [ˋbɛnəfɪt] 名 利益
☐ eventually [ɪˋvɛntʃʊəlɪ] 副 終於
☐ reward [rɪˋwɔrd] 動 報酬
☐ command [kəˋmænd] 名 命令
☐ summary [ˋsʌmərɪ] 名 摘要
☐ applause [əˋplɔz] 名 鼓掌（喝采）

☑ 113

Registration forms for season tickets ------- before March 31 will go in the draw to win a Vista Rosa Hotel package for two.

(A) have received
(B) received
(C) were received
(D) receiving

在 3 月 31 日前收到的季票登記表，將抽籤抽出維斯塔玫瑰飯店 （Vista Rose Hotel） 的雙人住宿券。

答案 (B)　　動詞型態

如果可以看出整句的主詞是Registration forms for season tickets ------- before March 31，述語動詞是will go，就知道空格不是填述語動詞。------- before March 31是為了要修飾前面的名詞（Registration forms for season tickets），因此空格適用分詞。加上「在～之前收到的登記表」，這句是被動關係，所以(B)的過去分詞是正確答案。

☐ registration [ˌrɛdʒɪˋstreʃən] 名 登記

☑ 114

Debating is really a battle of wits and words between two teams, each of which ------- to persuade the audience to its point of view.

(A) practices
(B) mistakes
(C) attempts
(D) resists

辯論真的是一場 2 隊間的機智與唇舌之戰，雙方都試圖說服觀眾接受其觀點。

答案 (C)　　字彙

空格前面的(each of) which是關係代名詞，先行詞是two teams（2隊）。因為後面是接to persuade（去說服），所以用to加原形動詞的不定詞句型來看，只有(C)的attempt to do（試圖做～）最符合。attempt與try同樣有「試圖、嘗試」之意。(A)和(D)後面只能接動名詞形式，後面不接to，而是practice ～ing（練習～），resist ～ing（反抗～）。
☐ wit [wɪt] 名 機智
☐ persuade [pəˋswed] 動 說服
☐ point of view　觀點

☑ 115

Distland Corp recently installed a database system that allows all their dealers ------- customer and sales information.

(A) share
(B) being shared
(C) sharing
(D) to share

迪士蘭德公司 （Distland Corp） 最近安裝了資料庫系統，允許所有的經銷商共享客戶及銷售資訊。

答案 (D)　　動詞型態

allows all their dealers是「允許所有的經銷商」，a database system（資料庫系統）則是相當於allows（允許）的主詞。再從「共享」與「客戶及銷售資訊」的關係去思考，如果用allow～to do...（允許～做……；（主詞）使～可以……）的句型，整句就是語意通暢的「資料庫系統使所有的經銷商可以共享客戶及銷售資訊」，所以(D)用to的不定詞最正確。

試題與翻譯	解答與解析

☑ 116

Hally Textiles' net income rose ------- the increase in the price of some of their raw materials.

(A) in spite of
(B) as far as
(C) while
(D) whereas

儘管有部分的原料價格上漲，哈利紡織 （Hally Textiles） 公司的淨利仍然增加。

答案 (A)　〔慣用語〕

主詞是Hally Textiles' net income（哈利紡織公司的淨利），述語動詞是rose（增加）。句子到這邊可以算完成，所以空格後面算是副詞子句。想一下有肯定意味的「淨利增加」和否定意味的「部分的原料價格上漲」的關係，就知道(A)的in spite of～（儘管～）最正確。

☐ net income　淨利
☐ as far as～　達到～程度
☐ while [hwaɪl] 連 當～時候
☐ whereas [hwɛrˋæz] 連 然而

☑ 117

Many firms nowadays are conscious of ------- social responsibility and develop their own community commitment programs.

(A) corporately
(B) corporation
(C) corporate
(D) corporatism

當今很多公司意識到企業的社會責任，並發展他們自己的社區回饋計畫。

答案 (C)　〔詞性〕

be conscious of～是指「意識到～」，of後面要接名詞。social（社會的）是形容詞，responsibility（責任）是名詞。所以符合這2個單字的是(C)corporate（法人的、企業的）。最好把corporate social responsibility（企業的社會責任）這個慣用語記住。

☐ corporately [ˋkɔrpərɪtlɪ] 副 共同地
☐ corporation [͵kɔrpəˋreʃən] 名 法人
☐ corporatism [ˋkɔrpərə͵tɪzm] 名 集團主義

☑ 118

Mr. Jones is expected to be relocated to the office in China unless another ------- candidate is found.

(A) suitable
(B) durable
(C) incapable
(D) accessible

瓊斯 （Jones） 先生預期會被調至中國辦公室，除非找到其他合適的人選。

答案 (A)　〔字彙〕

unless是以「除非」為條件式的連接詞。選項全是形容詞，而符合整句語意「瓊斯先生預期將有異動，除非找到其他～的人選」的，就是(A)suitable（合適的）。

☐ relocate A to B　將 A調往B
☐ candidate [ˋkændədet] 名 候選人、應徵者
☐ durable [ˋdjʊrəbl̩] 形 耐用的
☐ incapable [ɪnˋkepəbl̩] 形 無能的
☐ accessible [ækˋsɛsəbl̩] 形 容易得到的

☑ 119

------- entering the factory, visitors are asked to sign their names at the reception desk and put on visitors' badges.

(A) Though
(B) Nearly
(C) Whereby
(D) Before

進入工廠之前，訪客被要求在接待處簽名並配戴訪客證。

答案 (D)　〔選項混合型〕

空格後面的entering the factory不是子句而是分詞片語，所以當連接詞的(A)Though（儘管）可以先排除。though也可以當副詞，但不放在句首。想一下「進入工廠」和「訪客簽名並配戴訪客證」的關係，就知道(D)的介系詞Before（在～之前）最正確。(B)的Nearly（幾乎）是副詞。(C)的Whereby（因此）是關係副詞（＝by which）。

☑ 120

Howard Electronic Gallery grants visitors ------- to download and display copyrighted materials for private purposes.

(A) permit
(B) permitted
(C) permission
(D) permitting

霍華德電子藝廊 （Howard Electronic Gallery） 允許訪客下載和展示受版權保護的素材做私人使用。

答案 (C)　〔詞性〕

grant A B是「給予A B」之意。visitors是A，填入空格的字即是相當於B的名詞。雖然選項除了(B)之外都可當名詞，但也要顧及後面是帶to的不定詞「下載和展示受版權保護的素材」，用來修飾空格內的名詞，所以(C)的permission（許可）是正確答案。

☐ copyrighted [ˋkɑpɪ͵raɪtɪd] 形 受版權保護的

試題與翻譯	解答與解析

☑ 121

Miners at Iron Supplies Co. will soon have to ------- other job opportunities because the local mines are closing down.

(A) pursue
(B) initialize
(C) endure
(D) implicate

因為當地的礦井要停業，艾隆供應公司（Iron Supplies Co.）的礦工很快必須尋求其他的工作機會。

答案 (A) 〔字彙〕

符合受詞other job opportunities（其他的工作機會）的動詞是(A)的pursue（尋求～）。從because（因為）後面的原因，可確定語意是「不找工作不行」，不過如果知道其他選項的意思，即使只看 ------- other job opportunities 的部分應該也能作答。

☐ miner [ˈmaɪnɚ] 名 礦工
☐ initialize [ɪˈnɪʃəlˌaɪz] 動 初始化
☐ endure [ɪnˈdjʊr] 動 忍受～
☐ implicate [ˈɪmplɪˌket] 動 牽連

☑ 122

All candidates that ------- their application forms can now proceed to the interview.

(A) submits
(B) be submitted
(C) have submitted
(D) have been submitted

已提交申請表的所有應徵者，現在可以進行面試。

答案 (C) 〔動詞型態〕

看選項就知道空格是要填動詞，前面的that是關係代名詞引導出的子句主格。All candidates（所有應徵者）是整句的主詞，their application forms（他們的申請表）是受詞，所以可想而知空格內要填動詞的主動語態(A)或(C)，但是因為主詞為複數，所以選(C)而不選(A)。

☐ application form 申請表
☐ proceed to～ 進行～

☑ 123

------- to reprint the first edition of *Handyman's Handbook* or to publish a second edition will be decided at the editors' meeting today.

(A) Which
(B) If
(C) Whether
(D) Nothing

今天在編輯會議上將決定《巧手達人指南》（*Handyman's Handbook*）一書是要初版再刷或是發行第二版。

答案 (C) 〔文法〕

重點在or，(C)的whether A or B（是A或B）的句型最適合。A和B都是加to的不定詞型態，whether to *do*意即「是否做～」。whether是連接詞，帶出的字句可當主詞、受詞或補語。這題從開始到第2個edition為止才是主詞。(A)的which和or看似相關，但which to *do*（做哪一個）的用法不符整段語意。(B)的if也有「哪一個」之意，但後面不接to不定詞型態，也無法成為主詞。

☑ 124

The mountain routes are shut down this winter owing to the ------- snowfall in November.

(A) extreme
(B) feasible
(C) vague
(D) utmost

由於11月極大的降雪，今年冬季山區路線封閉。

答案 (A) 〔字彙〕

適合snowfall（降雪）的形容詞是(A)的extreme（極端的、極度的）。owing to～是「由於」之意，連接前後因果關係。是怎樣的雪讓道路封閉，從這方面思考，就可確定答案是(A)，不過如果知道其他選項的意思，即使只看the ------- snowfall的部分應該也能作答。

☐ feasible [ˈfizəbl] 形 可行的
☐ vague [veg] 形 模糊的
☐ utmost [ˈʌtˌmost] 形 最大的（限度、可能）

☑ 125

------- of a reservation must be made at least seven days prior to your scheduled date of arrival, otherwise a charge is incurred.

(A) Cancel
(B) Cancellation
(C) To cancel
(D) Cancelled

取消預約須至少在你預定抵達日的前7天提出，否則會產生費用。

答案 (B) 〔詞性〕

------- of a reservation（預約的-------）是主詞，must be made（必須被提出）是述語動詞。空格後面有of，所以用名詞最適當，(B)的Cancellation（消去、取消）最正確。這題的用法是make a cancellation（消去、做取消）的被動式。

☐ prior to～ 在～之前
☐ otherwise [ˈʌðɚˌwaɪz] 副 否則
☐ charge [tʃɑrdʒ] 名 費用
☐ incur [ɪnˈkɝ] 動 招致、帶來～

試題與翻譯	解答與解析

☑ **126**

The World Library Conference in Cleveland has been ------- indefinitely because the university staff is having a strike at the planned venue.

(A) postponed
(B) continued
(C) addressed
(D) featured

因為大學職員正在會議預定場地進行罷工，在克里夫蘭 （Cleveland） 舉行的世界藏書研討會已被無限期延期。

答案 (A) 字彙

因為職員罷工造成會議如何，從這方面思考，即可知(A)的postponed（被延期）是正確答案。後面的indefinitely是「無限期」之意，但是答案並不會受這個字影響，所以不認識這個單字也不要緊張。

☐ continue [kən`tɪnjʊ] 動 繼續
☐ address [ə`drɛs] 動 向～演說、致力於～
☐ feature [fitʃə] 動 以～為特色

☑ **127**

------- of the two interviewees found it difficult to explain what they were seeking in their job opportunities.

(A) All
(B) Neither
(C) Those
(D) Between

2 位應試者都能輕易闡述自己在工作機會中尋求的是什麼。

答案 (B) 選項混合型

空格後面是接of，所以可先排除(D)。其他選項都是可接of的代名詞，但是(A)的all不能用於像the two interviewees（2位應試者）只有兩者的情況。(B)的neither of～用於兩者時，意思是「～之中兩者都不……」，符合整句語意，所以是正確答案。(C)的those of～是that of～的複數形，of後面已是複數名詞，要避免重複使用。

☑ **128**

Gourmet Fresh sales manager Peter Wong said the business had grown ------- by word of mouth.

(A) variously
(B) mostly
(C) faithfully
(D) responsibly

美食家新鮮公司 （Gourmet Fresh） 的銷售經理彼得翁 （Peter Wong） 說，業務成長主要是靠口耳相傳。

答案 (B) 字彙

這是-ly的副詞字彙題。by word of mouth是指「靠口耳相傳」，從語意上來看，(B)的mostly（主要地）最正確。另外，動詞後面的副詞大多是修飾動詞，不過這題的mostly則是和後面的by word of mouth相關。

☐ variously [`vɛrɪəslɪ] 副 各式各樣地
☐ faithfully [`feθfəlɪ] 副 忠實地
☐ responsibly [rɪ`spɑnsəblɪ] 副 有責任感地

☑ **129**

In order to complete the ------- list of tasks by the project deadline, all members of the Sycos Design team worked overtime.

(A) longest
(B) length
(C) lengthy
(D) lengthen

為了在計畫最後期限前完成冗長的工作事項，賽克斯設計 （Sycos Design） 團隊的所有成員都加班工作。

答案 (C) 詞性

空格是在冠詞the與名詞list之間，所以要填形容詞。可考慮的選項為(A)形容詞long（長的）的最高級longest，以及(C)的lengthy（冗長的），從語意上來看，正確答案是(C)。與long相比，lengthy包含了否定意味。「length（長度）＋-y」是在名詞字尾加-y使該字變成形容詞。(D)的「length（長度）＋-en」是在名詞字尾加-en使該字變成動詞。

☐ deadline [`dɛd.laɪn] 名 最後期限

☑ **130**

The system failure hit an ------- part of Longbeach Industry's business operations, which caused them to stop all orders for 24 hours.

(A) attentive
(B) oriented
(C) eccentric
(D) integral

系統故障衝擊了長灘產業公司 （Longbeach Industry） 商業營運上不可欠缺的部分，造成公司停止所有訂單 24 小時。

答案 (D) 字彙

哪一個形容詞最適合修飾part（部分）？從「系統故障衝擊了營運上～部分」來思考，即可知(D)的integral（不可欠缺的）最正確。which雖是關係代名詞，但只要字彙能力足夠，憑逗點前的部分就可以解答。

☐ operation [.ɑpə`reʃən] 名 營運
☐ cause～ to do （主詞是原因）造成～做……
☐ attentive [ə`tɛntɪv] 形 專心的
☐ oriented [`orɪɛntɪd] 形 以～為導向的
☐ eccentric [ɪk`sɛntrɪk] 形 古怪的、反常的

PART 6

Questions 131-134 refer to the following Web page.

Welcome to the National Film Archive

The National Film Archive features a collection of films that spans from the 1920s to the present day. Founded in 1979 as a section in the National Film History Museum, the Archive collects and ------- original copies along with films in digital format.
131.

Most of the open-shelf films are available to all registered users for one-week rentals. Please note that there is a limitation on the number of films you can rent at one time. -------, users can view **132.** these open-shelf films in audio-visual rooms on the third floor of the museum. Please review the recently updated terms and conditions posted on the bulletin board.

Closed-shelf films are only available to approved users for research ------- academic purposes. **133.**

134.

---

131. (A) develops
　　 (B) stores
　　 (C) borrows
　　 (D) signs

132. (A) Even so
　　 (B) Additionally
　　 (C) Nevertheless
　　 (D) As a result

133. (A) or
　　 (B) more
　　 (C) as
　　 (D) yet

134. (A) We hope you will soon create your own archives.
　　 (B) Unfortunately, we cannot allow users to take films home.
　　 (C) To register as a user, please sign up at the circulation desk.
　　 (D) You can submit as many films as you like.

試題翻譯

試題 131-134 請參考以下網頁。

歡迎進入國家電影資料庫 （National Film Archive）

國家電影資料庫的特色是收藏了從 1920 年代到現在的一系列影片。 資料庫創立於 1979 年，為國家電影歷史博物館的單位之一，蒐集與保存了原版與數位版影片。

已登錄的使用者能租借大部分的開架影片一週。 請注意我們有限制一次可租借影片的數量。此外，使用者可以在博物館三樓的視聽室觀看這些開架影片。 請至公告欄閱覽近期最新的規定及條款。

非開架影片僅提供經核准的使用者做研究或學術目的的使用。

134. 欲成為使用者，請洽租借櫃台登記。

131
答案 (B) ｜前後句關係

主詞是the Archive（資料庫），動詞是collects和-------（須選擇的答案）二者並列。從受詞original copies（原版）和films（影片）的關係可知，(B)的stores（保存）是正確答案。(A)的develop除了有「發展」的意思外，也有「沖洗（底片）」之意，但是不符前後語意。

132
答案 (B) ｜前後句關係

將每個選項帶入句中，用前後語意即可判斷出答案。前面的句子是有關登記使用者租借影片的說明。後面包括空格在內的句子是在說明可觀賞影片的地方。因此，連接這2句、用來表示前句的附加說明，選(B)的Additionally（此外）最正確。

□ even so　然而
□ nevertheless [ˌnɛvəðəˈlɛs] 副 儘管如此
□ as a result　因此

133
答案 (A) ｜句型結構

Closed-shelf films are only available to... for～是指「非開架影片僅提供予……做～」。research和academic都跟purpose有關，所以連結這2個字以(A)最正確。research or academic purpose意即「研究或學術目的」。

134
答案 (C) ｜語句插入

這是National Film Archive（國家電影資料庫）發出的通知。第1段是對資料庫做簡單說明，第2段之後是介紹已登錄之使用者（registered users）能如何利用資料庫。從這樣的說明流程可知，符合最後一句的是描述受理登記地方的(C)。
(A)「希望你們很快創設自己的資料庫。」
(B)「可惜的是，我們無法准許使用者將影片帶回。」
(D)「你可提交任意數量的影片。」

□ register [ˈrɛdʒɪstə] 動 登記
□ circulation [ˌsɝkjəˈleʃən] 名 （圖書館等的）租借處

Vocabulary

□ span from A to B　從A橫跨到B
□ present [ˈprɛznt] 形 現在的
□ found [faʊnd] 動 創立
□ format [ˈfɔrmæt] 名 樣式
□ open-shelf [ˈopənˌʃɛlf] 形 開架的
□ limitation [ˌlɪməˈteʃən] 名 限制
□ audio-visual room　視聽室
□ terms and conditions　規定及條款
□ closed-shelf [ˈklozd ˈʃɛlf] 形 非開架的
□ approved [əˈpruvd] 形 被准許的

試題

Questions 135-138 refer to the following memo.

It's the time of the year for our annual round of employee discounts. We hope you will take advantage of these great deals.

This year we have five of our most recent computer models ------- in the list. To review
135.
specifications and pictures of the listed products, you can pick up catalogs for free at the Sales Department. Please note that while all electronic accessories are 30% off, the discount rates -------
136.
to computers vary by type: desktops, laptops, and netbooks.

We have abundant supplies put aside for employees, but ------- items run out, we will not be re-
137.
stocking. -------.
138.

For more information, please contact the Sales Department.

135. (A) will include
(B) are included
(C) included
(D) including

136. (A) apply
(B) to apply
(C) application
(D) applicable

137. (A) in the event
(B) thanks to
(C) meanwhile
(D) now that

138. (A) They have resulted from discounts on bulk purchases.
(B) All orders will be processed on a first-come, first-served basis.
(C) You will not be charged for any items that go out of stock.
(D) A copy of the sales receipt and serial number are required.

試題翻譯

試題 135-138 請參考以下摘要。

又到了我們一年一度的員工折扣時刻。 希望各位利用這些划算的價格。

今年我們的商品清單內包括了 5 台公司最新的電腦機型。 各位可以在銷售部門索取免費的型錄，以便瀏覽列表產品的規格和照片。 另外提醒各位，雖然所有的電子配件一律 7 折，但適用於電腦的折扣率如桌上型、筆記型、小筆電等會因產品種類不同而異。

我們有專門留給員工的庫存，但萬一商品不足，將不再備貨。 138. 所有訂單將依下單先後順序處理。

若需更多資訊，請洽銷售部門。

解答與解析

135

答案 (C) 〔句型結構〕

主詞是we，動詞是have，接著five of our most recent computer models是受詞。「------- in the list」是在修飾前面的models，所以用(C)的過去分詞included最合適，意即「商品清單內包括了5台公司最新的電腦機型」。(D)的including（包括～）是介系詞，後面要接名詞（子句）。

136

答案 (D) 〔句型結構〕

Please note that...接的是while A, B（雖然A，但是B）的句型結構。因為逗點後面的主詞是the discount rates（折扣率），動詞是vary（變更），所以「-------＋to computers」用來修飾前面的名詞the discount rates最合適。(D)的applicable to～（可適用於～）是正確答案。當語句從後面來修飾前面的名詞時，除了像135題用過去分詞形式外，也有像這題用形容詞形式的情況。

137

答案 (A) 〔前後句關係〕

空格後面接子句items run out，所以(B)的thanks to～（託～的福）及(C)用副詞meanwhile（其間）無法成為正確的句型結構。(D)的now that是「既然」的意思，雖可接後面的子句，但不符合前後句的語意。而(A)的in the event (that)～（萬一～）不論前後句的語意或是句型結構上都是最適合的。另外提醒各位，如果後面要接名詞，也可寫成in the event of～。

138

答案 (B) 〔語句插入型〕

因為第2段在表達折扣商品的細節時，空格的前一句是「有專門留給員工的庫存」，因此第3段挑選的答案，要選擇有催促早點下訂單之意的(B)。(C)的go out of stock和本文的run out同樣意思，注意別因而誤選。
(A)「是因為大批購買有折扣所致。」
(C)「缺貨的商品不會被收取費用。」
(D)「需要銷售收據影本與序號。」

□ process [`prɑsɛs] 動 處理
□ on a first-come, first-served basis 依先後順序
□ out of stock 無庫存

Vocabulary

□ take advantage of～ 利用～
□ specification [ˌspɛsəfəˈkeʃən] 名 規格
□ abundant [əˈbʌndənt] 形 豐富的
□ put aside～ 儲存

Questions 139-142 refer to the following notice.

Kanyon R&D Center Visitor Policy

Given the need to ------- our security, Kanyon R&D Center will be revising its policy for visitor
139.
access to all buildings.

Currently, visitors are preregistered in the visitor management system by name and affiliation, as
well as the duration and purpose of their visit. However, starting December 1, visitors will also be
required to wear photo IDs issued at the front desk. Furthermore, all visitors will be accompanied
by at least one Kanyon staff member even ------- accessing non-restricted areas.
140.

-------. Please be sure to inform your visitors prior to their ------- and ensure that the rules are
141. **142.**
understood and respected.

---

139. (A) high
　　(B) height
　　(C) highest
　　(D) heighten

140. (A) though
　　(B) until
　　(C) when
　　(D) whatever

141. (A) All staff members must have the approval of their supervisor.
　　(B) Failure to abide by these rules constitutes a security breach.
　　(C) Visitors have already been made aware of these policies.
　　(D) You may choose to remain completely anonymous.

142. (A) arrival
　　(B) agreement
　　(C) purchase
　　(D) performance

試題翻譯

試題 139-142 請參考以下公告。

肯尼昂 （Kanyon） 研發中心訪客規範

鑒於提高各位安全之必要，肯尼昂研發中心將修訂訪客進入所有大樓的相關規範。

目前，訪客僅需在訪客管理系統事先登錄姓名和所屬單位，以及訪問期間和目的。 惟，自 12 月 1 日起，訪問者必須配帶由接待櫃檯發給的附有照片的識別證。 而且，所有訪客至少要由一名肯尼昂職員陪同，即使是在進入不受限制的區域時也不例外。

^{141.} 不遵守這些規定將會違反維安規定。 請務必在您的訪客到達前通知他們，並確保規範受到理解與尊重。

139
答案 (D) 〔句型結構〕

the need to do 意即「有～之必要」。空格處要填原形動詞，所以 (D) 是正確答案。heighten 是「height（高度）＋ -en」，在名詞字尾加 en 成為動詞。(A) 是形容詞，(B) 是名詞，(C) 是 high 的最高級。

140
答案 (C) 〔前後句關係〕

從 all visitors...到 one Kanyon staff member 為止是完整的一句，所以 even 之後是副詞子句。空格後面是接～ing 形式的 accessing，因此可推斷空格應該是連接詞，且省略了 they are。這題的連接詞之中，可省略進行式中的〈主詞＋be 動詞〉的是(B)until 或(C)when，但為了符合「即使是在進入不受限制的區域時也不例外」這樣的語意，所以正確答案是(C)。

141
答案 (B) 〔語句插入型〕

正確答案(B)的字彙程度高，所以最好用消去法來作答。(A)對於職員要取得主管什麼認可描述不清。(C)從空格後的指示內容來看，這句「訪客已了解這些規範」的語意很奇怪。(D)的 anonymous（匿名的）因話題唐突，所以不合適。剩下的(B)就是正確答案了。
(A)「所有職員必須取得主管的認可。」
(C)「訪客已了解這些規範。」
(D)「你可以選擇保持完全匿名。」

□ approval [əˋpruv!] 名 認可
□ failure to do　不～
□ abide by～　遵守（規則等）
□ constitute a breach　侵害、違反

142
答案 (A) 〔前後句關係〕

prior to～是「在～之前」，their 是指前面的 your visitors（你的訪客）。從「訪客在～之前要通知他們」的語意可知，(A)的 arrival（到達）是正確答案。

□ purchase [ˋpɝtʃəs] 名 購買
□ performance [pɚˋfɔrməns] 名 性能

Vocabulary

□ access to～　進入～
□ preregister [priˋrɛdʒɪstɚ] 動 預先登記
□ affiliation [əˏfɪlɪˋeʃən] 名 隸屬
□ duration [djʊˋreʃən] 名 期間
□ issue [ˋɪʃʊ] 動 發給、發行～
□ furthermore [ˋfɝðɚˏmor] 副 而且
□ be accompanied by～　由～陪同
□ access [ˋæksɛs] 動 接近（場所）、進入
□ non-restricted [ˏnɑnrɪˋstrɪktɪd] 形　不受限制的
□ ensure that～　確保～

試題

Questions 143-146 refer to the following letter.

September 2

Mr. B C Lanning
76 Seaview Rd
Avondale, Hastings

Dear Mr. Lanning,

Thank you for choosing HAL Insurance to protect your financial health. I am pleased to confirm that the protection you requested is now -------. We have enclosed several important documents
143.
relevant to your policy. -------.
144.

If you decide that the policy does not meet your needs, you have fourteen days from the date you receive this letter to write to us and request that we cancel your policy and refund any premiums you -------.
145.

We at HAL Insurance would again like to take this ------- to thank you for choosing to insure with
146.
us.

Sincerely,

John Andrews
General Manager
Customer Services

---

143. (A) at last
(B) of value
(C) in place
(D) on deposit

144. (A) We hope you will consider our insurance policy.
(B) Please take some time to read over these documents.
(C) It is always important to make premium payments on time.
(D) There is no cancellation fee to terminate your contract with us.

145. (A) paying
(B) to pay
(C) have paid
(D) have been paid

146. (A) confirmation
(B) acceptance
(C) recognition
(D) opportunity

試題翻譯

試題 143-146 請參考以下信件內容。

9 月 2 日
藍尼先生 （Mr. B C Lanning）
海景路 （Seaview）76 號
愛文戴爾 （Avondale），海斯廷斯 （Hastings）

親愛的藍尼先生：

感謝選擇哈爾 （HAL） 保險公司來守護您的財富健全性。 很高興向您確認，您要求的保險範圍現在已就定位。 隨信在內的是有關保單的幾份重要文件。[144.]請花點時間詳讀這些文件。

如果您判定這份保單未符合您的需求，從收到這封信的 14 天內可書面要求我們取消您的保單，並退回您已繳納的全額保險費。

哈爾保險公司想再次藉此機會，感謝您選擇投保本公司。

謹致問候
約翰 · 安卓斯 （John Andrews）
總經理
客服部

解答與解析

143
答案 (C) 前後句關係

the protection you requested（您要求的保險範圍）是主詞，is是動詞。從後面的句子「隨信在內的是有關保單的幾份重要文件」可知，(C)的in place（就定位）是正確答案。(B)的of value（有價值的）和valuable同樣意思。請記住〈of ＋抽象名詞〉會變成形容詞型態。

144
答案 (B) 語句插入型

銜接前面的「隨信在內的是……」，以(B)的「請花點時間詳讀這些文件」最通順。these documents（這些文件）是指前句提到的important documents（重要文件）。選項內如果有this (these)等指示代名詞出現，可先確認是銜接前面的什麼內容，會更有利作答。從整個內容可看出收信人已完成保管事宜，所以選項(A)不符合。
(A)「希望您考慮我們的保單。」
(C)「按時繳納保費總是很重要。」
(D)「終止與我們的合約不需支付違約金。」

☐ premium [ˋprimɪəm] 名 保險費
☐ terminate [ˋtɝməˌnet] 動 終止～

145
答案 (C) 句型結構

雖然這句話很長，但是從空格前面的子句細看，就能看出request that we... refund any premiums you ------- 的句型結構。refund any premiums是「退回全額保險費」，you ------- 是在修飾前面的any premiums，因此，空格要填入的是針對you的動詞。選項可做述語動詞的是(C)和(D)。但(D)的被動語態不對，填入(C)的「你已繳納的保險費」才是正確答案。

146
答案 (D) 前後句關係

這是在信件最後向對方選擇本公司表達感謝。正確答案為(D)。take this opportunity to～是常用短語，意即「藉此機會～、藉這個地方～」。

☐ confirmation [ˌkɑnfɚˋmeʃən] 名 確認
☐ acceptance [əkˋsɛptəns] 名 接受
☐ recognition [ˌrɛkəgˋnɪʃən] 名 認可

Vocabulary

☐ protection [prəˋtɛkʃən] 名 （保險的）保護（範圍）
☐ relevant to～ 有關～
☐ meet *someone's* needs 滿足～的要求
☐ insure [ɪnˋʃʊr] 動 投保

PART 7

試題文章	試題文章翻譯

Questions 147-148 refer to the following advertisement.

試題147-148請參考以下廣告。

19TH ANNUAL TRI-STATE ANTIQUE FAIR

Stevens County Fairgrounds

Friday Sept. 21–Sunday Sept. 23
9:00 A.M.–6:00 P.M., Rain or Shine

Come explore the largest antique fair in the tri-state area! From furniture to fireplaces, from toys to timepieces, come explore the vast array of historic treasures. This year's theme is glassware, with more than 20 specialist dealers attending.

From Highway 30 take Exit 10, and drive five minutes west. Spacious parking is available. Admission is $5 for all three days.

To register as a dealer and reserve a booth, please call the Tri-State Fair Planning Committee at (980) 555-7171 by Monday, Sept 10.

第19屆三州地區年度古董市集
史蒂芬斯（Stevens）郡市集場地
9月21日（週五）－9月23日（週日）
9:00 A.M.－6:00 P.M.，不論晴雨

歡迎來探索三州地區最大的古董市集！從家具到壁爐，玩具到時鐘，各式各樣的歷史寶藏等你來探索！
今年的主題是玻璃製品，有超過20家的專門業者加入。

從30號公路10號出口下來，向西行駛5分鐘車程。有寬敞的停車場可利用。入場費是3天5美元。
欲登記為業者以及預約攤位者，請於9月10日週一前，洽詢三州地區市集規劃委員會（980）555-7171。

Vocabulary

- [ ] tri-state [ˈtraɪˌstet] 形 鄰近三州的
- [ ] county [ˈkaʊntɪ] 名 郡（美國次於州的行政區）
- [ ] fairground [ˈfɛrˌɡraʊnd] 名 市集場地
- [ ] rain or shine 不論晴雨
- [ ] fireplace [ˈfaɪrˌples] 名 壁爐
- [ ] timepiece [ˈtaɪmˌpis] 名 時鐘
- [ ] vast [væst] 形 龐大的
- [ ] array of~ 系列~
- [ ] dealer [ˈdilə] 名 業者
- [ ] admission [ədˈmɪʃən] 名 入場費
- [ ] register [ˈrɛdʒɪstə] 動 登記
- [ ] booth [buθ] 名 （有棚的）攤位

試題	試題翻譯	解答與解析

☑ 147

When does the event end?

(A) September 10
(B) September 19
(C) September 21
(D) September 23

活動何時結束？

(A) 9 月 10 日
(B) 9 月 19 日
(C) 9 月 21 日
(D) 9 月 23 日

答案 (D)　其他細節

標題下寫了舉辦日期Friday Sept. 21-Sunday Sept. 23，所以正確答案是(D)。

☑ 148

What item will be featured this year?

(A) Furniture
(B) Glassware
(C) Toys
(D) Timepieces

今年以什麼東西為特色？

(A) 家具
(B) 玻璃製品
(C) 玩具
(D) 時鐘

答案 (B)　其他細節

題目的單字feature意即「以～為號召、以～為特色」，是多益考試常出現的動詞。第1段就提到今年的主題This year's theme is glassware, ...，所以(B)是正確答案。glassware是「玻璃製品」。這2道題都可在第1段找到解答，因此第2段可以快速跳過繼續寫下1道題。

試題文章	試題文章翻譯

Questions 149-150 refer to the following chain of text messages.

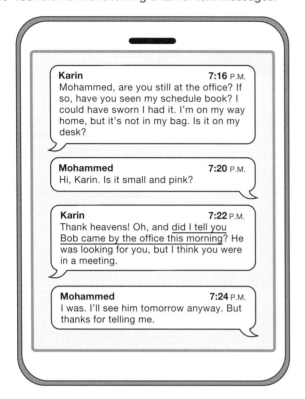

試題149-150請參考以下簡訊對話。

卡琳（Karin）7:16 P.M.
穆罕默德（Mohammed），你還在辦公室嗎？如果還在，有看到我的行程記事本嗎？我發誓我以為我拿了。我正在回家途中，才發現它不在包包裡。有在我桌上嗎？

穆罕默德 7:20 P.M.
嗨！卡琳。是粉紅色小本的嗎？

卡琳 7:22 P.M.
感謝老天爺！對了，我有告訴你鮑伯（Bob）今早有來辦公室嗎？他在找你，不過我想你當時在開會。

穆罕默德 7:24 P.M.
是的，我當時在開會。反正我明天會看到他。不過謝謝妳告訴我。

Vocabulary

□ sworn [sworn] 動 swear（宣誓、斷言～）的過去分詞　　□ on *one's* way home　在回家途中

試題	試題翻譯	解答與解析

☑ 149

Where is Mohammed?

(A) At an office
(B) On his way home
(C) In a taxi
(D) At a meeting

穆罕默德在哪兒？

(A) 在辦公室
(B) 在回家途中
(C) 在計程車內
(D) 在開會

答案 (A)　　其他細節

從卡琳開門見山的訊息就可知她在回家途中，詢問還在辦公室的鮑伯是否她的行程記事本還在她的桌上。

☑ 150

At 7:22 P.M., what does Karin most likely mean when she writes, "did I tell you Bob came by the office this morning"?

(A) Bob left the office early.
(B) Bob came to see Mohammed.
(C) Karin forgot to attend a meeting.
(D) Bob missed an appointment.

7:22 P.M.，卡琳說 「did I tell you Bob came by the office this morning?」，表示什麼？

(A) 鮑伯很早離開辦公室。
(B) 鮑伯來找穆罕默德。
(C) 卡琳忘了出席一場會議。
(D) 鮑伯錯過一場約會。

答案 (B)　　說話者的目的

這題是在詢問寫訊息者的意圖。先看問題，確認這個時間她說了什麼，然後再看看選項作答就行了。come by是「過來、來訪」。卡琳說He（＝鮑伯）was looking for you（＝穆罕默德）...，所以可知正確答案為(B)。

□ appointment [ə`pɔɪntmənt] 名 約會

Questions 151-152 refer to the following message.

While You Were Out . . .

TO: _Gene Simons_

FROM: _Brice Kammerick_

TIME: _9:15 A.M., Thursday_

MESSAGE:
Brice in Sales called this morning. He'd like to postpone next week's Monday staff meeting until Wednesday afternoon so he can meet with one of his clients. He will call back again tomorrow, but if possible could you contact him before then at 910-555-6644? It sounded urgent. Thanks!

Taken By: _Mindy Shue_

試題151-152請參考以下留言。

當您外出時……
留言對象：傑尼・西門子（Gene Simons）
聯絡人：布萊斯・卡梅里克（Brice Kammerick）
時間：週四9:15 A.M.

留言內容：
銷售部門的布萊斯早上來電。他想將下週一的員工會議延到週三下午，以便他可以約見一位客戶。明天他會再打來，不過如有可能，可否請你在那之前打910-555-6644跟他聯絡呢？聽起來這事似乎很急。謝謝！

留言人：敏蒂・薛（Mindy Shue）

Vocabulary

☐ postpone A until B　將A延期到B　　☐ so (that)~ can...　以便~可以……　　☐ taken by~　（留言）由~接收

試題	試題翻譯	解答與解析

151

When does Mr. Kammerick want to reschedule the meeting for?

(A) The next day
(B) Next Monday
(C) Next Wednesday
(D) Next Thursday

卡梅里克先生想把會議改到何時？

(A) 隔天
(B) 下週一
(C) 下週三
(D) 下週四

答案 (C)　　其他細節

卡梅里克先生是留言的人。這題是要問reschedule A for B（將A改期到B）的B。從He'd like to postpone next week's Monday staff meeting until Wednesday afternoon這句可知，他想將next week's Monday的會議改期到Wednesday afternoon，所以(C)是正確答案。

152

What does Ms. Shue advise Mr. Simons to do?

(A) Consult with a client
(B) Contact Mr. Kammerick as soon as possible
(C) Hold the meeting on Thursday
(D) Wait for Mr.Kammerick's call the next day

薛女士建議西門子先生做什麼？

(A) 諮詢一位客戶
(B) 儘快聯絡卡梅里克先生
(C) 週四開會
(D) 等卡梅里克先生明天的來電

答案 (B)　　其他細節

西門子先生是留言的對象。他收到這個留言後該怎麼辦才好。從He will call back again...後面的內容可知(B)是正確答案，因為卡梅里克先生似乎是急迫的（urgent），所以提出希望儘早聯絡的請求。同時卡梅里克先生也希望能在隔天來電之前有所連絡，因此(D)是錯的。

試題文章	試題文章翻譯

Questions 153-154 refer to the following book review.

What is the difference between "If I was you" and "If I were you"? Why does using "whom" instead of "who" sound stuffy? Why is there an "s" in "He eats" but not "I eat"? Jean Fortun's new book, *Why do they say it like that?* explores questions like these. Currently a professor of comparative linguistics at Lakewood State University, her eclectic background as a high school teacher, a social analyst and a regular columnist for the *Sun Times* gives her the ability to convey accurate, up-to-date research on linguistics and language teaching in a way that is easy to understand and fun to read. Not a formal reference manual like a dictionary or thesaurus, the book offers a down-to-earth, humorous look at some of the most commonly wondered-about words and phrases in the English language. Language scholars, teachers, students, as well as anyone who frequently wonders why we use the words we do, will find this book hard to put down.

試題 153-154 請參考以下書評。

「If I was you」和「If I were you」這兩句有何不同？為什麼用「whom」來代替「who」聽起來有很古板的感覺？為什麼s是加在「He eats」而不是加在「I eat」？珍‧佛頓（Jean Fortun）的新書《他們為什麼這麼說？》（*Why do they say it like that?*）探討了這類的問題。目前她是木湖（Lakewood）州立大學的比較語言學教授，過去曾任高中老師、社會分析家，以及《太陽報》（*Sun Times*）固定專欄作家等不拘一格的經歷，讓她能以易於理解且有趣的方式，傳達準確且最新的語言學和語言教學研究。這本書並不是字典或同義詞辭典般的正式參考書，它提供了一個實際又幽默的觀點來看英語中最常有疑惑的單字和片語。對於語言學者、教師、學生，以及經常對現行的語言使用方法有所好奇的任何人來說，這將是一本愛不釋手的好書。

Vocabulary

□ instead of～ 代替　　□ stuffy [`stʌfɪ] 形 古板的　　□ comparative linguistics 比較語言學
□ accurate [`ækjərɪt] 形 準確、正確的　　□ up-to-date [`ʌptə`det] 形 最新的　　□ formal [`fɔrml] 形 正式的　　□ reference [`rɛfərəns] 名 參考
□ thesaurus [θɪ`sɔrəs] 名 同義詞辭典　　□ down-to-earth [`daʊnə`ɝθ] 形 實際的　　□ humorous [`hjumərəs] 形 幽默的
□ commonly [`kɑmənlɪ] 副 一般地　　□ wondered-about [`wʌndəd·ə`baʊt] 形 感到疑惑的　　□ scholar [`skɑlə] 名 學者
□ frequently [`frikwəntlɪ] 副 頻繁地

試題	試題翻譯	解答與解析

☑ **153**

What was NOT one of Ms. Fortun's jobs in the past?

(A) A social analyst
(B) A high school instructor
(C) A college professor
(D) A newspaper columnist

佛頓女士以前沒有做過什麼工作？

(A) 社會分析家
(B) 高中教師
(C) 大學教授
(D) 報紙專欄作家

答案 (C) 　　是非題類型

佛頓女士是本書的作者。關於她的經歷，評論中提到了her eclectic background as a high school teacher, a social analyst and a regular columnist for the *Sun Times*。eclectic是「不拘一格的」，background有「經歷」之意。除了(C)以外，每個選項都有提到。大學教授是她現在的工作而不是過去的，所以(C)是正確答案。

☑ **154**

What does the reviewer suggest?

(A) Most people are not interested in English.
(B) The field of teaching is uninteresting.
(C) Ms. Fortun is an experienced college professor.
(D) The book will appeal to many kinds of people.

這位評論家提到什麼？

(A) 大部分的人對英文沒有興趣。
(B) 教學領域是無趣的。
(C) 佛頓女士是經驗豐富的大學教授。
(D) 這本書將吸引許多種人。

答案 (D) 　　何者正確類型

從文章最後一句就可知(D)是正確答案。因為選項內的many kinds of people就相當於該句的主詞，即Language scholars, ...we do。put down～是「將～放下」，...hard to put down則是「有趣到難以放下書（停止）」。評論家描述了很多佛頓女士的工作經歷，但是並未提及她是經驗豐富的大學教授，所以(C)是錯誤的。experienced意指「（在某個領域或職業上）很有經驗的」。

試題文章	試題文章翻譯

Questions 155-157 refer to the following information.

Startup Business?
We can help you get it off the ground!

Jorgensen CPA

Downtown Office:
21 N. 3rd St. Minneapolis, MN 54677
(612) 555-6969

Westside Mall Office:
47221 Brighton Ave. S. Egan, MN 54001
(653) 555-6969

Starting a small business can be challenging. Locally based and family owned and operated, Jorgensen CPA has been helping small businesses survive and thrive in the Greater Metro Area for more than 50 years.

We specialize in these services:
• Business and individual taxes • Personal financial planning
• Corporate bookkeeping • IRS representation (21 N. 3rd St. only)

We help individuals and businesses with tax returns, tax planning, payroll services, and IRS representation. We also audit, compile and review financial statements. Our Westside Mall Office offers free seminars monthly on financial planning, bookkeeping, and support and training for accounting software. Please call (653) 555-6969 for a current schedule.

Regular Business Hours*
Downtown:
Mon–Fri: 9:00 A.M.–5:00 P.M.

Westside Mall:
Mon: (closed)　Tue–Fri: 10:00 A.M.–8:00 P.M.
Sat: 10:00 A.M.–4:00 P.M.

* Closed Sundays and holidays.

試題155-157請參考以下資訊。

喬根森會計師事務所（Jorgensen CPA）
創業？
我們可以協助您順利開張！

市中心辦公室：
21北三路（N. 3rd st.）明尼阿波利斯（Minneapolis）明尼蘇達州（MN）54677
（612）555-6969
西區商場辦公室：
47221西布萊登大道（Brighton Ave.）明尼蘇達州南伊根市（S. Egan）54001
（653）555-6969

成立一家小企業很有挑戰性。深耕在地及家族經營的喬根森會計師事務所，在格雷特大都會地區（Greater Metro Area）協助小企業生存和繁榮成長已超過50年以上了。

本所的專業服務如下：
‧營業稅及個人稅 ‧個人財務規劃
‧公司記帳 ‧代理對應國稅局（IRS）相關事宜（僅市中心辦公室提供服務）
我們協助個人與企業納稅申報、稅務規劃、發薪服務及代理對應國稅局相關事宜。我們也提供帳冊查核、匯編及審閱財務報表。西區商場辦公室每月提供免費研討班，包括財務規劃、記帳，以及會計軟體的支援與訓練。欲洽詢目前課程表者請撥打（653）555-6969。

平日上班時間 *

市中心辦公室：
週一至週五：9:00 A.M.－5:00 P.M.
西區商場辦公室：
週一：（休息）　週二至週五：10:00 A.M.－8:00 P.M.
週六：10:00 A.M.－4:00 P.M.
＊每週日及例假日休息

Vocabulary

□ CPA 　（美國）註冊會計師（Certified Public Accountant的縮寫）　　□ get～ off the ground　使～順利開始
□ thrive [θraɪv] 動 繁榮成長　　□ specialize in～　專攻～　　□ bookkeeping [`bʊk͵kipɪŋ] 名 記帳
□ IRS 　（美國）國稅局（Internal Revenue Service的縮寫）　　□ tax return　納稅申報　　□ payroll service　發薪服務
□ audit [`ɔdɪt] 動 查核（帳冊）　　□ compile [kəm`paɪl] 動 （收集資料）匯編～　　□ financial statement　財務報表

試題	試題翻譯	解答與解析

155

What service is only available at the company's downtown location?

(A) IRS representation
(B) Individual tax help
(C) Seminars on bookkeeping
(D) Small business tax advice

哪一項服務僅在市中心的辦公室提供？

(A) 代理對應國稅局 （IRS） 相關事宜
(B) 個人稅協助
(C) 記帳研討班
(D) 小企業稅務建議

答案 (A)　〔其他細節〕

內文對Downtown Office和Westside Mall Office 2家辦公室都有明確描述，可看出其中有一項服務僅在Downtown Office提供，即是We specialize in these services: 的最後一項IRS representation（21 N. 3rd St. only），因括號內地址與上述的辦公室地址一致，所以(A)的IRS representation是正確答案。

156

When are both offices open?

(A) On Mondays
(B) On Fridays
(C) On Saturdays
(D) On Sundays

2處辦公室共同的營業時間是？

(A) 週一
(B) 週五
(C) 週六
(D) 週日

答案 (B)　〔其他細節〕

從2處辦公室的上班時間來看，市中心辦公室是週一至週五，西區商場辦公室是週一休息，週二至週六上班。所以選項中符合2家都有的上班時間是(B)「週五」。

157

What is indicated about the company?

(A) It has been in business for less than a decade.
(B) It is open seven days a week.
(C) It offers classes on financial planning.
(D) It is operated by a corporation.

關於這家公司，下列何者正確？

(A) 經營未滿 10 年。
(B) 一週上班 7 天。
(C) 提供財務規劃的課程。
(D) 它由法人經營。

答案 (C)　〔何者正確類型〕

選擇何者正確的問題，用消去法作答最適合。文中提到Jorgensen CPA has been helping... for more than 50 years. ，表示已有50年以上，所以(A)是錯誤的。而市中心辦公室是休週末，西區商場是休週一與週日，所以(B)敘述錯誤。選項(C)正好符合Our Westside Mall Office offers free seminars monthly on financial planning的描述。(D)是錯在它是家族經營的。

試題文章	試題文章翻譯

Questions 158-160 refer to the following advertisement.

"Exceed" your Expectations!

Would you like to cut down your work commute to just five minutes? — [1] —. By becoming a Client Support Professional with Exceed, you will be able to provide superior customer service from the comfort of your home. No suit, no commute! We have great opportunities available with premier online retailers, well-known cruise lines, the world's largest telecommunications company and many other Fortune 500 companies.

— [2] —. By becoming one of our affiliates you will be able to schedule your work around your life. You will finally have the flexibility to work as many or as few hours as you like while earning a competitive salary and performance bonuses. You will need strong computer skills, an adequate PC, excellent people skills, and a quiet workspace. — [3] —.

For more information, please call our main office at 1-800-555-7962 toll free, or contact Jacob Thatcher at jthatch@exceed.com. — [4] —. To apply online, please visit www.exceed.com/workfromhome and click on "Client Support Positions."

試題158-160請參考以下廣告。

「超越」（Exceed）你的預期！

你想把工作通勤縮短到只有5分鐘嗎？—〔1〕—。只要成為超越公司的一名客戶支援專家，你就能夠從舒適的家提供卓越的客戶服務。零制服，零通勤！本公司有很棒的職缺機會讓你可以跟一流的網路零售商、知名遊艇公司、世界最大的電信公司和其他許多全球500大企業共事。

—〔2〕—。成為我們的成員之一，你就可以依照自己的生活安排工作。在賺取有競爭力的薪水與績效獎金的同時，你終於能彈性選擇工作時數。你需要有強大的電腦技能、一台合用的電腦、優秀的社交能力，以及一個安靜的工作空間。—〔3〕—。有客服經驗者佳，但非必要條件。

欲知詳情，可撥打免付費電話1-800-555-7962至總公司，或以jthatch@exceed.com信箱聯繫雅各·柴契爾（Jacob Thatcher）。—〔4〕—。若是上網應徵，請到www.exceed.com/workfromhome網頁，點擊「客戶支援職務」。

Vocabulary

- commute [kəˋmjut] 名 通勤（距離）
- superior [səˋpɪrɪə] 形 卓越的
- comfort [ˋkʌmfət] 名 舒適
- premier [ˋprimɪə] 形 一流的
- retailer [ˋritelə] 名 零售商
- telecommunication [ˏtɛləˏmjunəˋkeʃən] 名 電信
- affiliate [əˋfɪlɪɪt] 名 成員
- flexibility [ˏflɛksəˋbɪlətɪ] 名 靈活性
- competitive [kəmˋpɛtətɪv] 形 有競爭力的
- adequate [ˋædəkwɪt] 形 合乎需要的、充足的
- toll free （電話）撥打免費

試題	試題翻譯	解答與解析

☑ 158

Where will employees who are hired for the advertised positions work?

(A) At Fortune 500 companies
(B) At the Exceed head office
(C) At their own home
(D) At the customer service center

廣告所招聘的職員要在哪裡工作？

(A) 全球 500 大企業
(B) 超越公司總部
(C) 自宅
(D) 客服中心

答案 (C) 〔其他細節〕

多益Part 7這個單元，不僅要先確認整篇的格式，還要預覽題目才有效率。這篇的格式是廣告，接著看問題就知道是「徵人廣告」。從 from the comfort of your home或No suit, no commute!、schedule your work around your life、have the flexibility to work...等語句就可知道(C)是正確答案。

☑ 159

How are interested people instructed to apply for the job?

(A) By going to the Exceed Web site
(B) By calling Client Support
(C) By visiting the Exceed corporate office
(D) By phoning Jacob Thatcher

對這項工作有興趣者該如何應徵？

(A) 上網到超越公司網站
(B) 打電話給客戶支援部門
(C) 拜訪超越公司辦公室
(D) 打電話給雅各·柴契爾

答案 (A) 〔其他細節〕

徵人廣告大致上都是以應徵期限及應徵方式等有關應徵的資訊作為總結。從最後的To apply online, please visit www.exceed.com/workfromhome...就可知道(A)是正確答案。

☑ 160

In which of the positions marked [1], [2], [3], and [4] does the following sentence best belong?

"Previous customer service experience is preferred, but not required."

(A) [1]   (C) [3]
(B) [2]   (D) [4]

下面這一句應該插入標記〔1〕、〔2〕、〔3〕、〔4〕中的哪一個位置？

「有客服經驗者佳，但非必要條件。」

(A)〔1〕   (C)〔3〕
(B)〔2〕   (D)〔4〕

答案 (C) 〔插入句〕

這道題是要把句子插入適當的位置，最好先掌握插入句的內容再閱讀文章。這題的插入句是描述有關應徵條件，因看到文章第2段的You will need...即是在敘述應徵條件，所以這句放在〔3〕的位置最適當。

Questions 161-163 refer to the following Web page.

Summer Open College

Summer Courses Available to all Leeston College Students
and Leeston County Residents

Monday–Friday: July 2–6, 9–13, 16–20

9:30 A.M.–4:00 P.M. daily; half-day & full-day courses

This summer we are pleased to offer a variety of practical courses for young people and the young at heart—from elementary school children to senior citizens. From family budget planning to beginning computing to cabinet-making, we've got something for you this summer. Courses are taught by a variety of qualified individuals from all over the state. Leeston College students are eligible to receive credits for some of these classes. Enrollment in the college is not necessary to register for these courses.

Each class has a maximum of 20 students, so if you're interested please register as soon as possible. Most half-day classes cost $15 per session, although some are slightly more expensive because of materials costs. Whole-day classes are also available at $25 per day. Lunch, snacks and drinks are available at $10 per day, or participants can bring their own. Bottled water is provided.

Our sincere thanks go to the Leeston District Council, whose ongoing and generous sponsorship helps keep our course fees at a minimum.

*For the full list of available classes, their descriptions, and how to register, **click here**.*
Or call our Summer Program Coordinator, Jennifer Ward, at 651-555-3131

試題161-163請參考以下網頁。

里斯頓（Leeston）商業暨技術學院
為更好的生活懷抱更好的理念
首頁／來訪路線／活動／聯絡我們／網站地圖

夏季開放學院
夏季課程提供給所有里斯頓學院的學生以及里斯頓郡的居民

週一－週五：7月2－6日，9－13日，16－20日
每日9：30 A.M.－4：00 P.M.；半天和全天課程

今年夏天，我們很高興能為年輕人以及擁有年輕之心的各類人士——從小學生到銀髮族，提供各種多樣的實用課程。從家庭預算的計畫、電腦入門到家具製作等等，都是我們今年夏天為各位用心安排的。課程由來自全州各地、多領域的合格人士講授。里斯頓學院的學生有資格從部分的這些課程取得學分。登記這些課程不需註冊入學。

每個課程的人數最大上限是20人，所以若有興趣的，請儘快登記。大部分的半天課程是每堂15元，但有些因材料費考量費用會稍微多一點。全天課程是一天25元。若需午餐、點心及飲料者，一天10元，參加者也可自備。我們有提供瓶裝水。

我們衷心感謝里斯頓區議會，持續不斷且慷慨的資金贊助，幫助我們的課程費用維持在最低的限度。

完整的課程表、相關說明，以及如何登記，請按此。
或是撥打651-555-3131洽夏季計畫統籌人，珍妮佛·華德（Jennifer Ward）。

Vocabulary

- resident [`rɛzədənt] 名 居民
- practical [`præktɪk!] 形 實用的
- senior citizen 老年人、銀髮族
- family budget 家庭預算
- qualified [`kwɑləˌfaɪd] 形 有資格的、合格的
- be eligible to *do* 具有～資格的
- credit [`krɛdɪt] 名 （修完）學分
- register for～ 登記～
- a maximum of～ 最大的～
- slightly [`slaɪtlɪ] 副 稍微地
- material [məˈtɪrɪəl] 名 材料
- participant [pɑrˈtɪsəpənt] 名 參加者
- sponsorship [`spɑnsəˌʃɪp] 名 資金贊助
- at a minimum 最低限度
- description [dɪˈskrɪpʃən] 名 說明

試題	試題翻譯	解答與解析

☑ **161**

What is the cost of a whole day class, including lunch?

(A) 10 dollars
(B) 15 dollars
(C) 25 dollars
(D) 35 dollars

包含午餐的全天課程要多少費用？

(A) 10 元
(B) 15 元
(C) 25 元
(D) 35 元

答案 (D)　　　其他細節

有關課程的費用請看第2段。a whole day class（全天課程），從Whole-day classes are also available at $25 per day.這句可知，一天25元。至於午餐，從Lunch, snacks and drinks are available at $10 per day這句可知，餐費是10元。因此，含餐費的全天課程費用為2者加起來，共35元。

☑ **162**

How does the Leeston District Council help the program?

(A) By teaching some classes
(B) By paying some of the costs
(C) By providing some equipment
(D) By providing the food

里斯頓區議會如何協助這項計畫？

(A) 教授部分課程
(B) 負擔部分費用
(C) 提供一些設備
(D) 提供食物

答案 (B)　　　其他細節

第3段有提到里斯頓區議會。ongoing是「持續的」，generous是「慷慨的、大量的」，help do是「幫助做～」。正確答案(B)用簡潔的說法來表現里斯頓區議會贊助很大筆的資金讓課程費用維持在最低的限度。

☑ **163**

What information is NOT provided on the Web page?

(A) Course dates
(B) Course fees
(C) Course times
(D) Course descriptions

這則網頁未提供下列哪一項資訊？

(A) 課程日期
(B) 課程費用
(C) 課程時間
(D) 課程說明

答案 (D)　　　是非題類型

這是問有關整篇的內容，用消去法來作答吧！(A)和(C)寫在本文最上端。(B)在第2段有提到。而(D)在整篇中並未提供，因為網頁最下方2行寫了For..., their descriptions, ..., click here.，所以是正確答案。

Questions 164-167 refer to the following letter.

World Excursion Incorporated
701 Bayside Drive
San Francisco, CA 61441

May 21

Ms. Ann Rodriguez
3077 NW 51st Ave.
Portland, OR 77313

Dear Ms. Rodriguez,

Thank you for choosing World Excursions. We are thrilled to have you aboard with us this summer.

This letter is to notify you that we have received your payment in full for our *July Eastern Mediterranean Cruise*. Your cabin has been reserved, and we are already making preparations for your arrival.

Enclosed please find a payment receipt and a copy of your cruise itinerary, as well as a booklet of helpful information about your upcoming cruise, including tips on packing, visiting ports of call, and popular sightseeing spots.

These and further details are also available on our Web site: www.worldexcursions.com. Log in using the account number and password listed below.

Account No.: 201307EMC   Cruise Dates: July 3–24
Password: XUM98C003   Starting/Ending Port: Venice
                                Cruise Guide: Ben Aldman

If you have any questions or concerns, or if you need to request changes to your itinerary, please don't hesitate to contact us toll-free: (800) 555-5050, 8 A.M.–6 P.M. Please note that cancellation requests become non-refundable 7 days before your date of departure.

We are looking forward to seeing you in July.

Regards,

Thomas Mulvey
Thomas Mulvey
World Excursions Incorporated

試題164-167請參考以下信件內容。

世界旅遊公司（World Excursion Incorporated）
701海灣區車道（Bayside Drive）
舊金山（San Francisco），加州（CA）61441

5月21日

安·羅德里格茲女士（Ms. Ann Rodriguez）
3077北西（NW）第51大道（51st Ave.）
波特蘭（Portland），奧勒岡（OR）77313

親愛的羅德里格茲女士：

感謝您選擇世界旅遊公司。很高興今夏有您與我們搭船同行。

這封信是通知您，我們已收到您參加7月東地中海航程（July Eastern Mediterranean Cruise）的全額款項。我們已為您保留客艙，並為迎接您的到來已開始各項準備。

隨函附上付款收據和一份行程表，以及一本對您即將啟程有所幫助的導覽冊，內容包括打包行李的訣竅、將拜訪的停靠港，以及熱門的觀光景點資料。

這些資訊與更多的細節也會在我們的網站上提供：www.worldexcursions.com。登入的帳號和密碼如下：
帳號：201307EMC
密碼：XUM98C003
航程日期：7月3－24日
啟程／終點港口：威尼斯
航程導遊：班·阿爾德曼（Ben Aldman）

如果您有任何問題或疑慮，或是需要更改行程，請別客氣用免付費電話聯繫我們：（800）555-5050，8 A.M.-6 P.M.。請注意出發前7日內要求取消預約者恕不退費。

期待7月與您相見。

謹致問候

湯瑪斯·穆爾維（Tomas Mulvey）
世界旅遊公司

Vocabulary

- □ be thrilled to *do*　非常高興～　　□ aboard [əˋbord] 副 上船（交通工具）　　□ cabin [ˋkæbɪn] 名（船）客艙
- □ make preparations for～　為～做準備　　□ Enclosed please find～　隨函附上～（也可說Please find enclosed～）
- □ booklet [ˋbʊklɪt] 名 小冊子　　□ tip [tɪp] 名 訣竅　　□ Please don't hesitate to *do*　請別客氣～
- □ non-refundable [ˌnɑnrɪˋfʌndəb!] 形 不能退款的

試題	試題翻譯	解答與解析

164

What is the main purpose of the letter?

(A) To confirm a reservation
(B) To request an itinerary
(C) To provide registration documents
(D) To request a payment

這封信的主要目的是什麼？

(A) 確認預約事宜
(B) 要求提供行程表
(C) 提供登記文件
(D) 要求付款

答案 (A) 　概述

寫信的目的通常都會一開始就提到，這封信是放在第2段This letter is to notify you that...（這封信是通知您……）。而we have received your payment in full for our *July Eastern Mediterranean Cruise*（我們已收到您參加7月東地中海航程的全額付款）說明已確定預約，所以(A)是正確答案。

165

Where most likely does Thomas Mulvey work?

(A) At a shipping company
(B) At a travel agency
(C) At a port of call
(D) At an airline company

湯瑪斯‧穆爾維最有可能在哪裡工作？

(A) 運輸公司
(B) 旅行社
(C) 停靠港
(D) 航空公司

答案 (B) 　推測

湯瑪斯‧穆爾維即是發信人。第2段是敘述航程付款事宜，接著第3段提到隨函附上收據及行程表、導覽冊。從以上細節來思考，就知道應該是(B)的旅行社。(C)的port of call是「停靠港、落腳處」之意，後者落腳處的說法可用在港口以外的地方。

166

According to the letter, what information is NOT in the booklet?

(A) How to prepare for a cruise
(B) What to do on the ship
(C) Details of ports of call
(D) Popular tourist attractions

根據信件內容，什麼資料不在導覽冊上？

(A) 如何為航程做準備
(B) 在船上能做什麼
(C) 停靠港的資訊
(D) 熱門觀光勝地

答案 (B) 　是非題類型

有關導覽冊的內容，就在第3段的a booklet of helpful information about your upcoming cruise, including tips on packing, visiting ports of call, and popular sightseeing spots。除了(B)以外，其他選項都有提到。上述的pack（打包）也可換成(A)prepare for～（為～做準備）的說法。(D)的attraction單獨意思雖是「吸引力」，但tourist attraction則是「觀光勝地」之意。

167

What is indicated in the letter?

(A) Ms. Rodriguez has paid for part of her cruise.
(B) Ms. Rodriguez has changed her itinerary.
(C) The cruise trip is a month long.
(D) The departure and arrival port are the same.

關於這封信，下列何者正確？

(A) 羅德里格茲女士繳了部分的旅費。
(B) 羅德里格茲女士已更改行程。
(C) 航程長達 1 個月。
(D) 啟程與終點港口相同。

答案 (D) 　何者正確類型

選項提到的羅德里格茲女士是這封信的收件人（＝參加航程的人）。第2段有說到全額付款，所以(A)的part of（部分）是錯的。至於itinerary（行程表）這個單字雖然在信中出現幾次，但並非要改行程，所以(B)也是錯的。而航程日期從7月3−24日，約3週左右，所以(C)的a month不符合。接著從Starting/Ending Port: Venice可知，啟程與終點都是威尼斯，所以(D)是正確答案。

Questions 168-171 refer to the following online chat.

Francesco, Alvarro [1:31 P.M.]
Did Doug send out the new sales data? Florence and I are working on the slideshow that we have to present at next week's meeting. We were going to try to include it.

Souk, Jasper [1:32 P.M.]
I haven't heard from him.

Francesco, Alvarro [1:34 P.M.]
Has he got it analyzed?

Binks, Florence [1:35 P.M.]
I wish I knew.

Kang, Lawrence [1:37 P.M.]
He just called me. He's on his way to the office, but traffic is heavy. It might be awhile.

Francesco, Alvarro [1:39 P.M.]
Did he say anything about the meeting or the presentation?

Kang, Lawrence [1:41 P.M.]
I didn't ask. Anyway, didn't Doug mention that sales data doesn't need to be discussed next week?

Souk, Jasper [1:43 P.M.]
I heard the same thing. The district meeting is three weeks from now. The district managers need that data, but next week is just a product review with sales representatives.

Binks, Florence [1:46 P.M.]
I've been a bit concerned it might require us to work overtime in order to include that data.

Francesco, Alvarro [1:48 P.M.]
Come to think of it, it might. I'll confirm that with Doug when he comes, but for now let's go ahead and finish the slideshow without that data. It'll actually make our job easier.

Binks, Florence [1:50 P.M.]
I'm all for that.

試題168-171請參考以下線上交談內容。

阿法洛・法蘭西斯科（Francesco, Alvarro）1:31 P.M.
道格（Doug）寄出新的銷售資料了嗎？佛羅倫斯（Florence）和我正在製作下週會議上報告用的簡報。我們打算把它加入簡報中。

賈斯柏・蘇克（Souk, Jasper） 1:32 P.M.
我沒聽他說過。

阿法洛・法蘭西斯科 1:34 P.M.
那他分析過資料了嗎？

佛羅倫斯・賓克斯（Binks, Florence） 1:35 P.M.
我要是知道就好了。

羅倫斯・康（Kang, Lawrence） 1:37 P.M.
他剛打電話給我。他在回辦公室路上，但現在塞車，可能要等一會兒。

阿法洛・法蘭西斯科 1:39 P.M.
他有提到任何有關開會或是簡報的事嗎？

羅倫斯・康 1:41 P.M.
我沒問。不過，他不是有提到下週不需要討論銷售資料嗎？

賈斯柏・蘇克 1:43 P.M.
我也聽到同樣的話。區會議距現在還有3週。雖然區經理們需要那份資料，但下週只是跟銷售代表進行產品討論。

佛羅倫斯・賓克斯 1:46 P.M.
我已經有點擔心，如果要加入那些資料，我們可能要加班。

阿法洛・法蘭西斯科 1:48 P.M.
這樣一想的話，是有可能的。道格回來時我會跟他確認，現在我們就不加入那些資料，繼續進行完成簡報製作。那會使我們的工作容易許多。

佛羅倫斯・賓克斯 1:50 P.M.
我完全贊成。

Vocabulary

□ awhile [əˋhwaɪl] **副** 一會兒　　□ come to think of it　這樣一想的話、這麼說　　□ for [fɔr] **介** 贊成

試題	試題翻譯	解答與解析

☑ 168

What will Mr. Francesco do next week?

(A) Analyze data
(B) Compile a report
(C) Attend a conference
(D) Give a presentation

法蘭西斯科先生下週要做什麼？

(A) 分析資料
(B) 彙整報告
(C) 出席會議
(D) 做簡報報告

答案 (D)　其他細節

從法蘭西斯科先生一開始提到Florence and I are working on the slideshow that we have to present at next week's meeting.，可知下週的會議要做簡報報告。而且他在第3次的發言說Did he say anything about the meeting or the presentation?，表示slideshow（簡報）即是在說presentation（報告），所以(D)是正確答案。

☑ 169

What is indicated about the product review?

(A) It will include sales data.
(B) It will require a lot of time.
(C) It will be held sooner than the district meeting.
(D) It will be held in three weeks.

有關產品討論，下列何者正確？

(A) 將包括銷售資料。
(B) 將需要花很多時間。
(C) 將比區會議更早舉行。
(D) 將在 3 週後舉行。

答案 (C)　何者正確類型

從next week is just a product review with sales representatives可知，product review（產品討論）是下週要舉行的會議。而在The district meeting is three weeks from now.這句則提到區會議是在3週後，也就是產品討論是在召開區會議之前，所以(C)是正確答案。另外根據這篇銷售資料是不是要放入下週會議流程的討論來看，(A)是錯誤的。

☑ 170

What does Mr. Francesco say he will do next?

(A) Contact sales staff
(B) Wait for sales data
(C) Go directly to a meeting
(D) Work on a slideshow

法蘭西斯科先生說他接下來要做什麼？

(A) 聯絡銷售人員
(B) 等銷售資料
(C) 直接去開會
(D) 準備簡報資料

答案 (D)　其他細節

法蘭西斯科最後發言時說…but for now let's… finish the slideshow without that data，所以(D)是正確答案。請大家要養成習慣意識到but之後會接續重要的內容。

☑ 171

At 1:50 P.M., what does Ms. Binks most likely mean when she writes, "I'm all for that"?

(A) She is happy that the job can be finished soon.
(B) She agrees with including data in a presentation.
(C) She is concerned that the meeting will take too long.
(D) She prefers to attend the meeting in three weeks.

1:50 P.M.，賓克斯女士寫到 「I'm all for that?」，她的意思是？

(A) 她很開心工作可以快點結束。
(B) 她贊成簡報包含銷售資料。
(C) 她擔心會議時間太長。
(D) 她比較希望參加 3 週後的會議。

答案 (A)　說話者的目的

for在這邊是「贊成～」之意，這樣解讀就可知賓克斯女士贊成什麼。賓克斯女士第2次的發言就提到擔心要加班，所以當法蘭西斯科先生說「不加入那些資料，繼續進行完成簡報製作。那會使我們的工作容易許多。」，她表示贊成。因為工作儘早完成就不用加班，當然值得高興，所以(A)是正確答案。

□ prefer to *do* 　（比起……更）喜歡～

Questions 172-175 refer to the following letter.

12 May

Mr. Sanjay Patel
EVX-Speed Logistics, Inc.
B-23, Connaught Place
New Delhi 110021

Dear Mr. Patel,

We may be interested in what your firm can do for us. At present, we ship all our products through our logistics department. — [1] —.

However, over lunch with Lucretia Hawkins, a former colleague of mine, I learned about your firm. She told me that her current employer, Trank Semiconductors, has benefitted substantially from outsourcing logistics to your firm. — [2] —. I was told that you have a very high on-time delivery rate and a sophisticated computer system linking you with clients. She also noted that you have an outstanding industry reputation. — [3] —.

To formally become one of our service providers, you would need to explain in detail how and why you could benefit us. To aid in this process, some of our company literature is enclosed. — [4] —. Please go through it to get a better idea of what we do; it is quite comprehensive.

If you are confident you could meet our requirements, please contact me at your first opportunity.

Kind regards,

Ivan Klimov
Ivan Klimov
Chief Operating Officer
Faisl Textiles, Inc.
i.klimov@faisltextiles.com

5月12日

桑杰・帕特爾先生（Mr. Sanjay Patel）
伊維克斯速達物流公司（EVX-Speed Logistics, Inc.）
B-23康諾特廣場（Connaught Place）
新德里（New Delhi）110021

親愛的帕特爾先生：

敝公司對於貴公司能提供的服務可能會有興趣。目前，我們所有產品的運送都是經由物流部門處理。—〔1〕—。

不過，透過與前同事盧克蕾蒂雅・霍金斯（Lucretia Hawkins）午餐的機會，我得知貴公司。她告訴我，她現在任職的托蘭克半導體（Trank Semiconductors）公司，將物流委外貴公司處理，受益匪淺。—〔2〕—我聽說貴公司有很高的準時交貨率和一套精密的電腦系統連結您和客戶。她也提到，貴公司在業界有非常傑出的聲譽。—〔3〕—。這些當然都是重要的成果標竿。

要正式成為我們的服務提供者之一，您需要詳細地解說該如何以及為什麼可以讓我們從中獲益。為了有助於這個過程，隨函附上一些敝公司的文宣資料。—〔4〕—。請您過目來更了解我們的業務內容；文宣內有很全面的介紹。

如果您有信心可以滿足我們的需求，請在第一時間與我聯絡。

謹致問候

伊凡・克里莫夫（Ivan Klimov）
營運長
飛索（Faisl）紡織品公司
i.klimov@faisltextiles.com

Vocabulary

□ at present　目前　　□ logistics [lo`dʒɪstɪk] 名 物流　　□ semiconductor [ˌsɛmɪkən`dʌktɚ] 名 半導體　　□ benefit [`bɛnəfɪt] 動 受益

□ substantially [səb`stænʃəlɪ] 副 大大地、相當地　　□ outsource A to B　將A外包給B　　□ high delivery rate　很高的交貨率

□ on-time [`ɑnˌtaɪm] 形 準時的　　□ sophisticated [sə`fɪstɪˌketɪd] 形 精密的　　□ link A with B　將A與B連結

□ outstanding [`aʊt`stændɪŋ] 形 傑出的　　□ reputation [ˌrɛpjə`teʃən] 名 聲譽　　□ formally [`fɔrm!ɪ] 副 正式地　　□ aid [ed] 動 幫助

□ literature [`lɪtərətʃɚ] 名（廣告等的）文宣、印刷品　　□ go through～　仔細過目　　□ meet *one's* requirements　滿足～的要求

試題	試題翻譯	解答與解析

☑ 172

Why was the letter written?

(A) To offer a new type of product
(B) To inform of operational changes
(C) To update a business account
(D) To suggest a business opportunity

為何寫這封信？

(A) 提供新的產品
(B) 通知營運上的變更
(C) 更新企業往來帳戶
(D) 推薦商機

答案 (D) 〔概述〕

第1句即開門見山說We may be interested in what your firm can do for us.來表示對對方公司有興趣，接著再敘述自己公司現況及聽到有關對方公司的相關訊息。從第3段的To formally become one of our service providers, ...，還有最後一段的If you are confident you could meet our requirements, ...可判斷在向對方推薦商機，所以(D)是正確答案。

☑ 173

According to the letter, what is true about Lucretia Hawkins?

(A) She leads a major logistics firm.
(B) She manages a textile business.
(C) She has worked with Mr. Klimov before.
(D) She consults on marketing techniques.

根據信件內容，有關盧克蕾蒂雅‧霍金斯的描述，下列何者正確？

(A) 她領導一家大型物流公司。
(B) 她經營一家紡織事業。
(C) 她曾與克里莫夫先生共事。
(D) 她諮詢行銷技巧。

答案 (C) 〔何者正確類型〕

第2段有提到，盧克蕾蒂雅‧霍金斯就是告訴他有關這封信收件人的公司資料的前同事。從a former colleague of mine可知(C)是正確答案。

☑ 174

The word "comprehensive" in paragraph 3, line 4, is closest in meaning to

(A) extensive
(B) secure
(C) limited
(D) reasonable

第 3 段第 4 行的單字 「comprehensive」意思最接近下列哪一個？

(A) 廣泛的
(B) 安全的
(C) 有限的
(D) 合理的

答案 (A) 〔同義詞〕

it is quite comprehensive中的主詞it是指前面說的some of our company literature。而將隨函附上文宣資料的理由是，因為寄件人要讓對方了解自己公司的業務，所以從前面內容可推測comprehensive有肯定的意思。comprehensive是「全面的」，(A)的extensive（廣泛的）意思最接近。(B)和(D)是錯在把所附上的資料視為secure（安全的）和reasonable（合理的），這說法很奇怪。至於(C)因為是否定意味的單字，所以可刪去不考慮。

☑ 175

In which of the positions marked [1], [2], [3], and [4] does the following sentence best belong?

"These are of course all critical performance benchmarks."

(A) [1]
(B) [2]
(C) [3]
(D) [4]

下面這一句應該插入標記 〔1〕、〔2〕、〔3〕、〔4〕 的哪一個位置？

「這些當然都是重要的成果標竿。」
(A) 〔1〕
(B) 〔2〕
(C) 〔3〕
(D) 〔4〕

答案 (C) 〔插入句〕

如果插入句裡面有this或these、that等代名詞，那麼敘述完具體內容之後空白處，就是插入句的正確位置。所以要從整篇文章找出表示「重要的成果標竿」的內容。第2段全部都在敘述對方公司的優點，因此在這段最後加入〔3〕最適當。〔2〕的位置前面雖然有提到優點，但是不符合插入句的these are及all。

□ benchmark [ˋbɛntʃˏmɑrk] 名 （判斷等的）標竿、基準

Questions 176-180 refer to the following article and memo.

June 1 (Lane City) —The 15th Annual Lane City Art Festival will be held from June 7 to June 14 in the Barnaby Plaza. Promoted by the city government and sponsored by Taki Sporting Goods, art fans will be able to view and purchase works from a variety of talent looking to raise their public profiles.

This year, over 50,000 visitors are expected to attend. There will be free outdoor painting classes for elementary school students, live folk music and clown shows. Food stands will also be located throughout the event, owned and operated by local vendors.

Over 300 artists will be participating, and showcasing paintings, photography, sculptures and other art forms. In *Art Wow Magazine*, art critic Sally Fromm termed the event "one of the best showcases of art in the region."

Memo
Lane City Government

From: Harold Byrd, Operations Director
To: Operations Managers
Date: June 19
Subject: Lane City Art Festival

I want to congratulate you on the successful completion of the recent Art Festival. I am pleased to inform you that over 1,200 art pieces were sold. After coming to see the event, Sally Fromm called me today to say that she found it simply outstanding in every respect.

This serves to increase national and international awareness of our city as a growing art hub. We hope to use the success of the event to attract more artists and art-related industries, including graphic design firms, galleries, and social media developers. This would be in line with our 10-year development plan that has so far been successfully implemented.

I know that you worked hard on this project, putting in long hours in addition to your normal departmental duties. As a small token of appreciation, I have ordered pizza and soft drinks to be delivered to the office at 12:30 P.M. Please stop by to have some.

試題176-180請參考以下報導及通知。

6月1日蘭市（Lane City）—第15屆年度蘭市藝術節將於6月7日到6月14日於巴納比廣場（Barnaby Plaza）舉行。由市政府推動，塔基（Taki）運動用品公司贊助，藝術迷們將能夠欣賞並購買各式各樣希望提升其知名度的人才的作品。

今年，預計將有超過50,000名參觀者。現場有針對小學生的免費戶外繪畫課程，還有現場民俗音樂和小丑表演。由當地小販擁有及經營的食品攤位也將分布在整個活動會場中。

300名以上的藝術家將參與活動，並展示其繪畫、攝影、雕塑和其他藝術作品。藝術哇雜誌（*Art Wow Magazine*）的藝術評論家莎莉‧佛羅蒙（Sally Fromm）還將這次的活動喻為「該地區最好的藝術展之一」。

通知
蘭市政府

發信者：營運總監　哈羅德‧白爾德（Harold Byrd）
收信者：營運經理們
日期：6月19日
主旨：蘭市藝術展

我想在此恭喜你們成功完成日前的藝術展。很高興通知大家，超過1,200件的藝術品已賣出。莎莉‧佛羅蒙來看了這場活動後，今日打電話給我說，她認為這個活動在每一方面都很出色。

這對逐漸成為藝術中心的本市來說，有助提高在國內及國際的知名度。我們希望藉由這個活動的成功來吸引更多藝術家、藝術相關企業，包括平面設計公司、畫廊和社群媒體開發者。這與我們目前已成功實行的10年發展計劃是目標一致的。

我知道你們為了這項任務非常努力工作，除了平常的部門職責外，還要額外投入很長的時間。我已訂了披薩和飲料，會在午後12點半送到辦公室，來做為一個小小的感謝之意。請各位過來享用。

Vocabulary

☐ promote [prə`mot] 動 推動～　　☐ a variety of～　各式各樣的～　　☐ raise *one's* profile　提高～的知名度

☐ showcase [`ʃo͵kes] 動 展示～；名 展示　　☐ sculpture [`skʌlptʃə] 名 雕塑品　　☐ term A B　把A稱為B

☐ region [`ridʒən] 名 地區　　☐ congratulate A on B　恭喜A有關B　　☐ completion [kəm`pliʃən] 名 完成

☐ awareness [ə`wɛrnɪs] 名 知名度、注意　　☐ hub [hʌb] 名 中心　　☐ in line with～　與～一致　　☐ so far　到目前為止

☐ in addition to～　除了～還有　　☐ as a token of～　～的象徵、之意　　☐ appreciation [ə͵priʃɪ`eʃən] 名 感謝　　☐ stop by　順路造訪

試題	試題翻譯	解答與解析

☑ 176

According to the article, what organization sponsored the event?

(A) An industry association
(B) A city charity
(C) A private corporation
(D) A media group

根據報導，是什麼組織贊助這項活動？

(A) 產業協會
(B) 城市慈善機構
(C) 私人企業
(D) 傳媒集團

答案 (C)　其他細節

sponsor是「贊助～」。報導內容第1段提到sponsored by Taki Sporting Goods，由此判斷Taki Sporting Goods（塔基運動用品公司）為私人企業，所以(A)是正確答案。

☑ 177

What was mentioned as available at the festival?

(A) Photography guides
(B) Talent recruitment
(C) Food contests
(D) Children's classes

文中提到藝術節有提供什麼？

(A) 攝影指南
(B) 人才招募
(C) 美食比賽
(D) 兒童課程

答案 (D)　何者正確類型

找出報導內在說明藝術節的部分，即是第2段free outdoor painting classes for elementary school students。所以(D)是正確答案。

☑ 178

In the memo, the word "respect" in paragraph 1, line 3, is closest in meaning to

(A) notice
(B) sense
(C) interest
(D) honor

通知文第 1 段第 3 行單字 「respect」 意思最接近下列哪一個？

(A) 通知
(B) 意義
(C) 興趣
(D) 名譽

答案 (B)　同義詞

單字前面的動詞為〈find it＋形容詞〉型態，是「認為它～」之意。it是前面描述的the event，也就是藝術節。從「認為藝術節在每一個～是出色的」的前後句關係來思考，respect有「（某）方面」之意。in every respect意即「在每一方面」。與這個意思最相近的是(B)的sense（意義）。in every sense意即「在每種意義上」。

☑ 179

Who contacted Harold Byrd on June 19?

(A) A magazine publisher
(B) An expert in the art field
(C) A film critic
(D) A producer of artwork

6 月 19 日誰聯絡了哈羅德‧白爾德？

(A) 雜誌社
(B) 藝術界專家
(C) 影評家
(D) 藝術品製造者

答案 (B)　其他細節

這題跟2篇文都有關係。哈羅德‧白爾德是通知文的發信者。第1段提到Sally Fromm called me today，根據通知的日期可知，莎莉‧佛羅蒙在6月19日聯絡他。接著再看報導內容，第3段提到art critic Sally Fromm。critic意為「評論家」，所以換一種說法的(B)「藝術界專家」是正確答案。

□ expert [`ɛkspɚt] 名 專家

☑ 180

What is suggested about the development plan of Lane City?

(A) It includes attracting creative types of firms.
(B) It centers on international trade companies.
(C) It consists of implementing political changes.
(D) It focuses on the food and beverage industries.

有關蘭市的發展計畫，下列何者正確？

(A) 包括吸引創意型企業。
(B) 聚焦於國際貿易公司。
(C) 由實施政治改革構成。
(D) 聚焦在食品飲料業。

答案 (A)　何者正確類型

關於蘭市的開發計畫，在通知文的第2段This would be in line with our 10-year development plan有提到。這邊的This是指前面提到的內容，從… attract more artists and art-related industries, including graphic design firms...這一小段就可知(A)為正確答案。industry意即「企業」，選項內是把graphic design firm（平面設計公司）用creative types of firms（創意型企業）來表示。

□ beverage [`bɛvərɪdʒ] 名 飲料

Questions 181-185 refer to the following letters.

試題181-185請參考以下信件內容。

Seltan Chemical Co.
www.seltanchem.net/jobs/
27 Wannake Avenue

May 3

Dr. Alejandro Gomez
Blakefort University

Dear Dr. Gomez,

We have several available paid positions in our Blakefort laboratories. These are ideal for senior students.

The open positions are:

Lab assistants: Help researchers with general tasks, such as preparing equipment.

Clerks: Manage, enter and file both digital and print information for researchers and technicians.

Assistant researchers: Help with basic testing and research tasks. Open only to exceptionally qualified candidates with at least three years of industry experience.

Test monitors: Take regular notes on test procedures, progress, and equipment condition. Update and inform researchers of significant changes or events.

Please feel free to share this letter with any of your students that you feel are qualified. They may apply directly online through the Web site above. Applications must be accompanied by at least three signed letters of recommendation, which may be mailed to the address above or e-mailed to the recruiter noted below.

Thanks very much in advance for your help.

Yours sincerely,

Harvey Betts
Harvey Betts
Human Resources Director

CC: Barbara Vick, Recruiter
barbara.vick@seltanchem.net

賽爾坦化學公司（Seltan Chemical Co.）
www.seltanchem.net/jobs/
27汪奈克大道（Wannake Avenue）

5月3日

亞利桑德羅‧戈梅茲博士（Dr. Alejandro Gomez）
布萊克福特大學（Blakefort University）

親愛的戈梅茲博士：

我們在布萊克福特實驗室有幾個有給薪的職務空缺。這些適合大四的學生。其空缺職務如下：
實驗室助理： 協助研究員做一般工作，諸如準備設備。
辦事員： 為研究員及技術員管理、輸入並歸檔數位與紙本的資料。
助理研究員： 協助基本測試及研究工作。僅開放給至少有3年業界經驗的特別傑出的合格應徵者。
實驗監控員： 定期記錄實驗的程序、進展及設備狀況。更新並通知研究員重要的改變或事件。

請別客氣將這封信分享給任何一位您覺得符合的學生。他們可以直接經由上方的網址在網上申請應徵。申請必須附帶至少3封有簽名的推薦函，可郵寄到上述地址或是用電子郵件傳至下方提到的招聘人員。

在此先跟您致謝。

謹致問候

哈維‧貝斯（Harvey Betts）
人力資源總監

副本：芭芭拉‧維克（Barbara Vick）招聘人員
barbara.vick@seltanchem.net

May 7

Mr. Harvey Betts
Seltan Chemical Co.

Dear Mr. Betts,

I am writing regarding the application of Ga-in Choi for the position of assistant researcher. Ms. Choi is in the final year of the Chemistry program at our school and otherwise fulfills all the listed qualifications for the aforementioned position.

She has been my student in four classes, where she received top grades and was a regular participant in class discussions. She was also the leader of two class teams that had to develop group projects. Moreover, Ms. Choi is active within our community, organizing student fundraisers for causes such as aid for elderly citizens.

I can therefore give Ms. Choi my highest recommendation. If you need further information, please do not hesitate to contact me. A copy of this letter has been sent to Barbara Vick.

Sincerely,

Alejandro Gomez
Alejandro Gomez
Blakefort University

5月7日

哈維‧貝斯先生
賽爾坦化學公司

親愛的貝斯先生：

我寫這封信是有關申請人崔家瑩（Ga-in Choi）應徵助理研究員一事。崔女士正在本校攻讀化學系最後1年，除此之外，她完全達到前述職務列出的應徵條件。

她有修過我開的4堂課，成績頂尖且經常參與班級討論。她也是2個必須發想小組計畫的班級團隊的領導者。此外，崔女士在我們的社群表現活躍，組織學生做例如為老年人提供援助等目的的募款活動。

因此，我強力推薦崔女士。如果您需要更詳細的資料，請連絡我不要客氣。我也傳了一份這封信的副本給芭芭拉‧維克。

謹致問候

亞利桑德羅‧戈梅茲
布萊克福特大學

Vocabulary

- □ paid [ped] 形 給薪的
- □ ideal [aɪˋdiəl] 形 理想的
- □ senior [ˋsinjɚ] 形 （美國）（大學或高中的）最高年級生的
- □ exceptionally [ɪkˋsɛpʃənəlɪ] 副 特別地
- □ procedure [prəˋsidʒɚ] 名 程序
- □ significant [sɪgˋnɪfəkənt] 形 重要的
- □ accompany [əˋkʌmpənɪ] 動 附帶～
- □ regarding [rɪˋgɑrdɪŋ] 介 關於～
- □ aforementioned [əˋforˋmɛnʃənd] 形 上述的、前述的
- □ fundraiser [ˋfʌndˏrezɚ] 名 資金募集的活動
- □ cause [kɔz] 名 目的、理由

試題	試題翻譯	解答與解析

181

Why does Mr. Betts write to Dr. Gomez?

(A) To offer a business service
(B) To recruit him for a research position
(C) To inquire about applicants for openings
(D) To request feedback on a proposal

貝斯先生為何寫信給戈梅茲博士？

(A) 提供業務服務
(B) 聘請他做研究職務
(C) 詢問有關適合職務空缺的求職者
(D) 請求對提案回饋

答案 (C) 概述

第1封是貝斯先生寫給戈梅茲博士的信。開頭提到We have several available paid positions後，具體地詳述4個職缺，最後說Please feel free to share this letter with any of your students...並描述應徵方法。所以(C)是正確答案。

☐ recruit [rɪˋkrut] 勔 招募、聘請～

182

What is NOT a requirement for the test monitors?

(A) Watching equipment
(B) Noting changes
(C) Relaying updates
(D) Making suggestions

哪一項不是實驗監控員的職務要求？

(A) 監看設備
(B) 記錄變更
(C) 傳達最新情況
(D) 提出建議

答案 (D) 是非題類型

這題是問有關實驗監控員的職務，所以用第1封信的Test monitors: 的部分來對照作答即可。(A)等同Take regular notes on... equipment condition.。(B)等同inform... significant changes。(C)等同Update and inform...。而(D)的部分並沒有被提到，所以是正確答案。

183

In the second letter, the word "fulfills" in paragraph 1, line 2, is closest in meaning to

(A) completes
(B) examines
(C) requires
(D) satisfies

第 2 封信第 1 段第 2 行單字 「fulfills」 意思最接近下列哪一個？

(A) 完成～
(B) 檢視～
(C) 需要～
(D) 滿足～

答案 (D) 同義詞

fulfills是動詞，主詞是這整句最前面的崔女士，意即「崔女士完全～前述職務列出的應徵條件」。寫信者推薦崔女士，因此可推測fulfill有肯定的意味。fulfill是「ful-（完全）＋fill（滿足～）」，所以與(D)的satisfy（滿足～）是一樣的意思。雖然qualification（資格、能力）與aforementioned（前述的）是有難度的單字，但是即使不懂也可以作答無礙。

184

What is true about the copy of the second letter?

(A) It has been sent to an alternate firm.
(B) It has been delivered to a company recruiter.
(C) It has been posted on a university Intranet page.
(D) It has been uploaded to a company Web site.

關於第 2 封信的副本，下列何者正確？

(A) 已寄到另一間公司。
(B) 已寄給公司的招聘人員。
(C) 已登在學校的內部網路上。
(D) 已上傳到一間公司網頁。

答案 (B) 何者正確類型

這題跟2封信都有關連。第2封信的最後有提到副本，A copy of this letter has been sent to Barbara Vick.。至於Barbara Vick是誰，第1封信的最後有註記CC: Barbara Vick, Recruiter，由此可知第2封信的副本是寄給招聘人員（recruiter），所以(B)是正確答案。

185

What is implied about Ga-in Choi?

(A) She has no industry experience.
(B) She has a student scholarship.
(C) She assisted a new professor.
(D) She wrote a recommendation.

有關崔家瑩的各項描述，表示著什麼？

(A) 她沒有業界經驗。
(B) 她獲得學生獎學金。
(C) 她協助一位新教授。
(D) 她寫了一封推薦信。

答案 (A) 推測

這題跟2封信都有關連。崔家瑩是第2封信中被推薦的學生，根據第1段，她被推薦為助理研究員，是大四學生，此外都達到應徵條件。但從第1封信的Assistant researchers: 來看，需要有業界經驗，而崔家瑩現在是大四學生，暗示著她沒有業界經驗，所以(A)是正確答案。

Questions 186-190 refer to the following letter, e-mail and floor plan.

試題186-190請參考以下信件、電子郵件、樓層平面圖。

Walton Hotel
555 North Seventh Street

October 11

Dear Ms. Semmens,

Thank you very much for your interest in our banquet rooms. Please find our brochure enclosed.

As you know, our hotel is one of the oldest and longest-running establishments in the city. Last year, we completed renovations to several rooms on our second floor for small and large gatherings. These had been previously converted to storage areas and private business offices in the 1960s. Now restored to their turn-of-the-century splendor, these rooms are currently available to lease for private events.

We recommend making year-end reservations in advance, as we expect these to be booked quickly this year. For any other inquiries, please call us toll-free at 800-555-6262, or you can e-mail me directly at tferrell@waltonhotel.com.

Yours sincerely,

Timothy Ferrell

Timothy Ferrell
General Manager
Walton Hotel
tferrell@waltonhotel.com

華頓飯店（Walton Hotel）
555北（North）第7街（Seventh Street）

10月11日

親愛的西門斯（Semmens）女士：

非常謝謝您對我們的宴會廳感興趣。隨函附上飯店指南。

如您所知，我們飯店是本市最古老、營運最久的企業之一。去年，我們完成了2樓幾個大、小型聚會空間的翻新工程。這些空間曾在1960年代時被改為倉庫及私人商辦。現在，我們恢復了它們的世紀輝煌，將這些房間出租給私人活動使用。

建議您預先做年終尾牙的預約，因為我們預期今年這些空間很快會被訂滿。若有任何其他需求，請撥免付費電話800-555-6262洽詢，或直接傳電子郵件至tferrell@waltonhotel.com給我亦可。

謹致問候

提摩西‧法洛（Timothy Ferrell）
總經理
華頓飯店
tferrell@waltonhotel.com

* E-mail *	✕
From:	Joyce Semmens <jsemmens@bryantcorp1.com>
To:	Timothy Ferrell <tferrell@waltonhotel.com>
Date:	October 17
Subject:	Bryant Corporation year-end banquet

Dear Mr. Ferrell,

Thank you for your prompt response. I can see what a great job you did with renovations. The rooms look gorgeous, and I loved the stained glass windows.

We have approximately 80 people attending, but we're planning on having a dance. I'm willing to cover the cost for a little more space. I'd like to know the number of people each room accommodates. Could you provide this information? That would be greatly appreciated.

Best,
Joyce

Joyce Semmens
Human Resources
Bryant Corporation
jsemmens@bryantcorp1.com

發信者：喬伊思‧西門斯（Joyce Semmens）
　　　　<jsemmens@bryantcorp1.com>
收信者：提摩西‧法洛
　　　　<tferrell@waltonhotel.com>
日期：10月17日
主旨：布萊恩特公司（Bryant Corporation）年終宴會

親愛的法洛先生：

感謝您的迅速回覆。我看得出來您的翻新工程做得很成功。房間看起來都很豪華，而且我很喜歡那個彩色玻璃窗。

我們約會有80位參加者，但我們正計畫辦場舞會。如果有大一點的空間，我願意負擔費用。我想知道每個房間可容納的人數。能否提供這些資料給我？由衷感激您！

謹致問候
喬伊思
‥‥‥‥
喬伊思‧西門斯
人力資源部
布萊恩特公司
jsemmens@bryantcorp1.com

試題文章	試題文章翻譯

Room Availability

Large Meeting Room
capacity: 80

FOYER

East Wing
capacity: 120

Banquet Room
capacity: 100
[RESERVED]

Small
Meeting Room
capacity: 40

房間使用狀況

大會議室
容納人數：
80人

門廳

東側廳
容納人數：
120人

宴會廳
容納人數：100人
（已預約）

小會議室
容納人數：
40人

Vocabulary

☐ banquet [`bæŋkwɪt] 名 宴會    ☐ establishment [ɪs`tæblɪʃmənt] 名 機構、企業   ☐ renovation [ˌrɛnə`veʃən] 名 翻新

☐ gathering [`gæðərɪŋ] 名 聚會    ☐ previously [`priviəslɪ] 副 以前、曾經   ☐ convert A to B　將A改成B

☐ restore [rɪ`stor] 動 修復（復原）～    ☐ turn-of-the-century [tɝn ɑv ðə `sɛntʃʊrɪ] 形 世紀末前後的   ☐ splendor [`splɛndɚ] 名 輝煌

☐ lease [lis] 動 出租～   ☐ year-end [`jɪrˌɛnd] 形 年終的   ☐ prompt [prɑmpt] 形 迅速的

☐ approximately [ə`prɑksəmɪtlɪ] 副 大約    ☐ be willing to *do*　願意去做    ☐ accommodate [ə`kɑməˌdet] 動 可容納～

☐ capacity [kə`pæsətɪ] 名 容納量、規定人數

試題	試題翻譯	解答與解析

☑ 186

What is the purpose of the letter?

(A) To advertise a new hotel
(B) To outline a strategy
(C) To respond to an inquiry
(D) To confirm a reservation

這封信的目的是什麼？

(A) 宣傳新的飯店
(B) 略述策略
(C) 回覆詢問事宜
(D) 確認預約

答案 (C) `概述`

從信件開頭前2句可知，這是回覆飯店客人詢問宴會事宜，並隨函附上飯店指南。所以(C)是正確答案。

☐ outline [`aʊt͵laɪn] **動** 略述～
☐ strategy [`strætədʒɪ] **名** 策略

☑ 187

What is suggested about the hotel?

(A) It is currently undergoing repairs.
(B) An area has been converted for storage.
(C) Some rooms can be used for private events.
(D) Enough rooms are available throughout the year.

關於飯店，下列何者正確？

(A) 目前整修中。
(B) 有一區已改為倉庫。
(C) 部分房間可作私人活動。
(D) 全年都有足夠房間可利用。

答案 (C) `何者正確類型`

用消去法來看，信中第2段we completed renovations to... ，表示翻新工程已完成，所以(A)不對。(B)與These had been previously...後面的2句內容不符，因為以前作為倉庫的空間在去年已翻新為大、小型房間。(C)的描述與these rooms are currently available to lease for private events相符，所以是正確答案。此外，從第3段可知，年終很難預約，所以(D)不對。

☑ 188

What is implied about the brochure?

(A) It includes photos of rooms.
(B) It includes a floor plan.
(C) It indicates room capacities.
(D) It was created recently.

有關隨函附上的指南，文中表示什麼？

(A) 附房間照片。
(B) 附樓層平面圖。
(C) 有標示房間可容納人數。
(D) 最近才製作完成。

答案 (A) `推測`

電子郵件是向飯店提出詢問的西門斯女士在看了對方寄來的指南後發送的。從第1段的The rooms look gorgeous, and I loved the stained glass windows.可推想指南上印有房間的照片，所以(A)是正確答案。本文第3部分是樓層平面圖，是西門斯女士送出電子郵件當時並不知道的資料，所以(B)和(C)都不正確。

☑ 189

Which room will Ms. Semmens most likely choose?

(A) Large Meeting Room
(B) Banquet Room
(C) Small Meeting Room
(D) East Wing

西門斯女士最可能選哪一種房型？

(A) 大會議室
(B) 宴會廳
(C) 小會議室
(D) 東側廳

答案 (D) `其他細節`

西門斯女士用電子郵件來詢問年終尾牙的宴會場地。先從第2段來掌握重點，「雖然大約有80位參加者，但因為要辦場舞會（以80位起算），所以需要更大空間」，然後再從平面圖選擇適合該條件的房型。大會議室雖可容納80人，但沒有跳舞的空間，因此不適合。而可容納100人的宴會廳雖符合條件卻已被預約。所以僅有可容納120人的East Wing（東側廳）最適合。

☑ 190

In the e-mail, the word "cover" in paragraph 2, line 2, is closest in meaning to

(A) wrap
(B) spread
(C) collect
(D) pay

電子郵件中，第2段第2行單字 cover 意思最接近下列哪一個？

(A) 包裹～
(B) 遍布～
(C) 蒐集～
(D) 支付～

答案 (D) `同義詞`

西門斯女士因為需要跳舞空間，所以即使要多花一點費用取得大空間也可以。cover也有(A) wrap (up)及(B)spread (over)的意思，但在這邊接the cost（費用）後，是「支付、負擔（費用）」之意，所以(D)是正確答案。

試題文章	試題文章翻譯

Questions 191-195 refer to the following advertisement, text message and e-mail.

Aspiring Chef Summer Courses

Want to do more than just make dinner? Want to try creating fine cuisine?
Impress your friends and family!
Kenmoor Culinary Academy is offering a short series of classes
for novice chefs next month at Circle Community Center.
The instructor, Allison Goodman, who has graciously volunteered her time,
is the head chef at Royton's Fine Dining in downtown Cincinnati.

> Saturdays: August 6, 13, 20, and 27
> 10:00 — 11:30 A.M.
> Ages 15 and up
> Limit: 12 students
> Fee: $149 (includes ingredients)

Participants will learn the basics of preparing several simple but popular
restaurant-quality dishes from scratch,
including where and how to buy the best ingredients.

For more information or to apply, please contact Julie Higgins
at Circle Community Center: 213 Boynton Way, (913) 555-4570,
or visit the center's Web site: www.circlecommctr.com.
Payment is required to reserve space. Hurry.
Space is limited, and every year this short course fills quickly.

From: Allison Goodman
Received: July 25, 10:43 A.M.
To: Julie Higgins

Hi, just a quick note. As usual the printed ad looks great. I wonder if I could ask a favor this year. Could you include the Web address to Royton's Fine Dining? It's www.roytons.com. I'd really appreciate that. Drop me an e-mail when you get a chance. Thanks, Julie!

試題191-195請參考以下廣告、簡訊及電子郵件。

有志於廚師者暑期課程

想做的不僅是一道晚餐嗎？想嘗試創作精緻美食嗎？
讓你的朋友及家人驚艷吧！
肯慕爾烹飪學院（Kenmoor Culinary Academy）下個月在圓弧（Circle）社區中心為新手廚師們提供短期系列課程。
講師是自願慷慨撥空的愛莉森‧顧德曼（Allison Goodman），目前是辛辛那提（Cincinnati）市中心羅伊頓美食（Royton's Fine Dining）的主廚。

週六：8月6、13、20及27日
10:00－11:30 A.M.
年齡15歲（含）以上
人數限制：12名
費用：149元（含材料費）

參加者將從頭開始學習製作數道簡單而受歡迎、如餐廳般品質的菜餚，包括在哪裡及如何購得上好食材。

想知道更多訊息或報名者，請洽圓弧社區中心：213伯因頓路（Boynton Way），（913）555-4570茱麗‧希金斯（Julie Higgins）或上中心網站：www.circlecommctr.com。
須完成繳費以預約名額，請從速。
名額有限，且每年這一短期課程都很快額滿。

發送者：愛莉森‧顧德曼
接收時間：7月25日10:43 A.M.
接收者：茱麗‧希金斯

嗨！簡短說一下。跟以往一樣，印刷廣告看起來很棒。不知是否今年可請妳再幫個忙？方便在廣告上加入羅伊頓美食的網址嗎？網址是www.roytons.com。真的很感謝妳。有空的時候傳個電子郵件給我。謝謝妳，茱麗！

＊E-mail＊   ✕

From:	Julie Higgins <jhiggins@coolmail.net>
To:	Allison Goodman <agoodman@royton.com>
Date:	July 25, 12:14 P.M.
Subject:	Web site link

Hey, Allison!

Sure, I'd be more than happy to. What I'm thinking for next year is, we could post photos of the course. I'll take a bunch of pictures and then we can decide which ones to upload. If you like, we could also include some pictures of Royton's, and some information as well. It's the least I could do for all your volunteer support at our center.

How about we talk it over on the last day of class? Let me know if you have some time.

Again, all our thanks,

Julie

發信者：茱麗・希金斯
　　　　<jhiggins@coolmail.net>
收信者：愛莉森・顧德曼
　　　　<agoodman@royton.com>
日期：7月25日12:14 P.M.
主旨：網站連結

嗨！愛莉森！

當然，我非常樂意去做。另外我正在想，明年我們可以貼出上課的照片。今年我會拍很多照，然後我們可以決定要上傳哪幾張。如果妳喜歡，我們還可以把一些羅伊頓餐廳的照片及相關資訊一起放進來。為回饋妳在我們中心所有自願付出的支援，這是我起碼能做的。

我們在課程最後一天來討論，如何？讓我知道你課後是否有空。
再次獻上我們所有的感謝！

茱麗

Vocabulary

- □ cuisine [kwɪˈzin] 名 菜餚
- □ novice [ˈnɑvɪs] 名 初學者、新手
- □ graciously [ˈgreʃəslɪ] 副 慷慨地；親切地
- □ volunteer [ˌvɑlənˈtɪr] 動 自願提供～；形 自願的
- □ ingredient [ɪnˈgridɪənt] 名 （烹調的）材料
- □ from scratch 從頭開始
- □ ask a favor 請求幫忙
- □ a bunch of～ 很多的
- □ upload [ʌpˈlod] 動 上傳

試題	試題翻譯	解答與解析

191

What is implied about the course?

(A) It is an annual event.
(B) The instructor is new this year.
(C) It does not have enough participants.
(D) The price has increased from last year.

有關課程敘述，文中表示什麼？

(A) 是一年一度的活動。
(B) 今年是新講師。
(C) 參加者人數不足。
(D) 費用從去年開始調漲。

答案 (A)　[推測]

題目問的the course（課程）是指廣告上說的烹飪課。廣告的最後提到... every year this short course fills quickly，可推測這是每年都有的課程，所以(A)是正確答案。至於(B)，身為講師的愛莉森在簡訊中說As usual...和... I could ask a favor this year，表示愛莉森不是新講師。

192

What is the purpose of the text message?

(A) To register a complaint
(B) To request a change
(C) To correct an error
(D) To promote a community center

簡訊的目的是什麼？

(A) 提出抱怨
(B) 請求更改
(C) 糾正錯誤
(D) 宣傳社區中心

答案 (B)　[概述]

先從簡訊中尋找表達請求的句子，講師在說了I wonder if I could ask a favor this year.後，具體地提出Could you include the Web address to Royton's Fine Dining?的請求。因為廣告中沒有列入羅伊頓美食的網址，所以可判斷(B)的請求更改是正確答案。刊登網址是為了宣傳羅伊頓美食，不是社區中心，所以(D)不對。

☐ register a complaint　提出抱怨
☐ error [ˋɛrə] 名 錯誤

193

What does Julie say she will do this year?

(A) Add a Web link
(B) Reprint an advertisement
(C) Change a classroom
(D) Hire more staff

茱麗提到今年會做什麼？

(A) 增加網站連結
(B) 重印廣告
(C) 更改教室
(D) 雇用更多職員

答案 (A)　[其他細節]

茱麗會做的事情在電子郵件中應該有暗示。開頭她說Sure, I'd be more than happy to.，究竟她樂意去做什麼？意即愛莉森的請求內容「把羅伊頓美食的網址加入廣告內」。因此(A)是正確答案。而且在電子郵件的主旨也寫了Web site link（網站連結）。

194

What does Julie propose to do next year?

(A) Work as a chef
(B) Expand the community center
(C) Help advertise a restaurant
(D) Change the instructor

茱麗提議明年做什麼？

(A) 擔任廚師工作
(B) 擴展社區中心
(C) 協助宣傳餐廳
(D) 變更講師

答案 (C)　[其他細節]

關於明年，茱麗在電子郵件中提到了What I'm thinking for next year is, ...。接著下一句可以看到她提議we could also include some pictures of Royton's, and some information as well.，意即在廣告上放入一些羅伊頓餐廳的照片和資料作為餐廳宣傳，所以(C)是正確答案。

195

When will Allison and Julie likely talk?

(A) August 6
(B) August 13
(C) August 20
(D) August 27

愛莉森和茱麗可能會在何時討論？

(A) 8 月 6 日
(B) 8 月 13 日
(C) 8 月 20 日
(D) 8 月 27 日

答案 (D)　[其他細節]

茱麗在電子郵件最後有建議How about we talk it over on the last day of class?，再對照廣告上的上課日期Saturdays: August 6, 13, 20, and 27，所以最後上課日是8月27日。

Questions 196-200 refer to the following advertisement and e-mails.

Room Type	Room/Night	Features
Economy	$49	Lowest prices in the region
Standard	$79	Includes continental breakfast
Deluxe	$109	Ocean view or mountain view
Suite	$179	Huge seaside balcony with BBQ equipment

For fastest reservations, please visit us online at www.seasideinn.com, or call our reservations desk at 800-555-1023.

* Summer rates apply at all U.S. Seaside Inn locations.

---

* E-mail *

From:	Tammy Dilinger <tdilinger@coolmail.com>
To:	Seaside Inn and Suites <reservations@seasideinn.com>
Date:	July 29
Subject:	Reservation confirmation

To Whom It May Concern:

I made a reservation online for the night of August 13 for one of your suite rooms in your Palo Alto hotel, but for some reason I haven't received a confirmation e-mail. I've tried calling, but the operator said that she didn't see any record, and that all rooms except one Deluxe ocean view room are booked for that weekend. If this is true, then we'd like to reserve that room, although to be honest our family was looking forward to a seaside cookout.

If you could look into this and get back to me, I'd appreciate it.

Regards,

Tammy Dilinger

試題 196-200 請參考以下廣告及 2 封電子郵件。

海濱旅館套房 （Seaside Inn and Suites）
夏季特惠指南 *

房型	房價／晚	特色
經濟型	$49	本地區最低價
標準型	$79	含歐陸式早餐
豪華型	$109	海景或山景
套房型	$179	大型海濱陽台附烤肉設備

做最快預約，請上網至 www.seasideinn.com 或撥打 800-555-1023 洽預約處。

* 夏季特惠適用於海濱旅館於全美的所有據點。

發信者：泰咪・ 狄林格 （Tammy Dilinger）
<tdilinger@coolmail.com>
收信者：海濱旅館套房
<reservations@seasideinn.com>
日期：7 月 29 日
主旨：確認預約事宜

敬啟者：

我昨天上網在你們飯店的帕羅奧多 （Palo Alto） 據點預約了 8 月 13 日晚上一間套房，但不知未何，我還沒有收到確認的電子郵件。 我嘗試打過電話，不過接線生說她沒有看到任何紀錄，而且除了一間豪華型海景房外，所有的房間在那週末都被訂滿了。 如果此事為真，那我們想預訂那間房，雖然老實說我的家人很期待在海濱野餐。

如果你可以深入調查這件事且回覆我，我會很感激你！

謹致問候

泰咪・ 狄林格

試題文章	試題文章翻譯

試題文章

```
* E-mail *                                            ✕

From:     Seaside Inn and Suites <reservations@seasideinn.com>

To:       Tammy Dilinger <tdilinger@coolmail.com>

Date:     July 30

Subject:  re: Reservation confirmation
```

Dear Ms. Dilinger,

We would like to sincerely apologize for the inconvenience with our online reservation system. We are currently experiencing server trouble. Our specialists are looking into the matter as I write this. However, I just checked with Palo Alto, and in fact it appears your reservation has gone through. I have attached a confirmation page to this e-mail. Further, in order to express our apologies, we'd like to offer you the Suite room at the Deluxe room rate for the night of August 13th. This is reflected in the attached confirmation page.

Please do not hesitate to contact me if you would like to make any changes. You can reply to this e-mail or call me directly at 800-555-9123, extension 4.

Yours sincerely,

Kareem Douglas
Manager, Seaside Inn and Suites
Palo Alto, California

試題文章翻譯

發信者：海濱旅館套房
　　　　　<reservations@seasideinn.com>
收信者：泰咪‧ 狄林格
　　　　　<tdilinger@coolmail.com>
日期：7 月 30 日
主旨：回覆：確認預約事宜

親愛的狄林格女士：

由於我們的網路預約系統造成您的不便，在此深表歉意。 旅館的伺服器現在發生問題。 當我寫這封信時，我們的專家們還在做深入調查。 不過我剛剛與帕羅奧多據點確認，其實您的訂房已順利完成。 我在這封電子郵件附上確認頁面。 另外，為了表示我們的歉意，我們想以豪華型房價提供您 8 月 13 日晚上的套房型房間。 這也顯示在附件的確認頁面上。

如果您想做任何變更，請別客氣聯絡我。 您可以用這封信回覆或是直接撥打 800-555-9123 分機 4 給我。

謹致問候

卡里姆‧ 道格拉斯 （Kareem Douglas）
海濱旅館套房經理
帕羅奧多，加州 （California）

Vocabulary

- deal [dil] 名 （表示大量時用複數形）這邊指特惠的交易
- cookout [`kʊkˌaʊt] 名 戶外烹調的野餐（的飲食）、烤肉
- reflect [rɪˋflɛkt] 動 反映〜、顯示〜
- for some reason　由於某些原因、不知為何
- look into〜　深入調查〜
- extension [ɪkˋstɛnʃən] 名 電話分機

試題	試題翻譯	解答與解析

☑ **196**

What is the purpose of the first e-mail?

(A) To ask about a reservation
(B) To confirm a location
(C) To offer feedback on a recent stay
(D) To point out a mistake on an advertisement

第 1 封電子郵件的目的是什麼？

(A) 詢問預約事宜
(B) 確認地點
(C) 提供有關最近住宿的意見回饋
(D) 指出廣告上的錯誤

答案 (A) 〔概述〕

從第1封電子郵件的開頭 I made a reservation...，可知發信者是用網路訂房。對於預約一事說了I haven't received a confirmation e-mail且要求確認，所以(A)是正確答案。

☑ **197**

What information does Ms. Dilinger receive by phone?

(A) Several room types are available.
(B) Her request does not appear online.
(C) An operator has processed her reservation.
(D) The hotel has sent her an e-mail.

狄林格女士從電話獲知什麼訊息？

(A) 有些房型還可預訂。
(B) 網路上沒有顯示出她的要求。
(C) 一名接線生已處理她的預約。
(D) 飯店已傳電子郵件給她。

答案 (B) 〔其他細節〕

狄林格女士是第1封電子郵件的發信者。從I've tried calling, but the operator said that she didn't see any record, ...這句即可知(B)是正確答案。Her request（她的要求）就是指預約飯店一事，「沒有看到紀錄」則是換成「網路上沒有顯示」的說法。而(A)跟郵件中提到的all rooms except one Deluxe ocean view room are booked...不一致。至於(D)則是跟郵件中提到的I haven't received a confirmation e-mail不符。

☑ **198**

Which hotel feature does Ms. Dilinger say interests her?

(A) Complimentary breakfast
(B) Beautiful scenery
(C) Barbecue facilities
(D) Inexpensive rates

狄林格女士說哪一種飯店特色吸引她？

(A) 贈送的早餐
(B) 美麗的景色
(C) 烤肉設備
(D) 低價格

答案 (C) 〔其他細節〕

狄林格女士在第1封電子郵件最後說our family was looking forward to a seaside cookout，可知她希望a seaside cookout（在海濱野餐）。從廣告中的各房型特色來看，Huge seaside balcony with BBQ equipment是符合的，因此(C)是正確答案。

☑ **199**

In the second e-mail, the phrase "has gone through" in paragraph 1, line 3, is closest in meaning to

(A) has been approved
(B) has been changed
(C) has been overlooked
(D) has been cancelled

第 2 封電子郵件第 1 段第 3 行的「has gone through」意思最接近下列哪一個？

(A) 已被核准
(B) 已被更改
(C) 已被忽略
(D) 已被取消

答案 (A) 〔同義詞〕

同義詞的問題不僅會問單字，也會問片語（phrase）。不管是哪一種都可以用前後句的關係來判斷。it appears (that)～有「看來好像～」的意思，而go through是「通過、順利完成」之意。或是從後面提到的「在這封電子郵件附上確認頁面」也可了解，「預約通過、被核准」的前後文意思是最適當的。

☑ **200**

How much will Ms. Dilinger most likely pay for the room?

(A) $49
(B) $79
(C) $109
(D) $179

狄林格女士最可能會付多少住房費用？

(A) 49 美元
(B) 79 美元
(C) 109 美元
(D) 179 美元

答案 (C) 〔其他細節〕

第2封電子郵件第1段後半部分有提到we'd like to offer you the Suite room at the Deluxe room rate，意即「用豪華型房價提供套房型房間」，也就是狄林格應該要付豪華型房價，因此再對照廣告上的Deluxe，房價為109美元。

TEST 2 模擬試題 解答＋完全解析

正確答案一覽表

題號	答案	題號	答案	題號	答案	題號	答案	題號	答案
1	B	41	D	81	D	121	C	161	B
2	D	42	D	82	C	122	D	162	B
3	B	43	A	83	B	123	B	163	C
4	A	44	B	84	C	124	D	164	D
5	C	45	D	85	B	125	B	165	C
6	B	46	A	86	C	126	A	166	A
7	B	47	C	87	B	127	C	167	C
8	C	48	D	88	D	128	C	168	C
9	B	49	C	89	C	129	D	169	B
10	B	50	D	90	A	130	A	170	D
11	A	51	B	91	B	131	C	171	B
12	B	52	A	92	B	132	B	172	B
13	C	53	B	93	D	133	A	173	D
14	A	54	A	94	B	134	D	174	C
15	C	55	C	95	D	135	A	175	A
16	B	56	C	96	B	136	C	176	C
17	C	57	D	97	A	137	D	177	A
18	A	58	C	98	C	138	B	178	A
19	C	59	C	99	A	139	B	179	C
20	B	60	A	100	C	140	C	180	A
21	A	61	B	101	D	141	D	181	C
22	B	62	C	102	C	142	A	182	B
23	C	63	B	103	D	143	B	183	D
24	B	64	B	104	B	144	C	184	C
25	B	65	D	105	B	145	D	185	B
26	C	66	C	106	A	146	A	186	A
27	A	67	D	107	A	147	D	187	B
28	A	68	B	108	C	148	C	188	B
29	C	69	C	109	B	149	D	189	D
30	B	70	A	110	A	150	D	190	C
31	A	71	B	111	C	151	B	191	B
32	C	72	D	112	A	152	A	192	C
33	B	73	A	113	B	153	C	193	A
34	A	74	A	114	A	154	A	194	A
35	B	75	B	115	D	155	D	195	A
36	D	76	C	116	A	156	C	196	A
37	A	77	D	117	C	157	B	197	C
38	A	78	C	118	D	158	A	198	A
39	C	79	A	119	A	159	B	199	D
40	B	80	A	120	D	160	C	200	C

PART 1 1-4

錄音原文與翻譯	解答與解析

☑ **1**

(A) He's pulling a cart.
(B) He's loading something into a car.
(C) He's parking an automobile.
(D) He's getting into the back seat.

(A) 他正在拉一台小推車。
(B) 他正把某些東西裝進一台車裡。
(C) 他正在停一台車。
(D) 他正要進入後座。

答案 (B)　　　　　人物（1人）

(B)適當表達男子的動作。load是「（貨物或人）進入（交通工具）；裝載～」。受詞something是指不確定的東西，和someone在PART 1經常出現。而(A)的cart（小推車）和car（車子）發音類似容易讓人誤選。(C)的parking（停車）和(D)的getting into（進入～）都是動作描述錯誤。

☐ automobile [ˋɔdəməˏbɪl] 名 自動車

☑ **2**

(A) A man is standing on the roof.
(B) A man is climbing the staircase.
(C) A ladder is being carried to the roof.
(D) A ladder is leaning against the building.

(A) 一名男子正站上屋頂。
(B) 一名男子正爬上樓梯。
(C) 梯子正被人抬到屋頂。
(D) 梯子正靠在建築物上。

答案 (D)　　　　　人物（1人）

(D)適當表達梯子的狀態。lean against～是「靠在～」，常出現在PART 1。(B)的staircase（樓梯）描述不適合，而且從照片中難以判斷是往上或往下，所以無法當正確答案。(C)的〈is being＋過去分詞〉是現在進行式被動語態，為「正被～」之意。

☐ staircase [ˋstɛrˏkes] 名（附一體成形的扶手）樓梯
☐ ladder [ˋlædɚ] 名 梯子

☑ **3**

(A) The shoppers are removing fruit from the baskets.
(B) Produce is displayed along the wall.
(C) The shelves are being stocked with vegetables.
(D) Some people are lined up to purchase groceries.

(A) 顧客正從籃子取出水果。
(B) 農作物沿著牆壁陳列。
(C) 架上正在備貨蔬菜。
(D) 有些人正在排隊買食品雜貨。

答案 (B)　　　　　人物（2人以上）

這題的焦點不是照片中間的人，而是陳列在店內的商品，所以描述一致的(B)是正確答案。display是「陳列～」。(C)是將stock A with B（進貨、備貨B放在A）的句型變成A（架上）是主詞的被動型態。(D)的be lined up是「排成一排」。另外像to purchase這類帶to的不定詞，希望大家也要能應對才行。

☐ produce [ˋprɑdjus] 名 農作物
☐ grocery [ˋɡrosərɪ] 名（常用複數形）食品雜貨

| 錄音原文與翻譯 | 解答與解析 |

(A) The man is washing a tractor with a hose.
(B) The man is watering the flower garden.
(C) The man is bending over to grab the handlebars.
(D) The man is pushing a machine in front of him.

(A) 男子正拿著水管洗牽引機。
(B) 男子正在花園澆水。
(C) 男子俯下身去抓住車手把。
(D) 男子正在推他面前的機器。

答案 (A)　　　　　人物（1人）

男子拿著水管向牽引機的輪胎上沖水，所以(A)是正確答案。(B)的The man is watering描述正確，但不是在flower garden（花園）。water是「澆水在～」，在這題是當動詞使用。(C)的bend over是表示彎腰前傾的樣子，也可用bend down（或bend forward）的說法，而屈膝的說法是bend one's knees。(D)的push（推）動作描述錯誤。

□ grab [græb] 動 抓住

 5

(A) The boat is approaching the harbor.
(B) The vessel is sailing out to sea.
(C) People are boarding the craft.
(D) Tourists are walking along the shore.

(A) 船正接近港口。
(B) 船正朝向大海航行。
(C) 人們正在登船。
(D) 觀光客們正沿著岸邊步行。

答案 (C)　　　　　人物（2人以上）

(C)適當表達要登船的乘客。board是「登上～」，用在上船、飛機、火車及巴士等交通工具。PART 1常出現水邊或船的照片，「船」不是只有ship、boat的說法，請牢記還有vessel（輪船、艦）、craft（船、飛機、太空船）、ferry（渡輪）及sailboat（帆船）等同類型的字彙。
□ approach [ə'protʃ] 動 接近～
□ sail [sel] 動 航行
□ out to sea　朝向大海
□ shore [ʃor] 名 岸邊

(A) The waterway is being drained by workers.
(B) Umbrellas have been placed alongside the pool.
(C) The scenery is reflected on the surface of the lake.
(D) The fountain has been turned off.

(A) 工人正在排掉水道的水。
(B) 沙灘傘沿著池邊設置。
(C) 美景倒映在湖面上。
(D) 噴泉已被關掉。

答案 (B)　　　　　無人物

這題的焦點是沿著池邊設置的沙灘傘，所以(B)是正確答案。雖然用的語句比較難，但是因為照片中沒有人物，所以聽到(A)有workers（工人）就可以先刪除。(C)描述的是lake（湖），不正確。照片中有拍到噴泉，但是有在噴水，所以(D) has been turned off（已被關掉）的說法是錯的。

□ drain [dren] 動 排掉～水
□ reflect [rɪ'flɛkt] 動 倒映～
□ surface ['sɝfɪs] 名 表面

PART 2 CD2 8-13

錄音原文與翻譯	解答與解析

☐ **7** M 🇦🇺 W 🇺🇸

M: Where is the conference going to be held?
W: (A) Tomorrow morning.
　　(B) In New York.
　　(C) Once a week.

M：會議要在哪裡舉行？
W：(A) 明天早上。
　　(B) 紐約。
　　(C) 一週一次。

答案 (B) 　　疑問詞

Where～?是問「場所」，所以(B)是正確答案。(A)是指「時間」，(C)是指「頻率」，所以這2個答案都不對。

☐ conference [`kɑnfərəns] 图 會議

☐ **8** W 🇬🇧 W 🇺🇸

W: Which position did Ben apply for?
W: (A) After he graduated.
　　(B) The cabinet over there.
　　(C) Marketing Coordinator.

W：班 (Ben) 應徵什麼職位？
W：(A) 在他畢業後。
　　(B) 那邊的櫥櫃。
　　(C) 行銷專員。

答案 (C) 　　疑問詞

Which～?就是在有限的選項中詢問「哪一個，哪一位（的）」？(C)說出具體的職位，所以是正確答案。問句說的position是指「職位、職業」，注意不要以為聽到的是「地點、場所」的意思而誤選(B)。

☐ apply for～ 應徵～

☐ **9** M 🇨🇦 M 🇦🇺

M: Sally will be giving today's presentation, won't she?
M: (A) Sure, it's a wonderful present.
　　(B) That's what I heard.
　　(C) I'll see if she's coming.

M：莎莉 (Sally) 今天要做簡報，對吧？
M：(A) 當然，它是個很棒的禮物。
　　(B) 我是這麼聽說的。
　　(C) 我來確認她是不是會來。

答案 (B) 　　特殊疑問句及對話表達

這是will的附加疑問句。will be giving是未來進行式，比will give更能表現明確的預定之意。「莎莉今天要做簡報＋對吧？」→「我是這麼聽說的」，(B)的回應最通順、合理。That's what I heard.可以當作慣用語記起來，其否定句是That's not what I heard.（我聽到的不是那樣）。(A)的present（禮物）與問句的presentation（簡報）有部分是相似的發音，注意不要混淆。

☐ **10** W 🇺🇸 M 🇨🇦

W: When did you change your mind about that policy?
M: (A) Within a few days.
　　(B) Right after the meeting.
　　(C) I'd suggest Monday.

W：關於那項政策，你是何時改變主意的？
M：(A) 在幾天之內。
　　(B) 就在會議之後。
　　(C) 我會建議週一。

答案 (B) 　　疑問詞

When did～?是詢問有關「過去的時間」。(A)和(C)都是未來式，所以不正確。(C)的I'd是I would的縮寫，有「如果可以建議的話……」之意，屬於保守型的表現法。(B)的right after～是「～之後馬上」，不但可以用在未來式，也可以用於過去式，所以是正確答案。

☐ change one's mind 改變主意

☐ **11** M 🇦🇺 M 🇨🇦

M: Can you tell me how to register for this course?
M: (A) Please fill out this form.
　　(B) You need to take a train.
　　(C) Of course you can do it.

M：你能告訴我該如何登記這門課嗎？
M：(A) 請填寫這份表格。
　　(B) 你需要搭火車。
　　(C) 你當然可以做到。

答案 (A) 　　特殊疑問句及對話表達

Can you～?（你能～嗎？）是表達請求的句型。how to do是指「用～方式、～的方法」，register for a course是指「登記課程」，所以具體描述登記方法的(A)是正確答案。(C)回應「你可以做到」是答不對題。

14-18

錄音原文與翻譯	解答與解析

☑ **12** W🇺🇸 M🇦🇺

W: What did you do with the invoices?
M: (A) I didn't hear anything.
　　(B) I gave them to Cindy.
　　(C) No, I haven't received them.

W：你怎麼處理發票呢？
M：(A) 我什麼都沒聽到。
　　(B) 我把它們給辛蒂 （Cindy） 了。
　　(C) 不，我還沒有收到。

答案 (B)　　　　　　　疑問詞

問句的do with～是「處理～」。What did you do with～?是指「怎麼處理～」，有時也會用在想問東西「到哪裡去了」。(B)回答「（發票）給辛蒂了」最符合。them是指the invoices（那些發票）。(A)要注意的是，不要從問句中invoices的voice（聲音）聯想到hear（聽）而誤選。而(C)是錯在這題的疑問詞不能用Yes / No的句型來回答。

□ invoice [`ɪnvɔɪs] 名 發票

☑ **13** M🇨🇦 M🇦🇺

M: Do those magazines on the table belong to you?
M: (A) Mine are size nine.
　　(B) Sorry, but I won't be long.
　　(C) They're probably Kevin's.

M：桌上的那些雜誌是你的嗎？
M：(A) 我的是 9 號尺寸。
　　(B) 很抱歉，但是我不會花太久時間的。
　　(C) 那些可能是凱文 （Kevin） 的。

答案 (C)　　　　　　　Yes / No

題目問桌上的雜誌是你的嗎？(C)回答「（不是）是凱文的」，具體的用人名來回答物主是誰最正確。They是指those magazines（那些雜誌）。(A)的mine（我的）雖然也是物主的代名詞，但是後面的size nine（9號尺寸）與題意不符。(B)的be long（久的）讓我們以為跟題目belong（屬於～的）發音相似而誤選。

☑ **14** W🇺🇸 W🇬🇧

W: How many inquiries have you replied to so far?
W: (A) About two-thirds of them.
　　(B) They haven't gone far.
　　(C) It required more than that.

W：目前你已回覆多少詢單了？
W：(A) 大約 3 分之 2。
　　(B) 他們尚未走遠。
　　(C) 它需要更多。

答案 (A)　　　　　　　疑問詞

問句的inquiry是指「詢單、詢問」。so far是指「目前」，常用於現在完成式。How many～?是問數目，正確答案(A)是用「3分之2」的比例來回答，因此，各位也要先了解分數的表達方式。them意即全部的inquiries。而(B)是故意跟問句用一樣的單字far（遠），(C)的required（需要）是故意跟問句的inquiries發音相似讓大家誤選，請多注意。

□ reply to～　回答～

☑ **15** W🇺🇸 M🇦🇺

W: Thanks so much for your hospitality this evening.
M: (A) In fact, there's a hospital nearby.
　　(B) Any time is good for me.
　　(C) The pleasure's all ours.

W：今晚非常謝謝你的款待。
M：(A) 事實上，附近有家醫院。
　　(B) 什麼時間我都可以。
　　(C) 是我們的榮幸。

答案 (C)　　　　　　　陳述句

從hospitality（款待）這個單字可想而知，這是被招待參加聚會，要回家時對主人表達感謝的場面。請記住正確答案(C)和The pleasure is mine.或It's my pleasure.（我的榮幸）都是表達感謝時的典型應答。(A)的hospital（醫院）是故意跟問句的hospitality發音相似。

□ in fact　實際上
□ nearby [`nɪr͵baɪ] 副 在附近

☑ **16** W🇬🇧 M🇨🇦

W: Has the executive committee reviewed the contract yet?
M: (A) I'll have him contact you right away.
　　(B) They'll discuss it next Wednesday.
　　(C) Yes, I saw it yesterday.

W：執行委員會已經審閱過合約了嗎？
M：(A) 我會讓他馬上聯絡你。
　　(B) 他們下週三會討論。
　　(C) 是的，我昨天看到它了。

答案 (B)　　　　　　　Yes / No

Has～ yet?（已經做～了嗎？）是現在完成式的句型。(B)回答（還沒有）日後會做的意思最正確。They是指執行委員會的委員。(A)的contact（聯絡）是故意跟contract的發音相似讓大家誤選。〈have＋受詞＋原形動詞〉是指「讓（受詞）做」。而(C)的Yes雖然有「已經審閱了」的意味，但是後面接的句子與問句不符。

□ review [rɪ`vju] 動 審閱～
□ contract [`kɑntrækt] 名 合約

| 錄音原文與翻譯 | 解答與解析 |

☑ 17 M 🍁 W 🇺🇸

M: We aren't allowed to park here, are we?
W: (A) It seems extremely long.
　　(B) The park used to be there.
　　(C) Not at this time of the day.

M：我們不准在這裡停車，對吧？
W：(A) 它似乎很長。
　　(B) 公園曾經在那裡。
　　(C) 只有這個時段不行。

答案 (C)　　　特殊疑問句及對話表達

這是be動詞的附加疑問句。「這裡不能停車＋對吧？」→「這個時段不行」，這樣的回答最通順，所以正確答案是(C)。allow～ to do（准許～做……），像這類把人當主詞，再用被動式表現的句子也不少。(B)雖然跟問句用一樣的單字park（公園、停車），但是詞性跟意思完全不同，注意不要因而混淆。

□ extremely [ɪk`strimlɪ] 副 非常

☑ 18 M 🇦🇺 W 🇬🇧

M: Why did you extend your stay to the fifth of next month?
W: (A) To meet several more clients.
　　(B) I'm afraid that's the date.
　　(C) I had to leave there by noon.

M：你為何延長停留到下個月5號？
W：(A) 為了見更多客戶。
　　(B) 很遺憾，就是這一天。
　　(C) 我必須在中午前離開那裡。

答案 (A)　　　疑問詞

Why～?是在問原因，正確答案(A)用To～直接說出目的。extend A to B是「將A延長到B」。(B)的date是指「日子、日期」，會讓人從問句的日期做聯想而誤選，要注意。

☑ 19 W 🇬🇧 M 🍁

W: I hear our department is moving to a new building.
M: (A) Not as much as you think.
　　(B) I haven't seen that movie yet.
　　(C) Yes, in the middle of next month.

W：聽說我們部門要搬到新大樓。
M：(A) 沒有你想像的那麼多。
　　(B) 我還沒看那部電影。
　　(C) 是的，聽說是下個月中旬。

答案 (C)　　　陳述句

對於詢問部門要搬家的傳聞，(C)在回答對方時附上「什麼時候」的答案最正確。(A)的much（多）意思不明確。(B)的movie（電影）跟問句的moving（搬移）發音相似，會誘使大家誤選。

□ in the middle of～　在～的中旬

☑ 20 M 🇦🇺 W 🇺🇸

M: Who submitted the analysis report to Mr. Walker?
W: (A) It's next to the copier.
　　(B) I handed it in.
　　(C) No, it's my turn.

M：是誰把分析報告交給沃克（Walker）先生的？
W：(A) 它在影印機旁。
　　(B) 我提交的。
　　(C) 不是，輪到我了。

答案 (B)　　　疑問詞

針對詢問「是誰做～的」，(B)直接回答「我做的」，所以最正確。submit A to B是「將A交給B」，hand it in只是換另一種說法而已。大家要多習慣使用不同說法改寫句子的題型。

□ analysis [ə`næləsɪs] 名 分析
□ hand～ in　提交～
□ one's turn　輪到～

☑ 21 W 🇬🇧 M 🇦🇺

W: Don't you think this room is a bit too warm?
M: (A) I'll turn on the air conditioner.
　　(B) I should warn her about that.
　　(C) It's down the hall, on the left.

W：你不覺得這個房間有點熱嗎？
M：(A) 我會去開冷氣。
　　(B) 我應該提醒她那件事。
　　(C) 走廊走到底，左手邊。

答案 (A)　　　特殊疑問句及對話表達

這題是否定疑問句。Don't you think～?（你不覺得～嗎？）常用於向對方請求認同時。Don't you think後面接的內容是重點，針對「不覺得～？＋這個房間有點熱」，(A)表示認同而提出「開冷氣吧！」，所以回答最正確。(B)的warn是「提醒～」，注意不要跟問句的warm（熱、暖）混淆了。

□ turn on～　打開（電器製品）

CD 2 24-28

錄音原文與翻譯	解答與解析

22 M 🇨🇦 W 🇬🇧

M: Do you want me to pick up anything from the café?
W: (A) Close to the grocery store.
　　(B) Some tea would be great.
　　(C) Thanks, I'll be there around six.

M：要我從咖啡廳幫你帶點什麼嗎？
W：(A) 靠近食品雜貨店。
　　(B) 來一些茶應該很棒。
　　(C) 謝謝你，我大約 6 點到那兒。

答案 (B)　　特殊疑問句及對話表達

Do you want me to～?這是提出建議的表現法。「我在咖啡廳要買什麼回來呢？」，針對這樣的提議，(B)具體希望對方買茶回來，所以是正確答案。pick up～在口語上是買（buy）的意思，但也有「用車搭載～」的意思，所以不要會錯意而選到(C)。(A)回答的是「場所」，所以不正確。

---

23 W 🇺🇸 M 🇨🇦

W: When do you think I should show the directors the sales figures?
M: (A) The seven o'clock show has begun.
　　(B) It'll be ready in half an hour.
　　(C) How about during the seminar?

W：你覺得我應該何時給董事們看銷售額？
M：(A) 7 點的表演開始了。
　　(B) 它會在半小時內準備好。
　　(C) 在研討會中如何？

答案 (C)　　疑問詞

這是When～?疑問句插入do you think（你覺得）的句型。對於「何時該給他們看」，(C)回答「研討會中」，明確地說出「時間」，所以是正確答案。不要被do you think混淆，掌握When should I show the directors...?的意思才是關鍵。(A)雖然跟問句有一樣的單字show（表演、給～看），但是詞性跟意思完全不同。而當問句改為「要多久能完成？」時，才會改為(B)的回答，而且it指的事物並不明確。

□ sales figure(s)　銷售額

---

24 M 🇦🇺 W 🇬🇧

M: Would you mind telling me when you sent the receipt?
W: (A) To your home address.
　　(B) On the eighteenth.
　　(C) I'll manage it by myself.

M：你能告訴我你是什麼時候寄出收據的嗎？
W：(A) 寄到你住的地方。
　　(B) 18 日。
　　(C) 我會自己設法完成。

答案 (B)　　疑問詞

要聽懂這題，重點是間接疑問句的疑問詞不是在開頭而是在句中。Would you mind ～ing?雖然是有禮貌的請求句型，但是關鍵在是否有聽懂When did you send the receipt?（你什麼時候寄出收據的呢？）。針對when，(B)回答「時間」，所以是正確答案。(A)是回答收件地址，如果把when跟where聽錯時，可能就會選錯答案了。(C)的manage意為「設法完成～」。

---

25 W 🇺🇸 M 🇦🇺

W: Whose proposal is the most user-friendly?
M: (A) As long as Grace said so.
　　(B) I like Mr. Robertson's idea.
　　(C) It's been revised by the area manager.

W：誰的提案最考慮使用者需要？
M：(A) 只要葛瑞絲 （Grace） 說了算。
　　(B) 我喜歡羅伯森 （Robertson） 先生的點子。
　　(C) 它已經被區經理修改了。

答案 (B)　　疑問詞

題目是問Whose～?（誰的～），(B)正確回答「羅伯森先生的」，只是把問句的proposal（提案）改說為idea（點子、構想）。(A)和(C)雖然都有提到人物，但是答案卻不符合題目問的「誰的提案」。問句的proposal會讓人聯想到revise（修改（原稿等）），要注意別誤選(C)。

□ user-friendly [`juzɚ`frɛndlɪ] 形 考慮使用者需要的
□ as long as～　只要～

---

26 M 🇨🇦 W 🇬🇧

M: Why didn't you visit our plant in Shanghai?
W: (A) It's growing well.
　　(B) To meet Ms. Wong.
　　(C) We ran out of time.

M：為什麼你沒來我們上海的工廠參觀？
W：(A) 它長得很好。
　　(B) 去見翁 （Wong） 女士。
　　(C) 我們沒有時間。

答案 (C)　　疑問詞

這是疑問詞和否定疑問句組合的句型。針對問句「為什麼沒來上海的工廠？」，(C)直接回答理由，所以是正確答案。run out of～是「用完～（沒有了）」。如果誤把plant解讀為「植物」可能就會誤選(A)。對於Why～?的問句，(B)回答的是目的To～，雖然算合理，但是內容答不對題。

□ plant [plænt] 名 工廠

錄音原文與翻譯	解答與解析

27 W 🇬🇧 M 🇦🇺

W: Would you like me to call Mr. Kim, or would you rather speak to him yourself?
M: (A) Could you take care of that?
(B) Some people call him John.
(C) He prefers to be alone.

W：你希望我打電話給金 （Kim） 先生，還是你寧願自己跟他說呢？
M：(A) 可否交給妳處理呢？
(B) 有些人叫他約翰 （John）。
(C) 他更喜歡獨處。

答案 (A)　　特殊疑問句及對話表達

這題是選擇疑問句。Would you like me to～?是提出建議的句型。這題是詢問要（代替當事人）打給金先生還是當事人自己打電話，(A)是當事人請求「想交給你打電話」，所以是正確答案。take care of～是「照顧～、處理～」，經常用於對話。(B)雖然跟問句有同樣的單字call，但是call A B是指「把A叫做B」。

☐ would rather *do*　更願意做～

---

28 M 🇨🇦 W 🇺🇸

M: Rebecca has formally accepted the overseas posting, hasn't she?
W: (A) Yes, she is well qualified for the job.
(B) Send your résumé with a cover letter.
(C) It doesn't matter what she thinks.

M：雷貝卡 （Rebecca） 已經正式接受外派職務，對吧？
W：(A) 是的，她非常能勝任這份工作。
(B) 請把你的履歷和求職信一起寄過來。
(C) 不管她是怎麼想的。

答案 (A)　　特殊疑問句及對話表達

附加疑問句要回答Yes / No，最好是用逗號前的部分來思考。(A)的回答最正確，「雷貝卡正式接受外派職務＋對吧？」→「是的（接受了）。因為可勝任那項工作」。(B)的內容雖然跟問句好像有關係，但是卻沒有回答是否有接受。

☐ formally [`fɔrml̩ɪ] 正式地
☐ qualified [`kwɑləˌfaɪd] 勝任的
☐ matter [`mætɚ] （常用於否定與疑問）有關係

---

29 W 🇬🇧 M 🇨🇦

W: We'll have three new people on our team next month.
M: (A) There were five of them altogether.
(B) Hopefully they'll forgive us.
(C) It'll help to have additional staff.

W：下個月將有 3 位新人加入我們團隊。
M：(A) 那時全部共有 5 位。
(B) 但願他們會原諒我們。
(C) 增加的工作人員將會有所幫助。

答案 (C)　　陳述句

聽到團隊增加新人，要回答什麼呢？(C)的additional staff（增加的工作人員）就是指three new people，所以是正確答案。(A)的five of them意思不明確，時態也不對。注意不要因為重複聽到數字而混淆誤選。

☐ altogether [ˌɔltə`gɛðɚ] 全部
☐ hopefully [`hopfəlɪ] 但願
☐ forgive [fɚ`gɪv] 原諒

---

30 M 🇨🇦 W 🇬🇧

M: What made you late for work this morning?
W: (A) Yes, it'll be finished by 11:30.
(B) I had a doctor's appointment.
(C) About an hour later than I expected.

M：什麼事讓你今天早上上班遲到？
W：(A) 是的，11 點半前會結束。
(B) 我跟醫生有約。
(C) 比我預期的晚 1 個小時。

答案 (B)　　疑問詞

What made you～?從字面直譯是「什麼事讓你～？」，意即問原因「為什麼～呢？」，這和Why were you late for...?是同樣意思，所以回答原因的(B)是正確答案。使用疑問詞的疑問句並不是用Yes / No來回答，因此(A)的答案不恰當。(C)則是錯在沒有說出遲到的原因。

☐ ～than I expected　比我預期的還～

---

31 W 🇬🇧 M 🇦🇺

W: Haven't you already met the new sales manager?
M: (A) No, I've been out of town.
(B) Yes, he sells old clothes.
(C) I probably won't attend it.

W：你不是已經見過新的銷售經理了嗎？
M：(A) 還沒，我最近人在外地。
(B) 是的，他賣舊衣服。
(C) 我可能不會出席。

答案 (A)　　特殊疑問句及對話表達

Haven't you already～?（不是已經～了嗎？）是現在完成否定疑問句，「見過」就回答Yes，「沒見過」就回答No。(A)回答No「沒見過」，並繼續說沒見到的原因，所以是正確答案。(B)的sells（賣）跟問句的sales（銷售）發音相似，會誘使大家誤選。

☐ out of town　出城、在外地

PART 3　CD2　34-35　M🇨🇦　W🇬🇧

錄音	原文翻譯
Questions 32 through 34 refer to the following conversation.	試題 32-34 請參考以下會話。

M: Hi. Could you tell me how far it is from here to the city center? This is my first time in Boston on business.

W: Well, it's not that far. If you take a taxi, you'll probably get there in about twenty minutes. The airport shuttle bus takes almost twice as long, but it's considerably cheaper.

M: In that case, I'll take the shuttle bus. Do you know how often it goes?

W: It departs every half hour from outside door five, which is at the end of the terminal by the foreign exchange counter.

M：嗨。你能告訴我這裡離市中心有多遠嗎？這是我第一次來波士頓（Boston）出差。

W：喔，沒有很遠。如果搭計程車，可能約 20 分鐘到那裡。機場接駁巴士幾乎要花 2 倍的時間，可是很便宜。

M：若是那樣的話，我搭接駁巴士。你知道它多久來 1 班嗎？

W：它每半小時從 5 號門外面出發，而 5 號門就在航廈盡頭靠近外幣兌換櫃台。

Vocabulary

□ on business　出差　　□ considerably [kən`sɪdərəblɪ] 副 相當　　□ in that case　若是那樣的話　　□ depart [dɪ`pɑrt] 動 出發
□ at the end of～　在～的盡頭、結束時　　□ foreign exchange counter　外幣兌換櫃台

試題	試題翻譯	解答與解析
32 Where does the conversation most likely take place? (A) At a public park (B) On a plane (C) At an airport (D) At a bank	這 1 則對話地點最有可能在哪裡？ (A) 公園 (B) 飛機上 (C) 機場 (D) 銀行	**答案 (C)** 概述 這是男性詢問往市區的交通方式。女性列舉了計程車和機場區間巴士。從door five及end of the terminal、the foreign exchange counter等句可想到是(C)「機場」。注意別因為聽到the foreign exchange counter而誤選(D)。
33 What will the man probably do next? (A) Take a taxi (B) Take a shuttle bus (C) Exchange money (D) Go to another terminal	男性接下來可能要做什麼？ (A) 搭計程車 (B) 搭接駁巴士 (C) 換外幣 (D) 去另一個航廈	**答案 (B)** 下一步動作 男性第2次的發言就提到I'll take the shuttle bus，所以正確答案是(B)。而接駁巴士發車的5號門就在航廈的盡頭，所以(D)與事實不符。
34 How many shuttle buses run per hour? (A) Two (B) Three (C) Four (D) Five	每小時有幾台接駁 1 巴士？ (A) 2 台 (B) 3 台 (C) 4 台 (D) 5 台	**答案 (A)** 其他細節 男性第2次發言時問了接駁巴士的行駛頻率，女性對此回答It departs every half hour。every half hour意即「每30分鐘」，所以可知1小時行駛2班。在多益測驗中，會出現像這種half（半～）或twice（2倍～）的數值替換或做很簡單的計算，大家要多練習並習慣這種題型。

錄音	原文翻譯

Questions 35 through 37 refer to the following conversation.

M: Excuse me, can you tell me where I can find a copy of a book by Eric Lockheed? It's called *Running for Glory*. It was published sometime in the '90s. I checked online, but everywhere seems to be sold out.

W: Let me check ... hmm, it looks like it's been out of print since last year, and ... unfortunately it doesn't look like we have a copy in stock right now. The library might have one.

M: OK, but ... I was hoping to get a copy for my friend. His birthday is next month.

W: I see. I'll call our other stores and ask if they have one.

試題 35-37 請參考以下會話。

M：不好意思，請問我可以在哪裡找到1本艾瑞克‧洛克希德（Eric Lockheed）的書？書名叫《為榮耀而跑》（*Running for Glory*）。出版於1990年代。我上網查過，但是似乎每個地方都賣完了。

W：我查看看……嗯，看起來好像從去年就絕版了，而且……很不幸地我們店裡現在似乎1本存貨都沒有。圖書館應該會有。

M：好的，不過……我其實是希望能買1本送給我朋友。他下個月生日。

W：了解。我會打給我們其他分店詢問是否有這本書。

Vocabulary

□ sold out　賣完　　□ out of print　絕版　　□ in stock　有存貨

試題	試題翻譯	解答與解析

☑ 35

What does the man want to do?

(A) Make a photocopy
(B) Purchase a book
(C) Borrow a book
(D) Use a printer

男性想做什麼？

(A) 影印
(B) 買書
(C) 借書
(D) 使用印表機

答案 (B)　　其他細節

男性一開頭就說can you tell me where I can find a copy of a book...?從詢問書在哪裡可知，這是客人和書店店員的對話，而且他第2次的發言也說I was hoping to get a copy，所以正確答案是(B)。copy有「（書籍類的）本、冊」的意思，用影印機影印則是像(A)的說法make a photocopy。

☑ 36

What does the woman suggest the man do?
(A) Check online
(B) Search in the store
(C) Place an order next month
(D) Go to a library

女性建議男性做什麼？

(A) 上網查看
(B) 在店內找
(C) 下個月訂購
(D) 去圖書館

答案 (D)　　請求、建議、提出

女性的建議通常是在她自己的說話內容裡。關於男性想買的書，她在第1次發言時就先說「很不幸地沒有存貨」，接著再說The library might have one.，由此可知她建議男性去圖書館，所以(D)是正確答案。

□ place an order　下訂單

☑ 37

What will the woman do next?

(A) Contact other stores
(B) Provide an address
(C) Check the stock list
(D) Search the Internet

女性接下來會做什麼？

(A) 聯絡其他的分店
(B) 提供地址
(C) 查看庫存清單
(D) 在網路上搜尋

答案 (A)　　下一步動作

女性下一步要做的，一般是聽她最後一次的發言內容而定。從I'll call our other stores這句可知(A)是正確答案。call（打電話給～）在選項內換成contact（聯絡～）的說法。而(D)是錯在男性一開始就已經說上網查過了。

錄音	原文翻譯
Questions 38 through 40 refer to the following conversation. **W**: Hello. I'm Nancy Bell from Satellite TV, and I'm calling to let you know about our special mid-summer promotion. If you're a TV viewer, this is a fantastic deal. <u>Have you got a minute?</u> **M**: Oh, yes. Go ahead and tell me about it. **W**: I'll be brief, sir. If you sign up this month on a twelve-month plan, you'll get free installation, the first two months will be half price, and you'll get two additional sports channels on top of the standard package. Would you be interested in that? **M**: That sounds quite good. Let me think about it and I'll get back to you if I decide to take the offer.	試題 38-40 請參考以下會話。 W：哈囉。我是衛星電視（Satellite TV）的南西‧貝爾（Nancy Bell），打電話過來是要通知您有關本公司的仲夏特別促銷活動。如果您有看電視的需求，這會是個很棒的交易。<u>您有一些時間嗎？</u> M：喔，好的。請繼續說明。 W：先生，那我就簡短說明一下。如果您這個月註冊 12 個月的方案，您將享有免費安裝、前 2 個月費用半價，以及除了標準全套節目之外，另有 2 個額外的運動頻道。您有興趣嗎？ M：聽起來很不錯。讓我想想，如果我決定接受提議再回電給你。

Vocabulary

☐ promotion [prə`moʃən] 名 （商品促銷的）宣傳活動　　☐ deal [dil] 名 交易　　☐ brief [brif] 形 簡短的　　☐ sign up　註冊
☐ installation [ˌɪnstə`leʃən] 名 安裝　　☐ take an offer　接受（交易）提議

試題	試題翻譯	解答與解析
☑ **38** Who most likely is the woman? (A) A telemarketer (B) A technician (C) A shop assistant (D) A sports journalist	誰最有可能是這位女性？ (A) 電話推銷員 (B) 技術人員 (C) 店員 (D) 運動記者	**答案 (A)**　概述 I'm Nancy Bell from Satellite TV, and I'm calling to...女性一開始就說明打電話的目的。從Have you got a minute?，或是第2次的發言提到If you sign up this month...，還有Would you be interested in that?等等的內容就可知(A)的「電話推銷員」是正確答案。telemarketer即是指用電話進行銷售活動的人。
☑ **39** What does the woman mean when she says, "<u>Have you got a minute</u>"? (A) She would like to know how much TV the man watches. (B) She is requesting the man to help her sign up. (C) She is asking if the man has some time available. (D) She needs the man to tell her what time it is.	女性說 「Have you got a minute?」 時，表示什麼？ (A) 她想知道男性看多少電視。 (B) 她要求男性幫忙她註冊。 (C) 她詢問男性是否有時間。 (D) 她要男性告訴她現在幾點。	**答案 (C)**　說話者的目的 Have you got a minute?是「你有一些時間嗎？」。minute（分鐘）和a一起使用時，有「一會兒」的意思。男性說了Go ahead and tell me about it.之後，女性才開始說明，所以可知(C)是正確答案。
☑ **40** What does the woman suggest the man do? (A) Install additional equipment (B) Sign up this month on a yearly plan (C) Try a new channel package (D) Watch some new channels	女性建議男性什麼？ (A) 加裝設備 (B) 這個月就註冊 1 年方案 (C) 嘗試新的全套節目 (D) 看一些新頻道	**答案 (B)**　請求、建議、提出 從女性第2次的發言If you sign up this month on a twelve-month plan就可知(B)是正確答案。a twelve-month plan（12個月方案）在選項內被換成a yearly plan（1年方案）的說法。兩人對話中雖有提到安裝免費，但是並無(A)說的加裝設備。channel（頻道）及package（全套）也是一樣，雖然對話中有提到，但是並沒有(C)和(D)提及建議新頻道及新的全套節目。

錄音	原文翻譯

Questions 41 through 43 refer to the following conversation.

W: Good morning, Robert. Have there been any developments on the year-end function?

M: Hi, Cindy. Actually, yes. We've booked the Pinehill Auditorium.

W: That big auditorium?

M: That's right. To be honest, it's a little expensive to rent, but it has enough space to accommodate the large numbers we're expecting, as well as plenty of free parking.

W: Wonderful. We had some issues with last year's venue, especially the fact that it wasn't easily accessible. A lot of people have told me Pinehill is very easy to get to. Have the tickets gone on sale yet?

M: They went on sale this morning. I heard around thirty percent have already been sold. We've managed to keep prices the same as last year, which is proving to be attractive.

W: Wow, that's great.

試題 41-43 請參考以下會話。

W：早安，羅伯特（Robert）。年終晚會有任何進展了嗎？

M：嗨，辛蒂（Cindy）。的確有喔！我們已經預約了派恩希爾禮堂（Pinehill Auditorium）。

W：那間大禮堂？

M：沒錯。老實說，租金有點貴，但是它有足夠的空間容納我們預期的大量人數，而且有很多免費的停車位。

W：太棒了。去年的場地有些問題，尤其是它不容易到達。很多人已經跟我說派恩希爾禮堂非常容易到達。入場券開賣了嗎？

M：今天早上開始了。我聽說已經賣出 3 成。我們設法維持去年的價格，這點顯然很有吸引力。

W：哇，真是太好了。

Vocabulary

□ development [dɪ`vɛləpmənt] 名 進展　　□ function [`fʌŋkʃən] 名 社交聚會、宴會　　□ auditorium [ˌɔdə`torɪəm] 名 禮堂、會堂
□ accessible [æk`sɛsəb!] 形 (場所)容易到達的　　□ manage to do 設法做到～　　□ attractive [ə`træktɪv] 形 有吸引力的

試題	試題翻譯	解答與解析

41

What are the speakers talking about?

(A) The cost of business travel
(B) Directions to an auditorium
(C) How to improve ticket sales
(D) Plans for an event

這 2 位在談論什麼？

(A) 出差的費用
(B) 去禮堂的方向
(C) 如何增加入場券的銷售
(D) 一場活動的計畫

答案 (D)　　概述

這篇對話次數雖多，不過也有像That big auditorium?這種簡單短句式的回答，這種題型在多益測驗中常出現，所以大家要習慣。對話的主題通常在一開始會提到。Have there been any developments on the year-end function?是女性詢問男性有關活動的籌備狀況，接著是場地和入場券的話題，所以可知正確答案是(D)。function（社交聚會、宴會）被換成event（活動）來表達。

42

What does the woman say about the previous year's event?
(A) It had free parking.
(B) Few people attended.
(C) It had enough space.
(D) It was hard to get to.

關於上次的年終活動，女性說了什麼？

(A) 有免費停車場。
(B) 很少人出席。
(C) 有足夠的空間。
(D) 很難抵達會場。

答案 (D)　　其他細節

關於上次的活動，女性在第3次發言時說了We had some issues with last year's venue，可知場地有問題，接著提到it wasn't easily accessible，正確答案(D)只是換另一種說法而已。至於今年預約的派恩希爾禮堂，對話中有提到very easy to get to（非常容易到達）。派恩希爾禮堂才符合(A)和(C)的描述。

43

What is indicated about the tickets?

(A) They are selling well.
(B) They are quite expensive.
(C) The prices are lower than before.
(D) They have already sold out.

關於入場券，下列何者正確？

(A) 賣得很好。
(B) 很貴。
(C) 比以前便宜。
(D) 已經賣完。

答案 (A)　　其他細節

關於入場券，男性在最後發言時說They went on sale this morning. I heard around thirty percent have already been sold.，意即雖然今早才開賣，但是已經（already）賣了約30%，由此可判斷「賣得很好」，所以(A)是正確答案。至於(B)和(C)因為票價是跟去年一樣，所以答案不符。(D)是錯在票只賣了30%。

錄音	原文翻譯
Questions 44 through 46 refer to the following conversation.	試題 44-46 請參考以下會話。

W: Excuse me, Dave. I have a dentist appointment after lunch. Are you going to be in the office?
M: Me in the office? What do you mean?
W: I mean, could you answer the phone for me while I'm out?
M: Oh, no problem. I don't have much going on this afternoon, so I can take all of your calls.
W: Thanks. My accountant's supposed to be getting in touch with me regarding some details he needs for a report. Also, I think he'd like to set up a meeting for next week.
M: Alright. I'll make sure to take a detailed message if he calls. I hope things go well at the dentist.
W: Yeah, I hope so, too. I really appreciate your help.

W：不好意思，戴夫 （Dave）。 我午餐後跟牙醫有約，你會在辦公室嗎？
M：我會在辦公室嗎？你的意思是？
W：我的意思是，我不在辦公室時，你可以幫我接電話嗎？
M：喔，沒問題。 今天下午我沒什麼事，所以可以幫你接所有的來電。
W：謝謝你。 我的會計師應該會跟我聯繫有關報告所需要的一些細節。 而且，我認為他想安排下週開個會。
M：好的。 如果他打來，我一定會做詳細的留言紀錄。 希望你看牙醫順利。
W：嗯，我也希望如此。 真的很感謝你的幫忙。

Vocabulary

□ answer the phone　接電話　　□ take *someone's* calls　接聽某人的電話　　□ accountant [əˋkaʊntənt] 名 會計師
□ get in touch with~　和~取得聯繫　　□ make sure to *do*　一定要做~　　□ detailed [ˋditeld] 形 詳細的　　□ go well　（事情）進行順利

試題	試題翻譯	解答與解析
☑ **44** What does the woman have to do today? (A) Attend a meeting (B) Go to the dentist (C) Visit her accountant (D) Have lunch with a client	女性今天一定要做什麼？ (A) 出席會議 (B) 看牙醫 (C) 拜訪她的會計師 (D) 和客戶吃午餐	**答案 (B)** ［其他細節］ 女性開頭就說I have a dentist appointment after lunch.，所以正確答案是(B)。男性最後說I hope things go well at the dentist.也是答題關鍵。
☑ **45** What does the man mean when he says, "I don't have much going on this afternoon"? (A) He does not have the energy to stay at work this afternoon. (B) He has quite a lot of work to do this afternoon. (C) He intends to go somewhere this afternoon. (D) He does not have a tight schedule this afternoon.	男性說 「I don't have much going on this afternoon」 時，表示什麼？ (A) 他今天下午沒有精力繼續工作。 (B) 他今天下午有很多工作要做。 (C) 他打算今天下午去某個地方。 (D) 他今天下午沒有很緊湊的行程。	**答案 (D)** ［說話者的目的］ 即使不太了解have much going on的意思，但從「今天下午我沒～，所以可以幫你接所有的來電。」這樣的前後文關係，可以推想男性今天下午不忙，所以答案是(D)。 □ intend to *do*　算（預定）做~
☑ **46** What does the woman plan to do next week? (A) Meet with her accountant (B) Schedule an interview (C) Set up a call center (D) Get in touch with a coworker	女性下週計畫做什麼？ (A) 和她的會計師見面 (B) 安排面試 (C) 設立一個電話客服中心 (D) 和同事取得聯繫	**答案 (A)** ［下一步動作］ 女性第3次的發言說會計師應該會打電話來，也提到he'd like to set up a meeting for next week（他想安排下週開會）。其中set up a meeting（安排會議）指的是跟女性的會議，所以答案是(A)。(C)雖然也用了同樣的set up，但意思是「設立」，請注意不要誤選。 □ coworker [ˋko͵wɝkɚ] 名 同事

錄音	錄音原文翻譯

Questions 47 through 49 refer to the following conversation.

M: Susan, how was the business trip you made last week? I'd like to hear how the international conference went.

W: Oh, the venue was packed. There were so many presentations! I was only able to attend a handful of them. A lot of them focused on advertising and public relations, but there was one on international trade laws that was especially interesting. There have been a few changes recently.

M: A few changes? Hmm, for example?

W: Well, for instance, I learned that recently there are more kinds of items that can be imported tax-free.

M: Wow, we were discussing import taxes in the managers' meeting just last month. I wonder, would you consider sharing some of what you learned at our next meeting?

W: I'd be glad to. I'll get started on a summary as soon as I can.

試題 47-49 請參考以下會話。

M：蘇珊 （Susan），上週出差如何？我想聽聽這次國際會議進行得如何。

W：喔，會場擠滿人。真的有很多的演講！我只能參加少數幾個。很多都聚焦於廣告和公關活動，但其中有一個在討論國際貿易法，特別讓我感興趣。最近這部分已有些改變。

M：有些改變？嗯，例如什麼？

W：是的，例如我得知最近有更多種進口商品開放免稅了。

M：哇，我們正好上個月經理人會議才討論進口關稅。我想知道，你是否考慮在我們下次開會時，分享一些你學到的？

W：我很樂意喔。那我會盡快開始做摘要整理。

Vocabulary

□ international conference　國際會議　　□ packed [pækt] 形 擠滿的　　□ a handful of～　少數、少量的　　□ focus on～　聚焦於～

□ public relations　公關活動　　□ international trade law　國際貿易法　　□ get started on～　開始做～

□ summary [ˋsʌmərɪ] 名 摘要

試題	試題翻譯	解答與解析

☑ 47

What type of business do the speakers most likely work for?
(A) A law firm
(B) A cleaning service
(C) A trading company
(D) A tax office

這 2 位最有可能從事什麼類型的工作？

(A) 律師事務所
(B) 清潔服務
(C) 貿易公司
(D) 稅務署

答案 (C)　概述

這篇對話是在談論女性出席的國際會議。從 international trade laws 及 items that can be imported tax-free、we were discussing import taxes in the managers' meeting 等句可知(C)是正確答案。注意不要被對話中的 tax(es)（稅）誤導而選(D)。

☑ 48

What presentation topic did the woman find interesting at the conference?
(A) Advertising
(B) International relations
(C) Marketing
(D) International trade laws

女性在會議上對什麼演講主題有興趣？

(A) 廣告
(B) 國際關係
(C) 市場行銷
(D) 國際貿易法

答案 (D)　其他細節

問句的 find～ interesting 意即「對～有興趣」，受詞（～）是 What presentation topic。因為女性一開始的發言就提及 there was one on international trade laws that was especially interesting，所以(D)是正確答案。

☑ 49

What will the woman do at the next meeting?
(A) Suggest a new advertising campaign
(B) Research public relations
(C) Give a report on a conference
(D) Propose a tax increase

女性在下週會議要做什麼？

(A) 提出新的廣告活動案
(B) 研究公關活動
(C) 提出參加會議心得報告
(D) 提出增稅方案

答案 (C)　下一步動作

對於男性提出的請求 would you consider sharing some of what you learned at our next meeting? 女性接受並回答 I'd be glad to.，所以(C)是正確答案。其中 sharing some of what you learned（分享一些你學到的）被換成 Give a report on a conference（提出參加會議心得報告）的說法。

□ give a report　提出報告
□ propose [prəˋpoz] 動 提議
□ tax increase　增稅

錄音	錄音原文翻譯
Questions 50 through 52 refer to the following conversation.	試題 50-52 請參考以下會話。

M: Hello, may I speak to the Distribution Manager?

W: I'm sorry, Mr. Jeffries is not in right now. He should be here later on this afternoon, though. May I take a message and ask who is calling, please?

M: Yes. This is Jim Riley from Western Newspaper Deliveries. I sent Mr. Jeffries an e-mail last Friday regarding changes that need to be made to the customer delivery list. I've just received the updated version from him in the mail, but seven new customers still haven't been added to it.

W: I'm very sorry to hear that. I'll let him know, and ask him to call you back today.

M：哈囉，請找配銷經理？

W：很抱歉，傑佛里斯 （Jeffries） 先生現在不在。 不過下午稍晚一點他應該會在。 我可以幫忙留言並請問您的大名嗎？

M：好的。 我是西方報社投遞公司 （Western Newspaper Deliveries） 的吉姆‧賴利 （Jim Riley）。 上週五我傳了 1 封電子郵件給傑佛里斯先生，是有關顧客配送名單需要改的地方。 我剛收到他郵寄來的修正版，但是仍然有 7 位新客戶沒有被加進來。

W：很抱歉有這樣的事。 我會讓他知道，並請他今天回電給您。

Vocabulary

□ distribution [ˌdɪstrəˈbjuʃən] 名 配銷　　□ updated [ʌpˈdetɪd] 形 （修改後的）最新的　　□ version [ˈvɝʒən] 名 ～版本

試題	試題翻譯	解答與解析
50 Who most likely is the woman? (A) An author (B) A delivery person (C) A news reporter (D) A personal assistant	女性最有可能是誰？ (A) 作家 (B) 配送員 (C) 新聞記者 (D) 個人祕書	**答案 (D)**　概述 因為接電話的女性說傑佛里斯先生不在，除了要求留言，還表示會轉達留言並會讓他回電話等等，所以(D)最適合。
51 When did the man send Mr. Jeffries an e-mail? (A) Last Monday (B) Last Friday (C) Yesterday (D) This afternoon	男性何時傳電子郵件給傑佛里斯先生？ (A) 上週一 (B) 上週五 (C) 昨天 (D) 今天下午	**答案 (B)**　其他細節 男性第2次的發言說I sent Mr. Jeffries an e-mail last Friday，所以(B)是正確答案。 在會話中表示「什麼時候」、「幾點」的語句，其出現多次的可能性很高，所以對於When～?及What time～?的問句，如果能先瀏覽一下問題，就可以集中精神聽「是什麼時候傳送的」。 另外，這篇對話有出現mail（郵遞的信件），注意不要和電子郵件混淆了。
52 What is the problem? (A) A list of customers is incomplete. (B) A manager is not available. (C) A delivery has not arrived yet. (D) Mail has been misplaced.	發生了什麼問題？ (A) 客戶名單不完整。 (B) 經理沒有空。 (C) 東西還沒有送到。 (D) 郵件被放錯地方。	**答案 (A)**　概述 從男性第2次的對話可知，話題是顧客配送名單，問題就在傑佛里斯寄來的最新版本卻沒有將7位新客戶追加進去。 所以(A)是正確答案。 對話中的customer delivery list（顧客配送名單）和still haven't been added（沒有被加進來）分別被換成a list of customer（客戶名單）和incomplete（不完整的）的說法。 □ available [əˈveləbl] 形 （人）有空的 □ misplace [mɪsˈples] 動 放錯地方

錄音	錄音原文翻譯

Questions 53 through 55 refer to the following conversation.

試題 53-55 請參考以下的會話。

M: Hello. I'd like to come in today to take a look at the dining table that is on sale now. What time do you close?

W: Our normal business hours are nine to five, but we're upgrading our computer system today, so unfortunately we will be closing at one.

M: I see. I'll come in tomorrow then. Do you have many left?

W: We just have the display model left in our store, but there are still several in our warehouse nearby, which we can easily have sent over.

M：哈囉。我今天想去看看你們目前正在特賣的餐桌。請問你們幾點打烊？

W：我們的正常營業時間是早上 9 點到下午 5 點，但是今天正好要升級電腦系統，所以很遺憾地我們 1 點就要打烊。

M：了解。那我明天再來。請問這項商品還有剩很多嗎？

W：店裡只剩下展示品，但是我們還有一些放在附近的倉庫，可以很容易運送過來。

Vocabulary

□ take a look at～　看一看～　　□ normal [`nɔrml!] 形 正常的　　□ business hours　營業時間　　□ upgrade [`ʌp`gred] 動 升級～
□ display [dɪ`sple] 名 展示（品）　　□ warehouse [`wɛr،haʊs] 名 倉庫

試題	試題翻譯	解答與解析

☑ 53

Where does the woman probably work?
(A) At a computer store
(B) At a furniture store
(C) At a shipping company
(D) At a clothing shop

女性的工作地點可能在哪裡？

(A) 電腦專賣店
(B) 家具店
(C) 運輸公司
(D) 服飾店

答案 (B)　概述

從一開頭的take a look at the dining table that is on sale now即可知(B)是正確答案。如果漏聽了dining table（餐桌），就無從得知是家具店。不過最後提到的have the display model left in our store和there are still several in our warehouse也可以成為答題關鍵點，所以要集中精神聽到最後。要小心(D)的clothing（服飾）和會話中的closing（打烊）有發音相似的陷阱。

☑ 54

Why does the man decide to go to the store tomorrow?
(A) It will close early today.
(B) The sale starts tomorrow.
(C) The item is out of stock.
(D) The item has sold out.

為何男性決定明天去這家店？

(A) 今天較早打烊。
(B) 明天才開始銷售。
(C) 商品已無庫存。
(D) 商品已賣完。

答案 (A)　其他細節

男性一開始就表示今天想去這家店。雖然正常營業時間是早上9點到下午5點，但是店家有提到今天1點就要打烊，所以他明天才要去。正確答案(A)只是換句話表達而已。

□ out of stock　無庫存

☑ 55

What does the woman say about the warehouse?
(A) It is closed today.
(B) It has a new computer system.
(C) It has more of the item in stock.
(D) It is far from the store.

關於倉庫，女性說了什麼？

(A) 今天關門了。
(B) 有新的電腦系統。
(C) 這項商品在那裡還有庫存。
(D) 離店很遠。

答案 (C)　其他細節

聽懂並掌握warehouse（倉庫）的敘述重點就能答對。從女性第2次的發言提到there are still several in our warehouse nearby可知(C)是正確答案。(C)的the item（這項商品）意即男性想買的dining table（餐桌）。(D)的far（遠）跟會話中提到的nearby（在附近）意思完全相反。

錄音	錄音原文翻譯

Questions 56 through 58 refer to the following conversation.

M: I'm really looking forward to hearing Mr. Jennings speak at tomorrow's medical conference. Did you know he's one of the world's leading experts on heart disease?

W: I know. I hope I get to hear his whole presentation. I have to leave to meet someone at five o'clock, and Mr. Jennings' presentation doesn't begin until four o'clock.

M: Four? Isn't he going to be the first speaker of the day—at nine in the morning?

W: Apparently his schedule changed and he can't make it to the morning session. He's expected to arrive at the conference center at two o'clock.

試題 56-58 請參考以下會話。

M：我真的很期待在明天的醫學會議上聽詹寧斯先生（Mr. Jennings）演講。你知道他是世界頂尖的心臟科權威之一嗎？

W：我知道。我希望可以聽到他全部的演講。我 5 點時必須離開去見某人，而他的演講要到 4 點才開始。

M：4 點？他不是當天第一位講者嗎——在早上 9 點？

W：顯然他的行程變更了，無法趕上早上的會議。他預計 2 點抵達會議中心。

Vocabulary

- 〈hear＋受詞＋原形動詞〉聽（受詞）做～
- medical [ˋmɛdɪk!] 形 醫學的
- leading [ˋlidɪŋ] 形 頂尖的、領導的
- expert on～ ～的專家
- heart disease 心臟疾病
- get to *do* （有機會）可以～
- whole [hol] 形 全部的
- apparently [əˋpærəntlɪ] 副 顯然地
- make it to～ 趕上～

試題	試題翻譯	解答與解析

56

Who is Mr. Jennings?

(A) A business owner
(B) A television presenter
(C) A medical expert
(D) An education specialist

詹寧斯先生是誰？

(A) 企業主
(B) 電視節目主持人
(C) 醫學專家
(D) 教育專家

答案 (C)　概述

除了正在對話的2人外，有時聽力測驗的Who is...? 也會問到對話中「某一段話」提到的第3人是誰。建議先看題目掌握人名最有利。有關詹寧斯先生的資訊，從hearing Mr. Jennings speak at tomorrow's medical conference可知他是在醫學會議上說話有份量的人，再從Did you know he's one of the world's leading experts on heart disease?可知他是世界頂尖的心臟科權威，所以(C)是正確答案。

- presenter [prɪˋzɛntɚ] 名 主持人
- specialist [ˋspɛʃəlɪst] 名 專家

57

What is the woman concerned about?

(A) Meeting a deadline
(B) Finding the conference center
(C) Being late for a conference
(D) Missing part of a presentation

女性擔心什麼事？

(A) 趕上最後期限
(B) 找到會議中心
(C) 會議遲到
(D) 錯過部分的演講

答案 (D)　概述

女性第1次的發言說I hope I get to hear his whole presentation.，從I hope...可以得知她不確定是否可以聽完詹寧斯先生全部的演講。(D)的a presentation就是指詹寧斯先生的演講，如果演講太長而超過5點，她就會錯過一部分，所以是正確答案。

- meet a deadline 趕上最後期限

58

What does the woman say about Mr. Jennings?

(A) He will be the first speaker.
(B) He will arrive in the morning.
(C) His schedule has changed.
(D) His presentation was canceled.

關於詹寧斯先生，女性說了什麼？

(A) 他將是第 1 位演講者。
(B) 他早上會抵達。
(C) 他的行程已經變更。
(D) 他的演說被取消了。

答案 (C)　其他細節

從女性第2次的發言提到his schedule changed可知(C)是正確答案。(A)說的是詹寧斯先生行程變更之前的情況。(B)是錯在因為對話中有說he can't make it to the morning session以及He's expected to arrive... at two o'clock.，所以詹寧斯先生中午以前不會抵達。(D)是錯在行程並無取消，只是變更而已。

錄音	錄音原文翻譯

Questions 59 through 61 refer to the following conversation with three speakers.

M-1 : Have you heard anything about the new proposal to combine department budgets?

W : Yes, and Ted, to be honest, some people aren't too happy about it. For example, there are a number of senior managers who don't like the idea of sharing their department resources.

M-2 : On the other hand, I personally think it's possible to allow minimum budget amounts to be distributed to certain individuals.

W : That way no one will feel like they're losing their money. What do you think, Ted?

M-1 : You have a good point there. Why don't we submit a revision of the proposal at the next meeting? Would that work for you, Mark?

M-2 : Sounds good. Then, we can present another option to everyone.

試題 59-61 請參考以下 3 人的對話。

M-1：有關結合部門預算的新提案，你們有聽到什麼嗎？

W：有啊，而且，泰德（Ted），老實說有些人不太開心。例如，有一些資深經理並不喜歡分享部門資源。

M-2：另一方面，我個人認為，可能可以容許將最低預算金額分配給某些個人。

W：那樣就不會有人覺得好像錢變少了。泰德，你覺得呢？

M-1：妳說的有道理。我們何不在下次開會時提交該方案的修正案？你覺得呢，馬克（Mark）？

M-2：聽起來不錯。那麼，我們就可以提出另一個選擇給大家了。

Vocabulary

□ combine [kəm`baɪn] 動 結合～　　□ budget [`bʌdʒɪt] 名 預算　　□ resource [rɪ`sors] 名 資源　　□ personally [`pɝsn̩lɪ] 副 就個人而言

□ distribute A to B　將A分配給B　　□ certain [`sɝtn̩] 形 特定的　　□ individual [͵ɪndə`vɪdʒʊəl] 名 個人

□ submit [səb`mɪt] 動 提交～　　□ present [prɪ`zɛnt] 動 提出～

試題	試題翻譯	解答與解析

☑ 59

What are the speakers mainly discussing?

(A) A salary reduction
(B) A conference schedule
(C) A proposal on budgets
(D) A department restructuring

談話者主要在討論什麼？

(A) 減薪
(B) 會議日程
(C) 有關預算的提案
(D) 部門重組

答案 (C) 〔概述〕

這是3個人的對話。話題就是一開始M-1泰德（Ted）說的Have you heard anything about the new proposal to combine department budgets?，由此可知(C)是正確答案。而且3個人在後面還討論了the new proposal（新的提案），M-1第2次發言時說Why don't we submit a revision of the proposal at the next meeting?，這邊又再次出現proposal這個字，可以讓大家再次確認。

□ reduction [rɪ`dʌkʃən] 名 減少
□ restructuring [ri`strʌktʃərɪŋ] 名 重組

☑ 60

According to the woman, what is the problem?

(A) Some people do not like the new idea.
(B) There will not be another meeting.
(C) Managers are making less money.
(D) The meeting was postponed.

根據女性所言，問題是什麼？

(A) 有些人不喜歡新的方案。
(B) 將不會有另一個會議。
(C) 經理們賺的錢變少了。
(D) 會議被延期。

答案 (A) 〔概述〕

從女性第1次的發言some people aren't too happy about it可知(A)是正確答案。it就是指前面M-1提到的the new proposal（to combine department budgets）。選項內的do not like及the new idea是把對話中的aren't too happy about及the new proposal換另一種說法而已。

□ make money　賺錢

☑ 61

What does Ted suggest?

(A) Submitting a rewritten budget
(B) Offering a revised proposal
(C) Keeping the budgets separate
(D) Asking the manager for help

泰德建議什麼？

(A) 提交重寫的預算
(B) 提出修改過的提案
(C) 維持預算分開
(D) 向經理求助

答案 (B) 〔請求、建議、提出〕

從M-1的第2次發言Why don't we submit a revision of the proposal...? 可知(B)是正確答案。選項內使用動詞的過去分詞revised（被修改過的）來代替revision（修正案）。

□ rewrite [ri`raɪt] 動 重寫
□ separate [`sɛprɪt] 形 分開的

CD2 45 M 🇦🇺 W 🇺🇸

錄音	錄音原文翻譯

Questions 62 through 64 refer to the following conversation and coupon.

M: Is your clothing department over there? I'm looking for it because I saw a newspaper ad about a sale on coats.

W: It's right over there, and yes, we're currently offering discounts. If you'd like to drop by our customer service counter, they'll give you all sorts of coupons you can use.

M: Oh, wonderful. Thanks. I wonder if there are any coupons for coats. There's a certain one I want that goes for ... uh ... I remember it sells for 120 pounds.

W: Well, I know we've definitely got discounts on coats, but I suggest you hurry. They're going pretty fast. We're down to about half of the inventory we started with before the sale.

試題 62-64 請參考以下會話和優惠券。

M：你們的服裝賣場在那邊嗎？因為我看到報上廣告有外套特賣，所以我正在找賣場位置。

W：它就在那邊，沒錯，我們目前正在打折。如果你願意順道去我們的客服櫃台，他們會給你各種可使用的優惠券。

M：喔，太棒了。謝謝。我想知道是否有任何外套可用的優惠券。有一件我想要的……嗯……我記得它賣 120 英鎊。

W：嗯，的確有外套的優惠，但是建議你要快點索取。外套賣得很快。我們大約只剩下特賣開始前的一半存貨而已。

衣服及配件　V 市場（V MART）
===================
適用所有標價 100 英鎊以上的衣服
現折 20 英鎊*
===================

* 11 月 20 日前有效

Vocabulary

☐ ad [æd] **名** advertisement（廣告）的縮寫　　☐ all sorts of～　各種、各樣的　　☐ be down to～　減少到～、只剩下～
☐ inventory [`ɪnvən͵tɔrɪ] **名** 存貨　　☐ valid [`vælɪd] **形** 法律上有效的

試題	試題翻譯	解答與解析

☑ 62

What does the man ask the woman about?
(A) The duration of a sale
(B) The size of a department
(C) The location of a section
(D) The price of deliveries

男性問了女性什麼？
(A) 特賣期間
(B) 賣場規模
(C) 某區的位置
(D) 運送費

答案 (C)　　其他細節

這是男性客人與女性店員的對話。從男性一開始的詢問 Is your clothing department over there? 可知 (C) 是正確答案。選項中的 section（區）是將 department（～部門、賣場）換成另一種說法而已。

☑ 63

Where does the woman suggest the man go?
(A) To a customer complaints office
(B) To a service desk
(C) To a clothing rack
(D) To a TV display

女性建議男性去哪裡？
(A) 客戶投訴辦公室
(B) 服務台
(C) 衣服貨架區
(D) 電視展示區

答案 (B)　　請求、建議、提出

女性說 If you'd like to drop by our customer service counter, ...，告訴客人如果到客服櫃台可以拿到優惠券。drop by～是指「順道拜訪～」，(B) 把 our customer service counter（我們的客服櫃台）用 a service desk（服務台）來表示，因此是正確答案。

☐ complaint [kəm`plent] **名** 抱怨

☑ 64

Look at the graphic. How much would the man have to pay for the coat?
(A) 20 pounds
(B) 100 pounds
(C) 120 pounds
(D) 140 pounds

依圖所示。 男性買外套應該付多少元？
(A) 20 英鎊
(B) 100 英鎊
(C) 120 英鎊
(D) 140 英鎊

答案 (B)　　圖表問題

這題是問如果男性有優惠券，他想買的外套要多少元？因為男性說 I remember it sells for 120 pounds，雖然外套價格是 120 英鎊，但是優惠券上印著「所有標價 100 英鎊以上的衣服現折 20 英鎊」，所以他要付 120-20=100 英鎊。如果能在聽會話前先讀一下問題，了解這題是要問金額，同時掌握 20 英鎊優惠券的關鍵點就可迎刃而解。

錄音	錄音原文翻譯

Questions 65 through 67 refer to the following conversation and sign.

W: Hello. I'm here for a 10 o'clock interview with Mr. Park, the head of housekeeping. My name is Suzanne Thomas.

M: OK, I'll call his office to let him know that you're on the way. After I do that, you can just go right on up to meet him.

W: Won't I need a visitor ID or something? That is … uh … to go into his office?

M: No, you won't need that. You'll see a sign above the doors that reads "employees only," but you can just go on in anyway. Just be sure to knock before you do.

W: Thanks for the advice. I'll certainly do that.

試題 65-67 請參考以下會話及告示牌。

W：你好。 我跟房務部主管派克（Park）先生約好 10 點面談。 我叫蘇珊娜·湯瑪士（Suzanne Thomas）。

M：好的，我會打電話到他辦公室轉達妳正要前往。 我打完後，妳就可以直接上去見他。

W：我不需要換訪客識別證或什麼證件嗎？那……嗯……直接進去他的辦公室嗎？

M：不用，不需要換證。妳會看到門上有個告示牌寫「限員工進出」，但是妳可以直接進去無妨。只是在進去之前務必敲門。

W：謝謝你的指點。 我一定會照著做。

NOKON HOTEL

Second Floor

Fitness Center	Room 238
Business Center	Room 240
Housekeeping	Room 262
Local Tours	Room 283

諾康飯店（NOKON HOTEL）

二樓

健身中心	238 室
商務中心	240 室
房務部	262 室
當地旅遊	283 室

Vocabulary

□ interview with～　和～面談（面試）　　□ let～ know　讓～知道　　□ be sure to *do*　務必～

試題	試題翻譯	解答與解析

65

Why did the woman come to the hotel?
(A) She wants to hire cleaners.
(B) She needs to reserve a room.
(C) She plans to interview some guests.
(D) She has a professional appointment.

女性為什麼來飯店？

(A) 她想雇用清潔人員。
(B) 她需要預訂一間房間。
(C) 她預計和一些客人面談。
(D) 她有個職業相關的約會。

答案 (D)　　其他細節

女性到飯店的目的就是開頭說的I'm here for a 10 o'clock interview with Mr. Park, the head of housekeeping.，從這句可知她跟房務部主管有面談約會（appointment），所以以(D)是正確答案。對話裡的interview是名詞，(C)的interview則是動詞。

□ professional [prəˈfɛʃən!] 形 職業上的

66

Look at the graphic. Where most likely will the woman go?
(A) To Room 238
(B) To Room 240
(C) To Room 262
(D) To Room 283

依圖所示，女性最有可能去哪裡？

(A) 238 室
(B) 240 室
(C) 262 室
(D) 283 室

答案 (C)　　圖表問題

和女性約好面談的人是the head of housekeeping（房務部主管）。依圖所示，Housekeeping在Room 262，所以(C)是正確答案。

67

What does the woman agree to do?

(A) Fill out an employee form
(B) Wear a visitor ID
(C) Try another hotel
(D) Knock at the entrance

女性同意做什麼？

(A) 填寫員工表格
(B) 配戴訪客識別證
(C) 到另一間飯店試試
(D) 在入口敲門

答案 (D)　　其他細節

對於男性的指點Just be sure to knock before you do.，女性接受並回答I'll certainly do that.。敲哪裡呢？就是前一句說的the doors，也就是Housekeeping部門的門。而(D)是用entrance（入口）來表達進入部門的門，所以是正確答案。

錄音	錄音原文翻譯

Questions 68 through 70 refer to the following conversation and card.

W: You have a much larger number of law books than I'd imagined. In fact, I was thinking I'd actually join the library since I plan on coming here a lot while I'm in law school.

M: We do have a fairly extensive collection. Anyway, I could sign you up right now, if you'd like. All I'd need you to do is fill out this form and then pay a two-dollar registration fee.

W: Just two dollars? I think I saw something in a brochure about … uhh, some kind of 20-dollar fee. Something about the Library Partner Program?

M: Oh. Right. That's kind of like a VIP program. It allows you to borrow double the number of books—up to 10 at a time, instead of the usual 5 under the standard card. One thing that's great about either card, though, is that it never expires.

試題 68-70 請參考以下會話及卡片。

W：你這裡的法律書籍超乎我想像的多。事實上，我有認真考慮要加入圖書館會員，因為我計畫在就讀法學期間要常來這裡。

M：我們的確有相當廣泛的藏書。總之，如果你想加入的話，我現在可以馬上幫你登記。我只需要你填寫這張表格，然後付一筆 2 元的登記費。

W：只要 2 元？我以為我在手冊上看到……嗯，什麼要 20 元的。關於某種圖書館夥伴方案？

M：喔，沒錯。那就像貴賓（VIP）方案。它可以讓你一次借出雙倍的書——也就是一次最多 10 本，而不是一般普通卡的 5 本。不過不管哪一種卡，都有個很棒的共通點，那就是沒有效期。

Iliz Library
Borrower Card
Eve Phillips
Status: Library Partner

> 伊莉茲 （Iliz） 圖書館
> 借書卡
> 依芙‧飛利浦斯 （Eve Phillips）
> 卡別：圖書館夥伴

Vocabulary

- □ extensive [ɪk`stɛnsɪv] 形 廣泛的
- □ collection [kə`lɛkʃən] 名 收藏
- □ registration fee 登記費
- □ double [`dʌb!] 形 2倍的
- □ up to～ （最大的）多達～
- □ instead of～ 代替～
- □ expire [ɪk`spaɪr] 動 到期

試題	試題翻譯	解答與解析

☑ 68

Why is the woman surprised?

(A) The school is open.
(B) The library's selection is broad.
(C) A fee is high.
(D) A reference book is missing.

為什麼女性很驚訝？

(A) 學校有開。
(B) 圖書館的藏書很廣泛。
(C) 費用很高。
(D) 遺失一本參考書。

答案 (B) 〔其他細節〕

先看圖卡，就可以預測這是有關圖書館的對話。一開始女性對圖書館有這麼多法律書籍相當驚訝，對此男性說 We do have a fairly extensive collection.。正確答案(B)把男性這句話換成另一種說法，將extensive（廣泛的）用broad（廣泛的）來表達。

☑ 69

Look at the graphic. How many books can the woman borrow at one time?
(A) 2 books
(B) 5 books
(C) 10 books
(D) 20 books

依圖所示，女性可以一次借多少書？

(A) 2 本
(B) 5 本
(C) 10 本
(D) 20 本

答案 (C) 〔圖表問題〕

從登記費相關的交談可知，女性想成為借書卡上所寫的Library Partner會員，男性對此也向其說明It allows you to borrow double the number of books... the usual 5 under the standard card.，意即成為圖書館夥伴會員的話，就能借到一般會員可借本數（5本）的雙倍，也就是10本。即使不懂double的意思，用up to 10 at a time也可判斷正確答案是(C)。

☑ 70

What does the man say is convenient about the library card?
(A) It can be used indefinitely.
(B) It comes with a customized brochure.
(C) It requires no payment.
(D) It eliminates overdue book fees.

關於借書卡，男性說什麼是方便的？

(A) 可以無限期的使用。
(B) 附有客製化的手冊。
(C) 不用付錢。
(D) 免除逾期圖書罰款。

答案 (A) 〔其他細節〕

這題重點在男性最後說One thing that's great about either card, though, is that it never expires.。正確答案(A)把never expires換成indefinitely（無期限）來表達。One thing～ is that...，意為「有個～的地方，那就是……（that...）」，這是固定句型，is that後面的內容才是重要關鍵。所以一旦聽到One thing～ is that的句子，就要仔細聽清楚that後面說什麼喔！

- □ eliminate [ɪ`lɪmə͵net] 動 消除～
- □ overdue [͵ovə`dju] 形 逾期的

錄音原文	錄音原文翻譯

Questions 71 through 73 refer to the following telephone message.

Hello, this is Rose Martinez from Clay Family Medical Center with a message for Mr. Wilson. When you called yesterday morning to make an appointment with Dr. Harris, our earliest opening was at 2 P.M. on Thursday. I just wanted to let you know that Dr. Harris has had a cancellation this morning at 10 o'clock, so if you'd like to move your appointment forward to this time, we can do that for you. Could you please give me a call at 555-5820 to confirm this? Thank you.

試題 71-73 請參考以下電話留言。

哈囉，我是克雷 （Clay） 家庭醫學中心的蘿絲‧馬丁尼茲 （Rose Martinez），要留言給威爾森 （Wilson） 先生。您昨天早上打電話來預約跟哈利斯 （Harris） 醫師看診的時間時，我們最快的空檔是週四的下午 2 點。現在我只是想通知您，哈利斯醫師今早 10 點的預約取消了，所以若您想把預約提前到這個時間，我們可以為您做更改。可否請您撥打 555-5820 回電確認？謝謝。

Vocabulary

- ☐ make an appointment　預約
- ☐ opening [`opənɪŋ] 名 空檔
- ☐ cancellation [ˌkænsl`eʃən] 名 取消
- ☐ move A to B　把A移到B
- ☐ forward [`fɔrwəd] 副 提前
- ☐ confirm [kən`fɝm] 動 確認（預約等）

試題	試題翻譯	解答與解析

☑ 71

When did Mr. Wilson call the medical center?
(A) Two days ago
(B) Yesterday morning
(C) Yesterday afternoon
(D) This afternoon

威爾森先生何時打電話到醫學中心？

(A) 2 天前
(B) 昨天早上
(C) 昨天下午
(D) 今天下午

答案 (B)　其他細節

從this is Rose Martinez... for Mr. Wilson可判斷出威爾森先生是電話留言的對象（聽留言的人）。you＝Mr. Wilson，所以從When you called yesterday morning可知正確答案是(B)。

☑ 72

What is the purpose of the telephone message?
(A) To apologize for a schedule change
(B) To suggest a treatment
(C) To cancel a doctor's visit
(D) To offer a new appointment time

這通電話留言的目的是什麼？

(A) 為了行程更改而道歉
(B) 建議做治療
(C) 取消醫生的約診
(D) 提供一個新的預約時段

答案 (D)　概述

打電話的目的通常都開門見山地說，但是這篇留言到一半時提到I just wanted to let you know that...，其後面內容才是這通電話的目的。因為更早的時段有空檔而詢問對方可否變更預約時間，所以正確答案是(D)。

- ☐ apologize for~　為了~道歉
- ☐ treatment [`tritmənt] 名 治療

☑ 73

What is Mr. Wilson asked to do?

(A) Return a phone call
(B) Drop by the clinic
(C) Give his telephone number
(D) Cancel an appointment

威爾森先生被要求做什麼事？

(A) 回電
(B) 順道拜訪診所
(C) 提供他的電話號碼
(D) 取消預約

答案 (A)　請求、建議、下一步動作

從最後的Could you please give me a call at 555-5820 to confirm this?可知(A)是正確答案。如果事先瀏覽題目在問什麼，就可以猜測來電者會在留言時向對方請求某些事，所以只要聽懂Could you please~?這類表達請求的句型，就會更仔細聽後面的內容。請求、建議或提議等會話表現法在Part 2、3、4屬於重要句型，大家藉著模擬試題的機會彙整一下吧！

錄音原文	錄音原文翻譯

Questions 74 through 76 refer to the following news report.

In business news today, the Devonport City Council has released its latest waste plan to move towards its goal of zero waste over the next thirty years. Alan Burgess, the project manager for the plan, says one of the main focuses is getting people to minimize waste. The idea involves introducing a user-pays system that charges people each time their household garbage is picked up by a garbage truck. The aim is to encourage people to recycle and reuse as much household waste as possible, such as uneaten food, which along with other organic waste makes up fifty percent of household garbage. This can be reused as compost for gardens, rather than adding to the large volume of garbage at landfills.

試題 74-76 請參考以下新聞報導。

以下為今日商業新聞，德文港 （Devonport） 市議會已發表最新的廢棄物計畫，期許未來 30 年朝向零廢棄物的目標。 這項計畫的專案經理艾倫‧柏吉斯 （Alan Burgess） 表示，主要的重點之一是讓人們做到廢棄物最少化。 這個想法包含推行每次家庭垃圾被垃圾車運走時，即收取費用的使用者付費系統。 其目的是鼓勵人們盡可能多回收及再利用家庭廢棄物，例如吃剩的食物和其他有機廢棄物就占了家庭垃圾的百分之 50。 這都可以再利用作為庭園堆肥，而不是增加垃圾掩埋場龐大的垃圾量。

Vocabulary

- □ user-pays [`juzə‚pez] 名 使用者付費
- □ household [`haʊs‚hold] 形 家庭的
- □ encourage~ to do　鼓勵~做……
- □ organic [ɔr`gænɪk] 形 有機的
- □ make up~　占~
- □ compost [`kɑmpost] 名 堆肥
- □ landfill [`lændfɪl] 名 垃圾掩埋場

試題	試題翻譯	解答與解析

☑ 74

What is the report mainly about?

(A) A waste minimization plan
(B) A new recycling plant
(C) A public health campaign
(D) A garbage collection site

這則報導主要在說什麼？

(A) 廢棄物最少化計畫
(B) 一個新的回收工廠
(C) 推行公共衛生的活動
(D) 垃圾收集站

答案 (A)　概述

新聞報導的目的通常會在開頭就說明。從its latest waste plan to move towards its goal of zero waste這句可知(A)是正確答案，並把its goal of zero waste用minimization來表達。minimization是動詞minimize（使減到最少）的名詞，getting people to minimize waste也是幫助作答的提示。

☑ 75

Who is Alan Burgess?

(A) A scientist
(B) A planner
(C) A journalist
(D) A researcher

艾倫‧柏吉斯是誰？

(A) 科學家
(B) 規劃者
(C) 新聞記者
(D) 研究員

答案 (B)　其他細節

注意聽人名艾倫‧柏吉斯，就會聽到報導中有提及Alan Burgess, the project manager for the plan，意即「這項計畫的專案經理」，也可說是(B)的「規劃者」。

☑ 76

According to the news report, what is proposed?

(A) Reducing the number of garbage trucks
(B) Changing food packaging
(C) Introducing waste disposal fees
(D) Limiting the amount of organic waste

根據新聞報導，什麼方案被提出來？

(A) 減少垃圾車的數量
(B) 改變食品包裝
(C) 推行廢棄物處理費
(D) 限制有機廢棄物的量

答案 (C)　請求、建議、下一步動作

關於該項方案，就是The idea involves introducing a user-pays system that charges people each time their household garbage is picked up by a garbage truck.，雖然這句很長，不過如果聽懂introducing a user-pays system that charges people的意思，就知道要選(C)。其他跟題目無關的內容可以不用理會，就能把握時間先看下一道題。

錄音原文	錄音原文翻譯
Questions 77 through 79 refer to the following announcement. Good afternoon and welcome aboard flight 632 bound for Queenstown. We'd like to apologize for our late departure. Due to an onboard computer problem, we are currently about twenty minutes behind schedule. However, the computer has been repaired, and <u>we should be able to make up for lost time</u> and arrive in Queenstown on schedule. Our attendants will be providing you with a light meal in around thirty minutes. In the meantime, if you need anything, please don't hesitate to let us know.	試題 77-79 請參考以下廣播。 午安，歡迎搭乘前往皇后鎮 （Queenstown） 的 632 班機。我們對於延遲起飛深感抱歉。 由於飛機上的電腦有問題，我們目前比預計時間約晚 20 分鐘起飛。 不過電腦已經修復了，我們應該可以把損失的時間彌補回來，並且準時抵達皇后鎮。 大約 30 分鐘後，我們的客艙服務人員將為您提供輕食。 在這段期間內，如果您需要什麼，請別客氣讓我們知道。

Vocabulary

□ bound for～　前往～　　□ due to～　由於～　　□ onboard ['ɑn‚bord] 形 飛機上的　　□ behind schedule　比預定時間晚
□ make up for～　彌補～　　□ on schedule　準時　　□ (flight) attendant [ə'tɛndənt] 名 （飛機）客艙服務人員
□ provide A with B　提供B給A　　□ in the meantime　在這段期間內

試題	試題翻譯	解答與解析
77 Where is the announcement taking place? (A) In a theater (B) In a store (C) On a train (D) On a plane	這則廣播在哪裡播放？ (A) 電影院 (B) 商店 (C) 火車上 (D) 飛機上	**答案 (D)**　概述 從一開始的welcome aboard flight...就知道這是機內廣播。接著後面提到如出發延遲的原因或抵達時刻、提供輕食等的內容，都可判斷(D)是正確答案。
78 What does the speaker mean when he says, "we should be able to make up for lost time"? (A) A device should be repaired. (B) A timetable can be altered. (C) The arrival time is unaffected. (D) Some equipment has been lost.	播報者說 「we should be able to make up for lost time」 時，表示什麼？ (A) 應該修理裝置。 (B) 時刻表可以變更。 (C) 抵達時間不受影響。 (D) 一些設備已經遺失。	**答案 (C)**　說話者的目的 make up for～是「彌補～」之意，這裡說的make up for lost time是「把損失的時間（=出發的延遲時間）彌補回來」。因為後面緊接著說arrive in Queenstown on schedule，由此可知飛機會準時抵達皇后鎮，所以(C)是正確答案。 □ device [dɪ'vaɪs] 名 儀器、裝置 □ alter ['ɔltɚ] 動 變更～、改變 □ unaffected [‚ʌnə'fɛktɪd] 形 不受影響的
79 What will happen in half an hour? (A) Food will be served. (B) The journey will begin. (C) A restaurant will open. (D) More details will be announced.	半小時後會有什麼事發生？ (A) 即將供應餐點。 (B) 行程即將開始。 (C) 餐廳即將營業。 (D) 即將宣布更多詳情。	**答案 (A)**　請求、建議、下一步動作 從Our attendants will be providing you with a light meal in around thirty minutes.可知，大約30分鐘後，客艙服務人員將為您提供輕食，所以正確答案是(A)。thirty minutes（30分鐘）在題目中被換成同樣意思的half an hour（半小時）。此外，上述句子雖然是主動語態，但選項內卻是將Food當作主詞而形成被動語態的句型，大家也要多習慣這種模式的語態轉換喔！

錄音原文	錄音原文翻譯

Questions 80 through 82 refer to the following talk.

Good afternoon, everyone. I am delighted to announce that our Employee of the Month Award program is in its third year now. This month, the awards committee would like to recognize the outstanding performance of someone who is an integral part of this company's success—Mr. Kevin Turner. Kevin's dedication to our company comes through in his every action. And all the committee members were impressed by his enthusiastic can-do attitude. Kevin, it is with great delight that I present to you August's Employee of the Month plaque, along with a gift certificate for a dinner for four at the restaurant of your choice. Congratulations, and a sincere thank you for your superb performance.

試題 80-82 請參考以下談話內容。

午安，各位。 我很高興在此宣布，我們的當月優秀員工獎勵計畫已經進入第 3 年。 這個月，授獎委員會想要表揚績效傑出的這位，他對公司的成功是不可或缺的一員——凱文‧特納先生 （Mr. Kevin Turner）。 凱文對公司的貢獻，從他的一舉一動表露無遺。 而且，所有的委員會成員都對他熱情、肯做的態度印象深刻。凱文，我非常開心頒贈給你 8 月的優秀員工表揚狀，以及你所選擇的餐廳 4 人份晚餐禮券。 恭喜，並由衷感謝你創造出色的業績。

Vocabulary

- □ be delighted to *do*　很高興做～
- □ recognize [ˋrɛkəgˏnaɪz] 動 （表揚功勞等）表揚
- □ outstanding [ˋaʊtˋstændɪŋ] 形 傑出的
- □ performance [pəˋfɔrməns] 名 績效
- □ integral [ˋɪntəgrəl] 形 不可或缺的
- □ dedication to～　對～的貢獻
- □ come through　（訊息）傳達、顯現出
- □ plaque [plæk] 名 （獎賞的）匾額、表揚狀
- □ superb [sʊˋpɝb] 形 極好、出色的

試題	試題翻譯	解答與解析

80

Why is Mr. Turner being congratulated?

(A) He is the recipient of an award.
(B) He has completed an important project.
(C) He is being promoted.
(D) He is retiring from the company.

特納先生為什麼被恭喜？

(A) 他是獲獎者。
(B) 他完成一項重要的計畫。
(C) 他獲得職位升遷。
(D) 他從職場退休。

答案 (A)　概述

題目問到的特納先生，在整個談話到一半時才出現這個人名，所以在一開始就必須要抓住談話的目的是什麼。從Award program（獎勵計畫）及the awards committee（授獎委員會）等字就可推測是表揚儀式的現場。特納先生的名字出現後，也說到他的好績效，由此可知(A)是正確答案。recipient是「獲獎者」。

81

What does the speaker say about Mr. Turner?
(A) He has never been absent from work.
(B) He is a devoted committee member.
(C) He has worked at the company for three years.
(D) He has a positive attitude.

對於特納先生，演說者說了什麼？
(A) 他從未缺勤。
(B) 他是 1 位有奉獻精神的委員會成員。
(C) 他在這家公司已經 3 年。
(D) 他擁有積極的態度。

答案 (D)　其他細節

請仔細聽Kevin's dedication to...之後的內容。從his enthusiastic can-do attitude就可知(D)是正確答案。positive attitude是將enthusiastic can-do attitude換成另一種說法而已。enthusiastic是「熱情的」，can-do是「肯做的」，positive是「積極的」。(C)錯在「3年」是指「當月優秀員工獎」相關的獎勵計畫，而不是工作年資。

82

What is given during the presentation?

(A) A bouquet of flowers
(B) A family holiday package
(C) A gift certificate
(D) A medal

頒獎時給了什麼？

(A) 一束花
(B) 家庭度假套裝行程
(C) 禮券
(D) 勳章

答案 (C)　其他細節

題目所說的presentation並不是「（為了宣傳的）演說」，而是指「頒獎儀式」。從I present to you August's Employee of the Month plaque, along with a gift certificate for a dinner for...這句可知，(C)是正確答案。along with～是「和～一起」，gift certificate是「禮券」。

錄音原文	錄音原文翻譯

Questions 83 through 85 refer to the following telephone message.

Hi, Steven. It's Lisa from Mayfair Flower Shop. I received your e-mail order for a bouquet to celebrate the opening of your friend's pastry shop. We don't usually deliver before 9 A.M., but we will accommodate your request and deliver it at 8:30 A.M. In this case, I don't think cash on delivery will work, as I presume you are paying, so please make an advance payment by credit card through our Web site. Also, can you let me know what message you would like added to the bouquet? You can either e-mail me or call me at 555-6457.

試題 83-85 請參考以下的電話留言。

嗨，史蒂芬 （Steven）。 我是梅菲爾 （Mayfair） 花店的麗莎 （Lisa）。 我收到您的電郵訂單，要以花束祝賀朋友的西式糕點店開幕。 雖然我們平時上午 9 點前不送貨，但仍會通融您的要求在上午 8 點半送達。 在這種情形下，我想貨到付款不可行，而我推測是由您這邊付款，所以要請您透過我們的網站用信用卡預先付款。 再者，可否讓我知道您想在花束隨附什麼留言嗎？您可以傳郵件或撥打電話 555-6457 告訴我。

Vocabulary

- [ ] accommodate *someone's* request　通融（某人）的要求
- [ ] presume [prɪˋzum] **動** 推測～
- [ ] make an advance payment　預先付款

試題	試題翻譯	解答與解析

83

Where does the caller probably work?

(A) At a courier service
(B) At a flower shop
(C) At a credit card company
(D) At a pastry shop

來電者可能在哪裡工作？

(A) 在宅配服務業
(B) 在花店
(C) 在信用卡公司
(D) 在西式糕點店

答案 (B) 　概述

電話留言一開始就說 It's Lisa from Mayfair Flower Shop.，接著提到對方訂購 bouquet（花束），由此可知(B)是正確答案。(D)是花束要送達的地方。留言中有提到 deliver（送貨）等字，容易讓人多做聯想而誤選(A)。另外，credit card（信用卡）也是一樣，別因而誤以為答案是(C)。

- [ ] courier [ˋkʊrɪə] **名** 宅配業者

84

How is the listener requested to make a payment?
(A) By check
(B) By cash
(C) By credit card
(D) By bank transfer

接聽留言者被要求如何付款？

(A) 支票
(B) 現金
(C) 信用卡
(D) 銀行轉帳

答案 (C) 　請求、建議、下一步動作

留言到一半時提到 please make an advance payment by credit card through our Web site，由此可知(C)是正確答案。注意不要因留言中提到 cash on delivery（貨到付款）而被混淆誤選(B)。

- [ ] check [tʃɛk] **名** 支票
- [ ] bank transfer　銀行轉帳

85

What does the caller want to know?

(A) The address of the pastry shop
(B) The message to be added to the bouquet
(C) Credit card information
(D) The requested time of delivery

來電者想知道什麼？

(A) 西式糕點店的地址
(B) 花束隨附的留言
(C) 信用卡資料
(D) 希望送達的時間

答案 (B) 　其他細節

從留言末段提到 can you let me know what message you would like added to the bouquet?，可知正確答案是(B)。add A to B 原指「把A加到（添入）B」，也有「隨附」之意。

CD 2　54　🇬🇧

錄音原文	錄音原文翻譯
Questions 86 through 88 refer to the following telephone message. Hello, this is Grace Aston. On January 10th, I browsed your Web site and found a mobile phone that I decided to purchase via the Internet. The total amount of the discounted phone was $169, which I paid for using my credit card. A few days ago I received my latest credit card statement which shows that I was charged $199 for the phone. An error must have occurred while processing my bill; <u>possibly the discounted price was not taken into account.</u> Could you please contact me at 555-1855 so we can resolve the matter? Thank you.	試題 86-88 請參考以下電話留言。 哈囉，我是葛瑞絲‧阿斯頓（Grace Aston）。1 月 10 日，我瀏覽貴網站並找到一支我中意的手機，因而決定透過網路購買。折扣後的手機總金額為 169 元，是用我的信用卡付款。幾天前，我收到最新一期的信用卡對帳單顯示，這支電話被收費 199 元。你們在處理我的帳款時一定有錯誤發生；<u>可能折扣價沒有被列入計算。</u>可否請你撥打 555-1855 與我聯繫以便解決問題？謝謝。

Vocabulary

- ☐ total amount of～　～的總金額　　☐ statement [`stetmənt] 名 對帳單　　☐ charge A B　向A（人）收取B（金額等）
- ☐ error [`ɛrɚ] 名 錯誤　　☐ process [`prɑsɛs] 動 處理～　　☐ bill [bɪl] 名 帳款、帳單　　☐ take～ into account　將～列入考慮（計算）
- ☐ resolve [rɪ`zɑlv] 動 解決～　　☐ matter [`mætɚ] 名 問題

試題	試題翻譯	解答與解析
☑ **86** Where did the caller make the purchase? (A) At a discount store (B) At a mobile phone shop (C) Online (D) At a hardware store	來電者在哪裡購物？ (A) 折扣商店 (B) 手機商店 (C) 網路上 (D) 五金店	**答案 (C)**　　概要 題目說的caller就是來電者。從I browsed your Web site and found a mobile phone that I decided to purchase via the Internet這句，就可知道這個人瀏覽網站並透過網路買手機。(C)是將via the Internet（透過網路）換成Online（網路上）的說法，所以是正確答案。
☑ **87** What does the woman imply when she says, "<u>possibly the discounted price was not taken into account</u>"? (A) She misread the discounted price. (B) She has been overcharged. (C) She has not received her bill. (D) She used an invalid account.	女性說 「possibly the discounted price was not taken into account」 時，表示什麼？ (A) 她讀錯折扣價。 (B) 她已被多收錢。 (C) 她沒有收到帳單。 (D) 她用了一個無效的帳戶。	**答案 (B)**　　說話者的目的 taken～ into account是「將～列入考慮（計算）」。雖然留言中沒有明白地說出「被多收錢」而有點難作答，但從「用信用卡支付折扣後的169元」→「對帳單為199元」→「處理帳款時是否有誤？」這樣的過程可判斷(B)是正確答案。(D)是用同字但意思相異的account（帳戶）誘使大家誤選。 ☐ misread [mɪs`rid] 動 讀錯～ ☐ invalid [ɪn`vælɪd] 形 無效的
☑ **88** What does the caller request? (A) To have an item replaced (B) To be contacted by e-mail (C) To get a refund (D) To be called back	來電者要求什麼？ (A) 更換商品 (B) 用電子郵件聯繫 (C) 退款 (D) 對方回電	**答案 (D)**　　請求、建議、下一步動作 向對方請求或要求時，大多會用Could you...? 或是Please... 等祈使句表達。從整篇的最後一句Could you please contact me at 555-1855...? 可知(D)是正確答案。選項的call（致電）是把contact（聯繫）改換另一種說法而已。

錄音原文	錄音原文翻譯

Questions 89 through 91 refer to the following announcement.

As director of AGG, I am pleased to announce that our company has successfully entered into a merger agreement with Hoffman Life. This partnership will further strengthen our position in the insurance industry and will take place over the next few months. In the meantime, we expect you all will continue to provide our customers with the same high quality service that you always have. We expect the transition will have very little impact on our daily operations, but we realize many of you may have questions or concerns. In that event, I encourage you to speak with your floor supervisor or area manager, who will be able to give you more details.

試題 89-91 請參考以下宣布內容。

身為艾格 （AGG） 的董事，我很高興在此宣布我們公司已經成功地與霍夫曼人壽 （Hoffman Life） 達成合併協議。 這項合作關係將更進一步鞏固我們在保險業界的地位，並在接下來幾個月的期間內進行合併。 這段期間，我們期待大家繼續為客戶提供一貫不變的高品質服務。 我們認為，這項轉變將對公司日常營運的影響甚微，但我們可理解你們之中的大多數人可能會有疑問或顧慮。 如果有的話，我鼓勵你們跟各位的樓層主管或區經理談談，他們可以提供你們更多的詳情。

Vocabulary

☐ further [`fɝðɚ] 副 更進一步地　　☐ strengthen [`strɛŋθən] 動 加強～　　☐ insurance industry　保險業界　　☐ take place　進行、發生
☐ continue to *do*～　繼續～　　☐ in that event　如果那樣的話　　☐ encourage～ to *do*　鼓勵～做……

試題	試題翻譯	解答與解析

89

What is the speaker announcing?

(A) A vacant position
(B) The opening of a new office
(C) A partnership with another company
(D) The launch of a new product

發言者宣布什麼？

(A) 空缺的職位
(B) 啟用新辦公室
(C) 與另一家公司的合作關係
(D) 發表新產品

答案 (C)　　概述

從our company has successfully entered into a merger agreement with Hoffman Life可知，這是宣布與霍夫曼人壽的合併協議，所以(C)是正確答案。接下來提到的partnership（合作關係）也是答題的主要關鍵。enter into a merger agreement with～是指「與～達成合併協議」，選項內的another company（另一家公司）是把霍夫曼人壽（Hoffman Life）換成另一種說法而已。

90

Who is the audience for the announcement?
(A) Company employees
(B) AGG directors
(C) Hoffman executives
(D) Floor supervisors

誰是這場宣布內容的聽眾？

(A) 公司員工
(B) 艾格的董事們
(C) 霍夫曼的重要主管們
(D) 樓層主管

答案 (A)　　聽眾與發言者

從As director of AGG, I am pleased to announce...這句可知，發言者是公司的董事，傳達了合併是開心的消息，並對當前的業務提出指示。由此可判斷他是對艾格的員工談話，所以(A)是正確答案。(B)是指發言者本人。(C)是此項合作關係的對方公司。(D)是員工有疑問或顧慮時商談的對象。

91

According to the announcement, what will happen to the company?
(A) New workers will be hired.
(B) It will carry on as usual.
(C) An area manager will be transferred.
(D) There will be a major operational change.

根據宣布內容，公司將發生什麼事？

(A) 雇用新職員。
(B) 如常運作。
(C) 一位區經理將被調職。
(D) 營運上將有重大的變化。

答案 (B)　　其他細節

題目說的the company是指艾格（AGG）公司。有關合作關係轉變期間的營運，在the transition will have very little impact on our daily operations這句有提到。transition是「轉變」，have impact on～是「產生～影響」，operation是「營運」的意思，而(B)是將這一整句簡化為「如常運作」，所以答案正確。(D)則是錯在說法完全相反。

CD 2 · 56 🍁

錄音原文	錄音原文翻譯

Questions 92 through 94 refer to the following advertisement.

Are you eager to start a career in the IT industry? A diploma from our one-year Software Development Course is designed to train high-quality programmers with cutting-edge job market competitiveness. Successful applicants for this course will not be disappointed. Last year, eighty-five percent of graduates found employment by April of this year. A significant part of our curriculum focuses on developing practical skills. Two days per week are devoted to hands-on training, both on-campus and off-campus, and our classes are small, with a maximum of sixteen students per class. For more information, or to complete an application form, please visit our Web site at www.careercourses.com.

試題 92-94 請參考以下的廣告。

你渴望從事資訊科技 (IT) 產業嗎？我們為期 1 年的軟體開發課程學位證書，旨在培養具備最尖端就業市場競爭力的高素質程式設計師。 成功申請上這門課程的人絕不會失望。 去年百分之 85 的畢業生，在今年 4 月前已找到工作。 我們的課程最重要的部分就是將焦點放在實用技能的養成。 每週 2 天致力於校內及校外的實務經驗培訓，而且我們是小班制課程，每班最多 16 位學生。 如要瀏覽更多訊息，或是要填寫申請表格者，請至我們的網頁 www.careercourses.com。

Vocabulary

- □ be eager to *do* 渴望的～   □ diploma [dɪˈplomə] 名 學位證書   □ cutting-edge [ˈkʌtɪŋ ɛdʒ] 形 最尖端的
- □ competitiveness [kəmˈpɛtətɪvnɪs] 名 競爭力   □ applicant [ˈæpləkənt] 名 申請人   □ significant [sɪɡˈnɪfəkənt] 形 重要的
- □ curriculum [kəˈrɪkjələm] 名 課程   □ focus on～ 焦點放在～   □ practical [ˈpræktɪkl] 形 實用的
- □ a maximum of～ 最大限度的～   □ application form 申請表格

試題	試題翻譯	解答與解析

☑ 92

What field should applicants have an interest in?
(A) Teaching
(B) Information technology
(C) Office management
(D) Sales

申請人應該對哪個領域有興趣？

(A) 教學
(B) 資訊科技
(C) 事務管理
(D) 銷售

答案 (B) 〔其他細節〕

從開頭的第1句，就知道正確答案是(B)。先找空檔預覽題目，應可推測是「招募」相關的英文內容。其次是播放前的標題指示，聽到這篇是advertisement的類別時，當下會知道這是推薦性質的「廣告」。甚至如果也先預看了第94題，那就更能從students這個字去推敲這是學校的宣傳廣告。

☑ 93

Why does the man say, "Successful applicants for this course will not be disappointed"?
(A) To highlight the start date of this year's course
(B) To outline the contents of various courses
(C) To describe competitive salaries for employees
(D) To emphasize a high employment rate for graduates

為何男性說 「Successful applicants for this course will not be disappointed」？

(A) 為強調今年課程的開始日期
(B) 為概述各種課程的內容
(C) 為描述員工具競爭力的薪資
(D) 為強調畢業生的高就業率

答案 (D) 〔說話者的目的〕

successful applicants（申請成功的人）是指通過某種申請資格的人。因為下一句有具體敘明畢業生的就業率，因此可知(D)是正確答案。選項內的a high employment rate（高就業率）是把eighty-five percent of...換成另一種說法而已。

- □ highlight [ˈhaɪ͵laɪt] 動 強調～
- □ content [ˈkɑntɛnt] 名 內容
- □ emphasize [ˈɛmfə͵saɪz] 動 強調～
- □ employment rate 就業率
- □ graduate [ˈɡrædʒʊɪt] 名 畢業生

☑ 94

What can students do two days a week?
(A) Receive individual instruction
(B) Get practical training
(C) Build a curriculum
(D) Visit different campuses

學生 1 週有 2 天可以做什麼？

(A) 接受個別教導
(B) 獲得實習
(C) 建立課程
(D) 參訪不同的校園

答案 (B) 〔其他細節〕

整篇中間的地方提到Two days per week are devoted to hands-on training，由此可知正確答案是(B)。devote A to B是「將A奉獻給B」，hands-on training是指「實地職業體驗的訓練」，而非知識，(B)是直接把該意思改說為practical training（實習）。

- □ individual [͵ɪndəˈvɪdʒʊəl] 形 個人的、個別的
- □ instruction [ɪnˈstrʌkʃən] 名 教導

錄音原文	錄音原文翻譯
Questions 95 through 97 refer to the following talk and map.	試題 95-97 請參考以下談話及平面圖。

Okay, gather around. This morning, we're going to start working with some of the driverless forklifts that were delivered last week. That's part of the big upgrade the company is making—you know, introducing more automation. Anyway, we're going to use these vehicles to move items around within the warehouse, and we should get a big boost in efficiency this way. Polly's section will be the only one using them to begin with—as sort of a field experiment. If her section does well with these machines, we'll probably order more. Remember that with or without the forklifts, we have to meet our packing and shipping targets. We failed to do that yesterday, and we can't have a repeat.

好，請大家集合一下！今天早上，我們要開始操作上週送來的一些無人駕駛堆高機。 這是公司正在進行重大升級的一部分，你們知道的，就是導入更多的自動化機器。 總之，我們將在倉庫內使用這些機器來移動商品，應該會讓我們的效率獲得很大的提升。 波莉（Polly）管理的區域是首先進行試用的唯一地方──當作是一種實地測試。 如果她的區域用這些機器可以做得很好，我們可能會訂購更多。 記住不管有沒有堆高機，我們都必須達到我們的包裝及出貨目標。 昨日我們未達成，今日不能再重蹈覆轍。

Warehouse Layout / 倉庫平面圖

Section 1 Quality Testing / 第1區域 品質測試
Section 2 Internal Deliveries / 第2區域 內部配送
Section 3 Administration / 第3區域 管理單位
Section 4 Cafeteria / 第4區域 自助餐廳
Security Desk / 保全櫃台
Break Room / 休息室
Restrooms / 洗手間

Vocabulary

- driverless [ˋdraɪvɚ·lɛs] 形 無人駕駛的
- automation [ˏɔtəˋmeʃən] 名 自動操作、自動化
- boost [bust] 名 提升、增加

試題	試題翻譯	解答與解析
☑ **95** What change is the company making? (A) It is hiring more drivers. (B) It is working in a new area. (C) It is introducing more suppliers. (D) It is using a more advanced system.	公司正在做什麼改變？ (A) 雇用更多的駕駛。 (B) 在拓展新的領域。 (C) 引進更多的供應商。 (D) 使用更先進的系統。	**答案 (D)** 〔概述〕 先看圖（倉庫的平面圖），可推測這是與倉庫內的配置等相關的談話。整段一開始就表達要使用上週送來的堆高機進行作業，接著又提到「效率獲得很大的提升」、「更進一步推行自動化」，也就是所謂的「更先進的系統」，所以(D)是正確答案。
☑ **96** Look at the graphic. Where will Polly's team work? (A) In Section 1 (B) In Section 2 (C) In Section 3 (D) In Section 4	請看地圖。 波莉這組在哪裡工作？ (A) 第1區域 (B) 第2區域 (C) 第3區域 (D) 第4區域	**答案 (B)** 〔圖表問題〕 注意聽人名波莉的部分，就是Polly's section will be the only one using them to begin with。這句的them是指無人駕駛的堆高機，但是從we're going to use these vehicles to move items around within the warehouse這句可知，那些堆高機是要用在倉庫內來回搬運物品的。因此再對照平面圖來看，只有第2區域的內部配送最適合。
☑ **97** According to the speaker, what took place yesterday? (A) A goal was unmet. (B) A plan was revised. (C) A standard was changed. (D) A group was organized.	根據發言者的說法，昨天發生了什麼？ (A) 目標未達成。 (B) 計畫被修正。 (C) 標準被改變。 (D) 組織了一個小組。	**答案 (A)** 〔其他細節〕 發言者在結尾前告訴大家「必須達到我們的包裝及出貨目標」，接著說We failed to do that yesterday。fail to do是「失敗～、做不到～」的意思，由此可知沒有達到包裝及出貨目標，所以(A)是正確答案。target（目標）只是被換成goal（目標）的說法而已。 □ unmet [ʌnˋmɛt] 形（要求等）未滿足的

錄音原文	錄音原文翻譯

Questions 98 through 100 refer to the following telephone message and order form.

Hello, Mr. Carver, this is Irina Kowalski, calling from Sindell Office Supplies. I'm responding to your text requesting we add two additional chairs to the order form you e-mailed us last night. We can certainly do that without any problems at all. However, you'd receive your items about three days later than scheduled. We could also send the items express, but there'd be an additional fee for that. When you get a moment, please call me back at 203-555-1483 to let me know which option you have decided on.

試題 98-100 請參考以下電話留言及訂購單。

哈囉，卡佛先生 （Mr. Carver），我是辛德爾 （Sindell） 辦公用品公司的依琳娜．科瓦爾斯基 （Irina Kowalski）。我來電是要回覆您的文字訊息，針對您昨晚用電子郵件傳來的訂購單，您要求再追加 2 張椅子。毫無疑問，我們當然可以做到。不過，您會比預計的日程還要晚 3 天收到。我們也可以用快遞方式配送，但是會產生額外的費用。您有空時，請撥打 203-555-1483 回電給我，讓我知道您決定採用哪一個選項。

Sindell Office Supplies

Order Form

Product	Number Ordered
Desk Lamps	4
Tables	2
Telephones	2
Photocopiers	1
Office Chairs	3

辛德爾辦公用品公司

訂購單

產品	訂購數量
桌燈	4
桌子	2
電話	2
影印機	1
辦公用椅	3

Vocabulary

□ express [ɪk`sprɛs] 勔 用快遞、用宅急便方式

試題	試題翻譯	解答與解析

98

Look at the graphic. How many chairs will Mr. Carver receive?
(A) 3
(B) 4
(C) 5
(D) 6

請看圖。卡佛先生會收到幾張椅子？
(A) 3
(B) 4
(C) 5
(D) 6

答案 (C) 圖表問題

從I'm responding to...這句可知，收聽留言的人，也就是卡佛先生，前一晚以電子郵件傳了訂購單並要求追加2張椅子。而我們看到的訂購單上是寫3張辦公用椅，所以卡佛先生要訂的數量是3+2=5張。建議答案步驟如下：1. 先看題目，掌握這是在問椅子的數量，2. 看訂購單確認辦公用椅（Office Chairs），3. 再從廣播聽懂要追加2張椅子（two additional chairs），從這樣的順序來解答就可以。

99

What does the caller indicate about the order?
(A) It will arrive later than planned.
(B) It could cause installation problems.
(C) It could require additional staff.
(D) It will contain discounted items.

關於訂購事宜，來電者說了什麼？
(A) 會比預定時間晚送達。
(B) 可能會發生安裝問題。
(C) 可能需要追加工作人員。
(D) 將包含打折商品。

答案 (A) 其他細節

整篇中間的地方提到However, you'd receive your items about three days later than scheduled.，由此可知正確答案是(A)。scheduled（預定的）只是被換成planned（預定的）的說法而已。However後面通常是講重要的內容，所以一旦聽到However，記得要好好地聽清楚後面的內容喔！

100

What is Mr. Carver asked to do?

(A) Wait for a phone call
(B) Take an express bus
(C) Make a selection
(D) Cancel a fee

卡佛先生被要求做什麼？

(A) 等電話
(B) 搭特快巴士
(C) 做選擇
(D) 取消費用

答案 (C) 請求、建議、下一步動作

整個段落的最後出現please call me back... which option you have decided on 這樣的祈使句，可知這是請求表現法。選項(C)Make a selection只是將which option you have decided on（您決定採用哪一個選項）換個簡單的說法，所以是正確答案。而所謂的option（選項），是指關於商品的送達，要選擇比預定日晚3天，還是要支付追加的費用改用快遞方式。

PART 5

<table>
<tr><td>試題與翻譯</td><td>解答與解析</td></tr>
</table>

☑ 101

Anyone ------- in volunteering to help out with the annual fun-run event is encouraged to contact Ms. Williams, the event coordinator.

(A) interests
(B) interesting
(C) interestingly
(D) interested

我們鼓勵任何有興趣幫忙年度公益長跑活動的志願者，聯繫活動的負責人威廉斯女士 （Ms. Williams）。

答案 (D) 　　　　　　　　詞性

Anyone是主詞，is encouraged是動詞，所以------- in volunteering... fun-run event是修飾前面的Anyone。空格填入(D)的interested，意即「對～有興趣的人……」，所以是正確答案。(B)的interesting也可以修飾前面的名詞當作分詞，但並不是用在「人」而是「事物」。這種情況，把Anyone who is interested in...的句型從省略who is的方向來思考，會更容易了解為何interesting不適合。

☑ 102

Hamilton Enterprises sells similar products for almost half the price at which Lengston Tech offers -------.

(A) it
(B) its
(C) theirs
(D) themselves

漢米爾敦企業 （Hamilton Enterprises） 以幾乎是冷斯頓科技 （Lengston Tech） 所提供產品的一半價格，銷售類似的產品。

答案 (C) 　　　　　　　　文法

這是人稱代名詞的問題。which是關係代名詞，Lengston Tech是主詞，offers是動詞。正確答案(C)的theirs（他們的產品）即是動詞的受詞。這裡的theirs＝their products，即代表they的所有格代名詞。(A)的it（它）雖然可當受詞，不過先行詞的名詞要單數才行。(B)its（它的）後面需要接名詞。(D)的意思會變成「提供他們自己」。

☑ 103

To ------- the optimum life of the machinery, regular cleaning and maintenance is essential.

(A) state
(B) deprive
(C) certify
(D) ensure

為了確保機械的最佳壽命，定期的清潔與保養是必要的。

答案 (D) 　　　　　　　　字彙

句首的〈to＋原形動詞〉大致上是表目的。為了什麼原因，要讓機械維持最佳壽命，所以必須定期清潔與保養，從這個角度思考，答案(D)的ensure（確保～）最適當。

☐ optimum [`ɑptəməm] 形 最佳的
☐ essential [ɪ`sɛnʃəl] 形 不可缺的
☐ state [stet] 動 陳述
☐ deprive [dɪ`praɪv] 動 剝奪～
☐ certify [`sɚtə͵faɪ] 動 證明～

☑ 104

The ------- of daily visitors to the Metro Web site went from two million in January to four million in August.

(A) launch
(B) number
(C) data
(D) statistics

捷運網站每日的到訪人數，已經從 1 月的 2,000,000 人次變為 8 月的 4,000,000 人次。

答案 (B) 　　　　　　　　字彙

The ------- of daily visitors (to the Metro Web site)是主詞部分，動詞部分是用went from A to B的型態。這裡的go意思是「變為（～的結果）」。from A to B的A和B都是數值，所以答案(B)的number（數量）最適當。the number of～是「～的數量」的意思，請和a number of～（很多的～）區分清楚。

☐ launch [lɔntʃ] 名 開始
☐ statistics [stə`tɪstɪks] 名 統計

☑ 105

Appointments for eye examinations at Woodbury Eye Clinic can be made either online ------- by phone.

(A) and
(B) or
(C) but
(D) not

伍德柏里 （Woodbury） 眼科診所的眼睛檢查預約，用網路或電話任一種方式皆可。

答案 (B) 　　　　　　　　選項混和型

either A or B是指「A或B任一」。所以一看到either，首先就要想到or。其他類似的片語包括both A and B（A和B都～）、neither A nor B（A和B都不～）、not A but B（不是A而是B），以及not only A but (also) B（不僅A還有B也是）等等，請大家都要記住。

試題與翻譯	解答與解析

☑ 106

Wilderness River Cruises, the world's leading river cruise line, offers travelers opportunities to explore spectacular destinations in a most ------- and comfortable way.

(A) relaxing
(B) relaxation
(C) relax
(D) relaxes

荒野河川巡航公司 （Wilderness River Cruises），是世界領先的河川遊輪業者，提供旅遊者以最放鬆及舒適的方式探索壯觀旅遊目的的機會。

答案 (A) 　　詞性

in a most ------- and comfortable way（以最～及舒適的方式），關鍵在於是否有看出這個重點。most是副詞（最高級），語法順序是〈a＋副詞＋形容詞＋名詞〉，也就是這句有-------和comfortable 2個形容詞。因此，形容詞的(A) relaxing（令人放鬆的）才是正確答案。

□ relaxation [ˌrilæksˈeʃən] 名 放鬆

☑ 107

The contract indicates that interest at a rate of five percent will begin to be charged for any ------- balances after thirty days.

(A) outstanding
(B) effective
(C) representative
(D) disposable

合約書指出，任何未付清的帳款餘額 30 天後將被收取 5% 的利息。

答案 (A) 　　字彙

修飾後面單字balances（餘額）的形容詞以(A)最正確。outstanding除了是指「顯著的、傑出的」，也有「未付清的、未解決的」意思，大家要先記牢才行。(C)的representative是「代表性的」，當名詞時是「代表人」，多益測驗的出現頻率高。

□ effective [ɪˈfɛktɪv] 形 有效的
□ disposable [dɪˈspozəbl̩] 形 用完即丟的

☑ 108

------- the company report, sales rose by 2.5 percent compared to the same time last year.

(A) Except for
(B) Rather than
(C) According to
(D) By way of

根據該公司的報告，銷售量比去年同期成長 2.5%。

答案 (C) 　　慣用語

將「公司的報告」和「銷售量成長2.5%」2者的關係做連結思考，(C)的According to～（根據～）是正確答案。

□ compared to～　與～比較
□ except for～　除了～以外
□ rather than～　而不是～
□ by way of～　經由～

☑ 109

------- by financial deficits, Imaginos Group announced job cuts in addition to the sale of its resin manufacturing plant.

(A) To hamper
(B) Hampered
(C) Hampering
(D) Been hampered

受財務赤字拖累，伊瑪巨洛斯集團 （Imaginos Group） 宣布除了賣掉樹脂製造工廠外，還要裁員。

答案 (B) 　　動詞型態

從選項的語詞來看，關鍵在於是否有看出-------by financial deficits是分詞構句。重點在by，讓句型成為被動式「受財務赤字阻礙」，選項(B)是過去分詞，所以是正確答案。放在句首的Being被省略了。即使不懂hamper（阻礙～）的意思也沒有關係，因為是by的分詞構句型態，所以只要知道是被動式就能解答。

□ deficit [ˈdɛfɪsɪt] 名 赤字
□ resin [ˈrɛzɪn] 名 樹脂

☑ 110

The ------- covers the cost of parts and labor to repair the product in the event it breaks.

(A) guarantee
(B) deadline
(C) correspondence
(D) segment

這項保證包括產品毀壞時，維修產品的零件費用與人工成本。

答案 (A) 　　字彙

如果了解(A)guarantee（保證）的意思，只要看到The ------- covers the cost的部分就知道答案應該選(A)。

□ cost of labor　人工成本
□ in the event (that)～　在～情況下
□ correspondence [ˌkɔrəˈspɑndəns] 名 通訊
□ segment [ˈsɛgmənt] 名 區段

☑ 111

Although risk management expenses seem unproductive, they may save a company from ------- damages in the case of a contingency.

(A) pay
(B) paid
(C) paying
(D) payment

雖然風險管理的支出似乎是無收益的，但若有意外事件時，它們可以挽救公司免於支付賠償金。

答案 (C) [詞性]

save A from B是指「挽救A免於B」。空格後面的damages（損害）是名詞，以「支付賠償金」這種動詞和受詞的組合最適當，所以空格置入動詞最正確。由於介系詞後面的動詞要用～ing型態，因此(C)的paying（支付～）是正確答案。

☐ expense [ɪkˋspɛns] 名 費用
☐ unproductive [ˌʌnprəˋdʌktɪv] 形 無收益的
☐ contingency [kənˋtɪndʒənsɪ] 名 意外事件

☑ 112

CDU Insurance is ------- to offering its customers the highest level of care and customer service possible.

(A) committed
(B) predicted
(C) subjected
(D) contributed

CDU 保險公司盡可能致力於提供客戶最高水準的照護和客戶服務。

答案 (A) [字彙]

因為選項內都是～(e)d的動詞型態，加上前面是is，所以這是被動句。而offering是動名詞，表示前面的to是介系詞。(A)的be committed to～（致力於～）符合這樣的文法，所以是正確答案。(B)的be predicted to *do*～（預測～），後面的不定詞to要接原形動詞才對。(C)的be subjected to～（被暴露於～），雖然這裡的to也是介系詞，但不符句意。

☑ 113

Please be forewarned that the tickets for the special showing are non-refundable and cannot be exchanged or ------- after purchase.

(A) replace
(B) replaced
(C) to replace
(D) replacing

請注意：特別加映場的門票是不可退款的，而且在購買後不能退換或補發。

答案 (B) [動詞型態]

not A or B的意思是「不能A，也不能B」。or是對等連接詞，要接對等的語句。先看or的前面，是be exchanged（被更換）的被動型態，因此or的後面也要接過去分詞，所以(B)的過去分詞是正確答案。

☐ Please be forewarned that... 請注意（有關that後面的內容）
☐ non-refundable [ˌnɑn rɪˋfʌndəbl] 形 不可退款的

☑ 114

Farmers in the far north ------- there will be a long-term impact if rain does not come in the next few weeks.

(A) fear
(B) fears
(C) to fear
(D) are feared

如果未來幾週內都不下雨，最北區北方的農民擔心會有長遠的影響。

答案 (A) [動詞型態]

Farmers in the far north是主詞，作答關鍵在於是否有看出重點，就是there will be...前面的連接詞that被省略了。fear帶出that後面的部分，意思是「恐懼～、擔心是否～」。原形的fear針對複數形主詞（Farmers）加以陳述而成謂語動詞，所以是正確答案。意思相近的be afraid（害怕）、be frightened（驚恐）及be scared（恐懼）等，則是用形容詞及被動型態表現法，請加以區別。

☑ 115

The terms and conditions of your employment are ------- on the following pages of this agreement.

(A) notified
(B) registered
(C) approved
(D) outlined

你的雇用條約及條款，概述於這份協議書接下來的頁數內。

答案 (D) [字彙]

因為有are，所以是被動句。(D)的「概述」符合「雇用條約及條款」與「協議書」的關係。(A) notified（通知）應該是用在employees are notified（員工被通知）。

☐ terms and conditions 條約及條款
☐ following [ˋfɑləwɪŋ] 形 接下來的
☐ agreement [əˋgrimənt] 名 協議書
☐ approve [əˋpruv] 動 核准

試題與翻譯	解答與解析

☑ 116

The Restaurant Recognition of Excellence Award represents consistency and quality ------- a series of categories.

(A) across
(B) during
(C) upon
(D) beneath

餐廳識別卓越獎 （The Restaurant Recognition of Excellence Award） 代表跨類別評比中展現的一致性與品質。

答案 (A)　 字彙

這題是考介系詞。The Restaurant Recognition of Excellence Award是主詞，represents是動詞，consistency and quality是受詞，從選項可判斷-------a series of categories是要接介系詞的語句。整句的意思以「橫跨一系列類別的一致性與品質」最符合，所以(A)是正確答案。

□ consistency [kən`sɪstənsɪ] 名 一致性
□ a series of～　一系列的～

☑ 117

General inquiries are first accepted at the Help Line, but when an inquiry proves to be -------, it can be transferred to Tech Support.

(A) technique
(B) technician
(C) technical
(D) technically

一般的詢問會先在服務專線受理，但如果該詢問證明是技術性的問題時，就會被轉到技術支援單位。

答案 (C)　 詞性

prove to be～意即「證明是～」，空格要填入的是對an inquiry（詢問）的補語。形容詞的(C)technical最正確。(A)「技術」和(B)「技術者」是名詞，雖然也可當作補語，但是an inquiry = technique，或是an inquiry = technician的前後關係會變得很奇怪。

□ technically [`tɛknɪk!ɪ] 副 在技術上

☑ 118

The community hall is inexpensive to rent and an ideal ------- for social functions and many kinds of recreational and leisure activities.

(A) source
(B) intention
(C) routine
(D) venue

社區大廳租金便宜，而且對社交活動及各種娛樂和休閒的活動而言，是理想的地點。

答案 (D)　 字彙

如果看懂The community hall is... an ideal -------是「主詞＋動詞＋補語」（SVC）的句型結構，應該就知道要選表示場所的單字(D)venue（地點）。

□ recreational [,rɛkrɪ`eʃən!] 形 娛樂的
□ source [sors] 名 來源
□ intention [ɪn`tɛnʃən] 名 意圖
□ routine [ru`tin] 名 例行公事

☑ 119

The future of the resort's run-down building will be in danger ------- some funding can be secured to help replace the old structure.

(A) unless
(B) however
(C) because
(D) whereas

渡假村破落建築的未來將十分危險，除非能確保有資金來幫助更換舊結構。

答案 (A)　選項混合型

選項內夾雜著連接詞和連接副詞。因為空格前後是各自獨立的子句，所以空格就是要填入連接詞。從整句的意思可判斷(A)unless（除非～）即是正確答案。(B)的however（然而）是連接副詞，但是不能用這種形式連接2個子句。(D)的whereas比while語氣堅定，有讓步語氣的「儘管～」和對比語氣的「～反之」的含意。

□ secure [sɪ`kjor] 動 確保～

☑ 120

At Satos Restaurant, you will find not only delicious food at ------- prices but quick, efficient service and a friendly atmosphere.

(A) approximate
(B) passionate
(C) considerate
(D) moderate

在莎多斯 （Satos） 餐廳，你會發現不僅有平價的美食，還有快速、有效率的服務及友善的氣氛。

答案 (D)　 字彙

符合at ------- price這種組合的字是(D)的moderate（平價的）。moderate除了「（數量或程度）適度的」之外，還有「（天氣）穩定的」意思。(C)的considerate是指「考慮周到的」，注意不要和considerable（相當大的）混淆。填入空格就變成at considerable price（相當高的價格）了。

□ atmosphere [`ætməs,fɪr] 名 氣氛
□ approximate [ə`praksəmɪt] 形 大約的
□ passionate [`pæʃənɪt] 形 熱情的

☑ 121

Owing to ------- demand for the award-winning book, all copies are currently sold out.

(A) authentic
(B) illustrious
(C) unprecedented
(D) monotonous

由於該獲獎書籍收到前所未有的需求，所有的書目前都銷售一空。

答案 (C) 字彙

owing to～是「由於～」，和due to～的意思及用法相同。是什麼樣的需求（demand）造成得獎作品全部銷售一空，從這方面思考，就可以確定選項(C)的unprecedented（前所未有、史無前例）最適合。

☐ authentic [ɔˋθɛntɪk] 形 真實的
☐ illustrious [ɪˋlʌstrɪəs] 形 輝煌的
☐ monotonous [məˋnɑtənəs] 形 單調的

☑ 122

Rhotrade Telecom's new line of smartphones features enhanced user-friendliness as well as wider color and design -------.

(A) vary
(B) variable
(C) various
(D) variations

羅崔德電信 （Rhotrade Telecom） 的新系列智慧型手機不只更人性化，色彩和設計也更多元。

答案 (D) 詞性

A as well as B（A和B都～，不只是B而且A也是）。wider color and design -------的wider是形容詞（比較級），修飾 color and design -------。(D)的variations（變化）為正確答案，是名詞與名詞並列的形式。

☐ enhance [ɪnˋhæns] 動 提高～
☐ vary [ˋvɛrɪ] 動 使多樣化
☐ variable [ˋvɛrɪəb!] 形 多變的
☐ various [ˋvɛrɪəs] 形 各式各樣的

☑ 123

The management, in an effort to reduce waste and cut costs, ------- a new workplace improvement program in line with the AXO-35000 requirements.

(A) introduce
(B) introduced
(C) introduction
(D) introducing

經營部門為了減少浪費及降低成本，引進了符合 AXO-35000 要求的新職場改善計畫。

答案 (B) 詞性

夾在 2 個逗點中間的是插入句，The management是主詞，-------是述語動詞，a new... program是受詞。(A)或(B)可當述語動詞，但是針對單數主詞，原形動詞的(A)並不合適。因此過去式的(B)才是正確答案。大家在閱讀英文時，如果常注意到主詞和動詞，即使遇到主詞和動詞分開的句子也能對應自如。

☐ in an effort to do　為了～
☐ in line with～　符合～

☑ 124

To access the archives, you must first submit a form that needs to be ------- by the director of the institute.

(A) admired
(B) accompanied
(C) abandoned
(D) authorized

要存取資料庫，你必須要先提出經該機構所長授權的表格。

答案 (D) 字彙

空格被be和by夾在中間，因此可判斷這是被動句。that是關係代名詞的主格，撇開that來解讀主述語的意思，a form needs to be ------- by the director of the institute以「需要該機構所長授權的表格」的意思最適，所以答案是(D)。

☐ admire [ədˋmaɪr] 動 欣賞～
☐ accompany [əˋkʌmpənɪ] 動 伴隨、陪同
☐ abandon [əˋbændən] 動 捨棄～

☑ 125

Marketing expert Jeff Coleman's new book *Business Momentum* provides an excellent road map to follow ------- sales and profits.

(A) increases
(B) to increase
(C) increasingly
(D) will increase

行銷專家傑夫 ‧ 柯爾曼 （Jeff Coleman） 的新書 《商業氣勢》 （*Business Momentum*），提供了應遵循的計畫準則，用以提高銷售和利潤。

答案 (B) 文法

從句首到follow（遵循）就能構成一完整句子，所以空格之後的部分可視為副詞片語。以全句的意思來看，表示目的的「用以提高銷售和利潤」最適當，因此不定詞to increase（增加、提高）的(B)最正確。(C)的increasingly是副詞，意思是「越來越」。

☐ momentum [moˋmɛntəm] 名 氣勢

試題與翻譯	解答與解析

☑ 126

Many financial analysts argue that the business environment today is ------- more complicated than ever before.

(A) much
(B) very
(C) so
(D) such

許多金融分析師認為，今天的商業環境比以往複雜得多。

答案 (A) [文法]

這是關於比較級與副詞的問題。空格後面的 more是比較級，(A)的much的功能是加強比較級，所以是正確答案。加強比較級的單字除此之外還有far（遠遠地）及a lot（非常）。

□ financial [faɪˋnænʃəl] 形 財政的
□ argue [ˋɑrgjʊ] 動 主張～
□ complicated [ˋkɑmpləˌketɪd] 形 複雜的

☑ 127

Delivery time will vary ------- the weight and size of the item and also the location of the shipping address.

(A) as for
(B) prior to
(C) depending on
(D) in contrast to

配送時間將因物品的重量、尺寸及送達地點而異。

答案 (C) [慣用語]

思考「配送時間不同」和「物品的重量、尺寸及送達地點」這2者的關係，就可知(C)為正確答案。depending on～（依～而定、全憑～）是 depend on～（取決於～、全憑～）的「ing 形」，扮演副詞的作用。

□ as for～ 至於～
□ prior to～ 在～之前
□ in contrast to～ 與～形成對比

☑ 128

Project team leaders will be asked to explain the ------- of delays in the construction of the Riverside Apartment Complex.

(A) processes
(B) upgrades
(C) causes
(D) apologies

專案團隊的主管們，將被要求解釋河岸複合式公寓 （Riverside Apartment Complex） 的建設延誤的原因。

答案 (C) [字彙]

要說明該建設延誤的什麼，當然是(C)的causes （原因）最正確。(B)upgrades是「升級」,(D) apologies是「道歉」，這2個字用在說明延誤的過程，意思都不對。

□ upgrade [ˋʌpˏgred] 名 升級

☑ 129

The main purpose of the document is to propose measures which will help reduce losses and increase -------.

(A) product
(B) producing
(C) productively
(D) productivity

這份文件的主要目的是提出有助於減少損失和增加生產力的措施。

答案 (D) [詞性]

撇開關係代名詞（主格）which來看，measures will help reduce losses and increase -------意即「措施將有助於減少損失和增加～」。空格字是increase（增加）不可缺少的受詞，名詞 (D)的productivity（生產力）為正確答案。(A)的 product（產品）雖也是名詞，不過增加產品的銷售及品質、需求等說法才對，產品本身是不用增加的。

□ productively [prəˋdʌktɪvlɪ] 副 有成果地

☑ 130

Rainbow Furniture & Fittings has decided to ------- two of its stores into one location early next year.

(A) consolidate
(B) validate
(C) diversify
(D) proclaim

彩虹家飾公司 （Rainbow Furniture & Fittings） 已經決定在明年初將 2 家店合併為一。

答案 (A) [字彙]

重點在into，從two of its stores和one location 這樣的關係來看，(A)的consolidate A into B （將A合併成B）最符合語意。

□ validate [ˋvæləˏdet] 動 確認～
□ diversify [daɪˋvɝsəˏfaɪ] 動 使～多樣化
□ proclaim [prəˋklem] 動 宣布～

PART 6

Questions 131-134 refer to the following advertisement.

Do you want your career to take off? International Travel Academy has ------- opened a new
131.
campus, complete with an airport training center, right in the heart of the city. -------. The training
132.
center simulates real-world airports, ------- check-in, customs, gate lounges, and even planes where
133.
students are trained in all aspects of in-flight service. Applications for this year are now -------. For
134.
more information on how to launch your career in the travel industry, contact our team at 216-555-
7670.

131. (A) ever
(B) yet
(C) recently
(D) often

132. (A) The training will cover a general
overview of major airlines.
(B) The facilities here are certainly
something special.
(C) Airport security systems are operating
at peak capacity.
(D) The airline industry is currently facing
a labor shortage.

133. (A) including
(B) relative to
(C) as soon as
(D) in order to

134. (A) to take
(B) taken
(C) taking
(D) being taken

試題文章翻譯

試題 131-134 請參考以下廣告。

想讓你的職業生涯起飛嗎？國際旅遊學院 （International Travel Academy） 最近在市中心開設了一個附設機場培訓中心的新校區。 ¹³². 這裡的設施非常特別。 培訓中心模擬真正的機場，包括登機報到、海關、候機室，甚至是訓練學員各個飛行服務的飛機。 目前正在受理今年課程的申請。 欲知更多訊息以了解如何在旅遊業開創職業生涯者，歡迎撥打 216-555-7670 洽詢我們團隊。

解答與解析

131

答案 (C) [句型結構]

從空格前後的has和opened可判斷這是現在完成式。這樣的句型結構加入副詞，以(C)的recently（最近）最正確。(A)ever和(B)yet雖然也是常用於現在完成時態的副詞，但不適合放在肯定句has和過去分詞中間。ever用於現在完成時態的疑問句或否定句，意為「曾經、至今」。yet則用於現在完成時態的疑問句，意為「已經」；用於否定句時，意為「還（沒～）」。另外還有一種用法是have yet to *do*（尚未做～）。

132

答案 (B) [語句插入型]

空格前面傳達的內容是，新設立的校區有機場培訓中心。(B)為正確答案，當主詞的The facilities（設施）意即a new campus（新校區）的設施，something special（特殊之處）的具體內容則是空格後面所說明的。(A)和(D)雖然能連接前面的內容，但不符合後面內容。對於語句插入型的問題，一定也要仔細閱讀空格後面的內容才行。
(A) 「培訓將涵蓋各大航空公司的整體概況。」
(C) 「機場的安全系統正以最高的性能運作。」
(D) 「航空產業目前面臨勞工短缺。」

□ general overview 整體概況
□ peak [pik] 形 最高的、最大的
□ labor shortage 勞工短缺

133

答案 (A) [前後句關係]

從空格後面的「登機報到、海關、候機室、飛機」和前面的real-world airport（真正的機場）的關係可知，(A)是正確答案。including是介系詞，意為「包括～」。(B)relative to（與～有關）在句型結構上行得通，但語意不符。(C)as soon as（一～就）後面要有一個子句接著才對。(D)in order to（為了～）後面要接原形動詞，無法放入這裡的句型結構。

134

答案 (D) [句型結構]

這是主詞Applications (for this year)，動詞are (now) -------的句型結構。意為「申請正被受理中」，所以現在進行式被動語態的(D)是正確答案。因為「受理中」表示正在進行中的事情，所以(B)的are (now) taken不符合。

Vocabulary

□ complete with～ 有～（而更完備）
□ simulate [`sɪmjə͵let] 動 模擬
□ customs [`kʌstəmz] 名 海關
□ aspect [`æspɛkt] 名 方面
□ launch [lɔntʃ] 動 （事業）開始
□ industry [`ɪndəstrɪ] 名 行業

試題文章

Questions 135-138 refer to the following notice.

NZS Bank wishes to inform our valued customers about the pending relocation and merger of our Belmont branch banking operations with those of our nearby Bayview branch. ------- . The facilities **135.** ------- at our Bayview branch will give you an exciting, innovative banking experience. It offers the **136.** very ------- in banking technology, along with a team dedicated to providing exceptional customer **137.** service. ------- you have any questions regarding this change, please call our contact center at **138.** 1-800-555-888.

135. (A) The change will take place on Friday, January 22.
(B) Consequently, some of our services will be suspended.
(C) Our Belmont branch will reopen the following day.
(D) Here is the analysis of a merger's impact on competition.

136. (A) offer
(B) offering
(C) offered
(D) have offered

137. (A) late
(B) later
(C) lately
(D) latest

138. (A) Whether
(B) Should
(C) Now that
(D) Even though

試題文章翻譯

試題 135-138 請參考以下通知。

紐西蘭標準銀行 （NZS Bank） 希望通知我們尊榮的客戶有關貝爾蒙特 （Belmont） 分行懸而未決的搬遷，以及其與鄰近的灣景 （Bayview） 分行合併銀行營運的事宜。¹³⁵˙這項改變將於 1 月 22 日週五進行。灣景分行提供的設施，都將給您一個令人興奮、創新的銀行體驗。它提供了最新的銀行業務技術，以及一個致力於提供卓越客戶服務的團隊。您對這項改變如果有任何疑問，請撥打 1-800-555-888 洽詢我們的聯絡中心。

解答與解析

135

答案 (A) 　語句插入型

這句要接在紐西蘭標準銀行決定搬遷及合併的通知內容後面，以傳達實施日期。作為基本日期情報的(A)最流暢適合。主詞The change（改變）指出前述的變更時間。和132題一樣，如果有選項是含定冠詞the的名詞，最好要想一想是否可以連結前句的內容。例如(C)的the following day（隔天），因為前述內容並未提到任何特定日期，由此可判斷不是答案。
(B) 「因此，我們的一些服務將暫停。」
(C) 「我們的貝爾蒙特分行將在隔天重新開幕。」
(D) 「這是合併對競爭會產生什麼影響的分析。」
□ take place　舉行

136

答案 (C) 　句型結構

答題重點在分辨主詞與述語動詞。The facilities ------- at our Bayview branch是主詞，will give是述語動詞。------- at our Bayview branch是在修飾前面的The facilities，所以空格要填分詞，由「灣景分行所提供的設施」這種被動關係可知，過去分詞的(C)是正確答案。

137

答案 (D) 　句型結構

這是考詞性。空格是在the very後面，接在in前面，所以應該填入名詞。選項中可當名詞的，(D)的latest加上前面的the意即「最新的事物」，因此是正確答案。the very latest in banking technology是指「最新的銀行業務技術」。latest除了是late「遲的、遲到」的最高級外，當作形容詞也有「最新的」意思。

138

答案 (B) 　前後句關係

光看選項會覺得句型結構上都行得通，所以要視前後句關係來作答。「您對這項改變如果有任何疑問，請撥打到～」這樣的「條件」最符合，所以正確答案是(B)。Should you～（如果～的話）是商業書信或電子郵件、通知等內容最後最常見到的表現法。這是將If you should～條件句的if省略後，動詞移到句首的倒裝句。
□ whether [`hwɛðɚ] 圉 不管是～
□ now that　既然～
□ even though　即使

Vocabulary

□ pending [`pɛndɪŋ] 圉 未定的、懸而未決的
□ relocation [rilo`keʃən] 图 遷移
□ merger [mɝdʒɚ] 图 合併
□ nearby [`nɪr,baɪ] 圉 附近的
□ innovative [`ɪno,vetɪv] 圉 創新的
□ （be）dedicated to～　專心、致力於～
□ exceptional [ɪk`sɛpʃən!] 圉 卓越的

Questions 139-142 refer to the following article.

Great weather, big crowds and a lot of ------- marked last Sunday's annual Waterfront Fun Run in
139.
Newcastle. Around 55,000 people turned out to enjoy the scenic ten-kilometer jog along the Ocean
Bay waterfront route. -------. In fact, just 1,500 runners participated when it was first held twenty-
140.
five years -------. This support for the event transforms into significant support for worthy causes, as
141.
funds raised from runners' registration fees go to several children's charities each year. Organizers
of the Fun Run were thrilled with the day's success and the goodwill of everyone -------.
142.

139. (A) enthusiast
(B) enthusiasm
(C) enthusiastic
(D) enthusiastically

140. (A) This scenic road took runners into the
town of Newcastle.
(B) Many more jogging courses could
have recently been constructed.
(C) The popularity of the event has grown
dramatically over the years.
(D) Running is the perfect pastime for
children as well as adults.

141. (A) after
(B) onto
(C) ahead
(D) ago

142. (A) involved
(B) employed
(C) reserved
(D) attended

試題 139-142 請參考以下文章。

大好的天氣、盛大的人群以及高漲的熱情都是上週日新堡 （Newcastle） 一年一度濱水區路跑 （Waterfront Fun-Run） 活動的標誌。約有 55,000 人沿著大洋灣 （Ocean Bay） 濱水路線享受景色秀麗的 10 公里慢跑。140. 這項活動受歡迎的程度多年來已飛躍性成長。事實上，25 年前活動第 1 次舉辦時只有 1,500 名跑者參加。由於從跑步者的報名費中所得的資金，每年都會捐給幾個兒童慈善機構，所以對這項活動的支持，已轉變為具有價值和意義的重大支援。路跑的主辦者對當天的成功及每位參與者的善意都興奮不已。

139

答案 (B) 句型結構

這是詞性問題。主詞有Great weather, big crowds, a lot of -------3個，動詞是marked，所以空格要填名詞。想一下有很多的什麼是這項活動的特徵（marked），名詞的(B)enthusiasm（熱情、熱心）即是正確答案。雖然(A)的enthusiast（熱心人士）是名詞，但是要與前面的big crowds意思交疊，因此空格必須要填複數形。

□ enthusiastic [ɪnˌθjuzɪˋæstɪk] 形 熱情的
□ enthusiastically [ɪnˌθjuzɪˋæstɪkl̩ɪ] 副 滿腔熱情地

140

答案 (C) 語句插入型

空格前面的內容在說路跑的馬拉松活動聚集多人，而可以跟後面的內容順利連結的即是(C)。In fact是作答重點，「（與開始的當年相比）年年人氣提高」→「實際上25年前首次活動參加的人數僅有1,500名」的接法最順暢。(A)雖然可以配合前面的內容，但與後面的In fact, ...無法連貫。
(A)「這條風景秀麗的道路將跑者帶入新堡。」
(B)「更多的慢跑路線最近應該已經完工了。」
(D)「對小孩以及成人而言，跑步是很理想的消遣活動。」

□ dramatically [drəˋmætɪkl̩ɪ] 副 飛躍性地
□ pastime [ˋpæsˌtaɪm] 名 消遣、娛樂

141

答案 (D) 句型結構

這是句尾副詞的問題。從when的子句來看，動詞was (first) held是過去式。要符合「25年前第1次舉辦時」的副詞，以(D)ago（～前）最正確。(B)的onto（到……之上）是介系詞，不符句型結構。

142

答案 (A) 前後句關係

the goodwill of everyone是指「每位的善意」。Organizers對the day's success以及the goodwill of everyone -------2件事都興奮不已，而整個意思能符合修飾everyone的單字是(A)的involved。involved放在名詞後面是「有關的」意思，當作形容詞。(D)的「參加」如果換成everyone who attended就對了。

Vocabulary

□ scenic [ˋsinɪk] 形 景色秀麗的
□ significant [sɪgˋnɪfəkənt] 形 重要的、重大的
□ worthy [ˋwɝˋðɪ] 形 有價值的
□ cause [kɔz] 名 目標、動機
□ raise funds 籌集資金
□ registration fee 報名費
□ goodwill [ˋgʊdˋwɪl] 名 善意

試題文章

Questions 143-146 refer to the following e-mail.

To: Angela Jenkins <ajenkins@triplestar.net>
From: Kevin Park <admin_kpark@orkson.com>
Subject: Orkson Special Bonus
Date: May 20

Dear Angela,

Congratulations on purchasing your new Orkson product. For making your purchase during our "Hot

Deals" summer promotion, Orkson Limited ------- to provide you with a bonus warranty certificate
                                          143.
which extends the standard warranty of your product by an additional year. To redeem this offer

you will need to provide proof of purchase of your product ------- a copy of the standard warranty
                                                            144.
certificate. -------. For full ------- of the standard warranty conditions, please visit www.orkson.com/
              145.   **146.**
warranty. Thank you for choosing Orkson.

Kind regards,

Kevin Park
Customer Service

---

143. (A) pleased
　　　(B) is pleased
　　　(C) was pleased
　　　(D) had been pleased

144. (A) as if
　　　(B) because of
　　　(C) as well as
　　　(D) in spite of

145. (A) When submitted, this certificate voids
　　　　any extended warranty.
　　　(B) If so, we would like to claim damages
　　　　for the loss suffered.
　　　(C) To reclaim this certificate, please sign
　　　　up for the standard warranty.
　　　(D) The standard warranty conditions
　　　　apply to this extended warranty.

146. (A) details
　　　(B) procedures
　　　(C) rates
　　　(D) accounts

試題文章翻譯

試題 143-146 請參考以下電子郵件。

收信者：安琪拉 · 詹金斯 （Angela Jenkins） < ajenkins@triplestar.net >
發信者：凱文 · 派克 （Kevin Park） < admin_kpark@orkson.com >
主旨：奧克森 （Orkson） 特別優惠
日期：5 月 20 日

親愛的安琪拉：

恭喜您購買全新的奧克森產品。 由於您在我們的 「熱賣」 夏季促銷活動中購買，奧克森有限公司很樂意提供給您額外優惠的保證書，將您產品的標準保固期延長 1 年。 要兌換此項優惠，不但需要一份標準保證書，還要您提供產品購買證明。[145.] 標準保固條款適用於這項延長保固。 欲知標準保固條款的所有詳情，請上 www.orkson.com/warranty。 感謝您選擇奧克森。

由衷的祝福
凱文 · 派克
客服部

解答與解析

143

答案 (B) 　　　句型結構

這是有關不定詞的問題。be pleased to do是「很樂意做～」，因此(B)是正確答案。在〈be ＋表示情感的形容詞＋to＋原形動詞〉的句型中，形容詞的部分就是這題的空格。就算空格是在〈to＋原形動詞〉的位置，大家也要能夠對應才行。

144

答案 (C) 　　　前後句關係

這是連接前後的慣用語問題。為了獲得保固，必須要提出什麼呢？proof of purchase of your product和a copy of the standard warranty certificate是並列關係。因此(C)的～as well as...（不但……還～）是正確答案。

☐ as if～　好像～
☐ because of～　由於～
☐ in spite of～　儘管～

145

答案 (D) 　　　語句插入型

空格前面在說明提供產品保固延長1年的服務。後面的句子則表示標準保固相關資料的參考網址。因此，中間加入(D)後的前、後句最連貫。this extended warranty（這項延長保固）是承接前句的內容。
(A) 「當這份保證書提交時，將會使延長保固無效。」
(B) 「如果是這樣的話，我們想要求賠償損失。」
(C) 「為重獲此保固，請註冊標準保固。」

☐ void [vɔɪd] 動 使～無效
☐ reclaim [rɪˋklem] 動 重新恢復
☐ apply to～　適用於～

146

答案 (A) 　　　前後句關係

這和Part 5出現的問題一樣，4種選項都是相同的詞性，所以必須從前後句關係來思考。整句語意是「欲知標準保固條款的～，請上網」，正確答案為(A)details（詳情）。full details是「所有詳情」的意思。

☐ procedure [prəˋsidʒə] 名 手續
☐ rate [ret] 名 費用
☐ account [əˋkaʊnt] 名 財務報表

Vocabulary

☐ warranty certificate　保證書
☐ redeem [rɪˋdim] 動 買回～、履行
☐ proof [pruf] 名 證明

PART 7

Questions 147-148 refer to the following postcard.

試題147-148請參考以下明信片。

Mighty Auto Pro
665 Clinton Ave. S.
Minneapolis, MN 55419

Dear _Mr. Schmidt_,

It's time for an oil change! Our records indicate your last oil change was on _July 14_. We recommend an oil change every six months. At your convenience, please schedule a service appointment with us. Our hours are:

Mon–Thurs:	7:00 A.M.–7:00 P.M.
Fri:	7:00 A.M.–5:30 P.M.
Sat:	8:00 A.M.–12:00 P.M.
	(Closed Sundays)

We look forward to serving you again.

Mr. Jacob Schmidt
2129 Field Parkway
St. Paul, MN 55108

強大汽車專業（Mighty Auto Pro）
665柯林頓大道（Clinton Ave.）南
明尼亞波利斯（Minneapolis），明尼蘇達州
（MN）55419

親愛的施密特（Schmidt）先生：
換機油的時間到囉！我們的紀錄顯示您上次換機油的時間是7月14日。建議您每6個月換一次機油。在您方便的時候，請跟我們安排服務預約事宜。我們的營業時間是：

週一～週四：	7:00 A.M.－7:00 P.M.
週五：	7:00 A.M.－5:30 P.M.
週六：	8:00 A.M.－12:00 P.M.

（週日休息）
期待再度為您服務。

雅各·施密特（Jacob Schmidt）先生收
2129 斐爾德公園大道（Field Parkway）
聖保羅，明尼蘇達州（MN）55108

Vocabulary

□ record [`rɛkəd] 名 紀錄   □ at your convenience　在您方便時   □ look forward to ～ing　期待～

☑ 147

Why was the postcard sent?

(A) To recommend a product
(B) To attract new customers
(C) To announce a change in business hours
(D) To remind a customer to make an appointment

為什麼寄明信片？

(A) 為了推薦產品
(B) 為了吸引新顧客
(C) 通知營業時間變更
(D) 提醒客戶預約

答案 (D)　概述

從開頭的第1句It's time for an oil change!可知，這是在通知換機油的時間。中間部分提到please schedule a service appointment with us並傳達營業時間以敦促客戶預約，所以正確答案是(D)。

□ remind～ to *do*　提醒～做……

☑ 148

On what day is the shop open only in the morning?

(A) Wednesday
(B) Friday
(C) Saturday
(D) Sunday

店家在哪一天只有上午營業？

(A) 週三
(B) 週五
(C) 週六
(D) 週日

答案 (C)　其他細節

On what day～?是問在星期幾。從營業時間可看到，只有上午營業的是8:00 A.M.-12:00 P.M.的Saturday（週六），所以(C)是正確答案。通常英文是以12小時制來表示時間，所以12:00 P.M.指的是正午12時。

試題文章	試題文章翻譯

Questions 149-150 refer to the following text message chain.

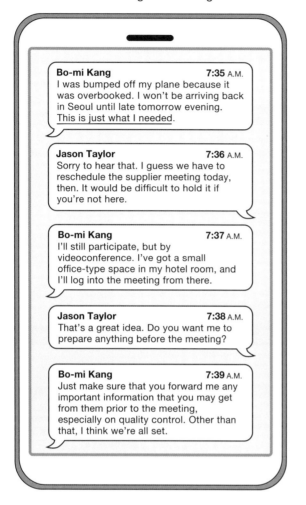

Bo-mi Kang　7:35 A.M.
I was bumped off my plane because it was overbooked. I won't be arriving back in Seoul until late tomorrow evening. This is just what I needed.

Jason Taylor　7:36 A.M.
Sorry to hear that. I guess we have to reschedule the supplier meeting today, then. It would be difficult to hold it if you're not here.

Bo-mi Kang　7:37 A.M.
I'll still participate, but by videoconference. I've got a small office-type space in my hotel room, and I'll log into the meeting from there.

Jason Taylor　7:38 A.M.
That's a great idea. Do you want me to prepare anything before the meeting?

Bo-mi Kang　7:39 A.M.
Just make sure that you forward me any important information that you may get from them prior to the meeting, especially on quality control. Other than that, I think we're all set.

試題149-150請參考以下一連串的文字通訊。

康柏米（Bo-mi Kang）　7:35 A.M.
因為機位超賣，我被擠掉機位了。明天深夜我才會回到首爾。怎麼偏偏讓我遇到這樣的事。

傑森・泰勒（Jason Taylor）　7:36 A.M.
聽到這消息真難過。我想我們得重新安排今日的供應商會議了，如果你不在，會議很難召開。

康柏米　7:37 A.M.
我還是會參加，但是要用視訊會議。我在飯店房間裡有個類似小辦公室的空間，我會從那裡參與會議。

傑森・泰勒　7:38 A.M.
這主意太棒了！在會議開始之前，你有想要我準備什麼嗎？

康柏米　7:39 A.M.
只要確保你在開會前，把你可能從他們那裡得到的任何重要訊息傳給我就行了，特別是品質控管方面的資訊。除此之外，我想我們都準備好了。

Vocabulary

- □ be [get] bumped off one's plane [flight]　（已訂位）卻被擠掉機位
- □ participate [pɑr`tɪsə‚pet] 動 參加
- □ videoconference [`vɪdɪo‚kɑnfərəns] 名 視訊會議
- □ quality control　品質控管
- □ other than~　除~之外
- □ be all set　都準備好了

試題	試題翻譯	解答與解析

☑ 149

At 7:35 A.M., why does Ms. Kang write, "This is just what I needed"?

(A) She is confused about a topic.
(B) She is opposed to a plan.
(C) She is unhappy about a price.
(D) She is irritated by a development.

7:35 A.M.，康女士為何寫了 「This is just what I needed」？

(A) 她對話題感到困惑。
(B) 她反對一項計畫。
(C) 她對價格不滿意。
(D) 事態的發展讓她不悅。

答案 (D)　　說話者的目的

畫底線的部分從字面上直譯是「這正是我需要的」，因為要搭乘的班機取消，讓她無法出席當日的會議，所以這是用來反諷的。正確答案 (D)就是指康女士的心情。

- □ be opposed to~　反對~
- □ irritate [`ɪrə‚tet] 動 引起不愉快~

☑ 150

What does Ms. Kang indicate that she will do?

(A) Move to another hotel
(B) Update an older schedule
(C) Revise a supplier contract draft
(D) Join a conference remotely

康女士表明她要做什麼？

(A) 搬到另 1 家飯店
(B) 更新舊的日程表
(C) 修改供應商合約草稿
(D) 遠端參加會議

答案 (D)　　其他細節

這題是在問康女士接下來的動作。她在上午7時37分的訊息表示，會在飯店的房間用視訊出席會議。因此(D)是正確答案。remotely是「遠距離地」，引申為「藉遠端操作、經由網路」。

- □ draft [dræft] 名 草稿

Questions 151-152 refer to the following notice.

試題151-152請參考以下通知。

Posted May 27

Please Note!

Due to unforeseen circumstances, the 17th Annual Employee Summer Party has been rescheduled for Saturday, June 23. We apologize to those of you who had already made plans to attend on June 16. Please call Suzanne Alderman in Marketing at extension 313 by Saturday, June 9 to inform her whether you will be able to attend. We have reserved the Downtown Pavilion so that, rain or shine, we will be able to enjoy a barbecue. All food and beverages will be provided. We sincerely hope to see you there.

發布日：5月27日
請注意！

由於發生不可預料的狀況，第17屆年度員工夏季派對已經改到6月23日週六舉行。我們對原預定6月16日出席的各位深表歉意。請於6月9日週六前撥打分機313給市場行銷部的蘇珊娜・奧德曼（Suzanne Alderman），通知她您是否會參加。我們已經預約了市中心大型帳篷（Downtown Pavilion），為了讓大家可以不論晴雨都能享受戶外烤肉。現場將提供所有的食品和飲料。誠摯地希望當天與您相見。

Vocabulary

- □ unforeseen [ˌʌnforˋsin] 形 不可預料的、意想不到的
- □ apologize to～ 向～道歉
- □ pavilion [pəˋvɪljən] 名 大型帳篷
- □ 〈so that S＋V〉 為了讓S做V
- □ rain or shine 不論晴雨

試題	試題翻譯	解答與解析

☑ **151**

What is the main purpose of the notice?

(A) To promote a downtown barbecue area
(B) To announce a change in plans
(C) To cancel a party
(D) To apologize to marketing employees

這則通知主要的目的是什麼？

(A) 宣傳市中心的戶外烤肉區
(B) 宣布計畫變更
(C) 取消派對
(D) 向行銷部的員工道歉

答案 (B) [概述]

整篇的目的在一開始就載明。從the 17th Annual Employee Summer Party has been rescheduled for Saturday, June 23可知派對的日期已變動，所以(B)是正確答案。rescheduled是「將～改期」。

☑ **152**

By what date should Ms. Alderman be contacted?

(A) June 9
(B) June 16
(C) June 17
(D) June 23

應該在哪天之前聯繫奧德曼女士？

(A) 6月9日
(B) 6月16日
(C) 6月17日
(D) 6月23日

答案 (A) [其他細節]

what date～?是在問日期。通知文中間的地方有出現人名奧德曼，Please call Suzanne Alderman... by Saturday, June 9，所以(A)是正確答案。(B)的June 16是派對變更前的日期，(D)June 23是派對變更後的日期。

試題文章	試題文章翻譯

Questions 153-154 refer to the following letter.

試題153-154請參考以下信件內容。

Outward Apparel, Inc.
101 Brisbane Drive
Chapel Hill, NC 27514
(919) 555-9158

May 16

Ms. Ayaka Kobayashi
332 W. Union Avenue
Wheaton, IL 60187
(630) 555-4038

Dear Ms. Kobayashi,

It is our pleasure to extend to you an offer of employment for the position of Associate Sales Representative in our Marketing Department.

Please review the following enclosed documents carefully:
1. Employment Contract and Non-compete Agreement: *Return by May 30*
2. Outline of Salary, Bonus/Commission and Benefits
3. Expenses and Travel Reimbursement Procedures
4. Outward Apparel Employee Handbook

This offer is contingent on passing a mandatory drug screening and our receipt of the Employment Contract, signed and postmarked by the date printed in bold above, in the pre-addressed envelope included with this letter. Please be aware that if we do not hear from you, this offer of employment will expire, and you will not be entitled to reapply.

If you have any questions or concerns, please do not hesitate to contact me at (919) 555-9158 ext. 2140.

Once again, congratulations. We look forward to hearing from you very soon.

Regards,

Jack Morris

Jack Morris
Director, Human Resources

奧特華德服飾有限公司（Outward Apparel Inc.）
101布里斯班大道（Brisbane Drive）
教堂山（Chapel Hill），北卡羅萊納州（NC）27514
（919）555-9158
5月16日

綾香‧小林女士（Ayaka Kobayashi）
332西聯合大道（W. Union Ave.）
惠頓（Wheaton），伊利諾州（IL）60187
（630）555-4038

親愛的小林女士：

很高興提供您本公司市場行銷部副銷售代表的職務。

請仔細檢查以下隨函附寄的文件：
1. 僱用合約書及競業禁止協議：**5月30日前寄回**
2. 薪資、獎金／佣金及福利概要
3. 支出及出差報銷手續
4. 奧特華德服飾員工手冊

本應聘有附帶條件，必須接受義務性藥物檢測，並將簽名的僱用合約書放入此信內附上的、寫有地址的信封內，郵戳日期須在前述粗體標記的日期前。請注意，如果我們沒有收到任何回音，這份聘僱函將失效，而且您將無法再有應聘的權利。

如果您有任何問題或疑慮，請別客氣撥打（919）555-9158分機2140聯繫我。

再一次恭喜您，期待很快能收到您的消息。

謹致問候

傑克‧莫里斯（Jack Morris）
人力資源部經理

Vocabulary

☐ outline [`aʊt͵laɪn] 名 概要　　☐ reimbursement [͵riɪm`bɝsmənt] 名 報銷　　☐ contingent on~ 視~條件而定

☐ mandatory [`mændə͵torɪ] 形 義務的　　☐ postmark [`post͵mɑrk] 動 在~上蓋郵戳　　☐ bold [bold] 名 粗體字

☐ expire [ɪk`spaɪr] 動（權利等）失效　　☐ entitle~ to *do* 給~做……的權利

試題	試題翻譯	解答與解析

153

What is the main purpose of the letter?

(A) To notify acceptance of an employment offer
(B) To give information about a company
(C) To offer an applicant a job
(D) To provide information on salary and benefits

這封信的主要目的是什麼？

(A) 通知接受錄取
(B) 提供有關公司的資料
(C) 給予應徵者錄取通知
(D) 提供薪資及福利資訊

答案 (C) 　概述

開頭那一句即是這封信的目的。It is our pleasure to~，對讀這封信的人而言，pleasure 是「高興」，所以會想像這是好的內容而繼續往下看。extend to~有「給予（祝賀等）」之意。從an offer of employment for...（職位錄取通知）可知(C)是正確答案。an applicant（應徵者）即是讀信的人小林女士。而(A)是以應徵者為立場的說法。

154

What information must Ms. Kobayashi send back to Outward Apparel, Inc.?

(A) A contract of employment
(B) An employee handbook
(C) An expenses procedure form
(D) A salary and bonus outline

小林女士必須要傳回什麼資料給奧特華德服飾有限公司？

(A) 僱用合約書
(B) 員工手冊
(C) 支出手續表
(D) 有關薪資及獎金概要

答案 (A) 　其他細節

在條列項目的下1段有提到，本應聘有附帶條件，our receipt of the Employment Contract, ...，受雇者被要求必須在隨函附上的僱用合約書上簽名並寄回公司。由此可知(A)是正確答案。receipt是receive的名詞形，是「收到」的意思。光憑項目1的Return by May 30（5月30日前寄回）應該也可以推測解答。

試題文章	試題文章翻譯

Questions 155-157 refer to the following news article.

試題155-157請參考以下新聞報導

KINGSTON, Jamaica, September 21—West Indies Lines Inc., Jamaica's premier cruise ship operator, announced Thursday that it will purchase the entire business assets of Sea Jewel, a Kingston-based company. Sea Jewel began its operations as a merchant shipping company in 1895, tapping into the tourism industry in 1955 as Jamaica's first independently owned cruise ship operator. The company had struggled under the economic downturn and civil unrest over the past decade, finally accepting the merger agreement in order to avoid bankruptcy. Under the agreement, Sea Jewel's fleet of older ships will be upgraded or replaced, and the number of Caribbean cruise routes and ports of call will be expanded. As a condition to the merger, West Indies Lines has agreed to guarantee retraining and rehiring of former Sea Jewel employees over a three-year period. Further details will emerge next week, following the filing of official documents with Jamaica's Ministry of Tourism. West Indies Lines expects the merger to be complete by the end of October; however, expansion of its routes and services is expected to require an additional six years to finalize.

牙買加（Jamaica），金斯敦（KINGSTON）市，9月21日——牙買加第一大郵輪公司西印度航線有限公司（West Indies Lines Inc.）週四宣布，它將收購總部位於金斯敦的海寶石（Sea Jewel）公司所有的商業資產。海寶石創設於1895年，以商船公司起家，1955年攻入觀光業成為牙買加首家擁有獨立經營權的遊艇業者。該公司在過去10年間受經濟衰退和國內動亂而苦苦掙扎，最後接受合併協議以避免破產。根據協議，海寶石的舊船隊將升級或汰換，而且加勒比海（Caribbean）的郵輪航線及停靠港口數量將有所擴展。作為合併的條件，西印度航線已同意保證再培訓及持續僱用前海寶石員工3年。牙買加旅遊局發布正式文件後，下週會有更多細節。西印度航線預計10月底前完成這項合併；不過預計其路線和服務的擴展需要額外的6年才能完成。

Vocabulary

- entire [ɪn`taɪr] 形 全體的
- asset [`æsɛt] 名 資產（用於複數形時）
- merchant [`mɝtʃənt] 形 商業的
- tap into～ 攻入～
- independently [ˌɪndɪ`pɛndəntlɪ] 副 獨立地
- struggle [`strʌg!] 動 掙扎
- economic downturn 經濟衰退
- civil unrest 國內動亂
- port of call 停靠港
- guarantee [ˌgærən`ti] 動 保證～
- rehiring [ri`haɪrɪŋ] 名 再僱用
- emerge [ɪ`mɝdʒ] 動 出現
- file [faɪl] 動 發布（文件）
- finalize [`faɪn!ˌaɪz] 動 使～結束

試題	試題翻譯	解答與解析

☑ **155**

What is the purpose of the article?

(A) To describe recent renovations to a cruise ship
(B) To report a company bankruptcy
(C) To advertise an investment opportunity
(D) To announce a business agreement

這篇報導的目的是什麼？

(A) 敘述最近郵輪的整修
(B) 報導一間公司破產
(C) 宣傳投資機會
(D) 宣布商業上的一件協議

答案 (D) 概述

報導的主題通常都置於開頭。文中一開始就說 West Indies Lines Inc., ..., announced Thursday that it will purchase the entire business assets...，(D)的business agreement（商業協議）即是在表示這件事，所以是正確答案。而整篇中間部分提到的accepting the merger agreement也可當解題關鍵。

☑ **156**

What is NOT a goal of West Indies Lines?

(A) To repair old cruise ships
(B) To expand cruise routes
(C) To hire new employees
(D) To add new ports of call

下列哪一項不是西印度航線的目標？

(A) 修繕舊郵輪
(B) 擴展航線
(C) 雇用新員工
(D) 增加新的停靠港

答案 (C) 是非題類型

什麼是西印度航線公司的合併目的？可以嘗試用消去法來解答是非題類型的題目。(A)的說法與Sea Jewel's fleet of older ships will be upgraded or replaced一致。(B)和(D)的說法則與the number of Caribbean cruise routes and ports of call will be expanded一致。至於(C)，雖然文中有提到舊海寶石員工再僱用一事，但並未提及新員工，所以是正確答案。

☑ **157**

How long is the expansion of the cruise routes expected to take?

(A) At least 3 years
(B) At least 6 years
(C) At least 10 years
(D) At least 60 years

遊輪新航線的擴展預期要多久？

(A) 最少 3 年
(B) 最少 6 年
(C) 最少 10 年
(D) 最少 60 年

答案 (B) 其他細節

expansion是「擴展、擴張」之意，從文中找出與郵輪航線相關的資料，除了中間部分提到的the number of Caribbean cruise routes and ports of call will be expanded，還有最後一句expansion of its routes and services is expected to require an additional six years to finalize。由此可知(B)是正確答案。

試題文章	試題文章翻譯

Questions 158-160 refer to the following itinerary.

試題158-160請參考以下日程表。

MONTEREY CLASSE HOTEL
- NEW EMPLOYEE ORIENTATION PROGRAM -
MONDAY, APRIL 30

8:00-9:00 A.M.
Our Human Resources (HR) Director, Janet Hills, will guide you through all the necessary Human Resources forms and paperwork to begin your employment.*

9:00-10:15 A.M.
Janet Hills will cover the most important and helpful points in the Hotel Associates' Handbook, including overtime wages, paid vacations, and 401k plans, as well as expected etiquette with hotel guests.

10:15-10:30 A.M.
Coffee break in the Employee Lounge

10:30 A.M.-12:00 P.M.
Associate Manager John Forsythe will give a guided tour of the Hotel, including guest accommodations, conference rooms, the recreation and fitness center, and our Hotel Shopping Plaza.

12:00-1:00 P.M.
Lunch will be provided in the hotel restaurant, following a short tour and explanation by Head Chef Tony Lambini.

1:00-1:30 P.M.
HR Assistant Director Eugene Provo will issue Associate ID badges, and explain the use of the time clock.

1:30-4:00 P.M.
Practical training: New associates will be assigned current associates as mentors, shadowing and assisting them where possible.

4:00-5:00 P.M.
Review, Q & A. Janet, John, and Eugene will be available to answer questions.

* Please bring a valid form of ID. This may include a driver's license, birth certificate, passport, or resident registration card.

蒙特利‧克拉斯（MONTEREY CLASSE）飯店
新進員工培訓日程
4月30日　週一

8:00-9:00 A.M.
由人事部長珍妮特‧希爾斯（Janet Hills）指導各位在開始這份工作時，所有必要的人力資源表格和文書工作*。

9:00-10:15 A.M.
珍妮特‧希爾斯將介紹飯店員工手冊中最重要和最有幫助的內容，包括加班費、有薪休假、退休福利（401k）計劃，以及與飯店客人應對的禮儀規矩。

10:15-10:30 A.M.
於員工休息室休息

10:30 A.M.-12:00 P.M.
由副理約翰‧佛賽斯（John Forsythe）帶大家導覽飯店，包括客房、會議室、休閒與健身中心，以及飯店購物廣場。

12:00-1:00 P.M.
午餐由飯店餐廳提供，主廚湯尼‧蘭比尼（Tony Lambini）做簡短的導覽及說明之後進行用餐。

1:00-1:30 P.M.
由人事副部長尤金‧普羅沃（Eugene Provo）發給員工識別證，並解說如何使用打卡鐘。

1:30-4:00 P.M.
實務訓練：新進員工會有現任員工當指導者，盡可能跟隨在旁及給予協助。

4:00-5:00 P.M.
總結與提問。由珍妮特、約翰和尤金解答。

＊請攜帶有效身分證件。如駕照、出生證明、護照或居民登記卡等。

Vocabulary

☐ associate [ə`soʃɪɪt] 名 同事、員工　　☐ overtime wage　加班薪資　　☐ paid vacation　有薪休假　　☐ etiquette [`ɛtɪkɛt] 名 禮儀規矩

☐ issue [`ɪʃjʊ] 動 發給～　　☐ practical [`præktɪk!] 形 實際的　　☐ assign A B　將B分配給A　　☐ mentor [`mɛntɚ] 名 指導者

☐ shadow [`ʃædo] 動 （如影般地）跟隨～學習　　☐ birth certificate　出生證明　　☐ resident registration　居民登記

試題	試題翻譯	解答與解析

☑ 158

What is required for the HR paperwork?

(A) A form of identification
(B) A training handbook
(C) An employee badge
(D) An orientation form

人力資源部門的書面作業需要什麼？

(A) 身分證明
(B) 培訓手冊
(C) 員工識別證
(D) 培訓表格

答案 (A)　其他細節

8:00-9:00 A.M.時段有提到HR paperwork（人力資源書面作業）。重點放在句尾最後「*」註記，再往整篇最下面看，寫著Please bring a valid form of ID。這個部分即是正確答案(A)的A form of identification。ID是identification（身分證明）的縮寫。

☑ 159

When will the employees most likely learn about workplace guidelines?

(A) From 8:00 A.M. to 9:00 A.M.
(B) From 9:00 A.M. to 10:15 A.M.
(C) From 12:00 P.M. to 1:00 P.M.
(D) From 1:30 P.M. to 4:00 P.M.

員工何時最有可能了解職場準則？

(A) 8:00-9:00 A.M.
(B) 9:00-10:15 A.M.
(C) 12:00-1:00 P.M.
(D) 1:30-4:00 P.M.

答案 (B)　推測

看到most likely（最有可能）的推測問題，如果整篇文章沒有很明顯的根據時，就要從可能性最高的選項來思考。9:00-10:15 A.M.有overtime wages（加班費）及paid vacations（有薪休假）等的說明，由此可判斷為workplace guidelines（職場準則）。如果只挑workplace（職場）來判斷，或許會誤以為是進行飯店導覽的10:30 A.M.-12:00 P.M.，總之，該時段不是正確選項。

☑ 160

Who will NOT be in the question-and-answer session?

(A) The HR director
(B) The associate manager
(C) The head chef
(D) The HR assistant director

誰不會參加問答時間？

(A) 人事部長
(B) 副理
(C) 主廚
(D) 人事副部長

答案 (C)　是非題類型

question-and-answer session是指「問答時間」，意即4:00-5:00 P.M.的Q&A。雖然這是由珍妮特、約翰和尤金解答提問，不過這題的選項都是職稱，從這3位的職稱來看，珍妮特是負責8:00-9:00 A.M.的人事部長，約翰是負責10:30 A.M.-12:00 P.M.的副理，尤金是負責1:00-1:30 P.M.的人事副部長。由此可知，不會參加提問的人是(C)。

Questions 161-164 refer to the following online chat.

Timoshenko, Galina [9:43 A.M.]
Okay, everyone seems to be online now. CMO Linda Franks wants an update on our marketing campaign to support our new cola release. <u>Tell me where we're at with that.</u>

Foster, Herbert [9:44 A.M.]
Our section has proposed that we run a campaign mainly focused on teens and young adults. That's actually our customer base.

Timoshenko, Galina [9:46 A.M.]
We're missing something. In many of those cases, parents are actually making the purchase decision ... for example, buying one case of cola or another.

Harris, Christopher [9:48 A.M.]
Then our marketing campaign should be big and broad enough to appeal to entire families.

Qureshi, Kadijah [9:49 A.M.]
That would mean going back and redesigning all of the work that we have done so far. It'd put a lot of pressure on my section.

Conseco, Jorge [9:50 A.M.]
Not necessarily. We could keep the advertisements that we already have—the ones that center on young people. Then we add more with parents and entire families. It would cost extra, but not too much. Rebecca Levy's research suggests that this marketing style would be successful.

Timoshenko, Galina [9:51 A.M.]
I hope so. Have her explain that idea to Ms. Franks in a formal proposal.

試題161-164請參考以下線上交談內容。

佳琳娜・季莫申科（Timoshenko, Galina）　9:43 A.M.
好，大家似乎都已上線了。市場總監琳達・法蘭克斯（Linda Franks）想要知道我們支援新品可樂發布會的行銷活動最新進展。告訴我目前我們進度到哪裡了。

赫伯特・佛斯特（Foster, Herbert）　9:44 A.M.
我們部門建議我們做一場主要針對青少年及年輕人的活動。實際上他們是我們的基本客戶群。

佳琳娜・季莫申科　9:46 A.M.
我們遺漏了某些重點。在許多情況下，實際上父母才是決定是否購買的人⋯⋯例如，要買1箱可樂或是買別的。

克里斯多福・哈里斯（Harris, Christopher）　9:48 A.M.
那麼我們的行銷活動應該夠大而廣泛，才足以吸引全家人。

卡地亞・庫雷斯（Qureshi, Kadijah）　9:49 A.M.
那意味著得回到原點且重新設計我們目前已做好的所有工作。這可是把很多壓力加在我的部門啊！

喬治・康賽科（Conseco, Jorge）　9:50 A.M.
不見得！我們可以保留我們已有的廣告，那些以年輕人為中心的廣告。然後再追加更多瞄準父母及整個家庭的內容。雖會增加額外成本，但不至於太多。根據雷貝卡・利維（Rebecca Levy）的研究建議，這樣的行銷模式將會成功。

佳琳娜・季莫申科　9:51 A.M.
希望如此。那就讓她用正式提案的方式向法蘭克斯女士解釋那個想法。

Vocabulary

☐ CMO　市場總監（Chief Marketing Officer）　　☐ put pressure on～　施加壓力於～

試題	試題翻譯	解答與解析

☑ 161

At 9:43 A.M., what does Ms. Timoshenko mean when she writes, "Tell me where we're at with that"?

(A) A project needs funding.
(B) An explanation is required.
(C) A plan has been delivered.
(D) A direction has been confirmed.

9:43 A.M.，季莫申科女士寫著 「Tell me where we're at with that」，這代表什麼？

(A) 一項計畫需要資金。
(B) 需要做說明。
(C) 計畫已被實行。
(D) 方向已被確認。

答案 (B) 〔說話者的目的〕

畫底線句的that是指前面提到的marketing campaign（行銷活動），從大家針對行銷活動陸續做意見交換可知，季莫申科女士希望其他成員做的是(B)。

☑ 162

In what sort of industry does Ms. Timoshenko most likely work?

(A) Health regulation
(B) Food and beverages
(C) Catering services
(D) Hospitality and travel

季莫申科女士最有可能在哪一種產業工作？

(A) 健康管理業
(B) 食品飲料業
(C) 餐飲服務
(D) 接待及旅遊業

答案 (B) 〔概述〕

季莫申科女士一開始就詢問其他職員有關「支援新可樂發布會的市場行銷活動」的意見。在9:46 A.M.時也提到cola（可樂），「決定要買1箱可樂或是買別的（飲料）是父母」，由此可判斷(B)是正確答案。

☐ regulation [ˌrɛgjəˈleʃən] 名 管理
☐ hospitality [ˌhɑspɪˈtælətɪ] 名 好客、接待

☑ 163

According to the discussion, whose department would be most affected by a change?

(A) Hebert Foster's department
(B) Christopher Harris' department
(C) Kadijah Qureshi's department
(D) Jorge Conseco's department

根據這場討論，哪個部門會因變更而受最大影響？

(A) 赫伯特 ・ 佛斯特的部門
(B) 克里斯多福 ・ 哈里斯的部門
(C) 卡地亞 ・ 庫雷斯的部門
(D) 喬治 ・ 康賽科的部門

答案 (C) 〔其他細節〕

卡地亞・庫雷斯對於克里斯多福・哈里斯提到行銷活動應該要大而廣泛並以全家人為對象時，說了It'd put a lot of pressure on my section，所以(C)是正確答案。

☑ 164

What will Ms. Levy most likely inform Ms. Franks about?

(A) The sales from a quarter
(B) The date of a confirmation
(C) The expansion of a budget
(D) The advantages of a project

利維女士最有可能向法蘭克斯女士報告什麼？

(A) 1 季的銷售額
(B) 確認的日期
(C) 預算的擴大
(D) 該計畫的優點

答案 (D) 〔其他細節〕

喬治在9:50 A.M.的發言提到了利維。「根據雷貝卡・利維的研究建議，這樣行銷模式將會成功的」，季莫申科對此回應Have her explain that idea to Ms. Franks in a formal proposal。her即是指雷貝卡・利維，所以(D)是正確答案。

Questions 165-167 refer to the following e-mail.

* E-mail *	✕
To:	Janet Simmons <jsimmons@ad-industrial.com>
From:	Ernest Puget <epuget@ad-industrial.com>
Subject:	Well done!
Date:	April 13

Dear Ms. Simmons:

I am writing to commend you on your work with the Andersen design committee last week. —[1]—. As you know, Andersen is one of our newest clients. Your attention to detail in your capacity as a planning consultant is exemplary, as your evaluation of Andersen's new rotor mechanism plan caught a hidden design flaw, helping our client to avoid some very costly production errors. —[2]—. Andersen committee's managing director called me personally to offer thanks, particularly for your suggestions to improve their design plan.

I am open to discussing the possibility of advancing you to top planning consultant in the near future. —[3]—. I would be grateful if you would verify any design improvement suggestions with me in advance, before formally offering them to the client. This will help me coordinate with Andersen's committee chairperson in the event you are temporarily unavailable.

—[4]—. I look forward to your detailed report on Andersen next week.

Sincerely,

Ernest Puget
Sales Director, Advanced Industrial Inc.

試題165-167請參考以下電子郵件。

收信者：珍妮特・席夢思（Janet Simmons）
<jsimmons@ad-industrial.com>
發信者：歐尼斯特・普吉特（Ernest Puget）
<epuget@ad-industrial.com>
主旨：做得好！
日期：4月13日

親愛的席夢思女士：

我寫這封信是想讚揚您上週與安德森（Andersen）設計委員會工作一事。—〔1〕—。如您所知，安德森是我們最新的客戶之一。身為設計顧問，您的能力中對細節的關注就是一個模範。您在評估安德森新型旋轉輪機械構造的設計圖時，發現了一個隱藏的設計缺陷，幫助我們的客戶避免一些代價極高的生產錯誤。—〔2〕—。安德森委員會的常務董事親自來電致謝，特別是對於您提出改進設計圖的建議。

我很樂意討論在不久的將來把您晉升到最高設計顧問的可能性。—〔3〕—同時，我有個請求。如果您能事先向我確認任何設計改進的建議，然後再正式提供給客戶，我將不勝感激。要是遇到您臨時不在的狀況，這會有助於我與安德森委員會主席進行協調。

—〔4〕—。期待您下週關於安德森的詳細報告。

謹致問候

歐尼斯特・普吉特
先進（Advanced）產業公司銷售主管

Vocabulary

□ commend A on B　因B讚揚A～　　□ exemplary [ɪgˋzɛmplərɪ] 形 模範的　　□ evaluation [ɪ͵væljʊˋeʃən] 名 評價

□ costly [ˋkɔstlɪ] 形 昂貴的　　□ advance A to B　將A提升為B　　□ coordinate with～　與～配合

□ chairperson [ˋtʃɛr͵pɝsn] 名 主席　　□ temporarily [ˋtɛmpə͵rɛrəlɪ] 副 一時地

試題	試題翻譯	解答與解析

☑ **165**

Who most likely is Ms. Simmons?

(A) A managing director
(B) A sales director
(C) A consultant
(D) A committee chair

席夢思女士最有可能是誰？

(A) 常務董事
(B) 銷售主管
(C) 顧問
(D) 委員長

答案 (C) 〔推測〕

席夢思女士是電子郵件的收信人。第1段的Your attention to detail in your capacity as a planning consultant is exemplary有提到「身為設計顧問」，所以(C)是正確答案。第2段的 advancing you to top planning consultant也是作答的線索。

☑ **166**

What is suggested about Ms. Simmons?

(A) She found a mistake in a client's plan.
(B) She acquired a new client.
(C) She met with the sales director.
(D) She gave a report.

關於席夢思女士，下列何者正確？

(A) 她在一位客戶的設計圖裡發現了一個錯誤。
(B) 她獲得一位新客戶。
(C) 她與銷售主管見面。
(D) 她做了報告。

答案 (A) 〔推測〕

從第1段的your evaluation of Andersen's new rotor mechanism plan caught a hidden design flaw可知(A)是正確答案。flaw是「瑕疵」之意，選項將它改成mistake（錯誤）。a client（一位客戶）即是指Andersen。

☐ acquire [əˋkwaɪr] 動 獲得～

☑ **167**

In which of the positions marked [1], [2], [3], and [4] does the following sentence best belong?

"Meanwhile, I have one request."

(A) [1]
(B) [2]
(C) [3]
(D) [4]

下面這 1 句應該插入標記 〔1〕、〔2〕、〔3〕、〔4〕 的哪一個位置？

「同時，我有個請求。」

(A) 〔1〕
(B) 〔2〕
(C) 〔3〕
(D) 〔4〕

答案 (C) 〔插入句〕

從插入句的Meanwhile（同時）可以看出，空格要放的位置是前、後句有相反意味的內容。看到one request先假設後面就是接具體的內容，所以如果放在〔3〕的位置，前句說的是帶給對方好消息的「想要晉升您做最高設計顧問」，後面接的即是要請求對方的事I would be grateful if you would...，因此正確答案就是(C)。

☐ meanwhile [ˋminˏhwaɪl] 副 同時

Questions 168-171 refer to the following information.

Addison *Insta-Print*™ Laser Printer
～ Statement of Limited Warranty ～

Thank you for purchasing an Addison printer.

This Limited Warranty guarantees to the consumer that Addison printers will be free from defects in material and workmanship for a period of 2 years from the date of purchase from an Authorized Addison Retailer. At the time of purchase, the consumer may elect to purchase an additional 3 years of coverage under the Extended Warranty plan (see Owner's Manual, p. 9).

The Limited Warranty and Extended Warranty are not valid unless registered with Addison by the original consumer. To register your printer, please fill in and mail the Registration Card (included in the Owner's Manual, p. 95) as well as a copy of your original Purchase Invoice using the postage-prepaid envelope immediately after purchase. Terms of Warranty cannot be honored if the product is not registered in advance.

To request warranty service or to report a defect, please call the Addison Technical Support Hotline at 1-800-555-1252 or send an e-mail to limitedwarranty@addison-printer.com. Please have your registration number ready as well as the last four digits of your original Purchase Invoice number.

For issues that cannot be resolved via telephone or e-mail, Addison will arrange to dispatch a technician from an Authorized Service Center nearest to your printer's location. For printers that cannot be repaired on-site, Addison may elect either to repair the printer at an Authorized Service Center, or to replace it, free of charge. However, please be advised that repair processes can take up to 5 business days.

試題168-171請參考以下資訊。

愛迪生（Addison）即時印刷（Insta-Prin）雷射印表機
限制保固書

感謝購買愛迪生印表機。

本限制保固，係針對愛迪生印表機在材料和製品上之瑕疵，自消費者從授權零售商購入印表機之日起2年內提供保固。在購買時，消費者可選購延長保固計畫（見使用手冊第9頁）以獲得額外3年的保固。

有限保固及延展保固除非由原消費者在愛迪生登錄，否則無效。為登錄您的印表機，請於購買後立刻填妥登錄卡（在使用手冊第95頁），連同原購買發票副本用郵資已付的信封寄出。產品若未事先登錄，保固條款將無法被履行。

需要保固服務或回報瑕疵，請撥打愛迪生技術支援熱線1-800-555-1252，或寄電子郵件至limitedwarranty@addison-printer.com。並請提供登錄號碼及原購買發票號碼後4碼。

若電話或電子郵件方式未能解決問題，愛迪生將安排離您印表機所在位置最近的授權服務中心，派遣一位技術人員前往服務。當場無法修復印表機者，愛迪生可以決定在授權服務中心修理或是免費更換印表機。但是，請注意修復過程可能需要5個工作日。

Vocabulary

- □ warranty [`wɔrəntɪ] 名 保固
- □ consumer [kən`sjumɚ] 名 消費者
- □ workmanship [`wɝkmən ʃɪp] 名 製品
- □ elect to *do* 決定做～
- □ coverage [`kʌvərɪdʒ] 名 保固項目
- □ honor [`ɑnɚ] 動 履行～
- □ on-site [`ɑn saɪt] 副 在現場

試題	試題翻譯	解答與解析

☑ **168**

How long is the optional Extended Warranty period?

(A) One year
(B) Two years
(C) Three years
(D) Four years

可選擇的延長保固期間是多久？

(A) 1 年
(B) 2 年
(C) 3 年
(D) 4 年

答案 (C)　　其他細節

這是1篇有關印表機的保固內容。針對Limited Warranty（限制保固）與Extended Warranty（延長保固）做說明。延長保固期間在第2段有提到an additional 3 years of coverage under the Extended Warranty plan，在購買時加購的話，有外加的3年期間，所以(C)是正確答案。(B)指的是有限保固的期間。

☑ **169**

The word "honored" in paragraph 3, line 5, is closest in meaning to

(A) modified
(B) guaranteed
(C) divided
(D) praised

第 3 段第 5 行的單字 「honored」 意思最接近下列哪一個？

(A) 被修改
(B) 被保固
(C) 被分割
(D) 被稱讚

答案 (B)　　同義詞

整句的語意是「產品若未事先登錄，保固條款將無法～」。從if後面的內容來看，推測cannot be honored是指「保固無效、不適用」。這句的honor是「遵守（協議、約定）、履行」之意，因此可判斷由(B)的guarantee（保固）來作為主詞warranty（保固）的動詞最合適。如果只單看honor而想成「稱讚～」的意思就會誤選(D)了。

☑ **170**

What must customers who need repairs do?

(A) Take the printer to Addison
(B) Wait five business days
(C) Call an Authorized Service Center
(D) Contact Addison Technical Support

需要維修的消費者一定要做什麼？

(A) 帶印表機到愛迪生
(B) 等 5 個工作日
(C) 打電話到授權服務中心
(D) 聯絡愛迪生的技術支援

答案 (D)　　其他細節

瑕疵的對應方法在第4段有指示，要撥打熱線與愛迪生技術支援聯絡或寄電子郵件。(D)將這2種方式統稱為contact（聯絡），所以是正確答案。(A)帶印表機到愛迪生的方法，文中並未提及。(B)這是維修可能所需的天數。(C)的Authorized Service Center是「授權服務中心」，但不是跟其連絡。

☑ **171**

What does Addison additionally offer to do?

(A) Send repair instructions
(B) Send a technician
(C) Extend the Limited Warranty
(D) Give the customer a refund

愛迪生額外提供什麼？

(A) 寄維修說明書
(B) 派遣技術人員
(C) 延長有限保固
(D) 退款給消費者

答案 (B)　　其他細節

第5段提到萬一用電話或電子郵件無法解決問題的狀況。從Addison will arrange to dispatch a technician from…可知(B)是正確答案。arrange to～是「安排～」，dispatch是「派遣～」。即使不知道dispatch的意思，從a technician from an Authorized Service Center nearest to your printer's location 也可以推測答案。

Questions 172-175 refer to the following article.

City OKs Funds for Downtown Landmark
Friday, March 30

Since its construction in 1891, the Mercantile Exchange building on 7th Street and 4th Avenue has been a city centerpiece. It was a hub of commerce and one of Easton's first department stores for more than half a century before a portion of it was destroyed by fire in 1955. The Mercantile closed and, in the years that followed, suburbanization took its toll on Easton's downtown vitality. The gradual relocation of people and businesses outside the city center blighted the once-affluent neighborhood, slowly turning majestic rows of Victorian mansions into crumbling tenements. —[1]—.

Easton's downtown revitalization projects turned the downtown neighborhood around in the 1990s. Mayor Robert Barker commented, "The rows of historic homes are beautiful again, and the streets much safer and cleaner." However, the Mercantile Exchange building was left out of the revitalization. It lay vacant as appeals to restore the building repeatedly faltered in year after year of legislative wrangling over thin budgets. —[2]—. On Thursday city officials approved long-awaited funding to restore the complex, with plans to convert the upper half into premium condominiums while furnishing the ground level with an array of shops and restaurants. Chief project engineer Glen Hill remarks, "We're really excited. At long last, the city center's jewel will shine again."

One problem remains. The building is crowned with a clock tower that, in a bygone era, rang out the time to downtown passersby. However, the clock has remained frozen in time, along with the building, since the 1955 fire. "We're going to fix the clock, but repairing the bells too might be a problem with our new residents," said Hill. —[3]—. The Easton Historical Society advocates preserving the building's originality as closely as possible. "The clock chimes were always a part of the neighborhood in the past, and they should be again," said society president Shawna Michaels, who proposes reducing chime volume or restricting the times when the clock would chime. —[4]—. But project managers and city officials aren't yet convinced. Barker comments, "Who would want to be reminded what time it is every 15 minutes by huge bells?"

市府批准商業區地標的資金
3月30日 週五

自1891年建設以來,第7街和第4大道的商業交易(Mercantile Exchange)大樓已成為城市的核心所在。在其中一部分於1955年被大火燒毀之前,它曾是商業中心,而且是伊斯頓市(Easton)歷經半個世紀之久的首家百貨公司之一。商業交易大樓關閉,在接下來的幾年中,郊區化對伊斯頓市中心的活力造成傷害。人們和商業逐漸往市中心以外遷移,使曾經富饒的鄰近地區受到破壞,慢慢地將宏偉成排的維多利亞時代豪宅變成破碎的廉價住宅。—〔1〕—這種情況一直持續了約一世代的時間。

1990年代伊斯頓市中心的重振計畫,讓市中心的鄰近地區有了轉變。市長羅伯特‧巴克(Robert Barker)表示:「歷史悠久的成排住宅再度美麗,而且街道更安全,更乾淨」。然而,商業交易大樓是被排除在重振計畫外的。在議院微薄預算的爭辯中,一再減弱的修復該建築的呼籲,使大樓持續空置。—〔2〕—。市府官員終於在週四批准了期待已久的資金來修復這棟綜合大樓,並計劃將上半部改為高級公寓,同時在1樓提供很多的商店和餐廳。該計畫的首席工程師格倫‧希爾(Glen Hill)談到,「我們真的很興奮。終於,市中心的寶石將再度閃耀。」

有個問題依然存在。這棟建築的頂樓為鐘樓,在逝去的歲月裡,它為市中心來往的行人敲響了時間。然而,自1955年火災以來,這座鐘已經與大樓一起被凍結在時間裡。希爾表示,「我們正在整修這座鐘,但回復的鐘聲也可能會對我們的新居民造成困擾」。—〔3〕—。伊斯頓歷史學會主張盡可能保持建築的原創性。該學會主席蕭納‧麥可斯(Shawna Michaels)說,「這座鐘的鐘聲過去一直是這個地區的一部份,它們應該再次如此。」,並建議減低鐘聲音量或限制鐘響的時間。—〔4〕—。但這部分尚未說服專案經理及市府官員。「我不認為有人會想每15分鐘就有鐘響來提醒現在幾點。」巴克市長對此下了評論。

Vocabulary

- commerce [`kɑmɚs] 名 商業
- suburbanization [sʌbˌɚbənɪ`zeʃən] 名 郊區化
- take *one's* toll on～ 對～造成損失
- vitality [vaɪ`tæləti] 名 活力
- affluent [`æfluənt] 形 富饒的
- turn A into B A變成B
- crumble [`krʌmbl̩] 動 粉碎
- tenement [`tɛnəmənt] 名 廉價公寓
- revitalization [riˌvaɪtəlɑɪ`zeʃən] 名 重振
- falter [`fɔltɚ] 動 衰退
- legislative [`lɛdʒɪsˌletɪv] 形 立法的
- wrangling [`ræŋglɪŋ] 名 爭辯
- complex [`kɑmplɛks] 名 綜合建築
- convert A into B 將A改為B
- an array of～ 大量的～
- advocate [`ædvəˌket] 動 主張
- convince [kən`vɪns] 動 說服～

試題	試題翻譯	解答與解析

 172

Why did the Mercantile Exchange close?

(A) Part of the building was a tenement.
(B) There was a fire in the building.
(C) The neighborhood became unsafe.
(D) The clock tower was too noisy.

為何商業交易大樓關閉？

(A) 部分建築物是廉價公寓。
(B) 因建築物火災。
(C) 鄰近地區變得不安全。
(D) 鐘塔太吵。

答案 (B) 〔其他細節〕

有關大樓關閉，在第1段的The Mercantile closed and...有提到。原因應是前句說的a portion of it was destroyed by fire in 1955，所以(B)是正確答案。a portion of～是「～的一部分」。

173

The word "blighted" in paragraph 1, line 13, is closest in meaning to

(A) conserved
(B) acknowledged
(C) renovated
(D) damaged

第 1 段第 13 行的單字 「blighted」 意思最接近下列哪一個？

(A) 保存
(B) 承認
(C) 修繕
(D) 受到破壞

答案 (D) 〔同義詞〕

the once-affluent neighborhood意指商業交易大樓曾使該市成為商業重鎮。而大樓關閉讓人們移往市郊和商業外流，曾經富饒的商業區變成如何？blight有「（都市等）受到毀壞」之意，(D)的damage（破壞）意思最接近。即使不知道blight的意思，因為第1段全部都是描述負面形象的語句，所以作答時可以推測答案是負面的單字，或是用消去法亦可，(A)、(B)、(C)都是正面形象單字，因此應該選(D)。

174

What will happen to the clock?

(A) It will be sold.
(B) It will be taken down.
(C) It will be repaired.
(D) It will be left as it is.

時鐘將會發生什麼事？

(A) 被賣掉。
(B) 被拆掉。
(C) 被修繕。
(D) 保持原貌。

答案 (C) 〔其他細節〕

請參考第3段有關大樓時鐘的描述。希爾先生表示，We're going to fix the clock, but repairing the bells too...，所以可知時鐘要修繕（鐘聲尚有討論空間）。因此(C)為正確答案。

175

In which of the positions marked [1], [2], [3], and [4] does the following sentence best belong?

"The situation stayed that way for nearly a generation."

(A) [1]
(B) [2]
(C) [3]
(D) [4]

下面這一句應該插入標記 〔1〕、〔2〕、〔3〕、〔4〕 的哪一個位置？

「這種情況一直持續了約一世代的時間。」

(A) 〔1〕
(B) 〔2〕
(C) 〔3〕
(D) 〔4〕

答案 (A) 〔插入句〕

插入句的The situation及that way是承接前面的內容。第1段提到了「1955年商業交易大樓關閉，富饒的商業區變為破碎的廉價公寓」。另外，接著第2段又說到「1990年代這個地區被重建」的內容。換句話說，一直到重建為止大約花了35年的時間（＝大約一世代），所以插入句放在第1段的最後最符合語意。因此(A)為正確答案。

Questions 176-180 refer to the following survey and report.

試題176-180請參考以下問卷調查及報告。

SOUTH SHORE CITY

SURVEY # 8010: AMENITIES & SERVICES

Dear Residents,

Your feedback on the following proposed changes to Town Council policy would be greatly appreciated. For each proposal, please choose: agree, disagree, or no opinion.

< Proposals >

1. A fee should be charged for use of public toilets.

   Agree ☐   Disagree ☐   or   No opinion ☐

2. The Community Swimming Pool needs better facilities for child care.

   Agree ☐   Disagree ☐   or   No opinion ☐

3. Park land at the north end of Beau Beach may be sold for privately owned low-density apartments.

   Agree ☐   Disagree ☐   or   No opinion ☐

4. Sidewalk boulevards bordering public roads and adjacent to residential properties will no longer be mowed by the Council.

   Agree ☐   Disagree ☐   or   No opinion ☐

These issues will be discussed at an open Town Council meeting on May 12 at 7 P.M. in the General Assembly Hall, which the public is welcome to attend and take part in.

[**Please post your survey response to PO Box 28, South Shore City, by May 7.**]

REPORT ON RESPONSES TO SURVEY #8010

(compiled on May 8, 4 P.M.)

Feedback was solicited from the general public on four proposals that will be debated in the open Town Council meeting next week.

Proposal 1   70% of respondents indicated they disagree with this proposal. The balance was evenly divided between the other two options.

Proposal 2   "Agree" and "Disagree" votes were 40% and 32% respectively. The number of people supporting the proposal or who indicate no opinion suggests this is a viable area for change.

Proposal 3   Respondents indicated that this would not be a popular move (80%).

Proposal 4   Positive response was 55%. Many residents already mow their own sidewalk boulevards.

These and any other issues that the Council may wish to advocate at the public meeting will have to be persuasively argued if the survey results can be considered an accurate picture of the wider public stance. It should be noted that the number of responses was smaller than anticipated, which raises questions about the level of interest of the residents as well as how the survey was distributed and collected.

南岸市（SOUTH SHORE CITY）
問卷調查編號＃8010：便利設施與服務

親愛的市民：
非常感謝您對以下擬議中的市議會政策變更提出回饋意見。每一項提案，請勾選同意、不同意或沒意見。

＜提案＞
1. 使用公廁應收取費用。
   同意☐　不同意☐　沒意見☐
2. 社區游泳池需要更好的孩童托育設施。
   同意☐　不同意☐　沒意見☐
3. 博海灘（Beau Beach）最北端的公園土地可以出售為私人擁有的低密度公寓。
   同意☐　不同意☐　沒意見☐
4. 與公共道路相鄰且毗鄰住宅物業的人行道，將不再由議會安排割草。
   同意☐　不同意☐　沒意見☐

上述提案將於5月12日晚上7時在大會堂開放的市議會上討論，歡迎大家出席並參與。

〔請於5月7日前將您的調查回覆郵寄到南岸市28號郵政信箱〕

有關問卷調查編號＃8010結果報告
（於5月8日下午4時彙整）

將於下週的開放市議會上進行辯論的4項提案，已收集到公眾的相關意見回饋。

提案1　70％的回覆者表示不同意此提案。其餘均勻分布在其他兩個選項。
提案2　同意和不同意的票數分別為40％和32％。從支持該提案或沒意見的人數顯示，這是一個可執行改變的領域。
提案3　回覆者表示這不是一個受歡迎的改變（80％）。
提案4　正面支持的答案是55％。許多市民已經在自己修剪他們人行道的草坪。

如果調查結果可以被認為是對更廣泛的公眾立場的準確描述，那麼議會可能希望在公開會議上討論的任何其他問題都必須以有力的辯論來說服民眾。該注意的是，問卷調查回覆的數量比預期的少，隨之而來問題是居民關注的程度及這項調查如何分發與收集。

Vocabulary

- amenity [əˈmɛnɪtɪ] 名 （常用複數形）（都市等的）便利設施、環境
- low-density [loˈdɛnsətɪ] 形 低密度的
- boulevard [ˈbuləˌvɑrd] 名 大道
- adjacent to～ 與～毗鄰的
- mow [mo] 動 割（草坪）
- solicit [səˈlɪsɪt] 動 徵求～
- respectively [rɪˈspɛktɪvlɪ] 副 各自地、分別地
- persuasively [pəˈswesɪvlɪ] 有說服力地
- anticipate [ænˈtɪsəˌpet] 動 預期～
- distribute [dɪˈstrɪbjʊt] 動 分發～

試題	試題翻譯	解答與解析

☑ 176

When will the survey results be discussed?

(A) May 7
(B) May 8
(C) May 12
(D) May 28

何時要討論調查結果？

(A) 5 月 7 日
(B) 5 月 8 日
(C) 5 月 12 日
(D) 5 月 28 日

答案 (C)　其他細節

從第1篇「問卷調查」文件的下方有1句These issues will be discussed at an open Town Council meeting on May 12 at 7 P.M. in...，意即5月12日要討論調查結果。因此(C)是正確答案。雖然這2則都有出現日期，不過憑第1篇就可作答。(A)是指提出問卷調查的最後日期，(B)是指第2篇「報告」，彙整調查結果的日期。

☑ 177

What do the results suggest about the Community Swimming Pool?

(A) It is likely to get new facilities for kids.
(B) The proposal to improve it will be rejected.
(C) A large number of people use the pool.
(D) A fee should be charged for using the pool.

社區游泳池的調查結果建議為何？

(A) 很可能為孩童們提供新設施。
(B) 改進的提議將被拒絕。
(C) 許多的人使用游泳池。
(D) 使用游泳池應收取費用。

答案 (A)　推測

這題跟2篇內容都有關係。有關社區游泳池的議案是放在「問卷調查」的提案2「需要更好的孩童托育設施」。另外就是「報告」中對於提案2的調查結果，同意和不同意者分別為40％和32％，若是同意者和沒意見的人數合計，就形成this is a viable area for change（這是一個可執行改變的領域），所以(A)為正確答案。viable是「可執行的」。(B)可能是提案1和3的內容，(D)的收費是與提案1的公廁議題相關。

☑ 178

What percent of respondents indicated no opinion toward public toilet fees?

(A) 15%
(B) 30%
(C) 40%
(D) 55%

百分之幾的回覆者對公廁收費沒有意見？

(A) 15%
(B) 30%
(C) 40%
(D) 55%

答案 (A)　其他細節

這題跟2篇內容都有關係。提案1有提到公廁的相關議題。Disagree（不同意）是70%。evenly是「均勻地」，the other two options是指Agree和No opinion，意即「同意」和「沒意見」各佔一半。換句話說「沒意見」的是（100-70）÷2＝15，所以(A)是正確答案。

☑ 179

What proposal was least popular among residents?

(A) Fees for public toilets
(B) Better facilities for the swimming pool
(C) The sale of park land for apartments
(D) Private responsibility for lawnmowing

哪個提案最不受居民歡迎？

(A) 公廁收費
(B) 更好的游泳池設施
(C) 售出公園用地作為公寓大樓
(D) 對草坪修剪的私人責任

答案 (C)　其他細節

這題跟2篇內容都有關係。選項(A)～(D)的內容分別與「問卷調查」的提案1～4相符。在「報告」中分別可看到每項提案的調查結果，提案3有80%反對，可以說是最不受歡迎的提案。所以代表提案3所述內容的(C)為正確答案。

□ responsibility for～　對～的責任
□ lawnmowing [lɔn`moɪŋ] 名 草坪修剪

☑ 180

What is NOT indicated about the survey?

(A) It was collected through the Internet.
(B) Results will be available to the public.
(C) There were fewer responses than expected.
(D) The response was negative to some proposals.

有關這項問卷調查，下列何者沒有被提到？

(A) 透過網路回收。
(B) 結果將對民眾公開。
(C) 回覆人數少於預期。
(D) 對某些提案的回答是否定的。

答案 (A)　是非題類型

「問卷調查」的最後指示要用郵寄方式回覆，所以(A)不是這項調查的方法。(B)符合「問卷調查」末尾提到的an open Town Council meeting以及the public is welcome to attend。(C)的說法則符合「報告」的最後一句the number of responses was smaller than anticipated。(D)從「報告」中可看出提案1及提案3有很多反對意見。

Questions 181-185 refer to the following press release and e-mail.

RIO DE JANEIRO, Brazil, December 1 — Bahia Industrial, based in Brasilia and specializing in small appliance production, announced Thursday plans to construct a new factory in Rio de Janeiro. The expansion is expected to generate as many as 700 new jobs, as well as improve production time for its new line of small refrigerators, whose sales have surged more than 230 percent since their introduction in April of last year. According to a Bahia Industrial representative, sales of other small electric appliances have enjoyed similar increases, thanks to the company's investment in newer, more efficient production equipment, and focus on attracting and retaining skilled labor. The Rio de Janeiro facility is expected to be operational by April of next year. Further details will be announced at the next Bahia Industrial shareholders' meeting on December 27.

里約熱內盧（RIO DE JANEIRO），巴西（Brazil），12月1日——總部位於巴西利亞（Brasilia），專門從事小型設備生產的巴伊亞工業（Bahia Industrial）於週四宣布計畫在里約熱內盧建造一座新工廠。公司的擴張預計將產生多達700個的新職位，並降低新系列小冰箱的生產時間，自去年4月導入以來，其銷售額激增230%以上。據巴伊亞工業的代表表示，由於公司投資更新、更有效率的生產設備，並致力於吸引與留住熟練的工人，讓其他小型電力設備的銷售額也有類似的成長。里約熱內盧工廠預計明年4月前開始營運。更多細節將於12月27日的下一次巴伊亞工業股東會上公布。

E-Mail Message ✕

To:	Janice Cleveland <jaycee4me@bahiaind.co.br>
From:	Steven Pallin <spallin@sales-bahiaind.co.br>
Date:	December 3
Subject:	Thank you

Dear Ms. Cleveland,

I just received the draft copy of the press release you sent me. Wonderful work. I'd like to commend you on your efforts as our chief marketing representative.

Before we send it off to press, I have a couple of revisions. First, can we add the brand name for our small refrigerators? Specifically, the EconoCold™ line. Second, I just got word that sales for this line have increased 250 percent over the last 8-month period. Let's include those figures.

Also, I'd like to meet with you regarding the ad campaign we're planning for next January. I'll be unavailable until the middle of this month, but I will contact you as soon as I am in the office. If you need to contact me before then, don't hesitate to e-mail me.

Once again, thanks for all of your hard work.

Warmly,

Steven Pallin

收信者：珍妮絲・克利夫蘭（Janice Cleveland）<jaycee4me@bahiaind.co.br>
發信者：史蒂芬・帕林（Steven Pallin）<spallin@sales-bahiaind.co.br>
日期：12月3日
主旨：謝謝您

親愛的克里夫蘭女士：

我剛收到您寄給我的新聞稿草稿。做得真好。我想讚揚您身為我們的首席市場行銷業務所作的努力。

在我們發送新聞稿之前，我有幾個地方要修改。首先，我們可以為我們的小冰箱加上品牌名稱嗎？具體來說，就是節能保冷（EconoCold™）系列。其次是，我剛剛聽說這條產品線的銷售額在過去8個月增長了250%。讓這些數字也包括在內吧！

另外，我想與您當面討論我們正在計畫的明年1月廣告活動。我到本月中旬前都不在，但我一回到辦公室就會與您聯絡，如果您需要在此之前與我聯絡，歡迎傳送電子郵件給我。

再次感謝您工作上所有的努力。

親切地，
史蒂芬・帕林

Vocabulary

□ generate [ˋdʒɛnəˏret] 動 產生～   □ introduction [ˏɪntrəˋdʌkʃən] 名 導入   □ thanks to～ 由於～   □ retain [rɪˋten] 動 留住～
□ specifically [spɪˋsɪfɪklɪ] 副 具體來說   □ figure [ˋfɪgjɚ] 名 數字

試題	試題翻譯	解答與解析

☑ **181**

What is the subject of the press release?

(A) A surge in production costs
(B) An increase in advertisements
(C) The planned opening of a new factory
(D) The introduction of a new product

新聞稿的主題是什麼？

(A) 生產成本的激增
(B) 廣告的增加
(C) 新工廠的建造計畫
(D) 新產品的介紹

答案 (C) 概述

新聞稿一開頭就提到主題。Bahia Industrial, ..., announced Thursday plans to construct a new factory in Rio de Janeiro.從該句可知一家名為 Bahia Industrial的公司要建造新工廠，因此(C)是正確答案。

□ surge [sɝdʒ] 名 激增

☑ **182**

What is indicated about Bahia Industrial?

(A) Its sales are declining.
(B) It is headquartered in Brasilia.
(C) It employs unskilled laborers.
(D) It is refurbishing its equipment.

關於巴伊亞工業，什麼描述是對的？

(A) 銷售額下降。
(B) 總部設在巴西利亞。
(C) 雇用非熟練的工人。
(D) 它正在翻新設備。

答案 (B) 何者正確類型

這題同樣是要看看開頭第1句。Bahia Industrial, based in Brasilia and specializing in small appliance production, announced...，插入句（畫底線部分）是在說明前面的巴伊亞工業。從based in～（總部位於～）可知，(B)是正確答案。headquarter當動詞是「設立～的總部〔總公司〕」之意，當名詞時是指「總公司」。

□ decline [dɪˋklaɪn] 動 衰退
□ refurbish [riˋfɝbɪʃ] 動 翻新

☑ **183**

What does Mr. Pallin want Ms. Cleveland to do?

(A) Create a title for the press release
(B) Send the press release to him
(C) Send the press release to the newspaper
(D) Amend the press release

帕林先生希望克里夫蘭女士做什麼？

(A) 為新聞稿設計標題
(B) 把新聞稿寄給他
(C) 把新聞稿寄給報社
(D) 修改新聞稿

答案 (D) 其他細節

帕林先生寫的電子郵件，第1段是先讚美克里夫蘭女士完成新聞稿，接著第2段提到Before we send it off to press, I have a couple of revisions，依序（First, ... Second, ...）要求修改新聞稿。因此(D)為正確答案。revision是「修改」之意，動詞形式是revise，和(D)的amend（修改）同樣意思。

☑ **184**

What does Mr. Pallin suggest about refrigerator sales figures?

(A) Including them in the ad campaign
(B) Omitting the fact that sales have decreased
(C) Showing the higher figure in the press release
(D) Reporting them at the shareholders' meeting

關於冰箱銷售數字，帕林先生建議什麼？

(A) 將它包括在廣告內
(B) 忽略銷售額已減少的事實
(C) 在新聞稿上秀出更高的數字
(D) 在股東會中報告那些數字

答案 (C) 其他細節

這題跟2篇內容都有關係。關於冰箱的銷售額，帕林先生在電子郵件說「過去8個月增長了250％」（sales for this line have increased 250 percents...），希望將這個數字放在新聞稿。另一方面，原新聞稿是「去年4月以來增加了230％以上」（whose sales have surged more than 230 percent...）。(C)將250％用the higher figure（更高的數字）來表示，所以是正確答案。

☑ **185**

When will Mr. Pallin return to the office?

(A) In early December
(B) In mid-December
(C) In late December
(D) In early January

帕林先生何時回到辦公室？

(A) 12 月初
(B) 12 月中旬
(C) 12 月下旬
(D) 1 月初

答案 (B) 其他細節

電子郵件的第3段提到I'll be unavailable until the middle of this month。從電子郵件的日期可知這個月是12月，所以(B)是正確答案。

Questions 186-190 refer to the following list, schedule, and e-mail.

 Makkus Plastics, Inc.
176 Smythe Street
Melbourne

Major production facilities*

Factory Number	Location	Percentage of Total Company Production	Manager
27	Kuala Lumpur	18.5%	Jadwiga Kowalski
16	Tegucigalpa	11.2%	Enrique Gonzales
41	Warsaw	9.8%	Rachel Whittinger
19	Nairobi	14.3%	Ellison Fraser
34	Toronto	8.1%	Harriet Coombs

*Other facilities are responsible for the remainder of production, and are concentrated primarily in Australia and New Zealand.

 Makkus Plastics, Inc.
Production managers meeting
Location: Headquarters building, Room 372F

Goal: Striving to become a market leader
Presenter: Hilene Consulting Group
Tunis-Cairo-Bucharest
North Africa and Global
Schedule created by Frank Hollis
E-mail: f.hollis@hileneconsulting.com

October 23

9:00 A.M. Overview: The importance of benchmarking industry best practices.

10:00 A.M. Quality Control: How our firm compares to others in our field, our strong and weak points.

11:00 A.M. Cost Management: What we are doing right, and what we are doing wrong.
Special focus on achievements of Factory 16, the best performer in this segment.

12:30 P.M. Lunch: Nila's Restaurant

1:30 P.M. Automation: Analysis of cutting-edge equipment and systems.
Special focus on Factory 41, both achievements and challenges.

3:00 P.M. Question and Answer Session

4:00 P.M. Close

馬庫斯（Makkus）塑料公司
176新里街（Smythe Street）
墨爾本（Melbourne）

主要生產設施＊

工廠編號	地點	佔公司總產量百分比	經理
27	吉隆坡（Kuala Lumpur）	18.5%	賈德維加・科瓦爾斯基（Jadwiga Kowalski）
16	德古斯加巴（Tegucigalpa）	11.2%	恩里克・岡薩雷斯（Enrique Gonzales）
41	華沙（Warsaw）	9.8%	瑞秋・懷廷格（Rachel Whittinger）
19	奈洛比（Nairobi）	14.3%	艾里森・佛雷澤（Ellison Fraser）
34	多倫多（Toronto）	8.1%	哈里特・庫姆斯（Harriet Coombs）

＊其他設施負責其餘部分的生產，並且主要集中於澳洲和紐西蘭。

馬庫斯塑料公司
生產經理會議
地點：總部大樓，372F室

目標：努力成為市場領導者
主講人：希林顧問集團（Hilene Consulting Group）
突尼斯（Tunis）－開羅（Cairo）－布加勒斯特（Bucharest）
北非及全球
製表人：法蘭克・霍利斯（Frank Hollis）
電子信箱：f.hollis@hileneconsulting.com

10月23日
9:00 A.M. 概述：業界最佳學習的基準評價之重要性。

10:00 A.M. 品質管理：公司與同領域的其他業者相較，我們的強勢與弱點。

11:00 A.M. 成本管理：我們做對了什麼，又做錯了什麼。
特別聚焦於16號工廠的成績，其在這部分是最佳的執行者。

12:30 A.M. 午餐：尼拉餐廳（Nila's Restaurant）。

1:30 P.M. 自動化：最先端設備及系統的分析。
特別聚焦於41號工廠，亮眼成績與艱鉅課題並存。

3:00 P.M. 提問與回答

4:00 P.M. 結束

試題文章	試題文章翻譯

＊E-mail＊

To:	Frank Hollis [f.hollis@hileneconsulting.com]
From:	Lakshmi Gupta [lakshmi.gupta@makkusplasticsinc.net]
Subject:	October 23 meeting
Date:	October 9

Frank,

I've gone over your proposed schedule, and it basically looks okay. However, I'd like you to make a couple of changes. Specifically, I'd like your 10:00 A.M. presenter to confer with the manager in charge of the factory with the largest percentage of total company production. That is the one with the highest levels of automation. Virtually everything there is highly sophisticated. This way, your presenter at that period will be much better informed.

Also, I'd like the question and answer session to be longer, so our close would be around 30 minutes later than originally scheduled.

Otherwise, we all look forward to a productive meeting and presentations with staff from your firm.

Thanks,

Lakshmi Gupta
Operations Director
Makkus Plastics, Inc.

收信者：法蘭克・霍利斯
[f.hollis@hileneconsulting.com]
發信者：拉克希米・古普塔（Lakshmi Gupta）
[lakshmi.gupta@makkusplasticsinc.net]
主旨：10月23日的會議
日期：10月9日

法蘭克：

我已經看完你提出的時間表，基本上看起來沒問題。不過，我希望你做一些修改。具體來說，我想讓你們上午10時的主講人和負責我們公司總生產量佔最高百分比的工廠經理一起商談。該工廠的自動化水準最高。幾乎每一樣東西都是非常尖端的。用這樣的方式，那段時間的主講人能取得更多的資訊。

再者，我希望提問與回答的時段久一點，所以我們的結束時間會比原定時間約晚30分鐘。

除此之外，我們全體都期待與貴公司員工進行一場有成效的會議及報告。

感謝，

拉克希米・古普塔
營運部長
馬庫斯塑料公司

Vocabulary

- □ remainder [rɪˋmendɚ] 名 剩下的部分
- □ concentrate [ˋkɑnsɛn‚tret] 動 集中於～
- □ primarily [praɪˋmɛrəlɪ] 副 主要地
- □ achievement [əˋtʃivmənt] 名 成績
- □ confer with～ 與～商談
- □ virtually [ˋvɝtʃʊəlɪ] 副 實際上、與～差不多
- □ productive [prəˋdʌktɪv] 形 有成效的

試題	試題翻譯	解答與解析

☑ **186**

According to the list, what is true about Makkus Plastics, Inc.?

(A) Its biggest production facilities are spread out internationally.
(B) Its headquarters has relocated from Australia.
(C) Its construction of new factories has rapidly increased.
(D) Its newest investments are primarily in New Zealand.

根據工廠名單，關於馬庫斯塑料公司，下列何者正確？

(A) 前幾大生產廠房分布於全球各地。
(B) 總部已搬離澳大利亞。
(C) 新工廠的建設迅速增加。
(D) 最新的投資主要在紐西蘭。

答案 (A) 〔何者正確類型〕

這題看工廠名單就能知道答案。從馬庫斯塑料公司主要生產設施的地點可以看到，上面寫著各個國家的城市名稱。而(A)將這些用 spread out internationally（分布於全球）來表示，所以是正確答案。

☑ **187**

What is indicated about the Tegucigalpa factory?

(A) It has the biggest share of total company production.
(B) It maintains the best cost management processes.
(C) It gets most of its supplies from North Africa.
(D) It faces challenges in automation.

關於德古斯加巴工廠，下列何者正確？

(A) 占公司總生產量最高百分比。
(B) 保持最好的成本管理流程。
(C) 大部分的原料供應來自北非。
(D) 面臨自動化方面的挑戰。

答案 (B) 〔何者正確類型〕

根據工廠名單，德古斯加巴工廠是編號16。再看時間表（第2篇），上午11時的成本管理（Cost Management）有提到，編號16的德古斯加巴工廠在成本控制這方面取得最佳的成績。因此(B)是正確答案。

☑ **188**

Where is the factory with special automation issues located?

(A) In Kuala Lumpur
(B) In Warsaw
(C) In Nairobi
(D) In Toronto

有特殊自動化問題的工廠在哪裡？

(A) 吉隆坡
(B) 華沙
(C) 奈洛比
(D) 多倫多

答案 (B) 〔其他細節〕

時間表1:30 P.M.的安排提到了有關 automation（自動化）的資訊，Special focus on Factory 41, both achievements and challenges.，所以可推測41號工廠需要面對 challenges（課題、問題）。再對照工廠名單，41號工廠地點在華沙，因此正確答案是(B)。

☑ **189**

What does Ms. Gupta want Mr. Hollis' team to do?

(A) Visit the largest production center
(B) Add another presenter for 30 minutes
(C) Wait to be contacted by Ellison Fraser
(D) Consult with Jadwiga Kowalski

古普塔女士希望霍利斯團隊做什麼？

(A) 參訪最大的生產中心
(B) 增加 30 分鐘給另一位主講人
(C) 等待艾里森‧佛雷澤聯絡
(D) 與賈德維加‧科瓦爾斯基一起商談

答案 (D) 〔其他細節〕

古普塔女士在電子郵件第1段第2句說I'd like you to...，後面即是要求霍利斯先生做些修改。要求的內容是希望上午10時的主講人和負責公司總生產量占最高百分比的工廠經理一起商談。從工廠名單來看，「占公司總生產量百分比最高的工廠」就是吉隆坡工廠，負責該工廠的是賈德維加‧科瓦爾斯基。而「上午10時的主講人」可確定就是時間表製表人霍利斯先生的團隊，因此(D)是正確答案。

☑ **190**

In the e-mail, the word "sophisticated" in paragraph 1, line 4, is closest in meaning to

(A) difficult
(B) expensive
(C) advanced
(D) unpredictable

電子郵件中，第 1 段第 4 行單字「sophisticated」 意思最接近下列哪一個？

(A) 困難的
(B) 昂貴的
(C) 先進的
(D) 無法預測的

答案 (C) 〔同義詞〕

sophisticated是形容詞，意為「（技術等）高度發展的、尖端的」，(C)的advanced（先進的）意思最接近。可以從前面句子That is the one with the highest levels of automation.的the highest level（最高等級）看出這是正面含意的內容。所以猜測接在Virtually everything there is highly後面的sophisticated也是正面含意的字。因此，帶有負面含意的(A)和(B)可以採消去法不列入考慮。

試題文章	試題文章翻譯

Questions 191-195 refer to the following product information, online review, and response.

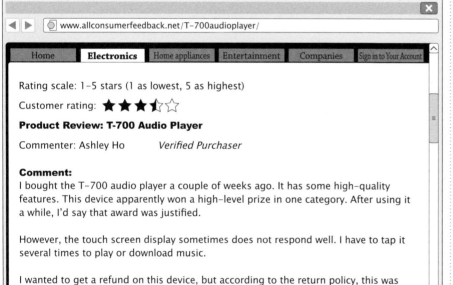

Major features include:
● **Wi-Fi capability**
● **Storage capacity of 8GB**
● **Voice-command functions (can be set to your language)**
● **Award-winning sound quality**

Use with any Baslink Electronics Co. headphones.
Share your music with your other Baslink Electronics Co. products.
Internal components warranty: 9 months from date of purchase.
Return period: Return for any reason for complete refund within 15 days.

www.allconsumerfeedback.net/T-700audioplayer/

| Home | Electronics | Home appliances | Entertainment | Companies | Sign in to Your Account |

Rating scale: 1-5 stars (1 as lowest, 5 as highest)

Customer rating: ★★★☆☆

Product Review: T-700 Audio Player

Commenter: Ashley Ho　　　*Verified Purchaser*

Comment:
I bought the T-700 audio player a couple of weeks ago. It has some high-quality features. This device apparently won a high-level prize in one category. After using it a while, I'd say that award was justified.

However, the touch screen display sometimes does not respond well. I have to tap it several times to play or download music.

I wanted to get a refund on this device, but according to the return policy, this was no longer possible. This is the main reason I gave this item a somewhat low rating.

試題文章翻譯

試題191-195請參考以下產品訊息、線上評論及回覆。

貝斯林克（Baslink）電子公司
T-700音樂播放器
適用於下載和播放音樂

主要特色包括：
●無線上網（Wi-Fi）功能
●8GB儲存容量
●聲控功能（可設定自選語言）
●屢獲殊榮的音質

可使用任何貝斯林克電子公司出品的耳機。
可與其他貝斯林克電子公司的產品共享你的音樂。
內部零件保固：自購買日起9個月。
退貨期限：15天內不論任何理由全額退款。

www.allconsumerfeedback.net/T-700audioplayer/
主頁／電子產品／家用電器／娛樂／企業客戶／登入帳戶

評價標準：1至5顆星（1最低，5最高）
客戶評價：（3顆半星）
評論產品：T-700音樂播放器
評論者：艾希莉・何（Ashley Ho）已驗證的購買者

評論：
幾週前我買了一台T-700音樂播放器。它有一些高品質的特色。這個裝置顯然獲得了某個類別的高級獎。使用過一段時間後，我認為能得那項獎是實至名歸。

但是，有時它的觸控螢幕感應不佳。我必須要點擊幾次後才能播放和下載音樂。

我想要退還這項裝置，但是根據退貨規定，已經不可能了。這是我為何給予這款產品偏低評價的主要原因。

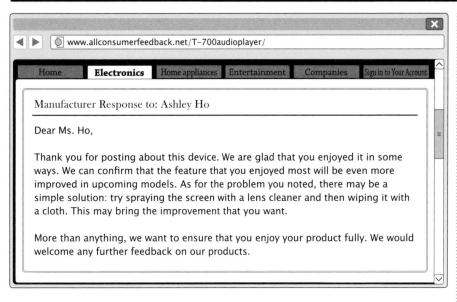

製造商對客戶的回應：艾希莉·何

親愛的何女士：

感謝您對這台裝置的留言。我們很高興您在某些方面上喜歡它。我們可以確定，您最喜歡的功能在即將推出的型號中會得到進一步的改善。至於您提到的問題，可能有個簡單的解決方式：試著用鏡頭清潔劑噴在螢幕上，然後用布擦拭。這應該能帶給您想要的改善。

更重要的是，我們希望確保您能充分地享受產品。歡迎您對我們的產品提供進一步的回饋意見。

Vocabulary

☐ capability [ˌkepəˈbɪlətɪ] 名 能力、功能　　☐ internal [ɪnˈtɜ˙n!] 形 內部的　　☐ component [kəmˈponənt] 名 零件、組成

☐ rating scale 評價標準　　☐ verified [ˈvɛrəˌfaɪd] 形 已驗證（證明）的　　☐ while [hwaɪl] 名（用a while形式）一段（短的）時間

☐ somewhat [ˈsʌmˌhwɑt] 副 有點、稍微

試題	試題翻譯	解答與解析

☑ 191

What can be customized on the audio player?

(A) Storage capacity
(B) Interactive features
(C) Language translation
(D) Wi-Fi functions

音樂播放器上可以自訂什麼？

(A) 儲存容量
(B) 互動功能
(C) 語言翻譯
(D) 無線上網 （Wi-Fi） 功能

答案 (B) 其他細節

customize是指「（依自己的要求）調整（訂做）～」。商品說明（第1篇文章）的主要特色中，Voice-command functions (can be set to your language)符合這種敘述，意為「可將聲控功能調成自己喜歡的語言」，(B)的interactive（互動的、雙向對話的）即是表達這樣的意思，所以是正確答案。(C)似乎會讓人瞬間迷惘，但畢竟這台裝置沒有翻譯的功能，所以不適合當答案。

☑ 192

In the online review, the word "justified" in paragraph 1, line 3, is closest in meaning to

(A) legalized
(B) moral
(C) correct
(D) responsible

在線上評論中，第 1 段第 3 行單字「justified」 最意思接近下列哪一個？

(A) 合法化的
(B) 道德的
(C) 正確的
(D) 負責的

答案 (C) 同義詞

這一段陳述了對商品的高度評價。justified意為「有正當理由的、理所當然的」，選項中可替換的字是(C)的correct（正確的）。即使不知道justified的意思，也會發現從高度評價到「認為那項獎是正確的」這樣的語意是很自然流暢的。

☑ 193

What is indicated about Ms. Ho's audio player?

(A) It was bought more than 15 days ago.
(B) It was purchased from an online retailer.
(C) It was sent in for a cash refund.
(D) It was repaired by the manufacturer.

關於何女士的音樂播放器，下列何者正確？

(A) 已購買超過 15 天。
(B) 購自網路零售商。
(C) 被寄回以要求現金退款。
(D) 由製造商修理。

答案 (A) 何者正確類型

請參考何女士寫的評論。第3段提到I wanted to get a refund...。意即「根據退貨規定無法退貨（指音樂播放器）退款」。有關退貨規定，在商品說明最後的Return period:有說明，這也意味著何女士沒有在15日內退貨（已購買超過15天）。

☑ 194

What feature of the audio player will be improved in future versions?

(A) Sound quality
(B) Download speeds
(C) Music selection
(D) Display size

音樂播放器在未來版本將會改善什麼功能？

(A) 音質
(B) 下載速度
(C) 音樂選曲
(D) 螢幕尺寸

答案 (A) 其他細節

製造商在線上評論的回答中提到We can confirm that the feature that you enjoyed most will be even more improved in upcoming models.，由此可知何女士最喜歡的功能在未來推出的型號會做改進。何女士在評論提到「獲得了某個類別的高級獎」，而這個類別，可以從商品說明的Award-winning sound quality中知道是指「音質」，所以(A)是正確答案。這題必須跨3篇文章才能找出正確答案。

☑ 195

What is suggested to Ms. Ho?

(A) Cleaning may be effective.
(B) A machine part needs to be fixed.
(C) Her complaint is not significant.
(D) Her problem might not be easily solved.

製造商給何女士什麼建議？

(A) 清潔可能有效。
(B) 機械零件需要修理。
(C) 她的抱怨不重要。
(D) 她的問題可能不容易解決。

答案 (A) 其他細節

對何女士的建議當然就在製造商的回答中。第1段的As for the problem you noted, ...的部分，提到何女士提出的問題（觸控螢幕感應不佳）或許可以簡單解決，也說明了具體的方法，因此(A)是正確答案。

Questions 196-200 refer to the following notice, e-mail, and article.

Klandai Robotics

Our company maintains a policy of playing an active part in the local community. As part of this policy, we encourage employees to join any of the charity programs and clubs that we are involved with. All charity groups that we work with have been verified by local government entities as both licensed and effective.

Find out more through visiting the company's community relations section Web site, or by visiting the human resources department. Staff who devote more than 100 hours a year to any of our affiliated clubs or programs become Green Star staff, eligible to receive €50 in cash and one day off work—as well as the appreciation of the community.

* E-mail *	
To:	All Employees
From:	Melissa Hahn, Community Relations Director, Klandai Robotics
Date:	May 23
Subject:	Canned food program

Every year, we work with the non-profit Plus Food Organization on their canned food collection efforts. In fact, we are their largest helper in terms of both volunteers and collections. All cans collected are donated to the needy. This year, we are again asking as many employees as possible to join in. The organization hopes to collect at least 2,000 cans this time. There are several ways to participate:
• Bring as many food cans as you can to place in the collection boxes.
• Help with setting up collection boxes or with transportation of boxes.
• Volunteer time with other tasks in my department that are related to this program.

I will definitely be a part of these efforts. I hope you will, too.

Sincerely,

Melissa Hahn
Community Relations Director

試題196-200請參考以下公告、電子郵件及報導。

克蘭黛機器人工程（Klandai Robotics）

我們公司堅持在當地社區發揮積極作用的政策。作為此政策的一部份，我們鼓勵員工加入我們參與的任何慈善計畫和俱樂部。我們合作的所有慈善團體均已獲得當地政府許可並認證其成果顯著。

透過公司網站裡的社區關係頁面，或是到人事資源部都可以了解更多訊息。每年投入我們的關係俱樂部或計畫，超過100小時的員工將成為綠星員工，有資格獲得50歐元的現金和一天的休假——以及社區的讚賞。

收信者：所有員工
發信者：梅麗莎‧哈恩（Melissa Hahn），社區關係部長，克蘭黛機器人工程
日期：5月23日
主旨：罐頭食品計畫

我們每年都會與非營利的「額外食物組織」合作進行罐頭食品募集工作。事實上，我們是他們在義工和募集這2方面最大的幫手。所有募集來的罐頭都將捐給貧困的人。今年我們再次尋求盡可能多一點員工加入。該組織希望這次能募集到至少2,000罐。有幾種參與方式如下：
‧盡你所能多帶點食品罐頭來放入募集箱內。
‧協助設置募集箱或箱子的運送事宜。
‧排出志工時間參與我的部門有關此次活動的其他工作。

我一定會貢獻己力。希望你們也是。
謹致問候

梅麗莎‧哈恩
社區關係部長

試題文章	試題文章翻譯

April 7 (Grand Rapids) — The Plus Food Organization concluded its canned food collection drive today. Vicente Salgado, a spokesperson for the non-profit group, stated that the program was a success due to the special help of a local company that is its biggest donor and overall contributor. "That company has really helped us out year after year," he stated in an e-mail interview with our newspaper. "One of its staff members, Chandra Epstein, has devoted 135 hours of her time to helping out this year, and many of her coworkers have devoted similar amounts of time." Mr. Salgado reported that his organization collected slightly more than double the number of cans it had hoped for in its canned food drive this year. He stated that it hopes to do even better next year, in part by recruiting more corporate partners.

4月7日（大急流城Grand Rapids）—今天「額外食物組織」結束了其罐頭食品募集活動。該非營利組織的發言人維森特·薩爾加多（Vicente Salgado）表示，由於身為最大捐助者暨全面貢獻者的當地公司特別的支援，讓這項活動得以成功。「這家公司真的年復一年地幫助我們」，發言人在本報的電子郵件採訪中表示。「該公司員工之一，錢德拉·艾普斯坦（Chandra Epstein）今年已經投入135個小時來幫忙，而且她的許多同事也花了幾乎同樣的時間。」薩爾加多先生指出，他的組織今年募集的罐頭數量是原希望數量2倍再多一點。他表示，該組織希望明年做得更好，其一部分是藉由招募更多的企業合作夥伴。

Vocabulary

□ verify [ˋvɛrəˏfaɪ] 動 證明（查清）～屬實　　□ government entity　政府機關　　□ affiliate [əˋfɪlɪˏet] 動 隸屬、相關

□ non-profit [ˏnɑnˋprɑfɪt] 形 非營利的　　□ effort [ˋɛfət] 名 努力　　□ in terms of～　就～方面來說

□ needy [ˋnidɪ] 名 （常用the -形式）貧困的人　　□ drive [draɪv] 名 （籌款募捐等的）活動　　□ donor [ˋdonə] 名 捐助者

□ overall [ˋovəˏɔl] 形 全面的　　□ contributor [kənˋtrɪbjʊtə] 名 貢獻者　　□ devote A to B　將A奉獻給B

☑ 196

What is indicated about the Plus Food Organization?

(A) It has been reviewed by government officials.
(B) It has established branches in many locations.
(C) It has been changed from a non-profit to a private firm.
(D) It has nominated Green Star employees each year.

關於「額外食物組織」，下列何者正確？

(A) 已由政府官員審查。
(B) 在很多地方設立分支機構。
(C) 已從非營利轉為私人企業。
(D) 每年提名綠星員工。

答案 (A) 〔何者正確類型〕

「額外食物組織」這個名稱是在電子郵件的第1句才出現。該組織是與克蘭黛機器人工程公司合作進行慈善活動的團體。從公告的第1段可知，克蘭黛機器人工程公司合作的所有慈善團體均已獲得當地政府許可和有效的認證，(A)能適當表達這些資訊，所以是正確答案。

☐ private firm　私人企業
☐ nominate [`nɑmə,net] 動 提名～

☑ 197

What is NOT a suggestion in the e-mail?

(A) Contributing time to a different department
(B) Moving goods from one location to another
(C) Getting in touch by phone with potential donors
(D) Taking personal items in to give away to others

下列哪一項不是電子郵件中的建議？

(A) 為不同部門貢獻時間
(B) 將貨物從一個地點搬到其他地點
(C) 用電話與潛在捐助者聯絡
(D) 把個人的物品送給其他人

答案 (C) 〔是非題類型〕

符合這題的參考內容是在電子郵件逐條列出的地方。分別是(A)在第3項Volunteer time with... 的部分，(B)是第2項的Help with... with transportation of boxes.的部分，(D)是跟第1項的Bring as many food cans as... 的部分一致。而(C)在文中並未被提到，所以是正確答案。

☐ get in touch with～　和～取得聯繫
☐ give away （把不需要的東西）送人

☑ 198

What is true about Ms. Epstein?

(A) She may receive some rewards from her firm.
(B) She may give some members of her team at least one day off.
(C) She may write about her experiences helping the needy.
(D) She may recommend more staff members to participate.

關於艾普斯坦女士，下列何者正確？

(A) 她應該會收到公司的一些獎勵。
(B) 她可能會給她的團隊成員至少1天休假日。
(C) 她可能寫一些有關幫助窮人的經驗。
(D) 她可能會推薦更多的員工參加。

答案 (A) 〔何者正確類型〕

這題要參考2篇文章。在新聞報導的中間處有提到One of its staff members, Chandra Epstein，its是指前述所言的當地企業，意即「額外食物組織」最大的捐助者。而根據電子郵件內容，克蘭黛機器人工程公司是「額外食物組織」最大的合作者，所以可推斷艾普斯坦女士是克蘭黛機器人工程公司的員工。此外，報導提到艾普斯坦女士在志工活動投入了135個小時，但根據公告，1年內貢獻100小時以上於志工活動的員工將可獲得50歐元的現金和1天的休假。(A)將這些表達為some rewards（一些獎勵），所以是正確答案。

☑ 199

How many cans of food were collected?

(A) About one thousand
(B) About two thousand
(C) About three thousand
(D) About four thousand

募集了多少罐頭？

(A) 約 1,000 個
(B) 約 2,000 個
(C) 約 3,000 個
(D) 約 4,000 個

答案 (D) 〔其他細節〕

新聞報導的中間後段提到his organization collected slightly more than double the number of cans it had hoped for in its canned food drive。而從電子郵件可知今年期待募集到至少2,000個罐頭，所以今年最後是募集到2,000個的2倍再多一點。因此(D)為正確答案。

☑ 200

According to the article, what does the Plus Food Organization plan to do?

(A) Promote more managers to partner-level
(B) Extend the duration of its next food drive
(C) Find more companies to cooperate with
(D) Recruit staff with specialized skills

根據這篇報導，「額外食物組織」計畫做什麼？

(A) 把更多管理者晉升到合作夥伴階層
(B) 延長下一次食物募集活動的時間
(C) 尋找更多與之合作的公司
(D) 招募具有專業技能的員工

答案 (C) 〔其他細節〕

新聞報導最後一句說it hopes to do even better next year, in part by recruiting more corporate partners。從前後語意來看，主詞it是指「額外食物組織」，正確答案(C)只是把recruiting more corporate partners換成另一種表達方式而已。另外要注意(A)和(D)分別使用和句中單字一樣的partner（夥伴）及recruit（招募），請各位別上當而誤選。

☐ cooperate with～　與～合作

TEST 3 模擬試題 解答＋完全解析

正確答案一覽表

題號	答案	題號	答案	題號	答案	題號	答案	題號	答案
1	B	41	C	81	D	121	D	161	B
2	A	42	B	82	A	122	A	162	C
3	D	43	D	83	C	123	D	163	C
4	D	44	C	84	B	124	A	164	C
5	B	45	A	85	D	125	C	165	A
6	C	46	A	86	A	126	C	166	B
7	C	47	A	87	C	127	D	167	A
8	B	48	B	88	B	128	A	168	D
9	C	49	D	89	A	129	B	169	C
10	B	50	C	90	B	130	A	170	D
11	A	51	B	91	A	131	A	171	B
12	B	52	D	92	D	132	C	172	B
13	A	53	C	93	D	133	D	173	A
14	C	54	D	94	B	134	B	174	C
15	B	55	D	95	A	135	A	175	C
16	C	56	B	96	C	136	C	176	B
17	B	57	C	97	D	137	D	177	A
18	B	58	A	98	C	138	B	178	C
19	C	59	D	99	D	139	A	179	B
20	A	60	D	100	C	140	D	180	A
21	C	61	B	101	C	141	C	181	C
22	B	62	A	102	D	142	B	182	B
23	A	63	C	103	B	143	B	183	D
24	C	64	B	104	A	144	A	184	C
25	A	65	B	105	C	145	D	185	A
26	A	66	C	106	D	146	B	186	B
27	B	67	D	107	A	147	D	187	A
28	B	68	C	108	B	148	B	188	C
29	A	69	A	109	A	149	B	189	D
30	A	70	A	110	B	150	C	190	D
31	C	71	B	111	C	151	A	191	A
32	D	72	D	112	C	152	C	192	D
33	A	73	A	113	D	153	D	193	B
34	C	74	D	114	C	154	D	194	B
35	B	75	B	115	C	155	C	195	C
36	D	76	C	116	C	156	A	196	D
37	A	77	D	117	B	157	B	197	C
38	C	78	B	118	A	158	A	198	A
39	B	79	D	119	D	159	B	199	B
40	D	80	B	120	A	160	C	200	D

PART 1

| 錄音原文與翻譯 | 解答與解析 |

1 🇺🇸

(A) She's tasting a glass of wine.
(B) She's wearing sunglasses.
(C) She's pointing at a plastic bottle.
(D) She's opening a paper bag.

(A) 她正在品嚐一杯酒。
(B) 她戴了一副墨鏡。
(C) 她指著一個塑膠瓶。
(D) 她正打開一個紙袋。

答案 (B) 　人物（1人）

(B)適當表達女子的動作。wear表示是戴著的狀態。(A)的taste是「品嚐、體驗～」，雖然有拍到酒杯，但是並沒有在喝，所以是錯的。(C)是錯在桌上好像有寶特瓶的東西，不過沒有point at～（指著～）的動作。(D)是錯在opening，因為女性雖然拿著紙袋，但並無打開的動作。

2 🇬🇧

(A) The tables have been set.
(B) Lamps are hanging from the ceiling.
(C) The restaurant is filled with patrons.
(D) There are some ornaments on the tables.

(A) 桌子已經擺好了。
(B) 燈具從天花板懸掛下來。
(C) 餐廳內擠滿了老顧客。
(D) 有些裝飾品在桌上。

答案 (A) 　無人物

(A)適當表達桌上的狀態。set the table是餐桌上擺好餐具及料理並準備用餐的意思，因此(A)是被動表現法。(C)的patron意為「（餐廳等的）老顧客」，但照片並無人物。(D)是錯在on the tables，雖然櫃台好像有裝飾品（ornament）的東西，但不是擺在桌上。

□ hang from～　從～懸掛下來
□ be filled with～　充滿著～

3 🇨🇦

(A) The woman is adjusting a car seat.
(B) An automobile is being fixed in the garage.
(C) The customer is leaving the gas station.
(D) Fuel is being pumped into the vehicle.

(A) 一名女人正在調整汽車座椅。
(B) 一輛汽車在汽車修理廠內修理。
(C) 客人準備要離開加油站。
(D) 一輛車正在加油。

答案 (D) 　人物（1人）

(D)的Fuel（燃料）是主詞，適當表達女性在車旁加油的樣子。pump A into B（將A（燃料等）注入B），在選項內是採被動表現法。(B)的garage除了「車庫」的意思之外，也有「汽車修理廠」之意。而在英式英文還有「汽油站」的意思，但是不管哪一種意思，都是錯在動詞fix（修理）。

□ adjust [ə`dʒʌst] 動 調整～
□ fuel [`fjʊəl] 名 燃料

錄音原文與翻譯	解答與解析

  4

(A) All of the seats are occupied.
(B) Dishes are being cleared from the tables.
(C) Customers are eating in a straight row.
(D) A man is reading something in a paper.

(A) 全部的座位都被佔用了。
(B) 菜餚從桌上被清掉了。
(C) 客人們坐成一排吃東西。
(D) 一名男子正在看報紙上的某個內容。

答案 (D)　　人物（2人以上）

(D)適當表達了前面男子的狀態。照片裡有不少人，可以把重點放在動作比較清楚的人身上。因為還有空位，所以(A)的all（全部）形容錯誤。(B)是將clear A of B（從A（場所）清除B）的A變成主詞的被動句。(C)是錯在in a straight row的形容。straight是「直直的」。表示列或排的單字row及line在Part 1常出現。

□ occupy [ˋɑkjəˌpaɪ] **動** 佔用～、佔據～

 5

(A) Items have been piled onto a tray.
(B) A number of umbrellas have been stuffed into a cart.
(C) Tools have been deposited in the trash.
(D) Stacks of rain gear have been left in the hallway.

(A) 物品都被堆在文件匣上。
(B) 一些雨傘被塞進小推車裡。
(C) 一些工具被放在垃圾桶裡。
(D) 一堆雨具被遺忘在走廊上。

答案 (B)　　無人物

(B)適當表達雨傘被擺入小推車的狀態，所以為正確答案，這是stuff A into B（把A塞到B）的被動用法。(A)用items（物品）取代雨傘還算可以，但是用pile（堆疊在～）則錯誤。(C)的tool意思是「工具」。如果不知道deposit（放置～）的意思，看到trash（垃圾桶）也知道要排除這個選項。(D)的rain gear表示「雨具」，left（遺忘）的確是正確描述，但是最後的in the hallway（在走廊）錯誤。

□ hallway [ˋhɔlˌwe] **名** 走廊

6

(A) The people are looking in the same direction.
(B) The people are assembling some equipment.
(C) One woman is leaning on a chair.
(D) One woman is taking notes at a lecture.

(A) 人們正在看同樣的方向。
(B) 人們正在組裝一些設備。
(C) 一位女子靠在椅子上。
(D) 一位女子在演講中做筆記。

答案 (C)　　人物（2人以上）

這題的焦點是照片右邊靠著椅子的女子，所以描述一致的(C)是正確答案。lean on～是「倚靠著～、依靠」。(B)的assemble當及物動詞是「組裝」，當不及物動詞時另有「集合」的意思，大家要注意一下。(D)的take notes是「做筆記」，坐著的女子有可能是在做筆記，不過現場並不是在lecture（演講）。在2人（以上）的照片中，有one man [woman] is...的表達方式時，我們可以把焦點放在一個人的身上。像(C)和(D)都是以One woman...為開頭，因為這2個選項對女性動作都有描寫，所以要仔細聽動詞之後的內容。

□ direction [dəˋrɛkʃən] **名** 方向

PART 2

錄音原文與翻譯	解答與解析

☐ **7** W 🇬🇧 W 🇺🇸

W: Where's the annual convention being held?
W: (A) August 9th to 14th.
　　(B) Every year.
　　(C) In Seattle.

W：年度的代表大會在哪裡召開？
W：(A) 從 8 月 9 日到 14 日。
　　(B) 每一年。
　　(C) 在西雅圖 （Seattle）。

答案 (C)　　[疑問詞]

where～ ?是問「場所」，(C)回答具體的地名，所以是正確答案。因為不是問「時間」或「頻率」，所以(A)和(B)這2個答案都不對。這題只要有聽懂一開頭的Where就知道要選(C)了。

☐ annual [ˋænjʊəl] 形 每年的
☐ convention [kənˋvɛnʃən] 名 代表大會

☑ **8** M 🇨🇦 W 🇺🇸

M: Will you set up the projector for me?
W: (A) Yes, there are four.
　　(B) I'd be happy to.
　　(C) The project was canceled.

M：可以幫我準備投影機嗎？
W：(A) 是的，這裡有 4 台。
　　(B) 我很樂意。
　　(C) 這項計畫被取消了。

答案 (B)　　[特殊疑問句及對話表達]

Will you～ ?（可以幫我～嗎？）是向對方請求的句型。其中回答「我很樂意」的(B)最正確。問句的projector是「投影機」的意思，要注意(C)是用發音相似的project（計畫）來誤導。只要懂Will you～ ?是請求的句型，就知道要選(B)了。

☐ set up～ 將（機械等）準備好

☑ **9** W 🇬🇧 M 🇦🇺

W: I'm not sure where I left my glasses.
M: (A) Let's leave them as they are.
　　(B) I've found them unpleasant.
　　(C) Did you look in the bathroom?

W：我不確定我把眼鏡放哪了。
M：(A) 就讓它們保持原來那樣吧。
　　(B) 我發覺他們不高興。
　　(C) 你在浴室找過了嗎？

答案 (C)　　[疑問詞]

在間接疑問句中聽懂疑問詞很重要。針對「忘記把眼鏡放哪」這句，(C)回答「你在浴室找過了嗎」最正確。選項(A)雖然是用left（留下）的原形leave（使處於某種狀態），但是語意上無法當成答案。(B)的found若解讀為「找到了」，似乎I found them是可以符合答案的，但是因為後面又接了unpleasant（不高興的），所以這句的find是＜find＋O（受詞）＋C（補語）＞的句型，意為「發覺O是C」。

☑ **10** W 🇺🇸 W 🇬🇧

W: How many people are expected to attend the dinner?
W: (A) Take as many as you like.
　　(B) At least 40, I guess.
　　(C) I didn't expect that.

W：預計會有多少人出席這次的晚餐？
W：(A) 喜歡多少就拿多少。
　　(B) 至少 40 位，我猜。
　　(C) 我沒想到是那樣。

答案 (B)　　[疑問詞]

How many people～ ?是詢問人數，具體回答「至少40位」的(B)最正確。expect～ to do 雖然有「期待～做……」的意思，不過只要有聽懂How many people大概就會選(B)了。要注意(A)的money（錢）和(C)的expect（期望）都是故意使用和問題相似的單字來誤導大家。

☐ as many as you like 和你喜歡的（數量）一樣多

☑ **11** M 🇦🇺 W 🇬🇧

M: Daniel is being promoted next month, isn't he?
W: (A) Yes, his assistant said so.
　　(B) No, he did it himself.
　　(C) He should be proud of you.

M：丹尼爾 （Daniel） 下個月會被升職，不是嗎？
W：(A) 對啊，他的助理是這麼說的。
　　(B) 不是，他自己去做的。
　　(C) 他應該為你感到驕傲。

答案 (A)　　[特殊疑問句及對話表達]

這是be動詞的附加疑問句。對於「丹尼爾下個月會被升職＋不是嗎？」這樣的提問，(A)回答是的（會升職）之後，附加補充誰這麼說，所以是正確答案。(B)的No雖然是指「不會升職」，但是he後面的內容不符。(C)是錯在沒有針對是否會升職來回答。

☐ promote [prəˋmot] 動 使～晉升
☐ be proud of～ 為～感到驕傲

CD 3 14-18

錄音原文與翻譯	解答與解析

☑ **12** M 🇨🇦 W 🇺🇸

M: Do you have any idea when Mr. Key will be back?
W: (A) It wasn't his idea.
　　(B) In around thirty minutes.
　　(C) He returned it on Monday.

M：你知道齊先生 （Mr. Key） 何時會回來嗎？
W：(A) 那不是他的主意。
　　(B) 大約 30 分鐘。
　　(C) 他已在週一將它歸還。

答案 (B)　　疑問詞

這是間接疑問句，關鍵在要聽懂when Mr. Key will be back（齊先生何時會回來）的when。針對問「何時」，以(B)具體地回答時間「大約30分鐘」最正確。(A)故意使用跟問題一樣的單字idea（想法）讓人混淆。而(C)要注意不要從問句的be back做聯想而誤以為returned是答案。return後面有it，所以是及物動詞，為「歸還～」的意思。

☑ **13** M 🇦🇺 M 🇨🇦

M: I'd like to see the schedule, please.
M: (A) Sure, here you go.
　　(B) I'll be busy tomorrow.
　　(C) I wonder if they saw it.

M：請讓我看一下日程表。
M：(A) 好，在這裡。
　　(B) 我明天會很忙。
　　(C) 我想知道他們是否看見它了。

答案 (A)　　陳述句

I'd like to～, please.意為「我想～、請讓我～。」的請求表現法。(A)是依對方請求並遞上日程表，所以是正確答案。另外要注意(B)是故意用單字busy（忙碌的）讓人從問句的schedule（日程表）多做聯想，而(C)是用see（看）的過去式saw誘使大家誤選。

☑ **14** W 🇺🇸 W 🇬🇧

W: How would you describe the new accountant?
W: (A) We'd better catch a taxi.
　　(B) Explain in detail.
　　(C) Very friendly.

W：你會如何形容這位新的會計師？
W：(A) 我們最好攔一輛計程車。
　　(B) 請詳細地解釋。
　　(C) 非常友善。

答案 (C)　　疑問詞

問句的describe是指「形容、描述～」。How would you describe～？意為「如何形容（描述）～」，是要求對方對事物或人的描述或印象下定論的句子。被問及新會計師如何，以(C)回答「非常友善」最正確。(A)的We'd是We had的縮寫，had better do是「最好～」。

□ in detail　詳細地

☑ **15** W 🇺🇸 M 🇨🇦

W: Don't we have to sign these purchase orders?
M: (A) I brought the signs here.
　　(B) Oh, yes, I forgot.
　　(C) I'll have today's special.

W：我們不必簽這些採購單嗎？
M：(A) 我帶了招牌來。
　　(B) 喔，是的，我忘記了。
　　(C) 我要點今日特餐。

答案 (B)　　特殊疑問句及對話表達

這是否定疑問句。不要拘泥於句子的開頭，仔細聽we have to sign these purchase orders的部分。「我們必須簽這些採購單」→「是的，我忘記了」，(B)這樣的對話流程最通順，所以是正確答案。(A)雖然是跟問句一樣的單字sign（招牌），但是詞性跟意思都不同。(C)是誘使大家把orders（單據）認為是在餐廳的點餐，注意別誤選。

□ purchase order　採購單

☑ **16** M 🇦🇺 M 🇨🇦

M: Why don't you ask Kevin to help us?
M: (A) We'll meet in person.
　　(B) Yes, I'll try a new one.
　　(C) I'll think about it.

M：你為何不請凱文 （Kevin） 來幫我們？
M：(A) 我們將碰面。
　　(B) 是的，我會嘗試新的一個。
　　(C) 我會考慮的。

答案 (C)　　特殊疑問句及對話表達

Why don't you～？（你為何不～？），這是在表達建議。不管贊成或反對這項建議，(C)的回答「我會考慮的」最為正確。ask～ to do有「請求～來做……」的意思，但只要聽到Why don't you～？這種建議類的句型，幾乎都可以選(C)。

□ in person　親自、當面（直接地）

143

| 錄音原文與翻譯 | 解答與解析 |

☑ 17 W 🇬🇧 W 🇺🇸

W：Do you have change for a hundred-dollar bill?
W：(A) It's out of order.
　　(B) I don't have any cash at all.
　　(C) That's pretty expensive.

W：你有零錢換 100 元嗎？
W：(A) 它發生故障。
　　(B) 我沒有任何現金。
　　(C) 那非常昂貴。

答案 (B) 　　Yes / No

問句中的change是名詞，意為「零錢、兌換的錢」。bill是「紙鈔、鈔票」。在被問到可否換零錢時，以(B)「我沒有任何現金（所以無法兌換）」的回答最正確。cash是「現金」。要注意(C)是故意用單字expensive（昂貴）讓人從問句多做聯想，誘使大家誤選。

☐ out of order　發生故障

☑ 18 M 🇦🇺 W 🇺🇸

M：What was your hotel in Bangkok like?
W：(A) Sounds like a big place.
　　(B) The rooms were tidy and spacious.
　　(C) Yes, I have a reservation.

M：你在曼谷 （Bangkok） 的飯店如何呢？
W：(A) 聽起來似乎是個很大的地方。
　　(B) 房間很整潔且寬敞。
　　(C) 是的，我有預約。

答案 (B) 　　疑問詞

What was～ like?是一種詢問感覺的表現法。也可以用How was～ ?來表達。(B)說出具體的感覺，所以是正確答案。(A)的sounds like～（聽起來似乎～）是一種表達想像的說法，所以不符合實際經歷過的感覺。(C)是從問句的hotel（飯店）聯想而來的內容，對於疑問詞開頭的疑問句回答Yes / No是不對的。

☐ tidy [ˈtaɪdɪ] 形 整潔的
☐ spacious [ˈspeʃəs] 形 寬敞的

☑ 19 W 🇬🇧 M 🇨🇦

W：They didn't shut down their computers, did they?
M：(A) Yes, they logged in.
　　(B) Don't leave the door open.
　　(C) Actually, they did.

W：他們沒有關掉電腦，對吧？
M：(A) 對，他們登入了。
　　(B) 不要讓門開著。
　　(C) 實際上，他們有。

答案 (C) 　　特殊疑問句及對話表達

「他們沒有關掉電腦＋對吧？」對於這種尋求確認的句子，以(C)的回答「他們有（關）」最正確。Yes, they did.是最明確回答，但也因為考題過於簡單，所以反而不敢選，這就是多益測驗特別的地方。(A)是刻意使用與話題相關的片語logged in（登入）來混淆大家。而(B)是用單字open（打開）讓人從問句的shut（關）來做聯想，請注意不要誤選。

☑ 20 M 🇨🇦 W 🇺🇸

M：Is Kelly going to take up painting when she retires?
W：(A) She has started already.
　　(B) Something is wrong with the tires.
　　(C) Yes, I have lots of paintings.

M：當凱莉 （Kelly） 退休時，要開始學畫畫嗎？
W：(A) 她已經開始學了。
　　(B) 輪胎有些問題。
　　(C) 是的，我有很多畫作。

答案 (A) 　　Yes / No

這是在表達未來預計發生的be going to～疑問句。take up～是「開始學（有關興趣等）」。對於退休後是否要開始學畫畫的未來做出提問，以(A)「已經開始學了」最正確。注意(B)的tires（輪胎）與問句的retires（退休）發音類似。另外，問句中的painting是表示「畫畫」的行為，(C)的painting是指畫作。

☐ something is wrong with～　～有些問題

☑ 21 M 🇨🇦 M 🇦🇺

M：How much longer are you staying in Paris, Tony?
M：(A) It won't cost that much.
　　(B) I'm looking forward to it.
　　(C) I'm leaving tomorrow.

M：湯尼 （Tony），你還要在巴黎 （Paris） 待多久呢？
M：(A) 那不會花那麼多錢。
　　(B) 我很期待。
　　(C) 我明天就離開。

答案 (C) 　　疑問詞

How much longer～ ?是問還要待多久。(C)用「明天就離開」來取代回答明確的期間，所以最符合。如果只聽到How much而誤以為是問金額，可能會誤選(A)。(B)的it讓人不知道指的是什麼。

☐ look forward to～　期待～

錄音原文與翻譯	解答與解析

22 W 🇬🇧 M 🇨🇦

W: Whose sales presentation was chosen for this week?
M: (A) Jason says it starts at eleven.
　　(B) Mr. Brown's was, I think.
　　(C) Sales figures are up this week.

W：這週誰的銷售報告被選中？
M：(A) 傑森（Jason）說 11 點開始。
　　(B) 布朗（Brown）先生的，我認為。
　　(C) 本週銷售數字提高。

答案 (B) ［疑問詞］

針對Whose sales presentation（誰的銷售報告）這樣的提問，(B)具體回答出人物「布朗先生的（銷售報告）」，所以是正確答案。(A)也是有提到人名，但是內容不符。而(C)是使用與問句一樣的單字sales（銷售）和this week（本週）來誘使大家，請注意不要混淆。

---

23 M 🇦🇺 W 🇬🇧

M: Would you like to start with an appetizer or just a main course?
W: (A) It's up to you.
　　(B) Neither do I.
　　(C) If it's not satisfactory.

M：你想要先從開胃菜開始還是只要主菜？
W：(A) 由你決定。
　　(B) 我也不要。
　　(C) 如果它不是令人滿意的。

答案 (A) ［特殊疑問句及對話表達］

Would you like to～？（你想要～嗎？）是Do you want to～？的禮貌用法。or是連接an appetizer（開胃菜）和 (just) a main course（主菜）。對於這2種選擇，以直接交給對方判斷的(A)「由你決定」最正確。up to～是「取決於～」。在選擇性疑問句中，往往有很多就像這種，哪一邊都不選擇的答案才是正確答案。

□ satisfactory [ˌsætɪsˈfæktərɪ] 形 令人滿意的

---

24 W 🇺🇸 M 🇦🇺

W: Can this computer be used to edit video files?
M: (A) We watched them together.
　　(B) Mine used to run quite well.
　　(C) I've never tried that before.

W：這台電腦可以用來編輯影像檔案嗎？
M：(A) 我們一起看過他們。
　　(B) 我的過去曾經運轉得很好。
　　(C) 我從來沒試過。

答案 (C) ［Yes / No］

這台電腦可以用來編輯影像檔案嗎？針對這樣的提問，以(C)回答「沒有試過（所以不知道）」最正確。希望大家也要多習慣像這類沒有回答Yes或No而直接回應「不知道」的對答形式。注意(A)的watched（看）是要讓人從video（影片）做錯誤聯想。(B)雖然與問句都是用used to，但是意思不一樣。

---

25 W 🇬🇧 W 🇺🇸

W: Shouldn't you be attending the general meeting?
W: (A) I was told to work on this report instead.
　　(B) It's in Conference Room 3.
　　(C) Yes, I went there yesterday.

W：你不是應該在全體大會嗎？
W：(A) 我被告知要做這份報告代替參加。
　　(B) 在 3 號會議室進行。
　　(C) 是的，我昨天去那裡了。

答案 (A) ［特殊疑問句及對話表達］

Shouldn't you～?是「你不～嗎？」的意思。以(A)的回答「我被告知要做這份報告（所以不出席）代替（參加全體大會）」最正確。I was told to do是「我被告知～」，instead是「代替」。(C)的Yes雖然有「我一定會參加」的意思，但後面接的內容不符。

---

26 M 🇨🇦 W 🇬🇧

M: Who did the management choose for the manager position?
W: (A) They haven't decided yet.
　　(B) Indeed they did.
　　(C) I hear it's a difficult job.

M：管理層決定誰擔任經理職位？
W：(A) 他們還沒決定。
　　(B) 他們確實如此。
　　(C) 我聽說它是一項很難的工作。

答案 (A) ［疑問詞］

對於「要選誰？」這個問題，正確答案(A)回答「他們還沒決定」而不是說出具體的人物。They是指the management（管理層）。Who雖然是choose的受詞，但是在會話中一般都用Who而不用Whom。因此，對於Who～?的問句，大家要多練習區分是「執行動作的主詞」還是「承受動作的受詞」。

□ indeed [ɪnˈdid] 副 確實

錄音原文與翻譯	解答與解析

☑ 27 W 🇬🇧 M 🇦🇺

W: Do you mind if I leave a little early today?
M: (A) I'll keep that in mind.
(B) No, not at all.
(C) The latter is better.

W：你介意我今天稍微早點離開嗎？
M：(A) 我會把那個放在心上。
(B) 不，完全不介意。
(C) 後者比較好。

答案 (B) 　　特殊疑問句及對話表達

Do you mind if I～?（你介意我～？）是請求對方允許的表現法。(B)的答案最正確。mind是「反對、介意」，對於像Do [Would] you mind～?這類問句，在回答同意「好啊」的情況時，其回答方式是No (, I don't mind.)（我不介意。），這點要特別注意。而(A)的mind是名詞，keep～ in mind（把～記在心裡）。(C)的latter雖然是要讓人從early做錯誤聯想，但它是名詞，意思是「後者」。

☑ 28 M 🇨🇦 W 🇬🇧

M: Are these the invoices that we received today?
W: (A) We can file a complaint.
(B) No, those are yesterday's.
(C) Including delivery charge.

M：這些是我們今天收到的發票嗎？
W：(A) 我們可以投訴。
(B) 不，那些是昨天的。
(C) 包括運費。

答案 (B) 　　Yes / No

在包含關係代名詞的句子中，可以依照前面開始聽到的順序來訓練理解能力，「這些是發票嗎？」＋「我們今天收到的」。以(B)的回答「不，（不是今天）是昨天收到的」最正確。

☐ file a complaint　投訴

☑ 29 W 🇺🇸 M 🇦🇺

W: When do you think we should start working on the proposal?
M: (A) By next Tuesday, at the latest.
(B) We already have enough people.
(C) I'll be in the office then.

W：你認為我們應該何時開始忙這項提案？
M：(A) 最晚在下週二以前。
(B) 我們已有足夠的人。
(C) 我那時候會在辦公室。

答案 (A) 　　疑問詞

這是在疑問詞後面插入do you think（你認為）的句子。可忽略插入句，答題關鍵在於是否理解問題的內容是「應該何時開始這項提案」。(A)明確地回答時間「最晚在下週二以前」，所以是正確答案。at the latest是「最晚」。而(B)和(C)都不符合對when的回應。

☐ 30 M 🇨🇦 W 🇺🇸

M: I think I should leave for the airport at a quarter to four.
W: (A) What time is your flight?
(B) Don't leave it behind.
(C) Whenever you can get ready.

M：我覺得我應該在3點45分出發前往機場。
W：(A) 你的班機是幾點？
(B) 不要讓它留在原處。
(C) 你做好準備的任何時候。

答案 (A) 　　陳述句

針對談話對象說leave for the airport at...（～點出發前往機場），以(A)詢問班機幾點的回答最正確。a quarter to four是「再15分就4點（＝3點45分）」。「4點15分」是a quarter past four。不過即使沒有正確聽懂這個時間應該也會答(A)，所以不需要對時間太琢磨。(B)跟問句一樣都是用leave（留下），但意思不一樣。

☐ get ready　準備

☑ 31 W 🇬🇧 M 🇦🇺

W: Why weren't this year's profits as high as last year's?
M: (A) We are more efficient now.
(B) Maybe next year.
(C) Costs have increased.

W：為什麼今年的利潤不如去年那麼高呢？
M：(A) 我們現在更有效率了。
(B) 可能明年。
(C) 成本增加了。

答案 (C) 　　特殊疑問句及對話表達

Why weren't～ ?的意思是「為什麼不～呢？」。profit是「利潤」，句尾是指last year's profits。對於「今年的利潤不如去年那麼高的原因」，以(C)的具體回答「因為成本增加」最正確。(A)的效率看似跟主題相關，但是不適合當作利潤減少的原因。

☐ efficient [ɪˈfɪʃənt] 形 效率高的

PART 3　CD 3　34-35　M 🍁 W 🇬🇧

錄音原文	錄音原文翻譯
Questions 32 through 34 refer to the following conversation.	試題 32-34 請參考以下會話。
M: Hello, I just saw an ad on TV for this digital camera. I was wondering if you carry it.	M：哈囉！我剛剛在電視上看到這款數位相機的廣告，我想知道妳這是否有賣。
W: We do, yes, but unfortunately we're temporarily out of stock. Would you like me to put one on order for you?	W：是的，我們有賣，但遺憾的是我們暫時缺貨。我可以幫你訂購嗎？
M: Thanks, but I'd really like to get one today.	M：謝謝，可是我今天真的很想買到。
W: I see. Well, our other store in Bellvie might have one. It's about thirty minutes from here. Let me call them and check for you.	W：了解。那麼，我們在貝爾維（Bellvie）的分店可能還有。離這裡約 30 分鐘。我來打個電話幫你確認看看。

Vocabulary

□ ad [æd] 名 廣告（advertisement的縮寫）　　□ temporarily [`tɛmpəˌrɛrəlɪ] 副 暫時地
□ Would you like me to *do*?　你想讓我做～嗎？、（我）可以做～嗎？（提議）　　□ put～ on order　訂購～

試題	試題翻譯	解答與解析
☑ **32** What product is the man looking for? (A) A television (B) A computer part (C) Computer software (D) A camera	男性在找什麼產品？ (A) 一台電視 (B) 電腦零件 (C) 電腦軟體 (D) 一台相機	**答案 (D)**　　其他細節 從一開始男性的發言I just saw an ad on TV for this digital camera可知正確答案是(D)。後面接著I was wondering if you carry it.的it就是指「數位相機」。carry在這句的意思是「商店備有（貨品），銷售中」，與stock（存貨）一樣意思。注意不要因為聽到on TV就誤選(A)。
☑ **33** What is the problem? (A) The item is sold out. (B) The product is too expensive. (C) The appliance is defective. (D) The store is too far.	發生什麼問題？ (A) 商品賣完了。 (B) 產品太貴。 (C) 電器有瑕疵。 (D) 商店太遠。	**答案 (A)**　　概述 對於男性要找的數位相機，女性在第1次發言時就提到unfortunately we're temporarily out of stock。正確答案(A)的item（物品）即是數位相機，sold out（賣完）是將對話中說的out of stock（缺貨）換個說法而已。 □ appliance [ə`plaɪəns] 名 電器 □ defective [dɪ`fɛktɪv] 形 有瑕疵的
☑ **34** What does the woman offer to do? (A) Refund the cost of the item (B) Exchange the item (C) Telephone another store (D) Talk to the manager	女性提議做什麼？ (A) 退還物品的款項 (B) 換貨 (C) 打電話到其他店 (D) 跟店長說	**答案 (C)**　　請求、建議、提出 對於商品已缺貨，女性向顧客說our other store in Bellvie might have one表示其他店可能還有。從最後那句Let me call them and check for you.可知(C)是正確答案。our other store in Bellvie和call分別被換成another store和telephone的說法。 □ refund [`riˌfʌnd] 動 退還～ □ exchange [ɪks`tʃendʒ] 動 交換～

錄音原文	錄音原文翻譯

Questions 35 through 37 refer to the following conversation.

W: Say, John, did we get the mutual fund data for March yet? I've just about finished the first quarter report, and those are the only figures I don't have yet.

M: Right. Judy from Marketing called just a minute ago. She said she'd e-mail them to me later this morning. Would you like me to call her and tell her you're waiting?

W: No, that's fine. Could you just forward them to me as soon as you get them? Then I can finish the report this afternoon. I have to give it to the printer tomorrow morning. I thought I might not make the deadline.

M: I see your situation. I'll definitely do that.

試題 35-37 請參考以下會話。

W：嘿，約翰（John），我們拿到 3 月共同基金的數字了嗎？我剛完成第 1 季的報告，就只差那些我目前還沒有的數字。

M：對。市場行銷部茱蒂（Judy）幾分鐘前才剛打電話來。她說今天早上晚點會用電子郵件傳給我。妳希望我打給她說妳在等資料嗎？

W：不，沒關係。可以請你一收到它們，就馬上轉給我嗎？這樣我今天下午就可以完成這份報告了。我必須在明天早上交給印刷廠。我怕我可能趕不上最後期限。

M：我了解你的情況。我一定會那樣做的。

Vocabulary

□ say [se] 動 （此處為感嘆詞）嘿　　□ first quarter 第1季　　□ forward A to B 把A轉給B
□ as soon as～ 一～馬上就　　□ printer [`prɪntɚ] 名 印刷廠　　□ make a deadline 趕上最後期限

試題	試題翻譯	解答與解析
35 What is the woman waiting for? (A) A deadline (B) Some data (C) Some photocopies (D) A phone call	女性在等什麼？ (A) 截止期限 (B) 一些資料 (C) 一些影本 (D) 一通電話	**答案 (B)** 〔其他細節〕 女性一開頭就問男性did we get the mutual fund data for March yet?。從下一句接著提到those are the only figures I don't have yet，可知只缺少3月的共同基金資料（the mutual fund data for March）。由此可判斷女性在等的就是這份資料，所以(B)是正確答案。接下來男性的發言提到...and tell her you're <u>waiting</u>?也是答題關鍵。
36 What did Judy say she would do later this morning? (A) Contact a mutual fund company (B) Give some figures to the printers (C) Forward an e-mail to the woman (D) E-mail some information to the man	茱蒂說她今天早上晚點會做什麼？ (A) 連絡共同基金公司 (B) 給印刷廠一些數據 (C) 把一封電子郵件轉給女性 (D) 用電子郵件傳一些資料給男性	**答案 (D)** 〔其他細節〕 關於茱蒂，在男性第1次發言裡可聽到不少資訊。從這句She said she'd e-mail them to me later this morning可知，(D)是正確答案。them是指前面女性發言時提到的the (only) figures（＝3月的共同基金資料），選項則是將它抽象表達為some information（一些資料）。(C)是男性下一步即將要做的事。
37 What does the woman plan to do tomorrow? (A) Hand in a report (B) Attend a meeting (C) Meet with a client (D) Extend a deadline	女性預計明天要做什麼？ (A) 交一份報告 (B) 參加會議 (C) 與客戶會面 (D) 延長期限	**答案 (A)** 〔下一步動作〕 從女性的發言可以聽到有關tomorrow（明天）的訊息，她第2次發言時提到，I have to give it to the printer tomorrow morning.，因此(A)是正確答案。it即是前句提到的the report（報告）。選項是將give換成hand in～（提交～）來表達。 □ extend a deadline 延長期限

錄音原文	錄音原文翻譯
Questions 38 through 40 refer to the following conversation.	試題 38-40 請參考以下會話。

W: Hi. I bought these boots from the clearance shelf the other day, but when I got home I realized they're flashier than I thought, and they simply don't go with anything in my wardrobe. I wonder, can I get a refund?

M: Oh, I'm sorry, we can't offer refunds on clearance items. However, we can give you a coupon for the same value, which you can use on other merchandise. Do you have your receipt?

W: Yes, here it is. Could you tell me how long the coupon is valid for?

M: Twelve months, and it can be used at any of our locations.

W：嗨。前幾天我在清倉大拍賣的架上買了這雙靴子，但是回家後我才發現它們比我想像的更華麗，而且它們完全無法跟我衣櫃裡的任何一件衣服搭配。我想知道，我可以申請退款嗎？

M：喔，不好意思，我們無法對清倉大拍賣的商品退款。不過，可以為您提供可以使用在其他商品上的等值優惠券。您有收據嗎？

W：有的，在這裡。你能告訴我這張優惠券的使用期限嗎？

M：12個月，而且在我們的任何分店都可以使用。

Vocabulary

- ☐ clearance (sale) [ˋklɪrəns] 名 清倉大拍賣
- ☐ the other day　前幾天
- ☐ get a refund　得到退款
- ☐ value [ˋvælju] 名 價格
- ☐ merchandise [ˋmɝtʃənˌdaɪz] 名 商品
- ☐ receipt [rɪˋsit] 名 收據
- ☐ valid [ˋvælɪd] 形 有效的

試題	試題翻譯	解答與解析

38

What does the store sell?

(A) Books
(B) Groceries
(C) Footwear
(D) Hardware

這家店賣什麼？

(A) 書
(B) 食品雜貨
(C) 鞋類
(D) 五金製品

答案 (C)　其他細節

從開頭的 I bought these boots from... 可知女性買了靴子。(C) 是將 boots（靴子）換成 Footwear（鞋類）來表達，所以是正確答案。就算萬一漏聽了 boots 這個字，也可以用接在後面的 they(= boots) simply don't go with anything in my wardrobe 這個部分，來判斷什麼東西與衣服有關。建議大家可以用消去法來作答。

39

What is wrong with the woman's item?

(A) The size
(B) The style
(C) The quality
(D) The price

這名女性的商品有什麼問題？

(A) 尺寸
(B) 樣式
(C) 品質
(D) 價格

答案 (B)　其他細節

這題的 the woman's item 即是指女性買的靴子。對於這項商品，女性提到 I realized they're flashier than I thought, and they simply don't go with anything in my wardrobe（比想像的更華麗（flashier），而且完全無法跟衣櫃裡的任何一件搭配），這些都可視為是「樣式（有問題）」，所以 (B) 是正確答案。go with～是「與～相配」。

40

What does the man say about the coupon?
(A) It can be used to get a 12% discount.
(B) It must be used within one month.
(C) It can be exchanged for a free lunch.
(D) It can be used at any other branch.

男性對於優惠券有什麼說法？

(A) 可以獲得 88 折。
(B) 必須在 1 個月內使用。
(C) 可以兌換免費午餐。
(D) 可以在任何其他分店使用。

答案 (D)　其他細節

男性第 1 次發言時提到，無法給予退款但可以提供優惠券。第 2 次的發言則說 it can be used at any of our locations，(D) 是換另一種說法而已，所以是正確答案。it 是指優惠券。branch 是「分店」，any of our locations 改用 any other branch 來表達。與靴子等值的優惠券可以用於其他商品，並沒有提到 88 折的折扣，所以 (A) 是錯的。

錄音原文	錄音原文翻譯

Questions 41 through 43 refer to the following conversation.

W: Excuse me, I work for Johnson Brothers on the sixth floor. My door card doesn't seem to be working.

M: Yes, ma'am, sorry about that. The security card readers have been shut off this weekend for maintenance. I can let you through to the office elevators.

W: I see. Thank you. Also, two of my clients are coming to meet me today. Will you contact me when they come through the main doors? I'll come down to meet them here.

M: Of course, ma'am. If you could give me their names and tell me about what time they'll be here, I'll be sure to telephone you when they arrive.

試題41-43請參考以下會話。

W：不好意思，我是在 6 樓強森兄弟（Johnson Brothers）上班的人。我的門禁卡好像不能運作了。

M：好的，女士，非常抱歉。這週末門禁卡讀卡機為了進行保養已經關閉運作。我可以讓您到辦公室電梯那邊。

W：了解。謝謝。另外，我有 2 位客戶今天要來見我。當他們從大門進入時，可以請你聯絡我嗎？我會下來這裡見他們。

M：當然可以，女士。如果您可以給我他們的名字，並告訴我他們什麼時候到這裡，當他們到達時，我一定會打電話給您。

Vocabulary

☐ seem to *do* 好像～　　☐ shut off～ （機械等）關掉　　☐ maintenance [`mentənəns] 名 保養
☐ let～ through 讓人可以往～（某個場所）、通過

試題	試題翻譯	解答與解析
☑ **41** Where most likely is the conversation taking place? (A) In an elevator (B) In a hotel lobby (C) At the entrance of a building (D) In front of a client's office	這篇對話最可能發生在哪裡？ (A) 在電梯裡 (B) 在飯店大廳 (C) 在建築物入口處 (D) 在客戶的辦公室前面	**答案 (C)** 〔概述〕 女性說無法使用門禁卡（所以無法到6樓）。男性說明了原因並讓女性至大樓電梯，所以可推測這是在建築物入口處跟警衛的對話，故(C)是正確答案。另外從女性第2次發言內容提到「當客戶通過主要大門（the main doors）進入時我會下來這裡」，也可以想像該畫面的地點。
☑ **42** Where is the woman's office? (A) On the 2nd floor (B) On the 6th floor (C) On the 12th floor (D) On the 16th floor	女性的辦公室在哪裡？ (A) 2 樓 (B) 6 樓 (C) 12 樓 (D) 16 樓	**答案 (B)** 〔其他細節〕 從對話的第1句I work for Johnson Brothers on the sixth floor 即可知正確答案是(B)。注意不要因為對話中出現其他數字two of my clients而有所混淆。
☑ **43** What does the woman ask the man to do? (A) Phone her clients for her (B) Guide her clients to the elevators (C) Provide her clients with her name (D) Contact her when her clients arrive	女性請男性做什麼？ (A) 幫她打電話給客戶 (B) 引導她的客戶到電梯 (C) 提供她的名字給客戶 (D) 當她的客戶到達時聯絡她	**答案 (D)** 〔請求、建議、提出〕 注意聽女性的「請求」，是在第2次發言中說的請求表現式Will you contact me when they ...?。這裡的they是指前句的two of my clients，所以(D)是正確答案。

錄音原文	錄音原文翻譯
Questions 44 through 46 refer to the following conversation.	試題 44-46 請參考以下會話。

M: Hello, and welcome back to the lunch hour show here on Radio One. Today we're talking with documentary filmmaker Joan Ingel, who's just come back from an excursion to Kenya. Tell us about that, Joan.

W: It was an adventure. I got to go rafting on the River Tana. It's even more thrilling than the Colorado. Of course, my favorite thing was interacting with the locals, although it can be challenging when few people speak English.

M: Fantastic. Can you give us a hint of what's in your upcoming film?

W: Well, it'll feature a lot of interviews, mostly with very low-income people. There's still a lot of poverty even as the government and economy improve.

M：哈囉，歡迎回到第 1 電台（Radio One）午餐時間秀。今天我們要和紀錄片製作人瓊安·英格爾（Joan Ingel）聊聊，她剛從肯亞（Kenya）短途旅行回來。來告訴我們這趟旅程吧，瓊安。

W：這是一趟冒險。我去塔納河（River Tana）泛舟。它甚至比科羅拉多河（Colorado）更刺激。當然，我最喜歡的是與當地居民交流，雖然很少人會說英文這點頗具挑戰性。

M：太棒了。對於近期即將上映的影片，您是否可以給我們一些內容提示呢？

W：嗯，它將穿插許多訪談，主要是採訪低收入者。即使政府和經濟改善，仍然有很多貧困的人。

Vocabulary

☐ go rafting 去泛舟   ☐ thrilling [`θrɪlɪŋ] 形 令人興奮的   ☐ interact with～ 與～交流
☐ local [`lok!] 名 （常用複數形）當地居民    ☐ challenging [`tʃælɪndʒɪŋ] 形 挑戰性的   ☐ fantastic [fæn`tæstɪk] 形 （口語上）太棒了
☐ upcoming [`ʌp͵kʌmɪŋ] 形 即將到來的    ☐ mostly [`mostlɪ] 副 主要地   ☐ even as～ 即使～

試題	試題翻譯	解答與解析
44 What type of business does the woman work for? (A) A radio station (B) A tour service (C) A film production company (D) An economic research firm	女性是做哪一類型的工作？ (A) 廣播電台 (B) 旅遊服務業 (C) 影片製作公司 (D) 經濟研究公司	**答案 (C)** 概述 對於來談話的女性，男性開場白時就提到 we're talking with documentary filmmaker Joan Ingel，所以正確答案是(C)。選項是將 filmmaker（影片製作人）換成 film production company（影片製作公司）來表達。男性第2次發言說的 your upcoming film 也是提示關鍵。(A)指的不是女性的職業，而是男性的職業。注意不要因為聽到肯亞旅行而誤做聯想選(B)。
45 What has the woman recently done? (A) Returned from a trip abroad (B) Written an article (C) Studied another language (D) Attended an international conference	女性最近做了什麼？ (A) 從海外旅行回來 (B) 寫一篇報導 (C) 學習其他語言 (D) 參加國際會議	**答案 (A)** 其他細節 男性第1次的發言提到...Joan Ingel, who's just come back from an excursion to Kenya，由此可知女性瓊安·英格爾從肯亞旅行（拍攝）回來，所以正確答案是(A)。選項是將 come back（回來）及 excursion to Kenya（去肯亞短途旅行）分別換成 return（回來）及 trip abroad（國外旅行）來表達。excursion 主要是指團體方式的短途旅行，trip 是不論時間長短，都可表示觀光或商務上的旅行。
46 Who does the woman say she talked with? (A) Many poor people (B) Government officials (C) Newspaper columnists (D) Volunteer aid workers	女性說她和誰談了話？ (A) 很多窮人 (B) 政府官員 (C) 報紙專欄作家 (D) 志工人員	**答案 (A)** 其他細節 對於最新的影片（＝在肯亞拍攝的影片），女性第2次的發言說 it'll feature a lot of interviews, mostly with very low-income people，由此可知她訪談了收入非常低的人，意即與當地的窮人談話。(A)只是將 very low-income（收入非常低的）換成 poor（貧困）來表達，所以是正確答案。該句後面提到的 poverty（貧困）即是 poor 的名詞。

錄音原文	錄音原文翻譯

Questions 47 through 49 refer to the following conversation.

W: Hello, my name is Jane Winslow, and I'm calling because I think I left my handbag at the theater earlier this evening at the six o'clock performance. Is this where I can ask?

M: This is the ticket office, ma'am, but I might be able to help you. Let's see ... it looks like there's a small handbag here—I'd say navy-blue or dark blue, with a gold clasp ....

W: Oh. The one I'm missing is black, with a zipper. It's got my driver's license in a wallet inside.

M: I see. Well, our cleaning staff is going through the theater right now. If you can leave me your phone number, I'll call you immediately if anything turns up.

試題 47-49 請參考以下會話。

W：哈囉，我叫珍・溫斯洛（Jane Winslow），我來電是因為我想我在戲院觀賞今天晚上 6 點的表演時，把手提包留在那裡了。我可以詢問您這邊嗎？

M：這裡是售票處，女士，但我應該可以幫上忙。我來看看……有個小手提包——我想是海軍藍或深藍色的，還帶一個金屬扣環……

W：喔。我遺失的是黑色的，有拉鍊。我的駕照就放在裡面的一個錢包內。

M：好的。那麼，我們的清潔人員現在正在清掃戲院。如果您願意留下電話號碼，一旦有找到什麼，我立刻通知您。

Vocabulary

- □ performance [pɚˋforməns] 名 表演
- □ navy-blue [ˋnevɪˏblu] 形 海軍藍的
- □ clasp [klæsp] 名 鉤環
- □ miss [mɪs] 動 丢失
- □ zipper [ˋzɪpɚ] 名 拉鍊
- □ driver's license 駕照
- □ wallet [ˋwɑlɪt] 名 錢包
- □ right now 就是現在

試題	試題翻譯	解答與解析

☑ 47

Why is the woman calling?

(A) To inquire about a lost article
(B) To purchase tickets
(C) To ask about show times
(D) To get directions to the theater

女性為什麼打電話？

(A) 詢問遺失物
(B) 要購票
(C) 詢問表演時間
(D) 請教去電影院的路線

答案 (A) 概述

一開頭的I'm calling because...意即「我打電話來是因為……原因」，所以要仔細聽懂後面內容，也就是「打電話的原因及目的」。從I left my handbag at the theater...可知(A)是正確答案。選項是將handbag（手提包）這種明確物品的單字用抽象化名詞a lost article（遺失物）來表達。Part 3、4常會像這樣把具體跟抽象的說法交換使用。

☑ 48

What most likely is the man's job?

(A) A cleaner
(B) A ticket agent
(C) A photographer
(D) A performer

男性的工作最有可能是什麼？

(A) 清潔人員
(B) 售票人員
(C) 攝影師
(D) 表演者

答案 (B) 概述

女性打電話問在戲院遺失物一事，不過男性回說This is the ticket office，所以電話應該是接到售票處。所以(B)最正確。

☑ 49

What does the man offer to do for the woman?
(A) Sell her discounted tickets
(B) Guide her to the theater
(C) Exchange an item for another one
(D) Inform her if her item is found

男性對女性提出什麼幫忙？

(A) 賣她折扣票
(B) 引導她到電影院
(C) 改換別的物品
(D) 如果找到她的東西就通知她

答案 (D) 請求、建議、提出

男性第2次發言時說If you can leave me your phone number, I'll call you immediately if anything turns up.。will並非只單純表達未來行為及想法，也有很多情況是包含「我來做～吧！」和「建議」的意思。turn up是「（遺失物）被找到或出現」，所以(D)是正確答案。her item（她的東西）即是指女性的手提包。

- □ item [ˋaɪtəm] 名 物品、東西
- □ inform [ɪnˋfɔrm] 動 通知～

CD 3 · 41 · M 🇦🇺 W 🇬🇧

錄音原文	錄音原文翻譯

Questions 50 through 52 refer to the following conversation.

M: Good morning, Ms. Sandstone. This is Chris Simpson from Greenwood Architects. I was wondering if you have had time to check the layout for your new art gallery. I e-mailed it to you two days ago.

W: Yes, thanks for sending it. It looks impressive. <u>I have one concern, though.</u> Do you think the entrance hall is large enough? We're expecting a large number of visitors on the weekends and need to avoid any congestion. Could you make it a little more spacious?

M: Sure, I'll make the change and send you the revision later today.

W: That would be great. I'll give you my feedback once I receive it.

試題 50-52 請參考以下會話。

M：早安，山德斯頓（Sandstone）女士。我是格林伍德（Greenwood）建築師事務所的克里斯·辛普森（Chris Simpson）。我想知道您是否有時間確認新藝術畫廊的格局。2 天前我用電子郵件傳給您了。

W：是的，謝謝你傳過來。它令人印象深刻。<u>不過，我有一個疑慮。</u>你覺得門廳夠大嗎？我們預期週末時段會有很多的參觀者，所以必須避免任何擁擠。你能讓它更寬敞些嗎？

M：當然可以，我會做些修改並在今天晚些時候將修正版傳給您。

W：那太好了。 我一收到它， 就會給你我的意見。

Vocabulary

☐ architect [ˋɑrkəˌtɛkt] **名** 建築師　　☐ impressive [ɪmˋprɛsɪv] **形** 令人深刻印象的　　☐ concern [kənˋsɜn] **名** 擔心的事
☐ though [ðo] **副**（置於句中或句尾）然而～　　☐ avoid [əˋvɔɪd] **動** 避免～　　☐ congestion [kənˋdʒɛstʃən] **名** 擁擠
☐ feedback [ˋfidˌbæk] **名** 意見

試題	試題翻譯	解答與解析

☑ 50

What did the man send the woman two days ago?
(A) A change in schedule
(B) Information about an art exhibition
(C) A layout for a new art gallery
(D) Photographs of an event

2 天前男性傳送什麼給女性？

(A) 時間表的變動
(B) 有關藝術展的訊息
(C) 新藝術畫廊的格局
(D) 活動的照片

答案 (C)　　其他細節

男性第 1 次發言說，I e-mailed it to you two days ago.。這個 it 即是指前句的 the layout for your new art gallery，所以 (C) 是正確答案。聽力測驗是無法像閱讀測驗可以回頭確認該代名詞所代表的內容，所以如果能有時間預覽問題，把握問題重點再聽內容會更有效率。像這一題就要專心聽「2 天前傳送了什麼」。

☑ 51

What does the woman mean when she says, "<u>I have one concern, though</u>"?
(A) She will be late for a meeting.
(B) The hall size might need adjusting.
(C) A document is missing.
(D) There will not be enough visitors.

當女性說 「<u>I have one concern, though</u>」，表示什麼？

(A) 她開會會遲到。
(B) 大廳的大小可能需要調整。
(C) 文件遺失。
(D) 參觀者會不夠多。

答案 (B)　　說話者的目的

concern是指「擔心的事」。女性前面說了「有件擔心的事」後，具體描述了擔心的內容，Do you think the entrance hall is large enough?。接著她請求對方說Could you make it a little more spacious?，因此也可以從這邊推想「因為窄小所以想寬敞一點」→「需要調整尺寸」，所以(B)是正確答案。

☑ 52

What does the man say he will do?

(A) Send the woman a quote
(B) Visit the woman's office later today
(C) Get in touch with his colleague
(D) Send the woman the modified layout

男性說他將做什麼？

(A) 傳報價給女性
(B) 今天晚些時候去女性辦公室拜訪
(C) 和他的同事取得聯繫
(D) 將修正後的格局傳給女性

答案 (D)　　下一步動作

男性第2次的發言說I'll make the change and send you the revision later today。make a change是「做改變」，revision是「修正版」，談的正是2天前傳送的格局內容。因此(D)是正確答案。modified（被修改的）和revised意思一樣，請大家最好要記牢。注意(B)是故意使用與對話內一樣的later today（今天晚些時候）讓人混淆而誤選。

錄音原文	錄音原文翻譯

Questions 53 through 55 refer to the following conversation with three speakers.

W-1: Have you heard the news?

M: Heard what?

W-1: Janet Nelson is going to be promoted to Regional Sales Manager sometime next week!

W-2: Oh, I did! David just told me.

M: Wow, that's great news, although it's no wonder—she's so good with people. It's the first time anyone from our department has risen that far. Do you know when they'll make the news public?

W-2: Well, David said it'll be officially announced at the next All-Staff Meeting. Isn't that on Friday?

M: No, actually that's the Sales Department Meeting. The All-Staff Meeting is next Monday. Jack Henderson is in charge of that one, so if you want details, I suppose it'd be best to ask him.

試題 53-55 請參考以下 3 人的會話。

W-1：你們聽到消息了嗎？

M：聽到什麼？

W-1：珍妮特·尼爾森（Janet Nelson）下週將晉升為區域銷售經理！

W-2：哦，我有聽說！大衛（David）才剛剛告訴我。

M：哇，好棒的消息，不過那也難怪——她很擅長與人相處。從我們部門晉升到這麼高職位的，她是第一人。你們知道他們何時會公開這項消息嗎？

W-2：嗯，大衛說在下一次的全體員工大會會做正式宣布。那不就是週五嗎？

M：不是，實際上那是銷售部門會議。全體員工大會是在下週一。傑克·亨德森（Jack Henderson）負責該大會，所以如果妳想了解細節，我認為妳最好問他。

Vocabulary

- □ no wonder　難怪
- □ good with people　擅長與人相處
- □ make～ public　公開～
- □ officially [əˋfɪʃəlɪ] 副 正式地
- □ in charge of～　負責～
- □ detail [ˋditel] 名 細節

試題	試題翻譯	解答與解析

☑ **53**

What are the speakers discussing?

(A) A job posting
(B) A job interview
(C) A job promotion
(D) A job fair

這些對話者在討論什麼？

(A) 徵人啟事
(B) 工作面試
(C) 工作晉升
(D) 就業博覽會

答案 (C)　概述

這是3個人的對話內容。大家要多熟悉像開頭的 Have you heard the news?——Heard what?這樣的短句往來方式。女性1在第2次發言時說 Janet Nelson is going to be promoted to Regional Sales Manager sometime next week!，意即敘述有關珍妮特·尼爾森的晉升。promote是及物動詞「晉升～」，常用於被動式。正確答案(C)的promotion是promote的名詞。

☑ **54**

When will the announcement take place?
(A) Today
(B) Tomorrow
(C) This Friday
(D) Next Monday

何時會宣布？

(A) 今天
(B) 明天
(C) 本週五
(D) 下週一

答案 (D)　其他細節

題目的the announcement（宣布）就是指公布珍妮特·尼爾森職位晉升一事。男性問了何時公布，女性2說it'll be officially announced at the next All-Staff Meeting。而從男性接著說All-Staff Meeting（全體員工大會）是在next Monday（下週一）可知，正確答案是(D)。注意不要被女性2說的Isn't that on Friday?所誤導。

☑ **55**

What is Jack Henderson in charge of?

(A) The Sales Department
(B) The Marketing Department
(C) A Regional Managers' Meeting
(D) An All-Staff Meeting

傑克·亨德森負責什麼？

(A) 銷售部門
(B) 市場行銷部門
(C) 區域經理人會議
(D) 全體員工大會

答案 (D)　其他細節

傑克·亨德森這名人物是男性在最後發言時提到的。至於他負責什麼，就在這句The All-Staff Meeting is next Monday. Jack Henderson is in charge of that one, ...。that one即是指The All-Staff Meeting（全體員工大會），由此可知(D)是正確答案。這篇內容除了對話的3人之外，還提到另3位人物，所以如果能先預覽題目會更有利作答。

錄音原文	錄音原文翻譯

Questions 56 through 58 refer to the following conversation.

W: Paul? Can you help me with this copier? I've tried to fix it several times, but I just can't get it to stop jamming.
M: OK, I see you took out the jammed paper. Now, have you tried putting a new stack of paper in the tray?
W: No, I haven't tried that. Do you think that'll work?
M: This is an older copier. It's been serviced recently, but it's sensitive to the weather. When the air is humid like today, the paper tends to get stuck. Putting in new, drier paper usually works.

試題 56-58 請參考以下會話。

W：保羅（Paul）？可以幫我用這台影印機嗎？我已經試著修很多次了，但就是無法讓它停止卡紙。
M：好的，我看到妳取出卡到的紙張了。現在，妳有試過把一疊新的紙放入紙匣嗎？
W：沒有，我沒有試。你認為那樣就可運轉了嗎？
M：這是一台較舊的影印機。最近已經維修過了，但是它對天氣很敏感。當空氣像今天這樣潮濕時，紙張容易卡紙。加進新的、較乾燥的紙通常可以順利運轉。

Vocabulary

□ help～with... 幫～用……　□〈get＋物＋to *do*〉 讓（物）得以～　□ take out～ 取出～
□ a stack of～ 一疊～　□ sensitive to～ 對～敏感　□ humid [`hjumɪd] 形 潮濕的　□ tend to *do* 有～的傾向
□ get stuck （東西）被卡住

試題	試題翻譯	解答與解析

56

Why is the woman upset?

(A) There is not enough paper.
(B) The machine does not work properly.
(C) She is not familiar with her job.
(D) She cannot remove the paper.

女性為何心煩？

(A) 紙張不夠。
(B) 機器無法正常運轉。
(C) 她對自己的工作不熟悉。
(D) 她無法移除紙張。

答案 (B) 〔其他細節〕

這題的upset（心煩的）是表示女性第1句說話的樣子。(B)抽象地形容影印機卡紙，因此是正確答案。選項是將copier（影印機）改成machine（機器）。用機器塞住或卡住而無法運轉來表示jam，也就是影印機上的「卡紙」。

□ properly [`prɑpɚlɪ] 副 正確地
□ be familiar with～ 精通～、熟悉～

57

What does the man mean when he says, "It's been serviced recently"?
(A) He has just bought a new model.
(B) He has checked the weather forecast.
(C) The copier has been inspected recently.
(D) The copier has been fitted with a new tray.

當男性說 「It's been serviced recently」，表示什麼？

(A) 他才剛買新的型號。
(B) 他已確認天氣預報。
(C) 影印機最近已被檢修過。
(D) 影印機已裝上新的紙匣。

答案 (C) 〔說話者的目的〕

抓住整篇的流程是「影印機無法正常運作」→「最近才維修但是對天氣敏感」→「放乾燥的紙試試看」。這裡的 service 是動詞，意思是購買機器後「做～的售後服務（檢查、維修）」。(C)用同樣意思的字 inspect 來代表service，所以是正確答案。這題如果有捕捉到 service 的意思應該就會選(C)了。

58

What does the man suggest?

(A) Inserting dry paper
(B) Using a different machine
(C) Calling a repair service
(D) Ordering a newer model

男性建議什麼？

(A) 放入乾燥的紙張
(B) 使用不一樣的機器
(C) 打電話給維修服務
(D) 訂購更新的型號

答案 (A) 〔請求、建議、提出〕

男性在第1次發言時詢問對方 have you tried putting a new stack of paper in the tray?（你有試過把一疊新的紙放入紙匣嗎？）。而放入新紙張的理由在其第2次發言時即針對天氣（濕氣）做了說明。所以從 Putting in new, drier paper usually works. 可知(A)是正確答案。對話中的 put (in)～（放入～）在選項內則換成 insert（放入）來表達。

錄音原文	錄音原文翻譯

Questions 59 through 61 refer to the following conversation.

M: Quentin Law Offices, this is Adam speaking. How may I help you?

W: Hi, my name is LeAnn Streng, and I made an appointment with Mr. Quentin earlier today for tomorrow at one, but unfortunately it's not looking like I'll be able to make it by then. I really apologize, but does Mr. Quentin have anything else open, say, later tomorrow or the next day?

M: I see. Well, let's ... take a look here ... uhh, it looks like he's booked tomorrow, and the next day is Saturday, so that wouldn't ... oh, wait. It looks like he has an opening at four-thirty tomorrow. Would that do?

W: Really? Yes, that should work. I could make it by then. Thanks so much.

試題 59-61 請參考以下對話。

M：昆汀（Quentin）律師事務所，我是亞當（Adam）。有什麼地方能效勞的嗎？

W：嗨，我是雷安・史崔（LeAnn Streng），我今天稍早跟昆汀先生訂好面天一點的約，但遺憾的是我似乎無法趕上。真的很抱歉，昆汀先生有其他空檔時間嗎？例如，明天晚點或再隔一天呢？

M：我明白了。那麼，讓我們……來看看這個……嗯，看起來他明天已約滿，而且再隔一天是週六，所以應該無法……喔，等等。他明天 4 點半看起來是可以的。那時候可以嗎？

W：真的嗎？好的，應該可行。那時間之前我能趕上。非常感謝。

Vocabulary

□ make it　到達（目的地）、及時趕上　　□ say [se] 動（可當感嘆詞）（常用作插入語）例如

試題	試題翻譯	解答與解析
59 Why is the woman calling? (A) To complain about a service (B) To apologize for missing a meeting (C) To get directions to the office (D) To change an appointment	女性為什麼打電話？ (A) 客訴 (B) 為缺席會議而致歉 (C) 詢問到事務所的路線 (D) 更改預約時間	**答案 (D)** 概述 女性打電話到昆汀法律事務所，表示今天和昆汀先生約好面談時間後，因為發現會趕不及，所以再打來詢問其他有空的時間。從這狀況可知，(D)是正確答案。
60 What does the man imply when he says, "the next day is Saturday"? (A) Saturday is available for reservations. (B) Mr. Quentin is fully booked on Saturday. (C) He is at work on Saturdays. (D) The office is closed on weekends.	當男性說 「the next day is Saturday」，表示什麼？ (A) 週六有空檔可預約。 (B) 昆汀先生週六預約全滿。 (C) 他每週六要工作。 (D) 事務所週末休息。	**答案 (D)** 說話者的目的 掌握前後句的語意「他明天預約滿了，後天是週六無法預約」。由此推測週六（＝週末）無法預約→事務所休息，因此(D)是正確答案。
61 On what day will the woman visit the office? (A) Thursday (B) Friday (C) Saturday (D) Sunday	女性會在哪一天拜訪事務所？ (A) 週四 (B) 週五 (C) 週六 (D) 週日	**答案 (B)** 其他細節 對於男性提問It looks like he has an opening at four-thirty tomorrow. Would that do?，女性回答Yes, that should work.，所以她明天會去事務所。而從男性在提問的前一句有說到the next day is Saturday可知後天是週六，因此明天是週五。

錄音原文	錄音原文翻譯

Questions 62 through 64 refer to the following conversation.

W: Hello, my name is Cindy Rodriguez. I need to speak to Robert Johnson in Customer Service, please.

M: Oh, Mr. Johnson has just stepped away from his desk. Is there something I can help you with?

W: Well, I spoke with him last Thursday about a defective item I received. He said he would send a new one immediately. It's Tuesday now, but I still haven't received it. I'd really like to have it by the end of the week.

M: I'm sorry to hear that, Ms. Rodriguez. Mr. Johnson should be back this afternoon around two.

W: Well, the problem is that I might not be able to call him around that time or even later.

M: Then, what about if you describe the item you ordered? Then, I can contact our shipping department and try to trace the order for you. That might be quicker.

試題 62-64 請參考以下會話。

W：哈囉，我叫辛蒂・羅德里格斯（Cindy Rodriguez）。我需要找客服的羅伯特・強森（Robert Johnson），麻煩你了。

M：喔，強森先生剛剛離開辦公桌了。有什麼事我可以幫忙的嗎？

W：嗯，我上週四和他說了我收到一件有瑕疵的商品。他說會立刻寄一份新的給我。現在已經是週二了，但我還沒有收到。我真的很想在週末之前拿到。

M：很抱歉聽到那樣的事，羅德里格斯女士。強森先生應該今天下午 2 點左右才會回來。

W：嗯，問題是我可能無法在那段時間甚至更晚的時候打電話給他。

M：那麼，可否請您描述訂購的商品？這樣，我可以聯繫我們的送貨部門並試著追蹤您的訂單。這可能會快些。

Vocabulary

□ step away from～　遠離～　　□ immediately [ɪ`midɪɪtlɪ] 副 立刻　　□ be sorry to *do*　對～感到抱歉
□ trace [tres] 動 追蹤～

試題	試題翻譯	解答與解析

62

What is the woman's problem?

(A) A delivery is late.
(B) An item is not available.
(C) She cannot find the shop.
(D) She ordered the wrong item.

女性的問題是什麼？

(A) 送貨延誤。
(B) 買不到商品。
(C) 她找不到商店。
(D) 她訂錯品項。

答案 (A)　　概述

對於瑕疵商品（a defective item），女性第2次發言時提到在上週四聯絡當下，對方說要馬上寄新的，但是到今天週二了還未送到。這情形即是正確答案(A)所說的「送貨延誤」。a delivery（送貨）就是指女性應該收到的新商品。

63

What information does the man ask the woman to provide?

(A) Her telephone number
(B) Her shipping address
(C) A description of her order
(D) The date the order was placed

男性要求女性提供什麼資訊？

(A) 她的電話號碼
(B) 她的送貨地址
(C) 她的訂貨內容
(D) 訂單的日期

答案 (C)　　請求、建議、提出

從男性的第3次發言Then, what about if you describe the item you ordered?即可知正確答案是(C)。How [What] about if～是「可否～好嗎？」的請求表現法。describe是動詞，意為「描述～的特徵」，選項是使用該字的名詞形description。(D)的the order was placed是place an order（下訂單）的被動式。

64

What does the man offer to do?

(A) Call Mr. Johnson
(B) Contact the shipping department
(C) Refund the woman's money
(D) Return the item

男性提議要做什麼？

(A) 打電話給強森先生
(B) 聯繫送貨部門
(C) 退還女性款項
(D) 退貨

答案 (B)　　請求、建議、提出

從男性的第 3 次發言if you describe... Then, I can contact our shipping department and...即可知正確答案是(B)。If you..., (then) I can [I'll] ... 這樣的表達方式，can 或 will 並非只是假設能夠、可能性或未來，它還含有「給予建議」的意味。請多接觸這類的句型，就能學到那種感覺了。

錄音原文	錄音原文翻譯

Questions 65 through 67 refer to the following conversation and list.

W: Hi, I'm here to perform some maintenance for you. Mr. Patel dispatched me here as soon as he got your e-mail. Apparently, there's quite a bit of work that has to be done.

M: Oh, good, yes, I sent him a list of things that we need repaired. Do you have a copy as well?

W: Yes, and I'll get started right away. I've already prepared the right equipment, so it shouldn't take me long to finish.

M: Great! We'd like to make one slight change, though: could you switch the times of the first and last items on the list? That way, we can start using the most important office items more quickly.

Items for Repair

Item	Quantity	Time
Floor Lamps	3	10:00 A.M.
Computers	2	11:00 A.M.
Photocopiers	2	12:00 P.M.
Desk Lamps	4	1:00 P.M.

試題 65-67 請參考以下會話及清單。

W：嗨，我是來為您做一些修繕工作的。帕特爾（Patel）先生一收到您的電子郵件就派我到這裡。顯然是有很多工作需要完成。

M：喔，好的，沒錯，我傳給他一份我們需要維修的項目清單。妳是不是也有一份副本？

W：是的，我馬上就開始進行。我已經準備好合適的設備，所以應該不會花太長的時間完成。

M：太好了！不過，我們想稍作一些變動：妳能否把列表中的第一項和最後一項的時間調換呢？如此一來，我們就可以更快開始使用最重要的辦公用品。

維修項目

項目	數量	時間
落地燈	3	10:00 A.M.
電腦	2	11:00 A.M.
影印機	2	12:00 P.M.
桌燈	4	1:00 P.M.

Vocabulary

□ dispatch [dɪˋspætʃ] 動 派遣～　　□ quite a bit of～　很多的～、大量的～　　□ slight [slaɪt] 形 微小的
□ switch [swɪtʃ] 動 調換～

試題	試題翻譯	解答與解析

☑ 65

Who most likely is Mr. Patel?

(A) A customer
(B) A supervisor
(C) An IT analyst
(D) A care worker

帕特爾先生最有可能是誰？

(A) 客戶
(B) 主管
(C) 資訊科技 （IT） 分析員
(D) 護理人員

答案 (B) 〔其他細節〕

從開頭說的Mr. Patel dispatched me here as soon as he got your e-mail.可知，女性是受帕特爾先生的指示來做維修的。所以正確答案是(B)。supervisor雖有「監督人、指導人」之意，但經常用one's supervisor 的形式來表示是「～的主管」。

☑ 66

What does the woman say she has already done?
(A) Dispatched some products
(B) Finished a project
(C) Brought items for repair
(D) Sent an e-mail

女性說她已經做了什麼？

(A) 寄了一些產品
(B) 完成一項計畫
(C) 帶了修理要用的東西
(D) 寄了一封電子郵件

答案 (C) 〔其他細節〕

注意聽女性的發言，在她第2次發言時說了I've already prepared the right equipment。其中的equipment（設備）就是為了男性請求的修理而準備的，因此(C)是正確答案。注意(D)是指男性已做的行為。

☑ 67

Look at the graphic. What item will be repaired first?
(A) Floor lamps
(B) Computers
(C) Photocopiers
(D) Desk lamps

依圖所示，哪一項會先修理？

(A) 落地燈
(B) 電腦
(C) 影印機
(D) 桌燈

答案 (D) 〔圖表問題〕

選項是依照清單的4個項目排序。男性第2次發言說could you switch the times of the first and last items on the list?，意即向對方提出請求，希望把第1項（＝Floor Lamps（落地燈））和最後一項（＝Desk Lamps（桌燈））的時間對調。因此一開始會先修理的項目是桌燈。

M 🇦🇺 W 🇺🇸

錄音原文	錄音原文翻譯

Questions 68 through 70 refer to the following conversation and map.

M: So, this is the layout of the factory we're supposed to install the solar panels in, right?

W: Yes, the company that owns the factory is trying to reduce energy costs. That's a big ... a near-term target for them.

M: I see. Well, just looking at things, the locations seem ideal—like we could do the installation almost anywhere—I mean, the roof being so flat and everything.

W: Yes, but they only want us to cover the closest building to Saila Lake, since that catches the highest amount of average sunlight during the day year-round.

試題 68-70 請參考以下會話及地圖。

M：所以，這是我們應該安裝太陽能板的工廠格局，對吧？

W：是的，擁有該工廠的公司正在嘗試降低能源成本。這對他們來說是一項很大的……近期的目標。

M：了解。那麼，照目前看到的來說，這地點似乎是理想的——看起來我們幾乎在每個地方都可以進行安裝——我的意思是，屋頂是如此平坦，還有其他一切條件都很適合。

W：是的，但他們只希望我們安裝離塞拉湖（Saila Lake）最近的建築物，因為那裡一整年白天的平均日照量最高。

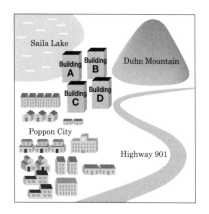

Vocabulary

□ near-term [`nɪr͵tɝm] 形 近期的　□ flat [flæt] 形 平的　□ year-round [`jɪr͵raʊnd] 副 一整年地

試題	試題翻譯	解答與解析

68

What does the woman say is a near-term goal of the company?
(A) Covering a work area
(B) Fixing the rooftop
(C) Reducing its expenses
(D) Producing more energy

女性說公司的近期目標是什麼？

(A) 包辦一處工作區域
(B) 修繕屋頂
(C) 降低支出
(D) 生產更多的能源

答案 (C)　〔其他細節〕

請大家要多習慣〈疑問詞＋does S say...?〉這樣的提問。女性說That's a big... a near-term target for them.，That即是指前面提到的the company... is trying to reduce energy costs。正確答案(C)是將energy costs（能源成本）用expense（支出）作抽象表達。

69

What does the man say is ideal?

(A) The worksite
(B) The sunlight angle
(C) Panel layouts
(D) Weather conditions

男性說什麼是理想的？

(A) 作業現場
(B) 日照角度
(C) 太陽能板格局
(D) 天氣狀況

答案 (A)　〔其他細節〕

仔細聽男性的發言即可掌握他說的關鍵字ideal（理想的）就是the locations seem ideal（地點似乎是理想的）的部分。這裡說的the locations（地點），從後續的內容可知是指安裝太陽能板的場所，所以(A)是正確答案。而對話中有提到安裝場所需要日照量多的地方，不是角度的問題，因此(B)的答案是錯的。

70

Look at the graphic. Where will the installation be done?
(A) On Building A
(B) On Building B
(C) On Building C
(D) On Building D

依圖所示，會在什麼地方安裝？

(A) 建築物 A
(B) 建築物 B
(C) 建築物 C
(D) 建築物 D

答案 (A)　〔圖表問題〕

從圖表和選項來看，可推測這是有關4棟建築物的問題。女性第2次的發言說they only want us to cover the closest building to Saila Lake，由此可知客戶端希望太陽能板安裝在離塞拉湖最近的建築物。再配合地圖來看，離塞拉湖最近的就是建築物A。

錄音原文	錄音原文翻譯

Questions 71 through 73 refer to the following advertisement.

After more than six happy years at its location in Henderson, Charisma Skin and Beauty Clinic is excited to announce it is relocating to new premises in the heart of Milford. Our ultra-modern clinic opens tomorrow on the corner of Omana Avenue and Cedric Road. Charisma utilizes the latest technology to help treat a variety of skin conditions caused by aging, sun damage and allergies. To celebrate our move, all customers who visit before the end of November will receive 25 percent off any treatment. To take advantage of this offer, or for a free consultation, phone 516-555-5821.

試題 71-73 請參考以下廣告。

在亨德森（Henderson）地區 6 年多的幸福歲月後，克莉斯瑪（Charisma）皮膚美容診所很高興宣布將遷往米爾福德（Milford）市中心的新址。我們的超現代化診所明日在奧瑪那（Omana）大道和賽德里克（Cedric）路的轉角處開幕。克莉斯瑪利用最新的技術幫助治療由老化、陽光傷害和過敏引起的各種皮膚狀況。為了慶祝我們搬遷，所有 11 月底前來訪的客戶，在任何療程將可享 75 折的折扣。要利用此優惠或免費諮詢，請致電 516-555-5821。

Vocabulary

- □ relocate to～ 搬到～
- □ ultra-modern [ˌʌltrəˈmɑdən] 形 超現代化的
- □ utilize [ˈjutlˌaɪz] 動 利用～
- □ help *do* 有助於～
- □ treat [trit] 動 治療～
- □ aging [ˈedʒɪŋ] 名 老化
- □ take advantage of～ 利用（優惠等）

試題	試題翻譯	解答與解析

☑ 71

What type of business is being advertised?
(A) A moving company
(B) A beauty clinic
(C) A fitness center
(D) A medical supply store

發廣告的是什麼類型的公司？
(A) 搬家公司
(B) 美容診所
(C) 健身中心
(D) 醫療用品店

答案 (B) 概述

一邊聽這篇內容，一邊就要捕捉相關業別的關鍵字。從Skin and Beauty Clinic、treat a variety of skin conditions caused by aging, sun damage and allergies和any treatment可知，(B) 是正確答案。

☑ 72

What will happen tomorrow?

(A) A new product will be introduced.
(B) A business will celebrate its anniversary.
(C) A special offer will end.
(D) New premises will open.

明天將會發生什麼事？
(A) 將推出新產品。
(B) 公司將慶祝週年紀念日。
(C) 特別優惠即將結束。
(D) 新址即將開幕。

答案 (D) 請求、建議、下一步動作

專注精神聽tomorrow那句，可以聽到Our ultra-modern clinic opens tomorrow...。由此可知(D) 是正確答案。選項是將Our ultra-modern clinic（超現代化診所）表達為New premises（新址），new premises在這篇前段內容也有出現。

☑ 73

What is offered at a 25 percent discount?
(A) Any treatment
(B) A consultation
(C) All products
(D) A training course

哪一項可得到 75 折的折扣優惠？
(A) 所有治療項目
(B) 諮詢
(C) 所有產品
(D) 研修課程

答案 (A) 其他細節

專注精神聽25 percent那句，可以聽到all customers who... will receive 25 percent off any treatment。由此可知(A) 是正確答案。treatment有「（生病的）治療」及「（肌膚等的）處理」之意。(B)是錯在consultation（諮詢）是可以免費的。

錄音原文	錄音原文翻譯
Questions 74 through 76 refer to the following telephone message.	試題 74-76 請參考以下電話留言。

Hey, Jerry, it's Dan. I'm sorry we weren't able to meet before lunch. Unfortunately, I'll be gone the rest of the day today. Just two things: Accounting called me yesterday afternoon. They need an expense report from your trip to Houston last month, including receipts. They also need the boarding passes for your flight to San Francisco last week. After you get back from lunch, would you give John Ackerman in Accounting a call? Extension 414. Oh, and also, if you could finish the report on the San Francisco branch by Tuesday, it would help me immensely. If you need any advice, I'll be in all day tomorrow if you'd like to get together briefly. OK then, Jerry, talk to you later.

嗨，傑瑞（Jerry），我是丹（Dan）。很抱歉，午餐前我們無法碰面了。很不幸地，今天剩餘的時間我也都不在。只有 2 件事：會計部昨天下午打電話給我，他們需要你上個月出差到休士頓（Houston）的支出報告，包括收據。他們也需要你上週搭機去舊金山（San Francisco）的登機證。你用完午餐後，可否打個電話給會計部的約翰・奧克曼（John Ackerman）？他的分機 414。喔，還有，如果你能在週二之前完成舊金山分公司的報告，這對我會非常有幫助。若需要任何建議，我明天一整天都在，能與你短暫碰個面。好，那麼，傑瑞，稍後再說了。

Vocabulary

- □ gone [gɔn] 形 （走了）不在
- □ rest [rɛst] 名 （the～）剩餘的部分
- □ Accounting [əˋkaʊntɪŋ] 名 會計部
- □ expense [ɪkˋspɛns] 名 支出
- □ boarding pass 登機證
- □ extension [ɪkˋstɛnʃən] 名 分機
- □ immensely [ɪˋmɛnslɪ] 副 非常地
- □ get together 聚會
- □ briefly [ˋbriflɪ] 副 短暫地

試題	試題翻譯	解答與解析
74 When most likely did the caller leave the message? (A) Last Monday evening (B) Last Tuesday morning (C) Yesterday afternoon (D) Around noon today	來電者最有可能在何時留言？ (A) 上週一傍晚 (B) 上週二早上 (C) 昨天下午 (D) 今天中午左右	**答案 (D)** 其他細節 來電者一開頭就說說I'm sorry we weren't able to meet before lunch. Unfortunately, ...，表示午餐前無法與留言的對象見面，且從聯絡當下就要外出。留言到一半左右時也提到After you get back from lunch, ...，由此推測這是午休前後的留言，所以(D)是正確答案。注意不要被留言內提到的yesterday afternoon（昨天下午）及Tuesday（週二）混淆了。
75 Who is the message for? (A) An accountant (B) A business employee (C) A university student (D) An airline agent	這一則留言是要給誰的？ (A) 會計師 (B) 公司的職員 (C) 大學生 (D) 航空公司代理	**答案 (B)** 聽眾與發言者 留言一開始就聽到非正式的稱呼，Hey, Jerry, it's Dan.。留言目的即是他所說的Just two things:，指示自己不在時要對方做的事。從內容可判斷聽留言的對象是公司同事或是部屬，所以(B)是正確答案。另外留言內有提到搭飛機的話題，不要被混淆而誤選(D)。
76 What will the listener most likely do first after lunch? (A) Go to another branch (B) Purchase an airline ticket (C) Make a phone call (D) Finish a report	聽留言的人午餐後最有可能先做什麼事？ (A) 去其他分公司 (B) 購買機票 (C) 打電話 (D) 完成報告	**答案 (C)** 請求、建議、下一步動作 有關午飯後的指示，就在這句After you get back from lunch, would you give John Ackerman in Accounting a call?。(C)將give John Ackerman in Accounting a call（打個電話給會計部的約翰・奧克曼）簡單表達為make a phone call（打一通電話），因此是正確答案。(D)的報告是在週二前完成就好，而不是午飯後要先做的事。

錄音原文	錄音原文翻譯
Questions 77 through 79 refer to the following excerpt from a meeting. OK, you all have your staff handbooks, right? I need you to detach the last page, page 71, sign it, and submit it to HR by this Thursday. Next, time cards: These need to be turned in by 7 P.M. each Friday, or on Monday morning if you work over the weekend, although that's not very common. Please do make sure these cards are filled out correctly. If not, your paycheck might get delayed or have errors. Like I said, overtime is pretty uncommon, and has to be approved by your department supervisor in advance. Payday is on the 15th of each month, or on the following Monday if it falls on a weekend.	試題 77-79 請參考以下會議摘要。 好的，你們都有員工手冊，對吧？我需要你們撕下最後一頁，也就是 71 頁，簽好名，然後在這週四前提交給人事部（HR）。接下來，出勤卡：這些需要在每週五晚上 7 點前交出，或是如果你週末有加班，就延至週一早上，雖然這並不常有。請確認這些出勤卡有正確填寫。如果不對，你的薪水可能會延遲或出現錯誤。就像我說的，加班是非常少見的，而且必須事先得到部門主管的批准。發薪日是每個月 15 日，如果 15 日正逢週末，發薪日則會在隔週的週一。

Vocabulary

□ detach [dɪˋtætʃ] 動 分離～　　□ fill out～ 填寫～　　□ correctly [kəˋrɛktlɪ] 副 正確地　　□ paycheck [ˋpe͵tʃɛk] 名 薪水（支票）
□ get delayed 延遲　　□ error [ˋɛrɚ] 名 錯誤　　□ approve [əˋpruv] 動 批准　　□ supervisor [͵supɚˋvaɪzɚ] 名 主管
□ payday [ˋpe͵de] 名 發薪日　　□ fall on～ 正逢～（日期）

試題	試題翻譯	解答與解析
☑ **77** What is the purpose of the talk? (A) To promote policy change (B) To update a work schedule (C) To solicit solutions to a problem (D) To explain office procedures	這段談話的目的是什麼？ (A) 促進政策改變 (B) 更新工作時間表 (C) 徵求問題的解決方案 (D) 說明辦公室常規	**答案 (D)** 概述 談話內容從確認員工手冊開始，並針對出勤卡、加班及發薪日等做了說明。(D)將這些內容抽象表達為office procedures（辦公室常規），所以是正確答案。 □ promote [prəˋmot] 動 促進～ □ solicit [səˋlɪsɪt] 動 徵求～
☑ **78** What should employees submit every Friday? (A) A staff handbook (B) A time card (C) A weekly report (D) An employee badge	員工每週五該提交什麼？ (A) 員工手冊 (B) 出勤卡 (C) 每週報告 (D) 員工識別證	**答案 (B)** 其他細節 有關每週五該提交的東西，從這句time cards: These need to be turned in by 7 P.M. each Friday可知，(B)是正確答案。turn in～是「提交（交）出～」之意，題目將它改用submit（提交）來表達。不僅是整篇文章和選項之間的同義詞，還有文章和每個問題之間的語句字彙改換，請大家要從平日的練習來多理解體會。
☑ **79** According to the speaker, what is uncommon? (A) Delays in payment (B) Errors on time cards (C) The absence of a supervisor (D) Working overtime	依說話者所言，什麼是不常有的？ (A) 延遲付款 (B) 出勤卡錯誤 (C) 主管不在 (D) 加班工作	**答案 (D)** 其他細節 uncommon是「不常有的」之意。從Like I said, overtime is pretty uncommon可知，(D)是正確答案。Like I said（就像我說的），就是指前面說的if you work over the weekend, although that's not very common。overtime如文字所言，「over（超過～）＋time（時間）」，代表的不只是晚下班做事的「加班」，還包括週末上班的「額外工作、超時上班」。

錄音原文	錄音原文翻譯

Questions 80 through 82 refer to the following telephone message.

Hi, this is George Falwell calling for Jeff Tucker. It's Friday, about two. Jeff, unfortunately it looks like I won't have time to meet you and Amy Peterson next Monday as we'd planned. I'm hoping we can reschedule for later next week. I'm available Tuesday and Wednesday morning, but Thursday works best for me. We could meet outside Amy's office as we'd planned. Please give me a call when you get this message. My mobile is 555-8787. Thanks so much, Jeff. Bye.

試題 80-82 請參考以下電話留言。

嗨,這是喬治 • 法爾維爾 (George Falwell) 打給傑夫 • 塔克 (Jeff Tucker) 的電話留言。 現在是週五大約 2 點。傑夫,很不幸地,看起來我應該沒有時間在預定的下週一與你和艾咪 • 彼得森 (Amy Peterson) 見面。 我希望我們可以重新安排到下週的其他時間。 我週二和週三早上都有空,不過週四對我來說最好。 我們可以依計畫在艾咪辦公室外面見面。 當你收到這則訊息時請打電話給我。 我的手機是 555-8787。 非常感謝,傑夫。 再見。

Vocabulary

□ I'm hoping (that)~　我希望~、你不能做~嗎？　　□ reschedule for~　重新安排~的時間

試題	試題翻譯	解答與解析

☑ 80

Why is the speaker calling?

(A) To explain an appointment cancellation
(B) To reschedule a meeting
(C) To change a meeting location
(D) To announce a client's arrival

為何來電者打這通電話？

(A) 說明約會取消
(B) 重新安排見面的時間
(C) 變更見面地點
(D) 通知客戶抵達

答案 (B) 〔概述〕

從這句 Jeff, unfortunately it looks like I won't have time to meet you and Amy Peterson next Monday as we'd planned.可知,這是在表達無法依預定日見面。接著後面提議其他日期,所以(B)是正確答案。

☑ 81

According to the message, when is ideal for the speaker?
(A) Later today
(B) Tomorrow
(C) Next Wednesday
(D) Next Thursday

根據留言,什麼時間對來電者是理想的?

(A) 當天晚一點
(B) 明天
(C) 下週三
(D) 下週四

答案 (D) 〔其他細節〕

在敘述要變更見面的日期後,來電者說了 I'm available Tuesday and Wednesday mornings, but Thursday works best for me.,由此可知(D)是正確答案。這裡提到的 work best 是指「最好、最合適的」,而題目中的 ideal 意即「理想的、最適當的」。

☑ 82

What does the speaker say about the meeting location?
(A) It can remain as scheduled.
(B) It will be closed next week.
(C) It should be inside the building.
(D) It is far from his office.

關於見面地點,來電者說了什麼?

(A) 可以維持已計畫的。
(B) 下週即將關閉。
(C) 應該在建築物內。
(D) 離他的辦公室很遠。

答案 (A) 〔其他細節〕

有關見面的地點,從 We could meet outside Amy's office as we'd planned.可知,並沒有特別提出變更,因此(A)是正確答案。as we'd planned 意思是「依我們已計畫的」,選項將其表達為 as scheduled。remain 是「維持~」。

錄音原文	錄音原文翻譯

Questions 83 through 85 refer to the following talk.

Good morning, everyone. I'd like to remind you that a new security system will be installed at the bank's main entrance starting this afternoon. A technician from the security company has informed me that it will take the workers around four hours to finish the job, and any disruption or noise should be able to be kept to a minimum. A temporary entrance adjacent to the main entrance will be used while construction is underway. This may create a little confusion for our customers, so please keep an eye out for people who may need assistance.

試題 83-85 請參考以下談話。

大家早安。我想提醒你們，今天下午銀行的主要入口要安裝一個新的保全系統。保全公司的技術人員通知我，這個工作大約要花 4 個小時完成，而任何干擾和噪音應該可以維持在最低限度。裝配正在進行時，鄰近正門旁邊的臨時入口將開放使用。這可能會給我們的客戶造成一些混亂，所以請留意可能需要協助的人。

Vocabulary

- □ inform~ (that)... 通知~……
- □ disruption [dɪsˋrʌpʃən] 名 干擾
- □ keep~ to a minimum 維持~在最低限度
- □ temporary [ˋtɛmpəˏrɛrɪ] 形 臨時的
- □ adjacent to~ 鄰近~
- □ underway [ˋʌndəˏwe] 形 在進行中的
- □ confusion [kənˋfjuʒən] 名 混亂

試題	試題翻譯	解答與解析

83

What are the workers going to do at the bank?
(A) Install electronic displays
(B) Enlarge an entry door
(C) Install a security system
(D) Upgrade a computer system

工作人員將在銀行做什麼？

(A) 安裝電子看板
(B) 擴大入口
(C) 安裝保全系統
(D) 升級電腦系統

答案 (C)　其他細節

從一開始的談話就提到a new security system will be installed at... starting this afternoon，由此可知(C)是正確答案。a new security system will be installed是被動式，選項是將它表達為主動語態。請大家也要多熟悉語態的轉換。

84

Where is the work taking place?

(A) At the reception desk
(B) At the main entrance
(C) At the customer service lounge
(D) At a temporary counter

這項作業在哪裡進行？

(A) 接待櫃檯
(B) 主要入口
(C) 客服大廳
(D) 臨時櫃台

答案 (B)　其他細節

這道題用現在進行式來問，是在表達已確定的未來事實。從 a new security system will be installed at the bank's main entrance可知，(B)是正確答案。main entrance 是指「主要入口」。本篇後段提到的 A temporary entrance adjacent to the main entrance will be... 也是答題關鍵。選項中故意使用跟談話內容一樣的單字 temporary（臨時的）& customer（客戶），注意不要混淆而誤選。

85

What does the man mean when he says, "This may create a little confusion for our customers"?
(A) The noise may annoy customers.
(B) The bank may need to close early.
(C) Some computers may not work.
(D) Customers may get confused at the entrance.

男性說 「This may create a little confusion for our customers」 時，表示什麼？

(A) 噪音可能困擾客人。
(B) 銀行可能需要提早打烊。
(C) 一些電腦可能無法運作。
(D) 客人可能對入口感到混亂。

答案 (D)　說話者的目的

這句意思是「這可能會給我們的客戶造成一些混亂」，This是指承受前句內容。意味著工程中的臨時入口可能會帶給客人混亂，因此正確答案是(D)。另外從any disruption or noise should be able to be kept to a minimum可知，多少都會有噪音發生，但是會維持在最低限度，所以(A)是錯的。

錄音原文	錄音原文翻譯

Questions 86 through 88 refer to the following radio announcement.

Fine Roast Coffee has issued a recall for its "Rich Blend" brand coffee, after it was reported Tuesday that some of the jars did not contain their 250-gram capacity. Analysis of the production facility indicated a packing equipment failure, which has since been corrected. Affected batch numbers are from K255 to K268. These numbers appear on the jar label. If you have one of these jars, you can exchange it for a free new jar at any participating retailer. Fine Roast Coffee offers its sincere apologies for any inconvenience this has caused.

試題 86-88 請參考以下廣播通知。

在週二被報導出一些咖啡罐未裝滿該有的 250 公克容量後，精緻烘培咖啡（Fine Roast Coffee）已發布收回旗下濃醇調味（Rich Blend）品牌的咖啡。根據生產廠的分析指出，是包裝設備產生的錯誤，現已經得到修正。受影響的批號是從 K255 到 K268。這些數字會出現在咖啡罐的標籤上。如果您有其中一罐，您可以在任何有合作的零售商店免費兌換新的一罐。精緻烘培咖啡對於由此造成的任何不便深表誠摯的歉意。

Vocabulary

- □ issue [`ɪʃjʊ] 動 發布
- □ recall [rɪ`kɔl] 名（瑕疵商品的）收回
- □ jar [dʒɑr] 名 廣口罐
- □ capacity [kə`pæsətɪ] 名 容量
- □ analysis [ə`næləsɪs] 名 分析
- □ indicate [`ɪndə͵ket] 動 指出～
- □ correct [kə`rɛkt] 動 修正～
- □ affected [ə`fɛktɪd] 形 受到影響的
- □ retailer [`ritelɚ] 名 零售商

試題	試題翻譯	解答與解析

☑ 86

What is the problem?

(A) Some coffee jars were not full.
(B) Some coffee is of inferior quality.
(C) Some coffee jars have been mislabeled.
(D) Some coffee jars are the wrong size.

發生什麼問題？

(A) 一些咖啡罐沒有被裝滿。
(B) 一些咖啡品質較差。
(C) 一些咖啡罐被貼錯標籤。
(D) 一些咖啡罐的尺寸錯誤。

答案 (A) 概述

如果有預覽題目，就能推測並聽到什麼是問題點。從一開頭的Fine Roast Coffee has issued a recall for...這段話，就可知道問題是商品收回一事。(A)是將some of the jars did not contain their 250-gram capacity（一些咖啡罐未裝該有的250公克容量）換成Some coffee jars were not full.（一些咖啡罐沒有被裝滿。）來表達，所以是正確答案。

- □ inferior [ɪn`fɪrɪɚ] 形（品質）較差的
- □ mislabel [mɪs`leb!] 動 貼錯～的標籤

☑ 87

What is mentioned about the packing equipment?

(A) It had been serviced before the incident.
(B) It is insufficient for production needs.
(C) It is no longer malfunctioning.
(D) It will require replacement.

關於包裝設備，通知文中提到什麼？

(A) 在問題發生前已經維修。
(B) 不足應付生產需求。
(C) 已不再故障。
(D) 需要更換。

答案 (C) 其他細節

這題關鍵在於是否能理解Analysis of the production facility indicated...這一句。掌握大致的內容為「packing equipment（包裝設備）發生故障」→「已修好」。把故障修好表示現在可以正常運轉了，所以(C)是正確答案。雖然malfunction（不能正常運轉、故障）本身就是含有否定意味的單字，但因為加了no longer（已經不再～）更重覆強化否定，所以整句是表示肯定的意思。

- □ insufficient for～ ～不足的
- □ replacement [rɪ`plesmənt] 名 更換

☑ 88

What will customers who return jars receive?

(A) A refund
(B) A new jar of coffee
(C) A free batch of coffee
(D) An apology letter

退罐的客人會收到什麼？

(A) 退款
(B) 一罐新的咖啡
(C) 一批免費咖啡
(D) 道歉信

答案 (B) 其他細節

從If you have one of these jars, you can exchange it for a free new jar at...可知，(B)是正確答案。exchange A for B的意思是「將A換成B」。如果有聽懂a free new jar，就可推斷是免費換新的一罐。

- □ refund [`ri͵fʌnd] 名 退款

錄音原文	錄音原文翻譯

Questions 89 through 91 refer to the following speech.

Ladies and gentlemen, esteemed colleagues, it is an enormous pleasure for me to be here, although admittedly I don't feel like I deserve being named "Employee of the Year." Frankly, I thoroughly enjoy doing what I do, and it has been wonderful to collaborate with you on so many projects over the years. I would also particularly like to thank one individual, our former executive director Scott Zelmer, whose hard schedule prevents him from joining us tonight in person. He is a model of leadership and generosity. So here's to our future successes, and to Scott, and once again to all of you from me, thank you.

試題 89-91 請參考以下演說內容。

各位女士、先生,以及尊敬的同仁們,我非常高興來到這裡,儘管無可否認地,我不覺得我該得「年度最佳員工」這項殊榮。坦白說,我完全享受我所做的事情,多年來在這麼多的案子上與您們共事真是太棒了。我還想特別感謝一個人,我們的前任執行總監思科特·澤爾默(Scott Zelmer),他的忙碌行程讓他今晚無法親自加入我們。他是一位具領導才能與寬宏大量的典範。因此,在這裡向我們未來的成功,向思科特,以及再次向您們大家表示感謝。

Vocabulary

☐ esteemed [əˋstimd] 形 受人尊敬的　　☐ enormous [ɪˋnɔrməs] 形 巨大的　　☐ admittedly [ədˋmɪtɪdlɪ] 副 無可否認地～
☐ deserve ～ing 該得～　　☐ frankly [ˋfræŋklɪ] 副 坦白地　　☐ thoroughly [ˋθɝolɪ] 副 完全地
☐ collaborate with～ 與～共事　　☐ particularly [pəˋtɪkjələlɪ] 副 特別　　☐ individual [ˏɪndəˋvɪdʒʊəl] 名 個人
☐ prevent... from ～ing 阻止……做～　　☐ model [ˋmɑd!] 名 典範　　☐ generosity [ˏdʒɛnəˋrɑsətɪ] 名 寬宏大量

試題	試題翻譯	解答與解析

☑ 89

What is the purpose of the speech?

(A) To accept an award
(B) To announce a competition
(C) To welcome a new employee
(D) To report a success in business

演說的目的是什麼?

(A) 接受獎賞
(B) 宣布競賽
(C) 歡迎新同仁
(D) 報告商業上的成功

答案 (A) 概述

從...admittedly I don't feel like I deserve being named "Employee of the Year." 可得知演說者是「Employee of the Year」(年度最佳員工)獎的得獎人,所以(A)是正確答案。雖然是用委婉的表現法來表示謙虛,而不直接說「得獎」,所以讓這題有點難度,不過從～of the Year(年度～獎)這個部分可判斷這是跟得獎有關的話,應該就會選(A)。

☑ 90

What is true about the speaker?

(A) He was late for the ceremony.
(B) He has good co-workers.
(C) He has just joined the company.
(D) He is unhappy with his career.

有關演說者的描述,何者正確?

(A) 他在典禮遲到。
(B) 他有很棒的同事。
(C) 他剛進入這家公司。
(D) 他並不滿意他的職業。

答案 (B) 其他細節

聽到it has been wonderful to collaborate with you on so many projects over the years這個部分,便可得知演說者認為多年來在這麼多的案子上與同事共事非常愉快。(B)將其表達為「他有很棒的同事」,所以是正確答案。這句的you在這裡即是指一起合作案子的co-workers(同事)。

☑ 91

Why does the man say, "He is a model of leadership and generosity"?
(A) To show gratitude to his former boss
(B) To praise his subordinate
(C) To introduce a new executive
(D) To demonstrate his company's achievements

為何男性說「He is a model of leadership and generosity」?

(A) 感謝他的前任上司
(B) 稱讚他的部屬
(C) 介紹新任高階主管
(D) 展現他公司的成就

答案 (A) 說話者的目的

generosity是「寬宏大量」的意思。主詞He是指前句說的our former executive director Scott Zelmer,意即演說者的前任主管。從I would also particularly like to thank one individual, ...以及後面的here's to our future successes, and to Scott, ...等可知對他感謝的心情,所以(A)是正確答案。gratitude是名詞,意為「感謝(之情)」。

☐ subordinate [səˋbɔrdɪnɪt] 名 部屬
☐ demonstrate [ˋdɛmənˏstret] 動 表明～、論證

錄音原文	錄音原文翻譯

Questions 92 through 94 refer to the following message and flight information.

Hi, Doug, it's Marty. Just wondering if you've arrived at the airport yet. Right now I'm in an Internet Corner in the South Wing, working on some documents for Chen-Wang's Chinese Restaurant. I just received a request for a few changes to the construction estimate this morning. The biggest thing is, they say they don't really need any extensive after-service on the refurbished kitchen, but they'd like to have it periodically checked. I'm thinking, like, once or twice a year, but I could use your opinion if we have a little time to talk about it before we board. Oh, and uhh, maybe you already know, but our departure gate's been changed. It's Gate 17, not 15. The Internet Corner I'm at is right next to the gate. Thanks, Doug!

FLIGHT	TO	GATE	TIME
6G 80	Boston	50	14:25
CK 198	Seattle	17	14:30
SZ 90	San Diego	34	14:40
XG 163	Florida	26	14:45

試題 92-94 請參考以下的留言和航班資訊。

嗨，道格（Doug），我是馬蒂（Marty）。我只是想確認你是否已經到達機場了。現在我在南側廳的一個上網區為陳王的（Chen-Wang's）中餐廳製作一些文件。我今天早上剛收到他們對施工估價提出的一些更改要求。最大的問題是，他們說他們對整修的廚房並不需要任何延伸的售後服務，但希望有定期檢查。我想，就一年一至兩次那樣。不過如果我們在登機前還有一點時間來討論一下，我會很希望有你的意見能參考。對了，嗯，也許你已經知道了，我們的登機門改了。在 17 號，不是 15 號門。我待的上網區就在這號門旁邊。謝謝，道格！

航班	前往	登機門	時間
6G 80	波士頓（Boston）	50	14:25
CK 198	西雅圖（Seattle）	17	14:30
SZ 90	聖地牙哥（San Diego）	34	14:40
XG 163	佛羅里達（Florida）	26	14:45

Vocabulary

☐ refurbish [rɪ`fɝbɪʃ] **動** 整修～　　☐ periodically [pɪrɪ`ɑdɪklɪ] **副** 定期地

試題	試題翻譯	解答與解析

☑ **92**

What is the speaker doing now?

(A) Checking in his baggage
(B) Looking for a gate
(C) Maintaining his computer
(D) Editing some paperwork

留言者正在做什麼？

(A) 辦理他的行李托運
(B) 找登機門
(C) 維修他的電腦
(D) 編輯一些文書作業

答案 (D) 　概要

留言者在前面留話時就說Right now I'm...來表示自己目前的狀況。(D)將這句的working on some documents（製作一些文件）改用意思雷同的Editing some paperwork（編輯一些文書作業）來表達，所以是正確答案。(C)雖然可推測是用電腦製作文件，但是maintain（維修）的說法是錯誤的。

☑ **93**

What field does the speaker most likely work in?
(A) Food service
(B) Recruiting
(C) Computer engineering
(D) Renovation

留言者最有可能在哪個領域工作？

(A) 餐飲服務
(B) 人力資源
(C) 電腦工程
(D) 翻新工程

答案 (D) 　概要

留言者幫目前的客戶，名為 Chen-Wang's Chinese Restaurant的餐廳製作文件，從construction estimate（施工估價）、after-service on the refurbished kitchen（整修廚房的售後服務），以及 have it periodically checked（定期檢查）等資訊來做綜合思考，就可推斷(D)的 Renovation（翻新工程）是正確答案。注意不要因為聽到 Restaurant（餐廳）和 kitchen（廚房）而誤選(A)。

☑ **94**

Look at the graphic. Where is the speaker's destination?
(A) Boston
(B) Seattle
(C) San Diego
(D) Florida

請看圖。留言者的目的地是哪裡？

(A) 波士頓
(B) 西雅圖
(C) 聖地牙哥
(D) 佛羅里達

答案 (B) 　圖表問題

看圖表可知題目是有關4個航班的問題。從整篇內容可想像留言者跟留言對象這2位是搭同一航班。後段提到maybe you already know, but our departure gate's been changed. It's Gate 17, not 15.。依圖表來看，從17號登機門出發的航班目的地是西雅圖，所以正確答案是(B)。另外，句型〈A, not B〉（是A＋不是B）的追加說明也可以用來確認答案喔！

錄音原文	錄音原文翻譯

Questions 95 through 97 refer to the following telephone message and itinerary.

Hi, Jack, Sandra here. Listen, I just got word that I need to attend an emergency meeting with one of our high-profile clients later this afternoon, so it looks like I'll be a day behind getting to Hong Kong. Unfortunately I won't make the conference, but I'll definitely be joining you at the office tomorrow. I'm looking forward to talking with Mr. Tseng, the director there. Anyway, I'd love it if you could fill me in on some of the presentations at the conference. Feel free to send me an e-mail when you get this message. Safe journey to you, and see you in Hong Kong, bye!

試題 95-97 請參考以下電話留言及行程表。

嗨，傑克（Jack），我是珊卓拉（Sandra）。聽好唷，我剛剛才知道我必須在今天下午晚一點時，跟我們的一位重量級客戶開緊急會議，所以看起來我將會晚一天才到香港。不幸的是，我無法參加會議，但我確定明天會在辦公室與你會合。我很期待與那裡的董事曾先生會談。無論如何，屆時我希望你能告訴我關於一些會議上的演講內容。當你收到這則留言時，歡迎隨時傳電子郵件給我。祝旅途平安，香港見，再見！

Business Travel Itinerary

Day 1 Monday	11:00 A.M. Arrive in Hong Kong
	2:00 P.M. East Asian Business Conference
Day 2 Tuesday	9:00 A.M. Visit Hong Kong Office
	1:00: P.M. Meeting with Chai Tseng

出差行程表

第 1 天（週一）	11:00 A.M. 抵達香港
	2:00 P.M. 東亞商務會議
第 2 天（週二）	9:00 A.M. 拜訪香港辦公室
	1:00 P.M. 與曾柴（Chai Tseng）會面

Vocabulary

□ emergency [ɪˋmɝdʒənsɪ] 名 緊急　　□ high-profile [ˏhaɪˋprofaɪl] 形 引人注目的、備受關注的　　□ fill *someone* in　告訴（某人）詳情

試題	試題翻譯	解答與解析

☑ 95

What problem does the woman mention?
(A) She has encountered an unexpected setback.
(B) She needs information about a branch office.
(C) She is looking for a conference venue.
(D) She has not completed a presentation.

女性提到什麼問題？

(A) 她遇到突如其來的計劃變更。
(B) 她需要有關分公司的資訊。
(C) 她正在找會議場地。
(D) 她還沒有完成簡報。

答案 (A) 概述

女性一開始就說I just got word that I need to attend an emergency meeting with...。 get word that～是指「接受～通知」，(A)只是將an emergency meeting（緊急會議）改用unexpected setback（突如其來的計劃變更）來表達，所以是正確答案。

□ encounter [ɪnˋkaʊntɚ] 動 遇到～
□ unexpected [ˏʌnɪkˋspɛktɪd] 形 意想不到的、突如其來的
□ setback [ˋsɛtˏbæk] 名 （事情進展等的）挫折、變故

☑ 96

Look at the graphic. When will the woman probably meet Jack?
(A) At 11:00 A.M. on Monday
(B) At 2:00 P.M. on Monday
(C) At 9:00 A.M. on Tuesday
(D) At 1:00 P.M. on Tuesday

請看圖表。 女性可能何時會見到傑克？

(A) 週一 11:00 A.M.
(B) 週一 2:00 P.M.
(C) 週二 9:00 A.M.
(D) 週二 1:00 P.M.

答案 (C) 圖表問題

圖表即是Itinerary（行程表），表上寫著4個行程。這題就是問女性（留言者）會在4個行程中的哪一個見到傑克（接聽者）。首先是女性說明今天下午因為急事而必須晚一天也就是明日（＝Tuesday）才會在香港。接著女性又說I'll definitely be joining you at the office tomorrow.，因此這個說法符合行程表的Tuesday的9:00 A.M. Visit Hong Kong Office。

☑ 97

What does the woman ask Jack to do?
(A) Return her call as soon as possible
(B) Advise her of travel itinerary changes
(C) Attend a meeting on her behalf
(D) Inform her about presentations

女性請傑克做什麼事？

(A) 儘快回電
(B) 通知她行程變更
(C) 代表她參加會議
(D) 告訴她演講內容

答案 (D) 請求、建議、下一步動作

後段出現I'd love it if you could～（我希望你能～）是表達請求的句型。後面接的fill me in on some of the presentations at the conference就是具體的請求內容，所以(D)是正確答案。fill me in on～是「告訴我有關～的詳情」，而(D)只是將其轉換成inform her about～（告訴她～）來表達而已。

□ advise *someone* of～　讓（某人）知道～
□ on *someone's* behalf　代表（某人）

錄音原文	錄音原文翻譯

Questions 98 through 100 refer to the following talk and graph.

I would like to thank everyone for coming here today. I know that I asked you here on short notice. The senior planning committee went over last quarter's operation report and unfortunately I can't say they were altogether happy with it. Specifically, they weren't pleased with the area where we performed the worst. They want us to develop a plan as to how we're going to do better in this area—and they want it by Monday morning. That means that we're probably going to spend the next three days here in the office. We'll spend a lot of time brainstorming this issue, then we'll draw up some proposals that Christopher Porter will then write up for a final submission.

試題 98-100 請參考以下談話及圖表。

我想先感謝在場的各位今天來到這裡。我知道我臨時招集大家。資深企劃委員會核查了上一季的營運報告書，很遺憾地，我不能說他們對整體感到滿意。具體來說，他們對我們表現最差的部分並不滿意。他們希望我們制定一個關於如何在這方面做得更好的計畫——而且希望能在週一早上之前收到。這意味著我們可能會在辦公室度過接下來的 3 天。我們將會花很多時間對這個議題集思廣益，然後擬定一些提案，讓克里斯多福·波特（Christopher Porter）屆時寫下最後要提交的內容。

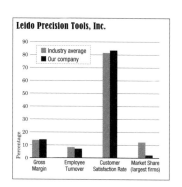

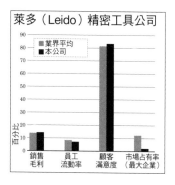

Vocabulary

☐ develop a plan　訂計畫　　☐ as to～　關於～　　☐ brainstorm [ˋbrenˌstɔrm] 動 對～集思廣益
☐ draw up a proposal　擬定提案　　☐ gross margin　銷售毛利　　☐ turnover [ˋtɝnˌovɚ] 名 （公司的）人員流動數（率）
☐ customer satisfaction　顧客滿意（度）　　☐ market share　市場占有率

試題	試題翻譯	解答與解析

98

Why does the speaker thank the listeners?
(A) They finished a quarterly report.
(B) They formed a committee.
(C) They gathered quickly.
(D) They distributed a notice.

為何說話者要感謝聽眾？
(A) 他們完成季報。
(B) 他們組成一個委員會。
(C) 他們迅速集合。
(D) 他們發布了一份通知。

答案 (C)　其他細節

說話者在開頭就說I would like to thank everyone for coming here today.，對於大家能集合過來非常感謝。從下一句的on short notice可知是突然召集大家，所以(C)是正確答案。

☐ quarterly [ˋkwɔrtɚlɪ] 副 每年4次地、按季地

99

Look at the graphic. What area does the board most want to improve?
(A) Gross margin
(B) Employee turnover
(C) Customer satisfaction rate
(D) Market share

請看圖。 委員會最想改善什麼部分？
(A) 銷售毛利
(B) 員工流動率
(C) 客戶滿意度
(D) 市場占有率

答案 (D)　圖表問題

問句的board即是談話文內提到的committee，從they weren't pleased with the area where we performed the worst及They want us to develop a plan... in this area可知，委員會想改善表現最差的部分。由圖表看來，該公司成效最差的就是Market Share（市場占有率）。

100

What will Christopher Porter have to do?
(A) Come back next weekend
(B) Submit an application
(C) Create a document
(D) Use a different office

克里斯多福·波特必須做什麼？
(A) 下週末回來
(B) 提出申請書
(C) 製作一份文件
(D) 使用不同的辦公室

答案 (C)　請求、建議、下一步動作

從We'll..., then we'll draw up some proposals that Christopher Porter will then write up for a final submission這句可知，(C)是正確答案。注意第2個then，同時按照聽到的順序來掌握它的流程是「說話者與大家擬定提案」→「克里斯多福·波特再將提案彙整成最後提出的版本」。

PART 5

☑ 101

All products in the store with a red tag will receive an ------- discount at the checkout counters.

(A) additionally
(B) adding
(C) additional
(D) addition

商店內所有紅色標籤的產品將在結帳櫃檯享有額外的折扣。

答案 (C) 〔詞性〕

冠詞和名詞之間填入形容詞最適當。所以(C)的 additional（額外的）是正確答案。(A)是副詞，意為「另外」，(B)是動詞add（增加～）加ing 的形式，或是作為名詞「增加」。(D)是名詞「增加」。

☑ 102

Let me introduce to you our new superintendent, Ms. Talisman, ------- will be responsible for the management of all Starline restaurants in the district.

(A) whether
(B) which
(C) that
(D) who

容我為你介紹我們的新任負責人，塔利斯曼（Talisman）女士，她將負責這地區所有史塔林（Starline）餐廳的經營。

答案 (D) 〔文法〕

這是關係代名詞的問題。先行詞是our new superintendent（我們的新任負責人），中間再插入同位語Ms. Talisman。即使不知道 superintendent（負責人）的意思，如果讀懂同位語Ms. Talisman和will be responsible for...（將負責……）是主詞、補語的關係，應該就會選代替先行詞是「人稱」的(D)who。雖然(C)的that也可用於代替「人稱」的先行詞，但是不能用在非限定用法。

□ be responsible for～　對～負責

☑ 103

Please ------- to Hobbyists DotCom's weekly newsletter for our latest offers and information about membership perks.

(A) browse
(B) subscribe
(C) conform
(D) resort

請訂閱業餘愛好者網路（Hobbyists DotCom）的電子週報，以獲得我們最新的特價及會員優惠資訊。

答案 (B) 〔字彙〕

句子的大致架構是「為了要……，請～」。要如何利用電子週報才能得到最新的特價和有關會員優惠的訊息呢？從這個角度思考，以答案(B)的subscribe（訂閱）最適當。注意這句的subscribe是不及物動詞，所以一定要加to。(A)的browse（瀏覽～）看似符合句意，但它是及物動詞，所以不對。(C)的conform to～意為「符合～」，(D)的resort to～意為「求助於～」。

□ perk [pɝk] 名 （用複數形時）優惠

☑ 104

The press conference is scheduled to ------- place at the Global Sound Maker Forum, where video and audio device developers gather annually.

(A) take
(B) put
(C) catch
(D) run

記者招待會預定於影像聲音設備開發商每年聚集的全球聲音製造商論壇（Global Sound Maker Forum）上舉行。

答案 (A) 〔慣用語〕

be scheduled to do的意思是「預定～」，思考主詞The press conference（記者招待會）和at the Global Sound Maker Forum（在全球聲音製造商論壇）的關係，空格以放入(A)的take變成take place（舉行）最適當。

□ device [dɪˈvaɪs] 名 設備
□ developer [dɪˈvɛləpɚ] 名 開發者

☑ 105

Since Tamara Varga had more than enough -------, she should have applied for the position of vice manager of Budapest Commercial Bank.

(A) qualify
(B) qualified
(C) qualifications
(D) qualifies

由於塔瑪拉・瓦爾加（Tamara Varga）有足夠的資格，她當初應該應徵布達佩斯商業銀行（Budapest Commercial Bank）的副理職位。

答案 (C) 〔詞性〕

以Since為首的從屬句，Tamara Varga是主詞，had是動詞，more than enough ------- 是受詞，more than enough（有足夠的）是用來修飾作為名詞的空格。所以名詞的(C) qualifications（資格）是正確答案。(B)和(D)是動詞qualify（取得資格）的變化形。

□ apply for～　應徵～
□ vice manager　副理

| 試題與翻譯 | 解答與解析 |

☑ 106

Spike Motors set up a new business contingency plan to protect ------- against unforeseeable threats and disasters.

(A) they
(B) their
(C) them
(D) themselves

斯派克汽車（Spike Motors）對於無法預料的威脅和災難，制定新的業務應變計畫來保護他們自己。

答案 (D)　　文法

這是人稱代名詞的問題。空格前面的protect（保護）是動詞，後面的against是介系詞，意為「對於無法預料的威脅和災難」。所以空格是protect的受詞，以(D)的themselves（他們自己）最適當。(C)的them也可以當受詞，但是在前後語句上還是以「保護自己公司（自己本身）」的意思最符合。

- □ contingency [kən`tɪndʒənsɪ] 名 突發事件
- □ unforeseeable [ˌʌnfor`siəbl] 形 無法預料的
- □ threat [θrɛt] 名 威脅
- □ disaster [dɪ`zæstɚ] 名 災難

☑ 107

To view all photography options, press ------- of the buttons on the screen to display the full list.

(A) any
(B) another
(C) every
(D) a lot

要觀看所有的照片選項，請按螢幕上任何一個按鈕來顯示所有的列表。

答案 (A)　　選項混合型

「看照片的選項，要按螢幕上的～按鈕」，而符合前後句意思的，以表示肯定句意味的(A)any（任何一個）最正確。(B)的another雖然也是後面接of的代名詞，但意思卻是「其他的東西」，不適合當答案。(C)的every（每一個的）是形容詞，後面應該接名詞。(D)套入空格後意為「按螢幕上很多的按鈕」，整個語意不符。

- □ view [vju] 動 觀看
- □ photography [fə`tɑgrəfɪ] 名 照相（術）
- □ display [dɪ`sple] 動 展示～

☑ 108

The world's population is growing so ------- that in the near future there may be food shortages on a global scale.

(A) commonly
(B) rapidly
(C) profoundly
(D) densely

世界人口正如此迅速地增加，以致於不久的將來可能會出現全球規模的糧食短缺。

答案 (B)　　字彙

這是so～ that...（如此～以致於……）的句型。空格應填入副詞來修飾動詞is growing（正在增加）。各選項以填入(B)rapidly（迅速地）最適當，意為「世界人口正在如此迅速地增加」。

- □ shortage [`ʃɔrtɪdʒ] 名 短缺
- □ on a global scale　全球規模
- □ commonly [`kɑmənlɪ] 副 一般地
- □ profoundly [prə`faʊndlɪ] 副 深深地
- □ densely [`dɛnslɪ] 副 密集地

☑ 109

When ordering the ------- parts for repair, mechanics are required to check the catalog for compatibility.

(A) necessary
(B) general
(C) lesser
(D) repeated

訂購維修必要的零件時，技師們需要參照型錄以確認零件的相容性。

答案 (A)　　字彙

句首When ordering省略了〈主詞＋be動詞〉，也就是When (mechanics are) ordering（當（技師們）訂購時）。而符合「（技師們）為了修理而訂購～零件時」的這句語意，以選項(A)的「必要的」最正確。

- □ be required to do　需要做～
- □ compatibility [kəm,pætə`bɪlətɪ] 名 相符
- □ general [`dʒɛnərəl] 形 一般的
- □ lesser [`lɛsɚ] 形 較小的
- □ repeated [rɪ`pitɪd] 形 重複的

☑ 110

While there is media speculation that there will ------- be a change of leadership in Merril Technologies, the company has not released any official announcement.

(A) already
(B) soon
(C) very
(D) just

雖有媒體猜測美利爾科技（Merril Technologies）領導階層很快會有變化，該公司並沒有發表正式的聲明。

答案 (B)　　字彙

speculation意為「猜測」，that表示同位語。符合「媒體猜測領導階層應該～有變化」這樣語意的副詞，以(B)的「很快地」最正確。soon（很快地）和表示未來式的will很常搭配在一起。(A)的already（已經）和(D)的just（剛剛）適合現在完成式。(C)的very（很）通常用來修飾形容詞和副詞，不適合用在助動詞和be動詞之間。

- □ release an announcement　做出聲明、發表
- □ official [ə`fɪʃəl] 形 正式的

☑ 111

Because the production line handles electronic parts, it is ------- for all workers to follow the procedures to prevent the generation of static electricity.

(A) exclusive
(B) mutual
(C) crucial
(D) eligible

由於生產線處理電子零件，因此所有作業員要遵守程序以防止靜電產生是很重要的。

答案 (C) 字彙

這是it is～ for A to do（A做……是～）的句型結構。所有作業員要遵守程序以防止靜電產生，你覺得這是如何的？從這角度思考可知，(C)的crucial（很重要的）是正確答案。

☐ handle [`hænd!] 動 處理
☐ generation [͵dʒɛnəˋreʃən] 名 （化學上的）產生
☐ static electricity　靜電
☐ exclusive [ɪkˋsklusɪv] 形 除外的
☐ mutual [`mjutʃʊəl] 形 互相的
☐ eligible [`ɛlɪdʒəb!] 形 有資格的

☑ 112

Since the launch of the health food campaign, the sales of organic and low-fat foods ------- at Texco Foods.

(A) increase
(B) was increased
(C) is being increased
(D) have been increasing

自從健康食品活動推出以來，德士科食品（Texco Foods）公司有機和低脂食品的銷售量已不斷增加。

答案 (D) 動詞型態

遇到述語動詞的問題，通常先看主詞及受詞、補語的關係，但這題的情形是由句首的since（自從～以來）來判定是現在完成式，所以正確答案是(D)。這題若沒有了解句子的意思是無法作答的。

☐ launch [lɔntʃ] 名 推出
☐ organic [ɔrˋgænɪk] 形 有機的
☐ low-fat [͵loˋfæt] 形 低脂的

☑ 113

Fillman Fashion proposes relocating stores to shopping malls so that they will be ------- situated in each of their urban markets.

(A) strategize
(B) strategy
(C) more strategic
(D) more strategically

菲爾曼流行（Fillman Fashion）公司提議將商店搬到購物中心，以便更有戰略地立足他們每個城市的市場。

答案 (D) 詞性

be situated是「位於」。就算沒有空格的字也可以跟前句意思相通，意即「立足他們每個市區的市場」，所以空格要填入副詞。由此可知(D)的more strategically（更有戰略地）是正確答案。

☐ relocate [riˋloket] 動 搬遷～
☐ so that～　以便於～
☐ urban [`ɝbən] 形 城市的
☐ strategize [`strætədʒaɪz] 動 制訂戰略
☐ strategic [strəˋtidʒɪk] 形 戰略上的

☑ 114

Quad Cycle Limited is currently negotiating with a supplier on prices and delivery time with the ------- of concluding an agreement next month.

(A) trial
(B) fact
(C) aim
(D) span

四循環有限公司（Quad Cycle Limited）目前正與一家供應商進行價格及送貨時間的交涉，並以下個月簽訂合約為目標。

答案 (C) 字彙

空格後的conclude an agreement是指「簽訂合約」。從整句的意思可知，(C)的aim（目的、目標）是正確答案。如果知道片語with the aim of～的意思是「以～為目標」，就更有利作答。

☐ negotiate [nɪˋgoʃɪ͵et] 動 交涉
☐ supplier [səˋplaɪɚ] 名 供應商
☐ trial [`traɪəl] 名 試驗
☐ fact [fækt] 名 事實
☐ span [spæn] 名 一段時間

☑ 115

The send-off party for members ------- the production team next month is scheduled for Saturday so most people can attend.

(A) leaves
(B) leaving
(C) left
(D) will leave

為下個月離開生產團隊成員們舉辦的歡送會訂於週六舉行，好讓大多數人都可以參加。

答案 (B) 動詞型態

The send-off party for members（為成員辦的歡送會）是主詞，is scheduled（被訂於）是述語動詞。空格 ------- the production team next month是修飾前面的members，整個意思是「下個月離開生產團隊的成員們」，其中以(B)的leaving（離開）最正確。(C)的left雖然也可以當過去分詞來修飾前面的名詞，但會變成被動和完成的意思。空格填入後的完整句是members (who will be) leaving the production team next month，由此可知left是不合適的答案。

試題與翻譯	解答與解析

☑ **116**

Please be informed that the south wing of the Middletown Hospital will be closed during November ------- renovations.

(A) in contrast to
(B) contrary to
(C) due to
(D) under

請注意，由於翻修作業，中城（Middletown）醫院的南側將於 11 月關閉。

答案 (C) 慣用語

Please be informed that～是發表公告的固定句型結構。renovation是「翻修」。思考「醫院」、「關閉」、「翻修」的關係，可推測「翻修是原因」。因此(C)的due to～（由於～）是正確答案。(D)的under renovation雖然是「翻修中」的意思，但這樣的表達必須是單數形式，所以不符原句的意思。

☐ in contrast to～　與～形成對比
☐ contrary to～　與～相反

☑ **117**

Our Web site, which was designed by Ms. Powell, ------- people with disabilities to use a screen reader to read all content.

(A) conducts
(B) enables
(C) lets
(D) shares

我們的網站，由鮑威爾（Powell）女士所設計，它讓殘障人士可以使用螢幕閱讀器來閱讀所有的內容。

答案 (B) 字彙

which was designed by Ms. Powell（由鮑威爾女士所設計）是插入句，所以這部分可視為Our Web site ------- people with disabilities。將重點放在to use時，就可理解(B)的enable～ to do（讓～可以……）是正確答案。to read是表「結果」的不定詞，意即「使用螢幕閱讀器是為了能夠閱讀所有的內容」。(C)的let（讓（人）做～）雖然看似符合原句的意思，但它不能接有to的不定詞，而是要直接接原形動詞。

☑ **118**

Should you have any questions or -------, do not hesitate to contact our Customer Support Desk.

(A) doubts
(B) doubtful
(C) doubtfully
(D) doubtless

如果您有任何問題或疑問，請不要客氣聯絡我們的客服支援櫃台。

答案 (A) 詞性

or 要連接一樣的詞性，所以和questions（問題）一樣詞性的(A)是正確答案。憑 any questions or -------的部分就能思考正確答案。Should you have～（如果有～的話）及 Do not hesitate to do（請不要客氣～）也是固定句型結構，要熟記。

☐ doubtful [ˋdaʊtfəl] 形 疑惑的
☐ doubtfully [ˋdaʊtfəlɪ] 副 懷疑地
☐ doubtless [ˋdaʊtlɪs] 形 無疑地

☑ **119**

The environmental conservation project that ------- by a group of companies in the automobile industry was covered in today's newspaper.

(A) leads
(B) had led
(C) was leading
(D) was led

今天的報紙報導了由數個汽車業公司組成的集團所領導的環境保護計畫。

答案 (D) 動詞型態

The environmental conservation project（環境保育計畫）是主詞，was covered（被報導）是述語動詞。that ------- by a group of companies in the automobile industry（由數個汽車業公司組成的集團-------）是關係子句，修飾主詞The environmental conservation project。重點放在by，就會了解「由～領導」的被動型態才是正確的，所以答案是(D)。

☐ environmental conservation　環境保護
☐ cover [ˋkʌvɚ] 動 報導（研究、主題）

☑ **120**

This year LTG Manufacturing has been awarded the Top CSR Award for their ------- to the community by hosting science programs for youths.

(A) contribution
(B) temptation
(C) affection
(D) perfection

今年 LTG 工業因為青少年主辦科學計畫，其對於社群的貢獻被授予最佳企業社會責任獎（Corporate Social Responsibility，簡稱CSR）。

答案 (A) 字彙

award A B for～是「因為～，將B授給A」。這種句型常用於被動式，也就是把A當主詞，再用被動式「因為～，A被授予（授獎）B」來表達。至為何得獎，其重點就在空格後面的to，意為「對社區的貢獻」。

☐ contribution [͵kɑntrəˋbjuʃən] 名 貢獻
☐ temptation [tɛmpˋteʃən] 名 誘惑
☐ affection [əˋfɛkʃən] 名 感情
☐ perfection [pɚˋfɛkʃən] 名 完美無缺

☑ 121

Bosworth's aggressive sales campaigns have been so successful that the company now ------- a leading regional market share in small electronics.

(A) cuts
(B) invests
(C) spoils
(D) boasts

伯斯沃斯（Bosworth）積極的銷售活動是如此成功，以致於公司現在在小型電子產品方面以擁有區域市場領先的占有率自豪。

答案 (D) 〔字彙〕

符合主詞the company（公司）和受詞a leading regional market share（區域市場領先的占有率）的動詞是(D)的boasts（以有～而自豪）。(A)的cuts填入後的意思是「削減市場佔有率」，與銷售活動大獲成功的結果不符。請各位要注意句型〈so～（原因）that...（結果）〉（如此～以致於……）的因果關係。

□ aggressive [əˋgrɛsɪv] 形 積極的
□ invest [ɪnˋvɛst] 動 投資～
□ spoil [spɔɪl] 動 破壞～

☑ 122

------- can improve workplace health and safety is creating operational procedures and a work environment based on identified risks.

(A) What
(B) Every time
(C) Who
(D) Anywhere

可以改善工作場所健康及安全的做法是，根據已知的風險建立操作程序和工作環境。

答案 (A) 〔選項混和型〕

------- can improve workplace health and safety（-------可以改善工作場所健康及安全）是主詞，is是動詞，creating（動名詞）之後是補語。(A)的What填入後的句意通順，意思是「可以改善工作場所健康及安全的做法是，建立～」。關係代名詞的what扮演主詞的角色，後面接續的動詞（can improve）則意指「什麼是可以改善的」。

☑ 123

------- its obscure location, the Rosero Villa resort has attracted photographers from all over the world with its strikingly beautiful natural landscapes.

(A) But for
(B) Nevertheless
(C) Ever since
(D) Despite

儘管其位置偏僻，羅塞洛（Rosero）別墅度假村以其出眾的自然美景吸引了來自世界各地的攝影師。

答案 (D) 〔選項混和型〕

obscure（偏僻的）是帶有負面含意的單字。而the Rosero Villa resort...後面卻是屬於正面的內容，所以(D)的介系詞Despite（儘管～）最正確。(B)的Nevertheless雖然也有「儘管如此」的意思，但因為它是連接副詞，並不適合放入這題的句型結構。而(A)的But for（要不是～）和(C)的Ever since（從～以來）都與整句意思不合。

□ strikingly [ˋstraɪkɪŋlɪ] 副 出眾地
□ landscape [ˋlænd͵skep] 名 景色

☑ 124

It was shortly ------- being assigned to the marketing department that Ms. Chang demonstrated her skills in market research and negotiation.

(A) after
(B) behind
(C) among
(D) without

張（Chang）女士被派到行銷部門後不久，就發揮了她在市場研究及談判交涉的能力。

答案 (A) 〔文法〕

重點放在that，就能理解it is～ that...（……就～）是強調句的句型。意即「張女士被派到行銷部門後不久，就發揮了她在市場研究及談判交涉的能力」，因此(A)是正確答案。shortly是「不久、馬上」，在這邊可換成另一個字soon。being assigned to～是assign A to B（將A派到B）的被動式，省略了A（＝Ms. Chang）。

☑ 125

Once ------- to a course, students are not allowed to withdraw without a valid reason or approval from the instructor.

(A) admit
(B) admits
(C) admitted
(D) admitting

一旦批准課程，學生就不能在沒有正當理由或講師未同意的情況下退選課程。

答案 (C) 〔動詞型態〕

once 是連接詞，意為「一旦～」。admit A to B 是「對A批准B」，Once ------- to a course 是省略了和主要子句一樣的 students are（學生被……）。意即這是 Once students are admitted to a course（學生被批准（上）課程）的短句型，因此空格填入(C)的過去分詞最適當。像這類接在連接詞後面的〈主詞＋be動詞〉不僅於現在進行式時會被省略，有時在被動式的表達時也會如此。

□ withdraw [wɪðˋdrɔ] 動 撤銷、退出
□ valid [ˋvælɪd] 形 正當的

試題與翻譯	解答與解析

☑ **126**

Company and union negotiators have reached a ------- agreement, but further discussions about the contract are pending.

(A) contractual
(B) quantitative
(C) tentative
(D) substantive

公司和工會談判者達成了暫定的協議，但是有關契約進一步的討論卻懸而未決。

答案 (C)　 字彙

reach an agreement是指「達成協議」。哪一個是修飾agreement（協議）的正確形容詞，可以從後半句的內容「但是有關契約進一步的討論是尚待決定的」來思考，因此(C)的tentative（暫定的）最正確。(A)的contractual（契約的）雖然與agreement有關，不過與but後面的內容不符。

☐ pending [`pɛndɪŋ] 形 懸而未決的
☐ quantitative [`kwɑntə,tetɪv] 形 與數量有關的
☐ substantive [`sʌbstəntɪv] 形 表示實在的

☑ **127**

Attendees of the business talk workshop were encouraged to ------- give their opinions on how the panel did in the simulated negotiation.

(A) candid
(B) candidness
(C) be candid
(D) candidly

商業談話研討會的與會者被鼓勵要坦率地發表自己對小組模擬談判的意見。

答案 (D)　 詞性

這是encourage~ to do（鼓勵~做……）的被動句。空格在to和原形動詞（give）之間，所以正確答案應該是副詞(D)candidly（率直地、坦白地）。即使不知道各選項內的意思，可以用to不定詞的觀念來了解插入to和原形動詞之間的字是副詞，應該就知道要選「-ly」型態的副詞了。如果有學到字尾規則就越有利作答。

☐ attendee [ə`tɛndi] 名 與會者
☐ candid [`kændɪd] 形 率直的、坦白的

☑ **128**

The newly developed products are currently in the testing ------- of the industrial redesign project.

(A) phase
(B) method
(C) attempt
(D) degree

新開發的產品目前正處於工業再設計方案的測試階段。

答案 (A)　 字彙

「~產品處於工業再設計方案的測試階段」，這樣的意思最通順，所以(A)是正確答案。phase（階段）也可以像in the last [early] phase of~（~最後的（最初的）階段）這樣跟形容詞一起使用。

☐ method [`mɛθəd] 名 方法
☐ attempt [ə`tɛmpt] 名 嘗試
☐ degree [dɪ`gri] 名 程度

☑ **129**

To apply for reimbursement, please submit the receipts ------- with the application form to the HR department.

(A) instead
(B) along
(C) as well
(D) to begin

請款時，請將收據與申請表一起呈交人力資源部門。

答案 (B)　慣用語

reimbursement意即「（費用的）退還、報銷」。重點放在空格後面的with，就可知正確答案是(B)的along with~（與~一起）。(A)的instead是副詞，意思是「作為替代」，而instead of~則是指「代替~」。(C)as well as B是「不但B，而且A」，如果這邊改用as well as the application form...就符合前後語意了。(D)的to begin with是指「開始、首先」。

☑ **130**

We created an online system to ------- the process of delivering large quantities of products from factories to warehouses.

(A) facilitate
(B) audit
(C) discard
(D) stimulate

我們建立了一個線上系統，是為了讓工廠配送大量產品到倉庫的過程更容易。

答案 (A)　字彙

這題的每個選項都是原形動詞，由此可知「to -------」是不定詞。這題大意是「這是為了讓大量的產品配送過程~的線上系統」，其中以(A)的「讓~容易」最符合。

☐ large quantities of~　大量的~
☐ audit [`ɔdɪt] 動 （財務等）查帳
☐ discard [dɪs`kɑrd] 動 丟棄~
☐ stimulate [`stɪmjə,let] 動 刺激~

PART 6

Questions 131-134 refer to the following memo.

Hi, Mark,

I wanted to thank you in advance for your hard work on next week's presentation. I took a look at the slideshow draft ------- sent me, and it looks great. -------. They make the slideshow so much
131.   **132.**
more engaging.

The only ------- problem I can foresee is that the presentation room doesn't have any up-to-date
133.
equipment. The building manager told me yesterday that new projectors will be installed, but that will be sometime next month. I have also heard that the computer in the room is quite old, so you might have to make some adjustments. -------, you might want to make a version of your slideshow
134.
with a simpler file format, to be sure that the older equipment can handle it.

As always, if you need any help, just let me know.

Regards,

Marjorie

---

131. (A) you
(B) your
(C) yours
(D) yourself

132. (A) I'll need the draft by tomorrow morning.
(B) You may have to edit it considerably.
(C) I love the embedded videos you created.
(D) You should specify the format for your presentation.

133. (A) thoughtful
(B) previous
(C) chronic
(D) potential

134. (A) As a rule
(B) In other words
(C) From now on
(D) All the same

試題文章翻譯

試題 131-134 請參考以下便箋。

嗨，馬克（Mark），
我想先感謝你為下週的簡報所做的努力。我看了你傳給我的投影片草稿，看起來很棒。132. 我喜歡你製作的嵌入影片。這樣讓投影片更具吸引力。

我唯一可預見的潛在問題是，簡報室沒有任何最新的設備。雖然大樓經理昨天告訴我將要裝新的投影機，不過那是在下個月某個時候。我也聽說簡報室的電腦很舊了，所以你可能需要做一些調整。換句話說，為了確保較舊的設備可以處理它，你或許需要製作一個格式更簡單的投影片版本。

一如往常，如果需要任何幫忙，請讓我知道。

謹致問候
馬喬莉（Marjorie）

解答與解析

131

答案 (A)   句型結構

空格前有完整的一句「我看了投影片草稿」，空格之後用you sent me（你傳給我）的接續結構，是對the slideshow draft（投影片草稿）的補充說明。因此，選(A)的you（你）來當sent（傳、寄）的主詞最適當。

132

答案 (C)   語句插入型

空格前面提到對方的投影片草稿做得很棒，後面的句子敘述了肯定的意見，由此可知表達喜歡embedded videos（嵌入影片）的(C)最正確。而後面句子的主詞They即是指(C)的the embedded videos。embedded是動詞embed（嵌入～）的過去分詞，即使不知道這個單字，只要理解I love the videos you created.的意思也可以答對。
(A)「我明天早上之前需要這份草稿。」
(B)「你可能需要相當程度地編輯。」
(D)「你應該明定你的簡報格式。」

☐ specify [`spɛsə͵faɪ] 動 指定（指明）～

133

答案 (D)   前後句關係

最適合修飾空格後面單字problem（問題）的形容詞是哪一個呢？problem後面I can foresee的foresee是「預測」的意思，因此選項中最符合前後句關係的是(D)的「可能的、潛在的」。potential用在未來可能性的狀況，不管是好是壞皆可。

☐ thoughtful [`θɔtfəl] 形 深思的
☐ chronic [`krɑnɪk] 形 慢性的

134

答案 (B)   文脈型

因為句型結構上要填入的是有連接功能的詞組，所以由前後句關係來決定。從「簡報室的電腦很舊，所以需要做一些調整」和「為了配合舊的設備，或許需要製作格式更簡單的投影片版本」這2句的關係來思考，可知後者與前者的內容相同，而且後者提出更具體的建議，因此以(B)的In other words（換句話說、總之）最為適當。

☐ as a rule　通常
☐ from now on　今後
☐ all the same　仍然

Vocabulary

☐ in advance　事先
☐ draft [dræft] 名 草稿
☐ up-to-date [͵ʌptə`det] 形 最新的
☐ make an adjustment　調整

試題文章

Questions 135-138 refer to the following letter.

July 5

Charles Grey
Spices Restaurant
5E/118 Victoria Street
Clevedon, Melbourne, 0620

Dear Mr. Grey,

Our records show that you have an outstanding balance dating back to April. Your April invoice
was for $1,325.00 and we have ------- to receive this payment.
　　　　　　　　　　　　　　　　135.

-------. If this amount has already been paid, please disregard this notice. -------, please forward us
136.　　　　　　　　　　　　　　　　　　　　　　　　　　　　　137.
the amount owed in full by July 20.

Thank you for your ------- and we hope to continue doing business with you in the future.
　　　　　　　　　138.

Sincerely,

Naomi Hughes
Account Manager

---

135. (A) yet
　　　(B) not
　　　(C) only
　　　(D) still

136. (A) Payment is due upon receipt of
　　　　invoice.
　　　(B) The refund will be credited to your
　　　　account.
　　　(C) Please find a copy of the invoice in this
　　　　letter.
　　　(D) You are required to complete this form.

137. (A) However
　　　(B) Besides
　　　(C) Therefore
　　　(D) Otherwise

138. (A) cooperated
　　　(B) cooperation
　　　(C) cooperative
　　　(D) cooperatively

試題文章翻譯

試題 135-138 請參考以下信件。

7 月 5 日
查理斯・葛雷（Charles Grey）
香料餐廳（Spices Restaurant）
5 東 / 118 維多利亞街（Victoria Street）
克里夫登（Clevedon），墨爾本（Melbourne），0620

親愛的葛雷先生：

根據我們的紀錄，您有一筆追溯到 4 月的未付款。您的4月發票金額是 1,325 元，而我們還未
收到這筆款項。

136. 請查收隨函附上的發票副本。 如果這筆金額已經支付，請不用理會這份通知。 否則，請
於 7 月 20 日前將欠款全額轉給我們。

感謝您的合作，希望未來繼續與您生意往來。

真誠問候
娜歐米・休斯（Naomi Hughes）
客戶經理

解答與解析

135
答案 (A) 句型結構

have跟不定詞之間若要填入副詞，以(A)的yet最正確。have yet to do意為「還沒做～」。即使句中沒有否定語詞，但仍然有否定的意思，這點要特別注意。這句與現在完成式we have not yet received...一樣意思。(B)的not如果是用have not變成現在完成的否定形；we have not yet received...就是正確的意思，不過以這句為例，後面就不接不定詞。

136
答案 (C) 語句插入型

第1段的內容是通知對方有未付款。這題是第2段的第1句，從接下來的句子來看，可知已付款的狀況以及未付款時的指定日期，所以(C)的「請查收隨函附上的發票副本」最適合。空格後面提到的this amount意即隨函附上的請款金額。
(A)「應在收到發票後付款。」
(B)「退款將會存到您的銀行帳戶。」
(D)「您需要填寫這份表格。」

☐ upon receipt of～　在收到～後
☐ credit [`krɛdɪt] 動 將～存入銀行帳戶
☐ account [ə`kaʊnt] 名 銀行帳戶

137
答案 (D) 前後句關係

句子一開頭就是空格，還用逗點隔開。所有的選項都是連接副詞，因此句型結構上要填入的答案，即是由前後句關係來決定。可以將「如果已付，請不用理會這份通知」和「請於7月20日前付款」這2句內容做連結的字，以(D)的Otherwise（否則）最正確。至於(B)的Besides，請大家要了解它有連接副詞「而且」和介系詞「除～之外」2種意思。

138
答案 (B) 句型結構

your（你的）後面要接名詞，所以正確答案是(B)。這題一看到your ------- and的瞬間就可作答。

☐ cooperative [ko`ɑpə͵retɪv] 形 合作的
☐ cooperatively [ko`ɑpəretɪvlɪ] 副 合作地

Vocabulary

☐ outstanding [`aʊt`stændɪŋ] 形 未付清的
☐ balance [bæləns] 名 結算餘額（金額）
☐ amount [ə`maʊnt] 名 金額
☐ disregard [͵dɪsrɪ`gɑrd] 動 不理會～
☐ owe [o] 動 欠款～
☐ in full　全部

Questions 139-142 refer to the following article.

Westfield Council is ------- to unveil their new designs for an ultra-modern, single level library
139.
in Burgundy Heights. The $9 million project involves demolishing the existing building and
constructing new facilities on the same site. The positioning of the new structure will create a
larger, more attractive public space. -------. An expansive glass window will allow library users to
140.
look out on to the reserve and will also ------- the building light, bright and inviting. The new library
141.
will have a wider range of services including space where digital media can be watched, listened to
and enjoyed, and an area dedicated to exhibiting local artwork. ------- is expected to commence in
142.
September and take approximately a year to complete.

139. (A) about
(B) subject
(C) unlikely
(D) reluctant

140. (A) At the new library, most reference
books can be checked out.
(B) Public library service is now accessible
to all residents in the community.
(C) The new facility currently features a
history of the institution.
(D) It will also provide quicker access to
the neighboring Kennedy Reserve.

141. (A) become
(B) hold
(C) make
(D) stay

142. (A) Relocation
(B) Construction
(C) Negotiation
(D) Administration

試題 139-142 請參考以下報導。

西田（Westfield）市議會即將對外公布他們在勃肯第高地（Burgundy Heights）的一個超現代化單層圖書館的新設計。這項斥資 9 百萬元的計劃包括拆除現有的建築物，並在同一地點建造新設施。新建築的的配置將創造一個更大、更有吸引力的公共空間。[140.] 它也提供了親近鄰近的甘迺迪保護區更快速的方法。寬敞的玻璃窗，讓圖書館使用者眺望保護區，並讓建築物有照明、明亮且迷人。新圖書館將提供更廣泛的服務，包括可以觀看、收聽和享受數位媒體的空間，以及專用空間展示當地藝術品。這棟建築物預計於 9 月動工，大約需要 1 年時間完成。

Vocabulary

☐ unveil [ʌn`vel] 動 使～公諸於世　　☐ single level 一層樓的
☐ involve [ɪn`vɑlv] 動 包含～　　☐ demolish [dɪ`mɑlɪʃ] 動 拆除
☐ existing [ɪg`zɪstɪŋ] 形 現有的　　☐ construct [kən`strʌkt] 動 建造～
☐ site [saɪt] 名 位置　　☐ structure [`strʌktʃɚ] 名 建築物
☐ expansive [ɪk`spænsɪv] 形 遼闊的　　☐ look out （從裡面）向外看
☐ reserve [rɪ`zɝv] 名 特別保留地、保護區　　☐ dedicate A to B 將 A 獻給 B
☐ exhibit [ɪg`zɪbɪt] 動 展示～　　☐ commence [kə`mɛns] 動 開始
☐ approximately [ə`prɑksəmɪtlɪ] 副 大約

139

答案 (A)　　前後句關係

在句型結構上，除了(B)以外的選項，都可以放入be動詞和帶to的不定詞之間。be about to *do* 是「即將要～」，be unlikely to *do*是「不太可能～」，be reluctant to *do*是「不願意做～」，從前後句關係來看，以(A)最正確。(B)的be subject to～是「取決於～」，這裡的to是介系詞，所以後面不是接原形動詞。

140

答案 (D)　　語句插入型

有關新圖書館的報導，空格前面的句子已描述了建築物在配置上的優點。(D)的It是指前句的 The positioning of the new structure，流暢的語意再追加優點的資訊，所以是正確答案。後面的那句An expansive glass window will allow... look out on to the reserve也連貫得很好。the reserve（保護區）就是指(D)的 Kennedy Reserve（甘迺迪保護區）。
(A) 「從新圖書館可以借出很多工具書。」
(B) 「社區所有居民現在都能使用公共圖書館的服務。」
(C) 「新設施目前展出該機構的歷史。」

☐ check out （從圖書館）借出
☐ accessible [æk`sɛsəb!] 形 （東西）易得到的
☐ neighboring [`nebərɪŋ] 形 鄰近的

141

答案 (C)　　句型結構

如果在and和will之間補上主詞An expansive glass window，可推測這句的意思是「寬敞的玻璃窗使建築物有照明、明亮且迷人」。the building（建築物）是受詞，light（有照明的）、bright（明亮的）、inviting（迷人的）是3個單字並列的形容詞。(C)的make（讓O成為C）形成了SVOC（主詞＋動詞＋受詞＋補語）的完整句型，所以是正確答案。其他選項雖然可形成SVC（主詞＋動詞＋補語），但無法做成SVOC的句子。

142

答案 (B)　　前後句關係

最後這句的意思是「～預計於9月開始，大約需要1年時間完成」。這篇主要是報導舊圖書館的拆除及重新建構，所以(B)的「建造工程」是正確答案。Part 6的題型大部分是從句型結構和前後句關係來作答，不過也有像這題一樣，如果沒有理解整篇的主旨，以及空格與稍有距離的句子內容，就無法解題。

☐ relocation [rilo`keʃən] 名 搬遷
☐ administration [əd͵mɪnə`streʃən] 名 行政

試題文章

Questions 143-146 refer to the following letter.

August 17

Ms. Avery Lansing
5175 Cinderland Parkway
Orlando, FL 32808

Dear Ms. Lansing,

Thank you for your inquiry. Regarding your concern about possible allergens in our recent product, Kun Yam Noodles, we have finally received a reply from our production manager. The noodles in ------- do contain soy products, specifically soy sauce and soy oil. -------. It is generally accepted
143.　　　　　　　　　　　　　　　　　　　　144.
that these processed soy products do not cause allergic reactions. In any event, you may still wish to consult your doctor to be sure.

Thank you again for your inquiry. We hope you find this response -------. We appreciate all
145.
questions and comments from our customers as we place your safety and well-being -------
146.
everything.

Sincerely,

Jeff Bridges
Customer Service Representative

---

143. (A) common
 (B) question
 (C) public
 (D) circumstance

144. (A) However, neither is in significant quantity per unit.
 (B) Reported food allergies have increased among people of all ages.
 (C) Moreover, more research is needed before results are conclusive.
 (D) If you are not aware of the situation, it could lead to further problems.

145. (A) help
 (B) helping
 (C) helpfully
 (D) helpful

146. (A) more than
 (B) ahead of
 (C) far from
 (D) little short of

試題文章翻譯

試題 143-146 請參考以下信件。

8 月 17 日
艾佛莉‧蘭辛 （Avery Lansing） 女士
辛德蘭 （Cinderland） 公園大道 （Parkway）5175 號
奧蘭多 （Orlando） 佛羅里達州 （FL） 32808

親愛的蘭辛女士：

感謝您的詢問。 關於您對我們的新產品昆陽麵條 （Kun Yam Noodles） 可能含有過敏原的擔憂，我們終於得到生產部經理的回應。 您詢問的麵條的確含有大豆製品，特別是醬油及大豆油。[144.] 但是，這 2 種原料每單位的含量都很少。 一般來說，這些加工大豆製品不會引起過敏反應。 無論如何，建議您諮詢家庭醫師來確保使用安全。

再次感謝您的詢問。 我們希望您覺得這個回覆是有幫助的。 我們感謝客戶的所有問題和意見，因為我們將您的安全和健康置於一切之上。

由衷的祝福
傑夫‧布里奇斯 （Jeff Bridges）
客服代表

解答與解析

143

答案 (B)　前後句關係

每個選項都可以和介系詞in一起變成片語。(A)in common是「共同」，(B)in question是「有問題的、詢問的」，(C)in public是「公開地」，(D)in any circumstances是「在任何情況下」。這封信的目的是在回答有關公司商品的詢問，「詢問的麵條的確含有大豆製品……」這樣的前後語意最符合，因此(B)為正確答案。

□ circumstance [ˋsɝkəmˏstæns] 名 情況

144

答案 (A)　語句插入

這封信是製造商對於顧客詢問某項產品的麵條是否含有大豆製品的回應。前面先承認「麵條的確含有大豆製品」的事實後，以(A)的「但是，含量都很少」最適合來表達這不是大問題。後面「它不會引起過敏反應」、「諮詢家庭醫師來確保使用安全」也都接續得很流暢。表示前後意思轉折的連接詞However（然而）及in any event（無論如何）也是重要關鍵。
(B)「有被報導的食物過敏已在各年齡層中增加。」
(C)「而且，在結果確定之前需要更多的研究。」
(D)「如果您不了解情況，可能會導致更多的問題。」

□ quantity [ˋkwɑntətɪ] 名 量
□ per unit　每單位
□ moreover [morˋovɚ] 副 並且、此外
□ conclusive [kənˋklusɪv] 形 決定性的

145

答案 (D)　句型結構

〈find＋O＋C〉意為「了解、認識、覺得O是C」。把(D)的helpful（有幫助的）放在C當作形容詞是最正確的。雖然也可能是〈find＋受詞＋副詞〉的句型，但如果選(C)的helpfully就變成「有助於找到這個回覆」，是沒有意義的。

146

答案 (B)　前後句關係

your safety and well-being是指「顧客的安全和健康」。(B)的ahead of～是「在～之前、超過～」，和place結合一起就是place A ahead of B（將A置於B之上）。ahead of everything（勝過一切），在這句也就是「以顧客的安全和健康為最優先」的意思。

Vocabulary

□ processed product　加工產品
□ allergic reaction　過敏性反應
□ consult [kənˋsʌlt] 動 諮詢～
□ to be sure　以防萬一、確保

PART 7

Questions 147-148 refer to the following coupon.

Fortnight Inn & Suites

Present this coupon and get 50% off our regular room rate[1] at
any of our participating locations in the continental U.S.[2]

(1) Does not include suite rooms or executive rooms.
(2) Restrictions apply. Void where prohibited, or with any other offers or discounts. Excludes Alaska and Hawaii. Offer does not include breakfast or dinner prices. Redeemable Monday night through Thursday night only, one room per coupon. Offer expires on March 31.

試題147-148請參考以下優惠券。

雙週酒店&套房（Fortnight Inn & Suites）

出示此優惠券，可得到普通房型5折的優惠[1]，適用於我們美國大陸上所有參與活動的據點[2]。

（1）不包括套房及行政客房。
（2）有適用限制。若有禁止情況，或有任何其他優惠或折扣時無效。不包括阿拉加（Alaska）和夏威夷（Hawaii）。本優惠券不含早餐或晚餐費用。僅限週一至週四晚可兌換，每張優惠券用於一房。優惠期限至3月31日。

Vocabulary

☐ present [prɪˋzɛnt] 動 提出～　　☐ continental [͵kɑntəˋnɛntl̩] 形 大陸的　　☐ restriction [rɪˋstrɪkʃən] 名 限制
☐ apply [əˋplaɪ] 動 適用　　☐ void [vɔɪd] 形 無效的　　☐ exclude [ɪkˋsklud] 動 不包括～　　☐ expire [ɪkˋspaɪr] 動 （期限）到期

| 試題 | 試題翻譯 | 解答與解析 |

☑ 147

Where was the coupon issued?

(A) From a business office
(B) From an apartment complex
(C) From a restaurant franchise
(D) From a hotel chain

優惠券是哪裡發行的？

(A) 商務辦公室
(B) 公寓大樓
(C) 特許加盟餐廳
(D) 連鎖飯店

答案 (D)　　其他細節

從標題的Fortnight Inn & Suites可推測這是用於飯店的優惠券。內文寫著有關住宿房價的折扣Present this coupon and get 50% off our regular room rate，因此正確答案是(D)。

☑ 148

When can the coupon be used?

(A) On Sunday
(B) On Wednesday
(C) On Friday
(D) On Saturday

何時可以使用優惠券？

(A) 週日
(B) 週三
(C) 週五
(D) 週六

答案 (B)　　其他細節

底下的（1）和（2）是說明優惠券的使用條件。從（2）的Redeemable Monday night through Thursday night only可找到「何時」可使用的資訊。符合條件的選項只有(B)的「週三」是正確的。redeemable雖然有「兌換錢」的意思，但即使不懂這個單字，用-able（可以～的）和only（只）應該也能判斷出「只有這個期間是有效的」。

180

試題文章	試題文章翻譯

Questions 149-150 refer to the following chain of text messages.

試題149-150請參考以下一連串的文字通訊。

布萊恩・柯爾（Brain Cole） 7:16 P.M.
妳能幫我嗎？我原定在明天的新進人員培訓上發表簡短的歡迎辭。雖然我不喜歡這麼臨時向妳提出這種請求，但我想知道妳是否可以代替我。我們的一位客戶打電話來，說她明天早上要見我。

優月・塚本（Yuzu Tsukamoto） 7:17 P.M.
應該是沒問題的。我以前做過這樣的致辭。有什麼特定的事需要我說的嗎？

布萊恩・柯爾 7:18 P.M.
我可以用電子郵件傳送我寫好的致辭給妳。大約只有5分鐘長度。相當標準，但妳可以修改任何地方。

優月・塚本 7:19 P.M.
沒關係。我會照著你寫的做。還有什麼我應該知道的事嗎？

布萊恩・柯爾 7:20 P.M.
沒有。這次是針對我們總公司僱用的大約百位新進員工。在31D禮堂，妳可以在上午9點15分左右開始。謝謝妳，優月。我真的很感激妳。

Vocabulary

☐ help *someone* out　幫助（人）　☐ specific [spɪ`sɪfɪk] 形 特定的　☐ standard [`stændəd] 形 標準的
☐ feel free to *do*　隨意做～　☐ auditorium [ˌɔdə`torɪəm] 名 會堂、禮堂

試題	試題翻譯	解答與解析

☑ 149

What does Mr. Cole indicate he will do?

(A) Gather new information
(B) Meet with a client
(C) Set up a presentation
(D) Wait for a speech

柯爾先生表明他要做什麼？

(A) 收集新資訊
(B) 見一位客戶
(C) 準備簡報
(D) 等待演說

答案 (B)　其他細節

柯爾先生一開始的訊息後面就提到，One of our clients called to say that she needs to meet me tomorrow morning.。因此(B)是正確答案。

☑ 150

At 7:20 P.M., what does Mr. Cole mean when he writes, "I really owe you"?

(A) He recognizes a business opportunity.
(B) He is offering an apology to the woman.
(C) He appreciates some assistance he received.
(D) He has approved a new funding plan.

7:20 P.M.，柯爾先生為何寫了 「I really owe you」？

(A) 他看到一項商機。
(B) 他向女性道歉。
(C) 他感謝受到的幫助。
(D) 他已核准新的籌資計畫。

答案 (C)　說話者的目的

owe有「支付～的義務」和「欠～錢」的意思，但口語上的I owe you.是在表達「得救了、實在虧欠、謝謝」的感謝心情。所以(C)是正確答案。即使不知道這樣的表現法，但是從前面的互動內容，如果有看懂是塚本女士答應了科爾先生想請求其代為致辭一事，應該也會選(C)。

Questions 151-152 refer to the following registration card.

試題151-152請參考以下註冊卡。

註冊證書編號 8033132

Registration Certificate No. ___8033132___

Thank you for purchasing a genuine IntelliWare^{-TM-} product. Please complete and mail this postage-paid registration card in order to activate your One-Year Worry-Free Warranty. If you would like to receive our monthly catalogue with coupons for special savings on software, hardware, games and more, please tick one or both of the boxes below.

Name* *Marion Wallace*

Product Serial No.* _A-771034BN_

Address _____

E-mail address* _mwall@coolmail.co.au_

*required

I would like to receive IntelliWare's monthly catalogue:

☐ By post ☑ By e-mail

IntelliWare Pty. Ltd., One Everworth Drive, Sydney, New South Wales 2029

感謝您購買正版的易達利威爾（IntelliWare）產品。為了啟用您的1年安心無虞保固，請填寫完整並郵寄這張郵資已付的註冊卡。如果您希望收到我們每月附有優惠券的目錄，包括軟體、硬體、遊戲及更多特別折扣優惠，請在下方框內勾選1或2個選項。

姓名 ＊ 瑪莉詠・華萊士（Marion Wallace）
產品序號 ＊ A-771034BN
地址 _____
電子信箱 ＊ mwall@coolmail.co.au
＊為必填項目
我想收到易達利威爾的每月目錄：
☐ 郵寄　☑ 電子信箱

易達利威爾有限公司，1號艾維爾沃斯大道，雪梨，新南威爾斯2029（IntelliWare Pty. Ltd., One Everworth Drive, Sydney, New South Wales 2029)

Vocabulary

☐ certificate [səˋtɪfəkɪt] **名** 證書　　☐ genuine [ˋdʒɛnjʊɪn] **形** 真正的　　☐ mail [mel] **動** 郵寄～

☐ postage-paid [ˋpostɪdʒˋped] **形** 郵資已付的　　☐ activate [ˋæktəˏvet] **動** 使～有效　　☐ tick [tɪk] **動** 在～打勾

試題	試題翻譯	解答與解析

☑ **151**

What type of products does IntelliWare sell?

(A) Computers
(B) Furniture
(C) Kitchen appliances
(D) Video equipment

易達利威爾銷售什麼類型的產品？

(A) 電腦
(B) 家具
(C) 廚房設備
(D) 影音設備

答案 (A) 〔其他細節〕

our monthly catalogue with coupons for special savings on software, hardware, games and more是「我們每月附有優惠券的目錄，包括軟體、硬體、遊戲及更多特別折扣優惠」的意思。可判斷是銷售電腦相關的產品，所以(A)是正確答案。

☑ **152**

What is true of Ms. Wallace?

(A) She has purchased a video.
(B) She is employed at IntelliWare.
(C) She will receive coupons from IntelliWare.
(D) She has requested a weekly e-mail newsletter.

關於華萊士女士，什麼描述是正確的？

(A) 她買了錄影機。
(B) 她受僱於易達利威爾。
(C) 她將會收到易達利威爾的優惠券。
(D) 她已要求每週收到電子報。

答案 (C) 〔何者正確類型〕

華萊士女士是填寫註冊卡的人。在I would like to receive IntelliWare's monthly catalogue: 的地方勾選了By e-mail（電子信箱），所以她希望以電子郵件方式收到目錄。而從our monthly catalogue with coupons for...可知目錄有附優惠券，因此(C)是正確答案。

試題文章	試題文章翻譯

Questions 153-154 refer to the following billing statement.

NORTHEASTERN UTILITY

709 N. Briarwood Lane (709) 555-6000
Dorchester, VT 12878
Hours: Mon–Sat, 9:00 A.M.–5:00 P.M.
www.northeasternutil.com

Account 554676	Service Area #4	Location No. 77889	Meter No. 19998	Statement March	Service electricity
COMPARISON		Days service	Total KWH	Avg. KWH/day	$/KWH
Current billing period		31	1251	40	0.12
Previous billing period		29	1055	36	0.12
Same period last year		31	1162	38	0.12
CURRENT CHARGES					
Previous amount due					$ 126.60
Payment—Thank You (March 24)					$ 126.60
TOTAL AMOUNT DUE					$ 150.12
				Payment Due By	April 30

Payments must be postmarked by the due date listed above. Payments received more than 30 days past the "Payment Due By" date will incur a Late Fee of $25.00. For more information on accounts payable, please contact us at the phone number listed above, or visit our Web site. Water, fuel oil and natural gas services will be billed separately.

試題153-154請參考帳單明細表。

東北公共事業（NORTHEASTERN UTILITY）

709北（N.）布萊爾伍德巷（Briarwood Lane）
（709）555-6000
多徹斯特（Dorchester），佛蒙特州（VT）12878
營業時間：週一～週六，9:00 A.M. - 5:00 P.M.
www.northeasternutil.com

客戶編號 554676	服務區域 #4	所在地編號 77889	儀表號碼 19998	明細表 3月	提供項目 電力
比較項目	用電日數	總度數 (Total KWH)	平均千瓦 (小時)／日 (Avg. KWH / day)	元／千瓦 (小時) ($ / KWH)	
本期計費期間	31	1251	40	0.12	
前期計費期間	29	1055	36	0.12	
去年同期	31	1162	38	0.12	
本期費用					
前期應繳金額				$ 126.60	
已付款—感謝配合（3月24日）				$ 126.60	
應繳總金額				$ 150.12	
			付款期限	4月30日	

付款的郵戳必須在上述截止日期之前。超過付款期限30天以上者，將收取25美元的延遲繳費罰金。有關更多應付帳款訊息，請撥打上述電話與我們聯繫，或瀏覽我們的網站。水費、燃油及天然氣服務將分別收費。

Vocabulary

- ☐ billing statement 帳單明細表
- ☐ utility [ju`tɪlətɪ] 名 （瓦斯、水、電等）公共事業
- ☐ comparison [kəm`pærəsn] 名 比較
- ☐ current [`kɝənt] 形 現在的
- ☐ period [`pɪrɪəd] 名 期間
- ☐ charge [tʃɑrdʒ] 名 費用
- ☐ postmark [`post͵mɑrk] 動 在～蓋郵戳
- ☐ past [pæst] 介 超過～
- ☐ incur [ɪn`kɝ] 動 遭受（處罰等）
- ☐ accounts payable 應付帳款
- ☐ bill [bɪl] 動 開帳單給～
- ☐ separately [`sɛpərɪtlɪ] 副 分別地

試題	試題翻譯	解答與解析

153

What is the deadline for the payment?

(A) March 24
(B) March 30
(C) April 15
(D) April 30

何時是付款的最後期限？

(A) 3月24日
(B) 3月30日
(C) 4月15日
(D) 4月30日

答案 (D) 〔其他細節〕

從表格最後一列Payment Due By的April 30可知，(D)是正確答案。due意為「應支付的、到期的」形容詞，by是「在～之前」，它們經常被使用在諸如付款及最後期限的語句。表格下方提到的due day就是「（支付）日期、截止日期、到期日」之意。另外，表格第7列和第9列的amount due即是「應繳金額」之意。

154

What is indicated on the statement?

(A) A previous payment has not been received.
(B) Detailed information is available only on the Web site.
(C) The service area will change.
(D) A penalty will be charged for late payments.

明細表上標示了什麼？

(A) 尚未收到前期的付款。
(B) 詳細資料只能從網站獲得。
(C) 服務區域即將改變。
(D) 逾期付款將被罰款。

答案 (D) 〔何者正確類型〕

這是涵蓋整篇內容的問題。依順序來看，(A)是錯在從表格內的Payment-Thank You (March 24)可知在3月24日已支付前期金額。(B)從表格下方描述的For more information on accounts payable, ...用電話詢問也可以，所以only（只）是錯的。(C)所說的是整篇都沒有提到的事。(D)是和Payments received more than 30 days...這句意思一致，因此是正確答案。而a Late Fee（延遲繳費罰金）則改為penalty（罰款）的說法。

Questions 155-157 refer to the following announcement.

Featured Speaker: Dr. Abby Wentworth "The Economy Today"

The 20th Annual International Economics Conference is pleased to welcome as its plenary speaker, one of the world's leading commentators on economic trends, Dr. Abby Wentworth. Currently a professor at Burlington University in Vermont, Dr. Wentworth's research into the modern economy is extensive. Her publications include a number of books, most notably the best-selling *Hard Knock Lives: The Modern American Economy, and How It Got That Way.*

Don't miss this year's International Economics Conference, to be held at the Civic Center in downtown Seattle, Saturday, November 23 (9:00 A.M.–6:00 P.M.) and Sunday, November 24 (10:00 A.M.–5:00 P.M.). Dr. Wentworth will open the conference on Saturday with her plenary session, titled "The Economy Today," in the Great Hall (Room 101). Admission is free. For complete conference details, schedules and access maps, please visit www.economicsconf.org.

試題155-157請參考以下公告。

特邀演講嘉賓：艾比‧溫特沃斯（Abby Wentworth）博士
「當今的經濟」

第20屆年度國際經濟會議很高興歡迎身為世界領先的經濟趨勢評論人之一，艾比‧溫特沃斯博士來擔任大會主講人。溫特沃斯博士目前是佛蒙特州（Vermont）伯靈頓（Burlington）大學的教授，對現代經濟的研究相當廣泛。她的出版物包括很多書籍，尤其是暢銷書《痛苦的生活：現代美國經濟，以及它如何演變至此》（*Hard Knock Lives: The Modern American Economy, and How It Got That Way*）。

可別錯過今年11月23日週六（上午9時至下午6時），以及11月24日週日（上午10時至下午5時）在西雅圖（Seattle）市區市民中心（Civic Center）舉行的國際經濟會議。溫特沃斯博士將在週六以「當今的經濟」為題，在大堂廳（101室）向全體演說來揭開大會序幕。免費入場。有關完整的會議詳情、日程安排和交通地圖，請上網至ｗｗｗ.economicsconf.org查看。

Vocabulary

- plenary [`plinərɪ] 形 全體的
- trend [trɛnd] 名 趨勢
- extensive [ɪk`stɛnsɪv] 形 廣泛的
- plenary session 全體會議
- title [`taɪt!] 動 加上～標題
- admission [əd`mɪʃən] 名 入場費

試題	試題翻譯	解答與解析

155

What is indicated about Dr. Wentworth?

(A) She will appear on TV.
(B) She has organized a conference.
(C) She has written a popular book.
(D) She works in downtown Seattle.

關於溫特沃斯博士，有什麼描述？

(A) 她即將在電視上露面。
(B) 她主辦了會議。
(C) 她寫了一本受歡迎的書。
(D) 她在西雅圖的市區工作。

答案 (C) 〔何者正確類型〕

這篇公告從標題和開頭就在介紹國際經濟會議和會議演說人溫特沃斯博士。從第1段最後的 Her publications include a number of books, most notably the best-selling可知，(C)是正確答案。選項是將the best-selling（暢銷書）表達為popular（受歡迎的）。publication意為「出版、刊物」，notably為「尤其」。

156

When will Dr. Wentworth give her presentation?

(A) November 23, at 9:00 A.M.
(B) November 23, at 10:00 A.M.
(C) November 24, at 9:00 A.M.
(D) November 24, at 10:00 A.M.

溫特沃斯博士何時進行演說？

(A) 11 月 23 日上午 9 時
(B) 11 月 23 日上午 10 時
(C) 11 月 24 日上午 9 時
(D) 11 月 24 日上午 10 時

答案 (A) 〔其他細節〕

根據第2段的Dr. Wentworth will open the conference on Saturday with her plenary session可知，週六的會議是以溫特沃斯博士的演說揭開序幕。由上述的會議日程來看，週六是11月23日，會議於上午9時開始。因此，博士進行演說是(A)的11月23日上午9時。

157

What is NOT mentioned in the announcement?

(A) The conference location
(B) Next year's conference schedule
(C) Dr. Wentworth's current employment
(D) The cost of attending the conference

下列哪一項不是這篇公告提到的？

(A) 會議的地點
(B) 明年的會議日程
(C) 溫特沃斯博士目前的職業
(D) 參加會議的費用

答案 (B) 〔是非題類型〕

是非題類型的題目，用刪除正確選項的方式最有把握。(A)所說的是在第2段的at the Civic Center in downtown Seattle。(B)整篇內容並未提到明年的會議日程，所以是正確答案。為了以防萬一，我們再確認(C)和(D)，(C)所說的是在第1段的Currently a professor at Burlington University in Vermont。(D)所說的是第2段的Admission is free。

試題文章

Questions 158-160 refer to the following advertisement.

Come be a part of the LabCorp Team!

Laboratory Corporation of Australia Holdings (LabCorp) is a pioneer in commercializing new diagnostic technologies.

LABORATORY FRONT DESK JOB OPENING — Adelaide, South Australia

Description:
We seek a motivated and responsible individual to answer incoming calls at the front desk in our Adelaide facility. You will communicate with clients to resolve requisition discrepancies or specimen issues, as well as provide pricing quotes in accordance with marketing guidelines.

Remuneration:
Our competitive remuneration package includes medical, dental and optical coverage, a retirement plan with matching company contributions, in addition to life insurance and short-term disability insurance for both you and your dependents.

Requirements:
- High school (Year 12) certificate or equivalent
- At least 3 years of client service experience
- Ability to communicate clearly with clients, scientists, and various levels of laboratory management
- Familiarity with computer databases and office applications
- Knowledge of medical terminology a definite plus

Please e-mail your cover letter and résumé to labcorp@coolmail.com.au by November 30.

For more information, contact Jenny Halls at (412) 555-0596, ext. 292.

試題文章翻譯

試題158-160請參考以下廣告。

　　成為實驗室公司（LabCorp）團隊的一員吧！
澳大利亞控股實驗室公司（Laboratory Corporation of Australia Holdings）（以下簡稱實驗室公司〔LabCorp〕）是商業化新型診斷技術的先驅。
實驗室櫃台接待人員空缺 ― 阿德萊德市（Adelaide），南澳

職務內容：
我們尋求一位積極主動且負責任的人接聽阿德萊德機構櫃台的電話。您將與客戶溝通以解決訂單出入或樣本問題，並根據行銷準則提供報價。

薪酬：
我們具競爭力的薪酬待遇包括醫療、牙科和眼科的保險項目、以與個人對公司的貢獻度相符的退休計畫，還有您和受扶養親屬的人壽保險與短期傷殘保險。

必要條件：
- 高中（12年級）證書或同等學力
- 至少3年客服經驗
- 能與客戶、科學家和各級實驗室管理人員明確地溝通
- 熟悉電腦資料庫及辦公室軟體
- 具醫學術語知識者尤佳

請於11月30日前將您的求職信及履歷電郵至labcorp@coolmail.com.au。
欲瞭解更多訊息，請致電（412）555-0596分機292的珍妮・霍爾斯（Jenny Halls）。

Vocabulary

- discrepancy [dɪ`skrɛpənsɪ] 名 不一致
- specimen [`spɛsəmən] 名 樣本
- in accordance with～ 根據～
- remuneration [rɪ͵mjunə`reʃən] 名 酬勞、薪資
- optical [`ɑptɪk!] 形 眼睛的
- dependent [dɪ`pɛndənt] 名 受扶養家屬
- equivalent [ɪ`kwɪvələnt] 形 同等的
- terminology [͵tɝmə`nɑlədʒɪ] 名 術語

試題	試題翻譯	解答與解析

158

What kind of position is being advertised?

(A) A receptionist
(B) A laboratory manager
(C) A government agent
(D) A computer technician

這是哪一種工作的徵才廣告？

(A) 接待人員
(B) 實驗室經理
(C) 政府職員
(D) 電腦技術人員

答案 (A) 〔概述〕

從標題和粗體字的說明可知，這是徵人廣告。招募的職業類別是LABORATORY FRONT DESK JOB OPENING，(A)將front desk（櫃台）用相同意思的receptionist（接待人員）來表示，所以是正確答案。另外，本篇內容包含有難度的專門用語，即使不知道那些單字的意思也可以作答，先別著急，把問題內容配合相關段落的位置來對照吧！

159

What is indicated about benefits?

(A) Wages are paid by the hour.
(B) It includes life insurance.
(C) Employees can buy company stock.
(D) It offers employee discounts.

有關福利部分，有提到什麼？

(A) 時薪支付。
(B) 包括人壽保險。
(C) 員工可買公司股票。
(D) 提供員工折扣。

答案 (B) 〔何者正確類型〕

題目問的benefits（福利），在廣告文的Remuneration（薪酬）這一項有詳細說明。remuneration package includes...（薪酬待遇包括……）提到了life insurance（人壽保險），所以(B)是正確答案。

☐ by the hour　依小時計算

160

What is NOT a requirement for the position?

(A) A high school degree
(B) Previous work experience
(C) Knowledge of medical terminology
(D) An understanding of computers

下列哪一項不是這項職位的必要條件？

(A) 高中學歷
(B) 以往的工作經驗
(C) 醫學術語知識
(D) 了解電腦

答案 (C) 〔是非題類型〕

必要條件也就是廣告文提到的Requirements（必要條件）。將選項與該標題底下的逐條內容做對照，(A)符合第1項。(B)符合第2項。(C)雖然在第5項有提到，但是a definite plus是指具有醫學術語知識者肯定有利。換句話說，不一定是requirement，所以答案是(C)。以防萬一再查看(D)，也符合了第4項。

Questions 161-163 refer to the following article.

Survey: More Americans deferring retirement

For decades, most people in the U.S. have been retiring around the age of 65. However, more and more Americans are ignoring that milestone. According to a survey conducted this June by the Assessment on Finance and Aging Committee, more than 60 percent of people ages 45 to 60 intend to defer retirement. —[1]—. The data highlighted the lingering effects of the economic recession. "A lot of people had to spend some of their retirement money early," says George Evans, professor of economics at Stanwick University and director of economic research for the Assessment on Finance and Aging Committee. "Even though the economy is beginning to recover, it's difficult for many people to recover the money they lost or used. They have to keep working."

Another reason for deferring retirement is the decline of U.S. interest rates. —[2]—. Interest-paying vehicles like government bonds and certificates of deposit yielded significantly lower interest rates compared to data from 10 years ago. "Older people are less risky," says Robyn Freeman, a retirement analyst for American Assets Inc., a securities firm that sponsors the Assessment on Finance and Aging Committee. "They like low-risk, low-return options. But this time they earned very little interest."

Finally, the age at which people can collect Social Security benefits is rising. —[3]—. However, the federal government is considering raising the age to 68. "What's happening is that there's more time when you're older that you can't afford not to work," commented Freeman. "Savings and pensions just aren't enough." On the other hand, rising longevity also means that many elderly people are physically able to work longer. —[4]—. The lesson among the statistics, perhaps, is an age-old one: learning to save money early is always a wise investment.

試題161-163請參考以下報導。

調查：更多美國人延後退休

　　幾10年來，美國大多數人都在65歲左右退休。然而，越來越多美國人不理會這一里程碑。根據財政及高齡化評估委員會（the Assessment on Finance and Aging Committee）今年6月進行的一項調查，有超過60%以上的45歲至60歲的人打算延後退休。一〔1〕一。這些數據凸顯了經濟衰退的長久影響。「很多人不得不提早用到一些退休金，」斯坦威克（Stanwick）大學經濟學教授暨財政及高齡化評估委員會經濟研究主任喬治·艾文思（George Evens）說。「即使經濟開始復甦，很多人還是很難賺回他們失去的和用掉的錢。他們必須繼續工作。」

　　延後退休的另一個原因是美國利率下降。一〔2〕一。與10年前的資料相比，像政府公債和銀行定存單等利息工具產生的利率顯著地降低。「年紀較大的人是較少冒險的，」一家贊助財政及高齡化評估委員會的證券公司美國資產公司（American Assets Inc.）的一名退休分析師羅賓·佛里曼（Robyn Freeman）說，「他們喜歡低風險、低報酬的選擇。但這一次，他們賺的利潤很少。」

　　最後，可以領取社會保障福利金的年齡正在提高。一〔3〕一目前，你可以從67歲開始領取退休福利金。但是，聯邦政府正在考慮將年齡提高到68歲。「屆時會發生的事情就是，當你老了卻不能不工作的時間會越來越長。」佛里曼如此評論，「儲蓄和退休金是不夠的。」另一方面，壽命提高也意味著從身體方面來看，許多老年人能夠工作更長的時間。一〔4〕一。或許，從這些統計資料得到的一課是老生常談：早點學習存錢始終是明智的投資。

Vocabulary

- □ retirement [rɪ`taɪrmənt] 名 退休
- □ milestone [`maɪl͵ston] 名 里程碑
- □ intend to *do* 打算做～
- □ highlight [`haɪ͵laɪt] 動 使～突出
- □ lingering [`lɪŋgərɪŋ] 形 長久的
- □ recession [rɪ`sɛʃən] 名 景氣衰退、不景氣
- □ assessment [ə`sɛsmənt] 名 評估
- □ decline [dɪ`klaɪn] 名 下降
- □ interest rate 利率
- □ vehicle [`viːk!] 名 工具
- □ government bond 政府公債
- □ certificate of deposit 銀行定存單
- □ yield [jild] 動 產生～
- □ social security benefit 社會保障福利金
- □ federal government 聯邦政府
- □ longevity [lɑn`dʒɛvətɪ] 名 壽命
- □ statistics [stə`tɪstɪks] 名 統計

試題	試題翻譯	解答與解析

☑ 161

What is the main purpose of the article?

(A) To list federal government finances
(B) To describe reasons for delaying retirement in the U.S.
(C) To report on economic recovery
(D) To promote investment opportunities

這篇報導的主要目的是什麼？

(A) 列出聯邦政府的財政
(B) 描述美國發生延後退休的原因
(C) 報導經濟復甦
(D) 宣傳投資機會

答案 (B)　　[概述]

報導一開始就描述了在美國有越來越多人不理會65歲是退休年齡，調查結果顯示，有超過60%以上的45歲至60歲的人打算延後退休。後面接著就說明原因，所以(B)是正確答案。而第2段開頭的Another reason for deferring retirement is...更讓我們可以確定內容。標題中也寫到的defer（延長～），在選項中用delay（延緩～）來表示。

☑ 162

Where most likely does Robyn Freeman work?

(A) At a bank
(B) At a government office
(C) At an investment company
(D) At a university

羅賓・佛里曼最有可能在哪裡工作？

(A) 銀行
(B) 政府機關
(C) 投資公司
(D) 大學

答案 (C)　　[推測]

提到羅賓・佛里曼這名人物是在第2段的Robyn Freeman, a retirement analyst for American Assets Inc., a securities firm that sponsors the Assessment on Finance and Aging Committee。a securities firm意為「證券公司」，從佛里曼先生前後句的談話可判斷是跟證券投資有關，所以正確答案是(C)「投資公司」。(D)提到的是第1段出現的人物喬治・艾文思任職的地方。

☑ 163

In which of the positions marked [1], [2], [3], and [4] does the following sentence best belong?

"Currently, you can start drawing retirement benefits at 67."

(A) [1]
(B) [2]
(C) [3]
(D) [4]

下面這一句應該插入標記〔1〕、〔2〕、〔3〕、〔4〕的哪一個位置？

「目前，你可以從 67 歲開始領取退休福利金。」

(A)〔1〕
(B)〔2〕
(C)〔3〕
(D)〔4〕

答案 (C)　　[插入句]

插入句是在說領取退休福利金（retirement benefits）的年齡。從整篇文章中來找提到年齡的地方可發現，第 3 段第 1 句的 Finally, the age at which people can collect Social Security benefits is rising，其話題就是在說社會保障福利金。所以〔3〕是正確答案，這句非常適合接在「年齡提高」的話題後面。

Questions 164-167 refer to the following online chat discussion.

Tran, Amy [8:21 A.M.]
Hi, all, thanks for logging in so early. It's good that we're getting things in order before the big meeting this afternoon. OK, so who's got what ready?

Olson, Ellen [8:22 A.M.]
I've already set up the projector and computer. My department just bought the computer, so it's brand-new and lightning fast. I tried out an older version of the slideshow software on it, just to make sure. Works fine.

Tran, Amy [8:24 A.M.]
Great! It's a relief to have someone from IT there.

Menckel, Richard [8:25 A.M.]
The slideshow is ready. Just waiting for data for two graphs on the last two slides.

Tran, Amy [8:26 A.M.]
David, you've got those graphs, right? With last month's data?

DeFavre, David [8:27 A.M.]
Last month's? I've made the graphs, but with data through October.

Tran, Amy [8:28 A.M.]
Didn't you get my e-mail? I wanted you to include that.

Boston, Kaleb [8:30 A.M.]
Actually, that data isn't available yet. I called Sales yesterday. Apparently they're not ready to release any figures yet. Some of them seem off, they say.

Tran, Amy [8:32 A.M.]
Oh. I should've checked. Sorry about that, David! We'll have to make do. Anyway, sales figures through October will definitely help market our product.

試題165-167請參考以下線上交談內容。

艾咪‧特倫（Tran, Amy）　8:21 A.M.
大家好，感謝大家這麼早登入。在今天下午的重要會議之前，我們把事情確認好，這是件好事。好的，有誰準備好了？

艾倫‧歐爾森（Olson, Ellen）　8:22 A.M.
我已經設定好了投影機和電腦。我的部門剛買了那台電腦，所以它是全新且速度非常快。我在電腦上試用了舊版本的投影片軟體，只是為了確認。運作正常。

艾咪‧特倫　8:24 A.M.
太好了！這裡能有來自資訊部門（IT）的人員真讓人安心。

理查‧門克爾（Menckel, Richard）　8:25 A.M.
投影片已準備就緒。只需再等要放在最後2張投影片的2張圖表資料。

艾咪‧特倫　8:26 A.M.
大衛（David），你有那些圖表，對吧？上面有上個月資料的？

大衛‧達法維爾（Defavre, David）　8:27 A.M.
上個月？我已經做好圖表，但是資料是到10月的。

艾咪‧特倫　8:28 A.M.
你沒收到我的電子郵件嗎？我有說希望把它包括在內。

卡雷布‧波士頓（Boston, Kaleb）　8:30 A.M.
事實上，那份資料還無法用。我昨天打給銷售部門，顯然他們還未準備好公布數字。他們說，還有一些錯誤的部分。

艾咪‧特倫　8:32 A.M.
喔。我應該要檢查過。很抱歉，大衛！我們必須將就使用了。無論如何，到10月為止的銷售數字肯定有助於行銷我們的產品。

Vocabulary

☐ lightning [`laɪtnɪŋ] 形 閃電的、快速的　　☐ just to make sure　只是為了確認　　☐ It's a relief to do　安心做～
☐ make do　將就使用、處理　　☐ market [`mɑrkɪt] 動 銷售～、在市場推出

試題	試題翻譯	解答與解析

☑ 164

What is the reason for the discussion?

(A) To review a conference schedule
(B) To generate data for a slideshow
(C) To prepare for an upcoming presentation
(D) To solicit opinions from several departments

有這段討論的原因是什麼？

(A) 重新探討會議的日程
(B) 為了製作投影片的資料
(C) 為即將進行的報告做準備
(D) 徵求多個部門的意見

答案 (C)　　[概述]

從特倫女士一開始的發言可知，當天下午有大型會議。接下來2個人的發言可視為在會議上要使用投影片做簡報，所以(C)是正確答案。

☐ generate [`dʒɛnə,ret] 動 製作～
☐ solicit [sə`lɪsɪt] 動 徵求～

☑ 165

According to the discussion, what is the problem?

(A) Some data has not been finalized.
(B) Some equipment has not been set up.
(C) Some graphs have not been included.
(D) Some important e-mails have been neglected.

根據討論，問題是什麼？

(A) 一些資料尚未確定。
(B) 一些設備尚未準備。
(C) 一些圖表未包括在內。
(D) 一些重要電子郵件被忽略了。

答案 (A)　　[概述]

這段討論的中間談到有關投影片的資料。對於特倫女士傳送的資料，雖然波士頓先生說that data isn't available yet，但是真正的理由是接下來說的they're not ready to release any figures yet和Some of them seem off，由此可知(A)是正確答案。這裡的off是形容詞，有「（計算等）錯誤」之意。

☐ neglect [nɪg`lɛkt] 動 忽略～

☑ 166

What department does Ms. Tran most likely work in?

(A) Sales
(B) Marketing
(C) IT
(D) Human Resources

特倫女士最有可能在什麼部門工作？

(A) 銷售部門
(B) 行銷部門
(C) 資訊科技部門
(D) 人力資源部門

答案 (B)　　[其他細節]

特倫女士是掌握這段討論的人物。從她最後的發言sales figures through October will definitely help market our product可知，最符合的答案是(B)。注意別被波士頓先生說的I called Sales yesterday.混淆而誤選(A)。至於(C)則是艾倫的所屬部門。

☑ 167

At 8:32 A.M., what does Ms. Tran mean when she writes, "We'll have to make do"?

(A) They will use the data through October.
(B) They will create a new slideshow.
(C) They must reschedule a presentation.
(D) They must get more information.

8：32 A.M.，特倫女士寫著「We'll have to make do」，表示什麼？

(A) 使用截至 10 月的資料。
(B) 他們將製作新的投影片。
(C) 他們必須重新安排報告時間。
(D) 他們必須獲得更多資訊。

答案 (A)　　[說話者的目的]

make do意為「將就使用、處理」。從最後一句可知，特倫女士認為即使沒有上個月的資料，如果有截至10月的銷售數據，這對產品的行銷是有利的，因此正確答案是(A)。

189

Questions 168-171 refer to the following notice.

試題168-171請參考以下注意事項。

Peponi Nature Reserve Tours
Great Rift Valley, Kenya

An unmatched tourist experience! Experience the breathtaking beauty of African nature firsthand! Visitors to one of Africa's oldest and largest reserves will have opportunities to see wildlife—zebras, elephants, lions and more—in its natural environment, as well as to encounter the daily lives of traditional peoples who have dwelled in the region for thousands of years.

Customize your itinerary. Due to the reserve's immense size, it is generally impossible to see everything. Accordingly, most tours focus on specific areas within the reserve. Total fees vary with each agency and tour. Tour packages are available in English, French, Spanish, Arabic, Mandarin Chinese, Japanese and Korean. Select the tour that is right for you.

Rules and Regulations
- All tours must be scheduled through a licensed agency. Lists of such agencies can be found through the National Association of Nature Tour Agencies: www.natnattour.ke.
- Tourists must strictly follow the directions of guides at all times.
- Cameras and video recorders are permitted, but devices that emit loud noises or other effects which could startle wildlife may be prohibited. Check with your agency regarding acceptable personal items that can be brought on a tour.
- Animals must not be approached under any circumstances.
- Fines may be imposed on violators of these rules.

佩波尼（PEPONI）自然保護區之旅
肯亞東非大裂谷（GREAT RIFT VALLEY, KENYA）

一趟無以倫比的旅遊體驗！直接體驗非洲大自然的壯觀之美！在非洲歷史最悠久且規模最大的保護區之一的遊客門，將有機會在自然的環境下看到野生動物——如斑馬、大象、獅子和更多——以及遇見在這個地區居住數千年的傳統民族日常生活。

訂製您的行程。由於保護區的規模廣大，一般不可能看到每樣東西。因此，大多數旅遊團都聚焦於保護區內的特定區域。每個代辦機構和旅行團的總費用各不相同。旅遊套裝行程提供英文、法文、西班牙文、阿拉伯文、中文、日文和韓文。請選擇適合您的行程。

規則與規定
- 所有行程必須經過有執照的代理機構安排。這些機構的名單可以透過全國自然旅遊機構協會（the National Association of Nature Tour Agencies）找到：www.natnattour.ke。
- 遊客必須隨時嚴格遵守導遊指示。
- 攝影機和錄影機是被允許的，但會發出噪音或其他效果讓野生動物受到驚嚇的裝置可能會被禁止。關於能在旅行中攜帶的個人物品，請與您的代理機構確認。
- 任何情況下都不准接近動物。
- 違反這些規則者可能會被處以罰款。

Vocabulary

- breathtaking [ˋbrɛθˏtekɪŋ] 形 壯觀的
- firsthand [ˋfɝstˋhænd] 副 直接地
- wildlife [ˋwaɪldˏlaɪf] 名 野生動物
- encounter [ɪnˋkaʊntɚ] 動 遇見～
- dwell [dwɛl] 動 居住
- accordingly [əˋkɔrdɪŋlɪ] 副 因此
- focus on～　聚焦於～
- vary [ˋvɛrɪ] 動 變更
- strictly [ˋstrɪktlɪ] 副 嚴格地
- direction [dəˋrɛkʃən] 名 指示
- at all times　隨時
- device [dɪˋvaɪs] 名 裝置
- emit [ɪˋmɪt] 動 發出（聲音或光）
- check with～　與～聯繫
- regarding [rɪˋgɑrdɪŋ] 介 關於～
- acceptable [əkˋsɛptəbl̩] 形 可以接受的
- approach [əˋprotʃ] 動 接近～
- under any circumstances　在任何情況下
- fine [faɪn] 名 罰款
- impose A on B　對B課加A
- violator [ˋvaɪəˏletɚ] 名 違反者

試題	試題翻譯	解答與解析

☑ **168**

What is mentioned as a feature of the nature reserve?

(A) Its size is modest.
(B) It offers hotel accommodations.
(C) It includes a history museum.
(D) It has wild animals.

什麼是自然保護區的特色？

(A) 區域不太大。
(B) 提供旅館住宿。
(C) 內有歷史博物館。
(D) 有野生動物。

答案 (D) 〔何者正確類型〕

(A)不符合第2段開頭的Due to the reserve's immense size, ...。immense是指「廣大的」，選項的modest則是指「不太大的」。(B)在整個通知中都沒有被提到。(C)從第1段的encounter the daily lives of traditional peoples...會讓人混淆而誤選。而第1段提到的wildlife—zebras, elephants, lions and more是自然保護區訪客可以見到的生物，由此可知，(D)是正確答案。

☑ **169**

According to the notice, what is included on the National Association of Nature Tour Agencies Web site?

(A) Lists of various nature reserves
(B) Applications for guide training
(C) Information on approved companies
(D) Schedules for each national tour package

根據注意事項，全國自然旅遊機構協會的網站包含什麼內容？

(A) 各種自然保護區名單
(B) 導遊培訓申請
(C) 被認可的公司資料
(D) 每個國家的旅遊套裝行程的時間表

答案 (C) 〔其他細節〕

第3段第1項提到有關全國自然旅遊機構協會的網站資訊，說明了旅遊要透過認可的旅遊代理機構安排，由此可知網站上有這些機構的清冊。因此(C)是正確答案。選項內把a licensed agency（有執照的代理機構）改用approved companies（被認可的公司）來表達。approve是「認可～」。

☑ **170**

The word "startle" in paragraph 3, line 6, is closest in meaning to

(A) identify
(B) monitor
(C) benefit
(D) scare

第 3 段第 6 行的單字 「startle」 意思最接近下列哪一個？

(A) 識別
(B) 監測
(C) 有利於
(D) 驚嚇

答案 (D) 〔同義詞〕

先看這一句在but後面的句型結構，devices（裝置）到wildlife（野生動物）是主詞，意思是「會發出噪音或其他效果使野生動物受到驚嚇的裝置」。may be prohibited（可能被禁止）是述語，可以從對野生動物做什麼會被禁止的這個角度來思考。startle意為「讓～驚嚇」，選項中以(D)的「驚嚇」意思最接近。

☑ **171**

What is NOT mentioned as a regulation of the reserve?

(A) Refraining from getting close to animals
(B) Avoiding dangerous outdoor zones
(C) Confirming acceptable devices
(D) Obeying all directions from guides

保護區的規定沒有提到什麼內容？

(A) 避免接近動物
(B) 避免危險的戶外區域
(C) 確認允許的裝置
(D) 遵守導遊的所有指示

答案 (B) 〔是非題類型〕

第3段是有關regulation（規定）的內容，除了(B)以外都提到了。分別是(A)符合第4項，(C)符合第3項的Check with your agency regarding...這一句。(D)符合第2項。

□ refrain from～　避免～
□ confirm [kənˋfɝm] 動 確認～
□ obey [əˋbe] 動 遵守～

Questions 172-175 refer to the following e-mail.

* E-mail *	✕
To:	John Middleton
From:	Jack Walters
Date:	March 11
Subject:	Warm Welcome
Cc:	Mindy Yang

Dear Mr. Middleton,

On behalf of all of us at United Financial Printing, I am thrilled to welcome you to our Financial Document Services division. We are fortunate to have someone with your qualifications and professional experience in financial document proofreading join our Document Production team. —[1]—.

Part of our new employee orientation program involves a week of on-site training. As this is your first position as proofreading team leader, we would like you to spend several days observing and assisting the managerial staff who oversee Document Production. Our senior manager, Mindy Yang, will be in charge of this. —[2]—. I will introduce you to her next Monday, and you can set up a schedule together.

Further, on Tuesday we will hold a new employee reception party from 4:00 to about 5:30. This will be a chance to get to know some of the Production staff you will be managing. —[3]—. Meanwhile, I have spoken to the Production floor leader, Deborah Falwell, about providing you with details about how the proofreading team has operated until now, and what changes your team members and others have proposed, for your consideration. —[4]—.

Once again, we are looking forward to seeing you on Monday.

Best Regards,

Jack Walters
Vice President of Operations, UFP Corporation

試題172-175請參考以下電子郵件。

收信者：約翰・米德爾頓（John Middleton）
發信者：傑克・沃爾特斯（Jack Walters）
日期：3月11日
主旨：熱烈歡迎
副本：明迪・楊（Mindy Yang）

親愛的米德爾頓先生：

我謹代表聯合金融印刷公司（United Financial Printing）全體人員，很高興歡迎您到我們的金融文件服務部門。很榮幸有像您這樣在金融文件校對方面有資歷與專業經驗的人加入我們的文件製作團隊。－〔1〕－

我們的新進員工培訓計畫包含一週的現場培訓，由於這是您第一次擔任校對團隊主管，我們希望您花數天的時間觀察和協助負責監督文件製作的管理人員。我們的資深經理，明迪・楊負責這一項。－〔2〕－。下週一我會把您介紹給她，您們可以一起安排時間表。

此外，我們將在週二的4點到大約5點半舉行新進員工歡迎會。這會是一個認識一些您將要管理的文件製作人員的機會。－〔3〕－他們很期待當面見到您。同時，我已跟生產樓層主管，黛博拉・佛維爾（Deborah Falwell）談過，我們會提供您有關校對團隊迄今為止如何運作的細節，以及您的團隊成員和其他人提出的改變提案，供您參考。－〔4〕－。

再一次，期待週一見到您！

謹致問候

傑克・沃爾特斯
聯合金融印刷公司營運副總裁

Vocabulary

☐ on behalf of～　代表～　　☐ be thrilled to *do*　對～感到非常高興　　☐ be fortunate to *do*　有幸做～

☐〈have *someone* ＋原形動詞〉　讓（人）做～　　☐ qualification [͵kwɑləfəˋkeʃən] 名 資格、資歷　　☐ involve [ɪnˋvɑlv] 動 包含～

☐ on-site [͵ɑnˋsaɪt] 形 現場的　　☐ observe [əbˋzɝv] 動 觀察～　　☐ managerial staff　管理人員　　☐ in charge of～　負責～

☐ further [ˋfɝðɚ] 副 另外　　☐ get to know～　認識～　　☐ consideration [kənsɪdəˋreʃən] 名 考慮、檢討

試題	試題翻譯	解答與解析

☑ 172

What is stated about Mr. Middleton?

(A) He has worked for the company before.
(B) He has previous experience in proofreading.
(C) He is exempt from the training program.
(D) He will oversee Document Production for a week.

下列哪一項是有關米德爾頓的描述？

(A) 以前曾任職這家公司。
(B) 他已有校對經驗。
(C) 他能免除受訓計畫。
(D) 他將監督文件製作團隊一週。

答案 (B) 〔推測〕

米德爾頓先生是電子郵件的收信人。從主旨的 Warm Welcome 以及第1段開頭的United Financial Printing可知，米德爾頓先生進入印刷公司工作受到歡迎。後面對他個人更提到 someone with your qualifications and professional experience in financial document proofreading，所以 (B) 是正確答案。proofreading是「校對」。

☐ exempt [ɪgˈzɛmpt] **形** 被免除的
☐ oversee [ˈovɚˈsi] **動** 監督～

☑ 173

According to the e-mail, what will happen next Monday?

(A) Mr. Middleton's training schedule will be decided.
(B) New employees will receive orientation.
(C) Changes to company policy will be announced.
(D) Mr. Middleton will meet the Production staff.

根據電子郵件，下週一將會發生什麼事情？

(A) 將會決定米德爾頓先生的培訓時間表。
(B) 新進員工將接受培訓。
(C) 將宣布公司政策變動。
(D) 米德爾頓先生將會見到文件製作人員。

答案 (A) 〔其他細節〕

第2段提到I will introduce you to her next Monday, and you can set up a schedule together.。而正確答案(A)是把後半句「你們（米德爾頓先生和楊女士）可以一起安排」換成「決定米德爾頓先生的培訓時間表」的說法而已。整篇內容並未明講培訓時間，所以(B)的說法不適合。至於(D)說的情況是週二歡迎會時才會發生。

☑ 174

What will Mr. Middleton do at the event on Tuesday?

(A) Learn about management techniques
(B) Receive training materials
(C) Meet his future subordinates
(D) Organize a reception party

米德爾頓先生在週二的活動將會做什麼？

(A) 學習管理技術
(B) 收到訓練資料
(C) 與他日後的部屬見面
(D) 籌畫一個接待會

答案 (C) 〔其他細節〕

所謂週二的活動，就是第3段第1句說的新進員工歡迎會。而在This will be a chance to get to know some of the Production staff you will be managing.這句提到的「您將要管理的文件製作人員」，也就是指日後會成為米德爾頓先生部屬的人員，因此(C)為正確答案。

☑ 175

In which of the positions marked [1], [2], [3], and [4] does the following sentence best belong?

"They are looking forward to meeting you in person."

(A) [1]
(B) [2]
(C) [3]
(D) [4]

下面這一句應該插入標記〔1〕、〔2〕、〔3〕、〔4〕的哪一個位置？

「他們很期待當面見到您。」

(A) 〔1〕
(B) 〔2〕
(C) 〔3〕
(D) 〔4〕

答案 (C) 〔插入句〕

插入句的meet *someone* in person意為「親自見到（某人）」。這句的主詞是They，可以想一下他們是誰，誰很期待見到新同事米德爾頓先生，同時再看整篇內容可知，第3段是在講新進員工的歡迎會，所以空格〔3〕的前一句 some of the Production staff you will be managing就是指他們。

Questions 176-180 refer to the following notice and e-mail.

Hakka Textile Co.
Now Accepting Managerial Submissions

Throughout our firm, many groups, teams and sections have done amazing work over the current fiscal year. We are calling on managers to submit stories that detail the efforts of these teams and the exceptional projects they have successfully completed.

The company will choose one of these teams to be our Team of the Year. Along with having their names mentioned prominently on our internal Web page, each member of the winning team will receive €500 and three paid vacation days. This is part of our continuing effort to show our appreciation for the valuable work that our employees do.

Each submission should be between 400 and 800 words long and explain the measurable effects the team and its work have had. It should be accompanied by 5-9 photos, images or slides related to the team and its work. Submissions are welcome from any department in any location.

Submissions are due by November 23. They should be sent to Ellen Gallagher in Global Human Resources.

E-Mail Message	✕
To:	Narasimha Balasubramaniam
From:	Ellen Gallagher
Date:	November 30
Subject:	Submission

Dear Narasimha,

We are pleased to inform you that the Building 4 Maintenance Team you submitted for consideration has won the Team of the Year Award. We were impressed with the work that they do, in particular the fact that nearly every maintenance issue is resolved within 24 hours. This is not only the best performance on the Chennai campus, but the best among all of our facilities worldwide.

We received six photos from you, all of them showing your team working on the Chennai campus, along with a 300-word story. The talent management committee needs you to comply with the submission guidelines in this area. After that, we can formally and publicly confirm you as the winners.

Regards,

Ellen Gallagher
Global Human Resources Director

試題176-180請參考以下通知及電子郵件。

哈卡紡織公司（Hakka Textile Co.）
即日起受理管理階層提出報告

在整個公司中，很多組別、團隊和部門已於目前會計年度完成令人驚豔的工作。我們號召管理人員提出詳述這些團隊的努力以及他們成功完成出色計畫的故事。

公司將從這些團隊選出其中一組成為我們的年度團隊。除了我們的內部網站會在明顯處提及他們的名字外，獲獎團隊的每一名成員也將獲得500歐元和3天的有薪休假。對於員工寶貴的工作表現，這是我們不斷努力地表達感激的一部分。

每份報告長度應在400字至800字以內，並解釋團隊完成工作成果所帶來的可衡量效益。它還需要附上5至9張與團隊及其工作有關的照片、圖片或投影片。歡迎來自任何地點的任何部門提出報告。

提出截止日期為11月23日。請傳送到全球人力資源部門的艾倫‧加拉格爾（Ellen Gallagher）。

收信者：納拉辛哈‧巴拉史布拉瑪尼安姆（Narasimha Balasubramaniam）
發信者：艾倫‧加拉格爾
日期：11月30日
主旨：提出報告

親愛的納拉辛哈：

我們很高興通知您，您提出報告的第4大樓維護團隊贏得了年度最佳團隊獎。我們對他們所做的工作印象深刻，特別是幾乎所有的維護問題都在24小時內得到解決。這不僅是在清奈（Chennai）廠區中表現最好，在我們的全球設施中也是最好的成果。

我們收到您提供的6張照片，所有照片都展示了在清奈廠區的團隊工作，還有300字故事。人才管理委員會需要您遵守該報告相關的規則。在一切符合之後，我們就可以正式公布您是贏家。

謹致問候

艾倫‧加拉格爾
全球人力資源部部長

Vocabulary

□ submission [sʌbˋmɪʃən] 图 提出　　□ fiscal year　會計年度　　□ call on~ to *do*　呼籲~做……　　□ along with~　和~一起

□ internal [ɪnˋtɝnl] 形 內部的　　□ paid vacation day　給薪休假日　　□ measurable [ˋmɛʒərəbl] 形 可衡量的

□ be accompanied by~　由~陪伴　　□ related to~　與~有關　　□ in particular　特別地

□ need~ to *do*　需要~做……　　□ comply with~　遵守（要求等）

試題	試題翻譯	解答與解析

☑ **176**

What is the main purpose of the notice?

(A) To invite feedback on a product
(B) To provide information about a contest
(C) To explain some process changes
(D) To outline some performance goals

這則通知的主要目的是什麼？

(A) 要求對產品的回饋
(B) 提供有關一場競賽的訊息
(C) 解釋一些過程變化
(D) 概述一些績效目標

答案 (B) 概述

先掌握通知的標題「即日起受理管理層提出報告」再來看整篇內容，第1段的We are calling on managers to submit...出現跟標題同樣的意思，從這一整句可知是提出報告詳細說明團隊的努力及完成的方案。接著再繼續看，從第2段得知是要選出年度最優秀的團隊，所以(B)將它表達為「競賽」是正確的。

☑ **177**

In the notice, the word "prominently" in paragraph 2, line 3, is closest in meaning to

(A) notably
(B) concisely
(C) frequently
(D) graciously

通知中的第 2 段第 3 行的單字「prominently」意思最接近下列哪一個？

(A) 顯著地
(B) 簡潔地
(C) 頻繁地
(D) 親切地

答案 (A) 同義詞

單字前面的結構是〈have＋受詞＋過去分詞〉。接在後面的prominently是副詞來修飾動詞。整句的意思就是「公司內部網頁將～提及最優秀團隊的成員名字」。prominently意為「明顯地」，以(A)的notably（顯著地）意思最接近。遇到同義詞的問題，即使不知道被問到的單字意思，不妨試著把各選項內的字替換看看，也是可以找出語意相通的答案。

☑ **178**

According to the notice, what is true about Hakka Textile Co.?

(A) It offers its managers large bonuses.
(B) Its production is centralized in Chennai.
(C) It recognizes the achievements of its staff.
(D) It pays employees competitive salaries.

根據通知內容，下列有關哈卡紡織公司的描述何者正確？

(A) 提供大量獎金給管理職。
(B) 其生產集中在清奈。
(C) 認可公司員工工作上的成就。
(D) 付給員工具競爭力的薪水。

答案 (C) 何者正確類型

從通知內容的第2段This is part of our continuing effort to show our appreciation for the valuable work that our employees do.可知(C)是正確答案。appreciation是「感謝之意」。選項是把show our appreciation for...（對……表達我們的感謝）換成recognize（認可～）來表達。the valuable work that our employees do（員工寶貴的工作表現）換成the achievements of its staff（其員工工作上的成就）來表達。
□ centralize [ˈsɛntrəlˌaɪz] 動 使集中在～

☑ **179**

What is indicated about Building 4 on the Chennai campus?

(A) Its repair technicians have been specially trained.
(B) Its maintenance issues are usually solved quickly.
(C) It is the most productive output center.
(D) It is the largest company structure.

對於清奈廠區第 4 大樓的描述何者正確？

(A) 其維修技術人員已接受專門訓練。
(B) 它的維護問題通常很快得到解決。
(C) 是最具生產力的輸出中心。
(D) 是最大的公司建築物。

答案 (B) 何者正確類型

從電子郵件一開頭的描述就知道第4大樓的維護團隊贏得年度最佳團隊獎。另外，從後面的內容可知該團隊是在清奈的廠區內。從第1段中間的the fact that nearly every maintenance issue is resolved within 24 hours就能看出(B)是正確答案。issue是「問題」的意思，選項內分別將該句的resolve（解決～）和within 24 hours（24小時內）換成solve（解決）和quickly（很快地）來表達。

☑ **180**

What is suggested about Mr. Balasubramaniam?

(A) He did not supply enough text.
(B) He did not comply with a maintenance directive.
(C) He did not formally enter a project submission.
(D) He did not agree with a committee decision.

關於巴拉史布拉瑪尼安姆先生，何者正確？

(A) 他沒有提供足夠的文字。
(B) 他沒有遵守維護指示。
(C) 他沒有正式提出企劃。
(D) 他不同意委員會的決定。

答案 (A) 推測

這是有關2篇文章的問題。巴拉史布拉瑪尼安姆先生是電子郵件的收信者。第2段的The talent management committee needs you to...提到他並沒有遵守報告相關的規則。從這句的前一句可以看到along with a 300-word story，意即他只提出300字的報告。但是根據上面通知所言，規定的字數是400字至800字以內。因此(A)的not supply enough text是正確答案。

Questions 181-185 refer to the following advertisement and book review.

Energy Going Forward

By Maleeha Noorzai

Cnoklin Publishing Co.
Available in print, e-book and audio format

This book deals with the major energy production problems the world faces today, from power outages to environmental damage. It then lays out a compelling vision of a clean energy future and how nations, companies and individuals can work together to get there. Relying on three decades of work in both the public and private sectors, Ms. Noorzai writes persuasively on how we can create a future of clean, abundant energy. The book is divided into five parts, each one containing four chapters.

Part 1: The history of energy since the industrial era
Part 2: Major environmental, output and price issues
Part 3: Alternative energy sources and research
Part 4: Policy recommendations for industries and governments
Part 5: Actions that ordinary citizens can take

This makes it much easier for readers to concentrate on areas that interest them the most.

About the Author: After working for seven years as Research Director for Anko Solar Energy Co. and three years as a governmental energy advisor, Ms. Noorzai now teaches at Alfreda University in Budapest. Readers can follow her social media site at www.socialcomglobe.eu/noorzai.

Book Pick of the Week: *Energy Going Forward* By Maleeha Noorzai
Review by Lester Colmes

Despite their critical importance to our lives, books that cover energy are often too complex for non-specialists to follow. This recent work by Ms. Noorzai is a welcome exception to this trend. It should therefore find a wider readership.

I found the work to be not only authoritative but well-written. Ms. Noorzai writes in clear, plain language, and takes the time to explain technical terms. This makes Parts 2-3 easy to get through. Part 5 of the book was also very useful, as it included the contact information of leaders, corporations, politicians and non-profit organizations. Readers can use this information to get involved in the clean energy movement.

I thought the chapters providing the background of energy development were a bit short. Nevertheless, I can certainly recommend this work to anyone.

試題181-185請參考以下廣告和書評。

　　前進吧！能源（Energy Going Forward）
瑪里哈・努爾扎（Maleeha Noorzai）著
克納柯林（Cnoklin）出版社
有紙本、電子書和有聲書格式

本書論及當今世界面臨的主要能源生產問題，包含停電到環境破壞。接著描述了一個令人十分振奮的乾淨能源未來，以及國家、企業與個人如何共同努力並達成目標。以其在公務與民間領域工作30年的經驗，努爾扎女士令人信服地寫下我們如何創造一個乾淨、富足能源的未來。本書分為5大部分，每篇包含4章。

第1篇：工業時代以來的能源歷史
第2篇：主要環境、產出和價格的議題
第3篇：替代能源的來源及研究
第4篇：對工業及政府的政策建議
第5篇：一般民眾可以做的行動

這種編排讓讀者能更容易集中閱讀感興趣的領域。

作者簡介：在擔任安科太陽能公司（Anko Solar Energy Co.）研究總監 7 年，以及擔任政府能源顧問 3 年之後，努爾扎女士目前在布達佩斯（Budapest）的艾爾菲達（Alfreda）大學任教。讀者可以關注她的社群媒體網站www.socialcomglobe.eu/noorzai。

本週選書：前進吧！能源 瑪里哈・努爾扎著
書評人：萊斯特・柯爾姆斯（Lester Colmes）

儘管能源對我們的生活極其重要，但是論及能源的書籍往往太過艱深而讓非專業人士無所適從。最近努爾扎女士的這本著作，對這種現象來說是個受歡迎的例外。因此，它應該會找到更廣泛的讀者群。

我發現這本著作不僅具權威性，還精心編寫。努爾扎女士用清晰、易懂的語言描述，並花時間來解釋專業術語。這讓讀者可以輕鬆理解第2至3篇。第5篇也是非常有用，因為它包含了領導者、企業、政治家及非營利團體的聯繫資訊。讀者可以利用這些資訊來參與乾淨能源運動。

我認為本書提供能源發展背景的章節有點短。僅管如此我肯定會向任何人推薦這本書。

Vocabulary

- deal with～　處理、論及～
- power outage　停電
- lay out～　描述（想法等）
- compelling [kəmˋpɛlɪŋ] 形 令人十分振奮
- clean energy　乾淨能源
- rely on～　依賴～
- sector [ˋsɛktə] 名 部門
- persuasively [pəˋswesɪvlɪ] 副 令人信服地
- abundant [əˋbʌndənt] 形 豐富的
- alternative [ɔlˋtɝnətɪv] 形 替代的
- concentrate on～　集中於～
- despite [dɪˋspaɪt] 介 儘管
- critical [ˋkrɪtɪk!] 形 重大的
- exception [ɪkˋsɛpʃən] 名 例外
- trend [trɛnd] 名 傾向
- authoritative [əˋθɔrəˏtetɪv] 形 權威性的
- technical term　專業術語
- get through～　通過～、完成
- non-profit organization　非營利團體
- movement [ˋmuvmənt] 名 運動
- nevertheless [ˏnɛvəðəˋlɛs] 副 僅管如此

試題	試題翻譯	解答與解析

☑ 181

What is probably true about *Energy Going Forward*?

(A) It is designed primarily for specialists.
(B) It is coauthored by a reporter.
(C) It is available in a digital format.
(D) It is published by a university.

關於《前進吧！能源》，什麼描述是可能對的？

(A) 主要是為專家而寫的。
(B) 與一位記者合著。
(C) 有提供數位版本。
(D) 由大學出版。

答案 (C) 〔推測〕

《前進吧！能源》是廣告和書評的標題，也是這本書的書名。從廣告上的Available in print, e-book and audio format可知(C)是正確答案。而從書評的第1段就知道(A)是錯的。(B)是錯在廣告和書評都提到這是瑪里哈·努爾扎的個人著作。至於(D)是錯在廣告一開頭就提到出版社為克納柯林出版社。

☑ 182

According to the advertisement, what CANNOT be found in the book?

(A) Other ways to get energy
(B) A cultural comparison of industrialized nations
(C) Suggestions for governmental policy change
(D) Ideas for how individuals can help

根據廣告，書上找不到什麼？

(A) 其他獲取能源的方式
(B) 工業化國家的文化比較
(C) 政府政策轉變的建議
(D) 個人如何盡一己之力的方法

答案 (B) 〔是非題類型〕

對照廣告上描述這本書第1篇到第5篇的內容來看，(A)符合第3篇。(C)符合第4篇，並將recommendation（建議）換成suggestion來表達。(D)符合第5篇，並將ordinary citizen（一般民眾）換成individual（個人）來表達。由此可知沒有描述到的(B)是正確答案。

☐ industrialized nation　工業化國家

☑ 183

Where does Maleeha Noorzai currently work?

(A) At a government office
(B) At an energy firm
(C) At a media company
(D) At an educational institution

瑪里哈·努爾扎目前在哪裡工作？

(A) 在政府機關
(B) 能源公司
(C) 媒體公司
(D) 教育機構

答案 (D) 〔其他細節〕

瑪里哈·努爾扎是這本書的作者。廣告最下方的簡介提到Ms. Noorzai now teaches at Alfreda University in Budapest，因此(D)為正確答案。university（大學）只是被換成educational institution（教育機構）來表達。至於(A)是指作者在大學執教前的經歷。

☑ 184

What does Mr. Colmes suggest about some textbooks?

(A) They are frequently overpriced.
(B) They are often hard to find.
(C) They are difficult to comprehend.
(D) They overlook key issues.

對於一些書籍，柯爾姆斯先生說了什麼？

(A) 它們經常價格過高。
(B) 它們通常很難找。
(C) 它們很難理解。
(D) 它們忽略了關鍵問題。

答案 (C) 〔何者正確類型〕

柯爾姆斯先生是書評人。題目說的textbooks在這兒是指能源相關的一般書籍。從書評一開始提到的books that cover energy are often too complex for non-specialists to follow就可知(C)是正確答案。選項分別將complex（複雜的）和follow（理解～）換成difficult（困難的）和comprehend（理解）來表達。

☐ frequently [`frikwəntlɪ] 圈 頻繁地
☐ overlook [ˌovəˈluk] 動 忽略～

☑ 185

What part of the book does the reviewer think is too short?

(A) Part 1
(B) Part 2
(C) Part 4
(D) Part 5

書評人認為書中哪一部份太短？

(A) 第 1 篇
(B) 第 2 篇
(C) 第 4 篇
(D) 第 5 篇

答案 (A) 〔其他細節〕

這是有關2篇文章的問題。書評人在最後一段說I thought the chapters providing the background of energy development were a bit short.。background是「背景」，energy development是「能源發展」。而哪一篇有說明能源發展的背景呢？由廣告可知，Part 1是寫有關能源的歷史，所以正確答案是(A)。

Questions 186-190 refer to the following brochure, form, and e-mail.

The International Machinery Convention (IMC)
www.imc_convo.net

Register online by June 30
Gain access to the most important business gathering of the year.

Attendees include:
  Global manufacturers
  Research institutes
  Materials producers
  Consulting agencies

This event is also regularly the focus of broad international business media coverage, providing a significant level of free publicity for companies and professionals who attend.

Individual registration fee: €175 per person Five or more individuals: €125 per person

This brochure includes prices for leasing booth space as well as advice on making travel arrangements. Feel free to share this document with colleagues everywhere.

The International Machinery Convention (IMC)
www.imc_convo.net
— Online Registration Form —

Date:	June 3
Applicant name:	Harriet Walters
Title:	Assistant sales manager
Employer:	Jarna Tool Corporation
Location:	Bucharest, Romania

I will be attending as a:

Business professional ☒
Member of the press ☐
Educator/analyst/researcher ☐

Contact information:	h.walters@jarnatools.net
Phone:	21-555-904-6000
E-mail:	h.walters@jarnatools.net

Others attending with you? Yes ☒ No ☐
If yes, number in group: 4

CLICK HERE TO SUBMIT **CLICK HERE TO SAVE AS DRAFT**

Note: This application is not complete and will not be processed until a deposit of €25 per person has been received. A confirmation number will be provided via e-mail.

試題186-190請參考以下手冊、表格及電子郵件。

國際機械大會（IMC）
www.imc_convo.net
6月30日前線上登錄
獲得參加年度最重要的商業聚會。

與會者包括：
全球製造商
研究機構
原物料製造商
諮詢機構

這個活動也經常成為國際商業媒體報導的焦點，為參加的公司和專業人士提供大規模的免費宣傳。

個人登錄費用：每人175歐元
5人（含）以上團體：每人125歐元

本手冊包括租賃攤位的價錢，還有旅遊安排建議。歡迎與各界同事分享這份文宣。

國際機械大會
www.imc_convo.net
線上登錄表格

日期：6月3日
申請人姓名：哈麗亞特・華特斯（Harriet Walters）
職稱：銷售副理
任職公司：賈納（Jarna）工具公司
所在地：布加勒斯特（Bucharest），羅馬尼亞（Romania）

我將以下列身分參加：
商務專業人士　　　　　　　☒
媒體成員　　　　　　　　　☐
教育工作者／分析師／研究員　☐

聯絡方式：h.walters@jarnatools.net
電話：21-555-904-6000
電子信箱：h.walters@jarnatools.net
是否有同行者：☒是 ☐否
若有，同行人數：4位

點擊此處提交 點擊此處儲存草稿
請注意：此申請程序尚未完成，待收到每人25歐元的訂金後才會受理。認證碼將用電子郵件發送。

試題文章	試題文章翻譯

＊ E-mail ＊　✕

To:	Harriet Walters
From:	Farhad Pahlavi
Date:	June 6
Subject:	IMC

Harriet,

I am writing to state that I have approved your trip to the IMC this year. Go ahead and complete the application process for the trip. Ga-in Lee in accounting will help you do that. I hope that you can return with multiple sales contracts. That would really make this entire venture worthwhile.

Be advised that I am also going to add two more people to your group, Lucy Wu and Owen Smith. They are new to the firm, but are eager, young salespeople and this would be a good experience for them.

Regards,

Farhad

\----------------------

Farhad Pahlavi
Sales Manager, Jarna Tool Corporation

收信者：哈麗亞特・華特斯
發信者：法哈德・帕拉維（Farhad Pahlavi）
日期：6月6日
主旨：國際機械大會

哈麗亞特：

我寫這封信是要說明我已經批准你今年出差參加國際機械大會。請繼續並完成出差的申請流程。會計部門的李加盈（Ga-in Lee）將會協助你。期待你能帶回好幾份的銷售合約回來。那就真的會讓這次的整個冒險嘗試值回票價。

另外要告知你，我也將增加吳露西（Lucy Wu）和歐文・史密斯（Owen Smith）這2個人到你的團隊。他們對公司來說是新人，但他們是熱忱的年輕銷售人員，這對他們來說將是一個很好的經驗。

此致

法哈德

\------------------

法哈德・帕拉維
賈納工具公司銷售經理

Vocabulary

☐ machinery [məˋʃinəri] 名 機械　　☐ gain [gen] 動 獲得～　　☐ gathering [ˋgæðərɪŋ] 名 聚集、聚會　　☐ attendee [əˋtɛndi] 名 與會者
☐ broad [brɔd] 形 廣泛的　　☐ media coverage　媒體報導　　☐ publicity [pʌbˋlɪsətɪ] 名 廣告、宣傳
☐ A as well as B　不僅是B還有A　　☐ deposit [dɪˋpɑzɪt] 名 保證金、訂金　　☐ multiple [ˋmʌltəp!] 形 多數的　　☐ entire [ɪnˋtaɪr] 形 全部的
☐ venture [ˋvɛntʃɚ] 名 冒險嘗試　　☐ worthwhile [ˋwɝθˋhwaɪl] 形 值得的　　☐ Be advised that～　請知悉～
☐ eager [ˋigɚ] 形 熱忱的　　☐ salespeople [ˋselzˌpip!] 名 銷售人員

☑ 186

What is available in the brochure?

(A) Advice on talking to the media
(B) Information on leases
(C) Prices of new products
(D) Tips on sharing travel information

手冊上記載了什麼？

(A) 與媒體交談的建議
(B) 租賃訊息
(C) 新產品的價格
(D) 分享旅遊資訊的祕訣

答案 (B)　其他細節

手冊（第1篇內容）的最後提到This brochure includes prices for leasing booth space，所以(B)是正確答案。

☑ 187

What is indicated about Ms. Walters?

(A) She has not yet completed her registration.
(B) She has registered for a company booth.
(C) She declined a press interview.
(D) She wants to recruit more analysts.

什麼是關於華特斯女士的描述？

(A) 她尚未完成登記。
(B) 她已登記一個公司的攤位。
(C) 她婉拒了新聞採訪。
(D) 她想招募更多分析師。

答案 (A)　何者正確類型

在給華特斯女士的電子郵件（第3篇內容）中，第2句說Go ahead and complete the application process for the trip.。後面也提到要變更人數，由此可推測華特斯女士尚未登錄完成。所以(A)是正確答案。

□ decline [dɪˋklaɪn] 動 婉拒～

☑ 188

What does Mr. Pahlavi tell Ms. Walters to do?

(A) Complete an analysis
(B) Increase a deposit
(C) Make an initial payment
(D) Approve a business trip

帕拉維先生告訴華特斯女士要做什麼事？

(A) 完成分析
(B) 增加存款
(C) 付訂金
(D) 批准出差

答案 (C)　其他細節

帕拉維先生在電子郵件中指示華特斯女士要完成參加國際機械大會的登錄後，說了「會計會協助妳」。而之所以會提到會計，是因為表格下方的Note（注意）提到This application is not complete...，如果有掌握到「請付訂金完成登錄」的指示，就知道(C)的an initial payment是付訂金的意思，所以是正確答案。(A)的an analysis（分析）要是改為a registration（登錄）就是正確答案了。

☑ 189

In the e-mail, the word "venture" in paragraph 1, line 3, is closest in meaning to

(A) organization
(B) market
(C) merger
(D) effort

電子郵件第1段第3行的單字「venture」意思最接近下列哪一個？

(A) 組織
(B) 市場
(C) 合併
(D) 努力

答案 (D)　同義詞

依字面翻譯的話，這句意思是「那確實讓這次所有的～是值得的」。That是指前句提到的「帶回好幾份的銷售合約」。雖然venture有「投機活動」等意思，但是在這裡是「冒險的嘗試（行動）」之意，其中以(D)的effort意思最接近。就算不知道venture的意思，也可以嘗試選擇符合worthwhile（值得的）這個單字的答案。

☑ 190

What is true about the people in Ms. Walters' group?

(A) They are members of the press.
(B) They have already registered online.
(C) They are all veteran employees.
(D) They may receive a discount.

關於華特斯小姐的小組人員，下列何者正確？

(A) 他們是媒體成員。
(B) 他們已線上登錄。
(C) 他們都是老經驗的員工。
(D) 他們可能會得到折扣。

答案 (D)　何者正確類型

從表格中看到If yes, number in group: 4 可知華特斯女士打算以4人小組參加，但根據電子郵件所述，因為追加了2人，所以合計6人參加。接著再看手冊，一個人費用是175歐元，5人（含）以上是每人125歐元，所以5人以上的每位參加費用比較便宜。(D)將這樣的情形用「折扣」來表達，所以是正確答案。至於(A)是錯在從表格的參加身分可看到是勾選Business professional（商務專業人士）而不是Member of the press（媒體成員）。(B)是錯在小組要追加的2位尚未申請登錄。另外，電子郵件提到追加的2位新人They are new to the firm, but are eager, young salespeople，所以(C)也是錯的。

| 試題文章 | 試題文章翻譯 |

Questions 191-195 refer to the following Web article, e-mail and text message.

試題191-195請參考以下網路文章、電子郵件及文字通訊。

Managerial Nuggets
"Getting the Best from Workers of All Ages"

Good performance is not an age-related outcome. Whether you're a novice fresh out of school or a veteran worker who learned it all on the job, attitude, aptitude, skills, and knowledge all count. A flexible team with a range of ages and a workplace culture that encourages cooperation means more efficiency and better productivity for everyone.

Efficient managers recognize the value of a workforce with diverse ages. For example, a young worker who is familiar with technology but lacks interpersonal skills and an older staff member who is good with people but lacks confidence with computers might make an excellent team.

Or, for example, offering older staff the opportunity to update their skills goes hand in hand with giving them chances to mentor younger workers. Technology changes, but learning how to communicate effectively comes with experience. Reduced or flexible schedules, meanwhile, can benefit all age groups.

Keeping yourself aware of the things different people have to offer can help you bring out the best in your workers.

管理金言（Managerial Nuggets）
「激發所有年齡層員工的潛能」

良好的表現無關年齡。無論是剛畢業的社會新鮮人或是已有工作經驗的老手，態度、天賦、技能及知識才是最重要的。一個由廣泛年齡層和鼓勵合作的職場文化組成的靈活團隊，對每個人而言，這意味著更有效率以及更高的生產力。

有能力的管理者了解不同年齡團隊的勞動效益。例如，一位熟悉科技但缺乏人際關係能力的年輕人，和一位擅長與人相處但對電腦缺乏自信的年長工作人員，或許能成為一支優秀的團隊。

或者，例如，為年長的員工提供更新技能的機會，並同時讓他們有機會指導年輕的員工。科技會改變，但如何有效溝通靠的是經驗。同時，減少或有彈性的工時可以讓所有年齡層受益。

隨時注意不同人所能貢獻的，會幫助你激發員工的潛能。

---

* E-mail *

From:	Annabel Kline <akline@di.co.ie>
To:	John Bauermeyer <jbauermeyer@di.co.ie>
Subject:	Mary Sanders
Date:	13 September, 10:15

John,

Have you seen the article on the Managerial Nuggets Web site? I immediately thought of what to do with Mary's sudden request to drop to half time starting next week.

Agreed, we can't always meet these requests. However, that article got me thinking. She's got such a way with people.

How about giving her a mentoring role during mornings, Mon-Fri? Kareem and Falik are both starting part-time mornings next week and could definitely use her guidance and expertise. Do you have time today to discuss this? I'm available in the morning, but will have a meeting after lunch, until 5:00. I'll be available again after that.

Regards,

Annie

發信者：安娜貝爾・克萊恩（Annabel Kline）
〈akline@di.co.ie〉
收信者：約翰・波爾梅爾（John Bauermeyer）
〈jbauermeyer@di.co.ie〉
主旨：瑪莉・桑德斯（Mary Sanders）
日期：9月13日10:15

約翰：

你看過管理金言網站的文章了嗎？我立刻想到，要如何處理瑪莉下週開始要減少一半工時的突然要求了。

我同意我們不能總是滿足這些要求。然而，那篇文章讓我思考。她對人是有那麼一套。

週一到週五早上時段讓她當一個職場導師的角色如何？卡里姆（Kareem）和法理克（Falik）2人都在下週開始早上兼職，肯定可以用得到她的指導和專業知識。你今天有時間討論這個問題嗎？我早上都有空，但午餐後有到5點的會議。之後就又有空了。

此致

安妮（Annie）

From: John Bauermeyer
Received: 13 September,
10:24 A.M.
To: Annabel Kline

Annabel,
Good idea, but actually
I've got more space on
other shifts. Could Ms.
Sanders do the P.M. shift
Mon-Fri? If so, I could
move the two new guys
there, too. Could you ask,
and then text me back? I'm
out of the office now and
will be back around 11:30.
Let's talk in person after
your meeting. Thanks!

發送者：約翰・波爾梅爾
接收時間：9月13日10：24 A.M.
接收者：安娜貝爾・克萊恩

安娜貝爾：
好主意，但實際上在其他輪班有比較多空缺。桑德斯女士可以在週一至週五做下午輪班嗎？如果可行，我也可以將這2位新人移到那時段。妳可以問問，再回傳訊息給我嗎？我現在不在辦公室，會在11點半左右回來。我們就在妳開完會後見面談談吧！謝謝！

Vocabulary

- □ age-related [`edʒ rı`letıd] 形 與年齡有關的　　□ outcome [`aʊt͵kʌm] 名 結果　　□ novice [`nɑvıs] 名 新手　　□ attitude [`ætətjud] 名 態度
- □ aptitude [`æptə͵tjud] 名 天賦　　□ count [kaʊnt] 動 有價值　　□ a range of~ 範圍廣泛的　　□ efficiency [ı`fıʃənsı] 名 效率
- □ productivity [͵prodʌk`tıvıtı] 名 生產力　　□ efficient [ı`fıʃənt] 形 有能力的　　□ workforce [`wɝkfors] 名 全體員工
- □ diverse [daı`vɝs] 形 多樣的、不同的　　□ lack [læk] 動 缺少~　　□ interpersonal [͵ıntɚ`pɝsən!] 人際關係的
- □ go hand in hand with~ 與~密切相關　　□ mentor [`mɛntɚ] 動 指導~　　□ meanwhile [`min͵hwaıl] 副 同時
- □ bring out~ 帶出~　　□ think of~ 腦中突然想到~　　□ drop to~ 下降至~　　□ agreed [ə`grid] 形 同意的
- □ have [have got] a way with~ 擅於和~打交道　　□ guidance [`gaıdns] 名 指導　　□ talk in person 親自見面談話

試題	試題翻譯	解答與解析

☑ **191**

What does the Web article say about age and employees?

(A) Different age groups can complement each other.
(B) Older workers excel at efficiency.
(C) Younger workers are more skillful.
(D) Maintaining distinct age groups is beneficial.

網路文章對年齡和員工有什麼評論？

(A) 不同年齡層彼此可以互補。
(B) 年長員工效率優。
(C) 年輕員工較熟練技巧。
(D) 維持有區別的年齡層是有利的。

答案 (A) 〔何者正確類型〕

這題說的age and employees（年齡和員工）即是網站文章的主題。從一開始大略看一下可知，第1段在描述成效和年齡沒有關係，第2段則指出有能力的管理者了解包含廣泛年齡層的人才價值之後，提到a young worker who... and an older staff member who is... might make an excellent team。因此(A)是正確答案。(A)的different（不同的）和文中提到的diverse（多樣的、不同的）是同樣意思。

☑ **192**

What is the purpose of the e-mail?

(A) To register a complaint
(B) To advocate hiring employees
(C) To propose adding staff
(D) To suggest granting a request

這封電子郵件的目的是什麼？

(A) 投訴
(B) 主張僱用員工
(C) 提議增加員工
(D) 建議答應一個要求

答案 (D) 〔概述〕

發信者在電子郵件一開始就提到，她看完文章想起了瑪莉‧桑德斯的要求。接著，後面再根據文章的內容提出問題的解決方案，所以(D)是正確答案。request（要求）指的就是第1段的Mary's sudden request to drop to half time starting next week。

☐ advocate [ˈædvə͵ket] 動 支持（主張）～

☑ **193**

In the e-mail, the word "meet" in paragraph 2, line 1, is closest in meaning to

(A) gather
(B) satisfy
(C) get to know
(D) suffer from

在電子郵件中，第2段第1行單字「meet」的意思最接近下列哪一個？

(A) 聚集
(B) 滿足 （要求等）
(C) 與～相識
(D) 遭受～

答案 (B) 〔同義詞〕

meet有各種不同的意思，這句的requests是受詞，所以meet是「滿足、因應（要求）等」的意思。與satisfy和fulfill同樣意思。雖然meet都有(A)、(C)、(D)的意思，但是它們都不適合放在這一句。

☑ **194**

How does Mr. Bauermeyer respond to Ms. Kline's suggestion?

(A) He agrees to her proposal.
(B) He offers an alternative.
(C) He denies her request.
(D) He asks that she reconsider.

波爾梅爾先生如何回應克萊恩女士的建議？

(A) 他同意她的提議。
(B) 他提供了一個替代方案。
(C) 他拒絕她的要求。
(D) 他要求她重新考慮。

答案 (B) 〔其他細節〕

請參考波爾梅爾先生傳給克萊恩女士的文字通訊內容。對於克萊恩女士建議讓瑪莉在上午的輪班做指導工作，波爾梅爾先生雖然一開始就說Good idea（好主意），不過在but後面隨即提出下午的輪班。(B)將該情況用alternative（替代方案）來表達，所以是正確答案。

☑ **195**

When will Ms. Kline and Mr. Bauermeyer have a meeting?

(A) Later this morning
(B) Over lunch
(C) Late this afternoon
(D) Tomorrow morning

克萊恩女士和波爾梅爾先生什麼時候開會？

(A) 今天早上晚些時候
(B) 在吃午餐的時候
(C) 下午晚些時候
(D) 明天早上

答案 (C) 〔其他細節〕

波爾梅爾先生在文字通訊的最後說Let's talk in person after your meeting.。而your meeting（你的會議）是何時呢？從克萊恩電子郵件最後的部分可知，會議是當天午餐後到下午5時。表示2人見面是在當天5點以後，因此(C)是正確答案。(B)的over在這裡不是「超過～」，而是「同時做～」的意思。

Questions 196-200 refer to the following e-mails and online form.

* E-mail *	✕
From:	rstevens@coolmail.com
To:	customer.care@homeworld.com
Date:	25 October
Subject:	Online order A-2625

Dear Customer Care Center,

Last week I ordered a set of shelves. The box it arrived in seemed undamaged, but when I opened it, I noticed that one of the shelves was broken in two. I have attached to this e-mail several pictures of the shelves and the box it arrived in.

I have ordered a number of items from your online site in the past with absolutely no incident. Rather than a refund, I would simply like to have new shelves. A prompt response would be appreciated.

Thank you,

Rachael Stevens

* E-mail *	✕
From:	customer.care@homeworld.com
To:	rstevens@coolmail.com
Date:	26 October
Subject:	Re: Online order A-2625

Dear Ms. Stevens,

We have received your correspondence regarding Order No. A-2625—damaged item. We wish to express our sincerest apologies, and will most gladly honor your request. Further, we will have the deliverers set up the shelves for you in your home, and remove the damaged item, all free of charge.

You may either call our Customer Care Center toll-free at 1-800-555-4821 between 9:00 A.M. and 5:00 P.M. Mon-Fri to schedule delivery, or you may use our online site 24 hours a day, 7 days a week. Just enter SHLF2045DMG in the item field.

Once again, we apologize for the inconvenience.

Sincerely,

Ron Wallace
Manager, Homeworld Customer Care Center

發信者：rstevens@coolmail.com
收信者：customer.care@homeworld.com
日期：10月25日
主旨：線上訂購A-2625

親愛的客服中心：

上週我訂了一組書架，外盒送達時似乎沒有損壞，但是當我打開它時，我注意到其中一個書架變成兩半了。我在這封電子郵件附上了幾張書架以及外盒送達時的照片。

過去我從你們的線上網站訂購了一些品項，完全沒有發生任何事。我不是要退款，只希望有新的書架而已。若迅速回應將不勝感激。

謝謝，

瑞秋・史蒂文森（Rachael Stevens）

發信者：customer.care@homeworld.com
收信者：rstevens@coolmail.com
日期：10月26日
主旨：回覆：線上訂購A-2625

親愛的史蒂文森女士：

我們已收到您有關訂單編號A-2625損壞品項的信件。我們希望表達最誠摯的歉意，並且非常樂意兌現您的要求。而且，我們會讓送貨人員在您家中為您組裝書架，並搬走損壞的品項，完全免費。

您可以在每週一到週五上午9時至下午5時之間撥打我們的客服中心免費電話1-800-555-4821安排送貨。或者您可以使用我們每週7天，每天24小時開放的線上網站。只需在品項欄位輸入SHLF2045DMG即可。

再次對給您造成的不便深表歉意。

謹致問候
羅恩・華勒斯（Ron Wallace）
家庭世界（Homeworld）客服中心經理

試題文章	試題文章翻譯

			✕

✤ Order Form ✤

Name:	Stevens, Rachael
Date:	Sat. 26 October, 5:54 P.M.
Order No.	3712-C

Item(s)	Item No.	Price
Wood Bookshelf	SHLF2045DMG	$ 0.00
Floor Lamp	LMP3309	$ 26.99
Shipping		$ 0.00
ORDER TOTAL		$ 26.99*

Payment	Credit Card
Preferred Delivery Date	Mon. 28 October
Preferred Delivery Time	2:00~5:00 P.M.

*Over $25.00 Free shipping!

＊訂購表格＊

姓名	史蒂文森，瑞秋（Stevens, Rachael）
日期	10月26日（週六）5:54 P.M.
訂購編號	3712-C

品項	品項編號	價格
木製書架	SHLF2045DMG	元
落地燈	LMP3309	26.99元
運費		元
訂購總金額		26.99元*
支付方式	信用卡	
希望送貨日	10月28日（週一）	
希望運送時間	2:00~5:00 P.M.	

＊超過25元免運費！

Vocabulary

☐ undamaged [ʌnˋdæmɪdʒd] 形 未損壞的   ☐ break~ in two ～折（裂）成兩半   ☐ with no~ 沒有～

☐ absolutely [ˋæbsəˌlutlɪ] 副 完全地、絕對地   ☐ incident [ˋɪnsədnt] 名 （附隨的）事件、插曲   ☐ rather than~ 而不是～

☐ prompt [prɑmpt] 形 迅速的   ☐ correspondence [ˌkɔrəˋspɑndəns] 名 通信、信件   ☐ sincere [sɪnˋsɪr] 形 衷心的

☐ apology [əˋpɑlədʒɪ] 名 道歉   ☐ further [ˋfɝðɚ] 副 而且   ☐ 〈have someone＋原形動詞〉 讓（人）做～

☐ remove [rɪˋmuv] 動 搬走～   ☐ free of charge 免費   ☐ enter [ˋɛntɚ] 動 輸入～

☐ field [fild] 名 （電腦）欄、欄位   ☐ preferred [prɪˋfɝd] 形 更喜歡的

試題	試題翻譯	解答與解析

☑ 196

What does Ms. Stevens say about online ordering?

(A) She cannot access the online order form.
(B) She experienced problems in the past.
(C) She prefers to order online.
(D) She has ordered online before.

關於線上訂購,史蒂文森女士說了什麼?

(A) 她無法進入線上訂購表格。
(B) 她過去曾遇到問題。
(C) 她偏好線上訂購。
(D) 她之前在線上訂購過。

答案 (D)　[何者正確類型]

從第1封電子郵件第2段的I have ordered a number of items from your online site in the past with absolutely no incident.可知,史蒂文森女士之前在線上網站訂購過。因此(D)是正確答案。(B)和這句說的with absolutely no incident(完全沒有發生任何事件)完全不符。

☑ 197

In the first e-mail, the word "incident" in paragraph 2, line 1, is closest in meaning to

(A) penalty
(B) access
(C) trouble
(D) opportunity

在第 1 封電子郵件中,第 2 段第 1 行單字「incident」 意思最接近下列哪一個?

(A) 處罰
(B) 入口
(C) 麻煩
(D) 機會

答案 (C)　[同義詞]

這一行第1句到past為止的意思是「之前在線上網站訂購過」,with接續後面,是指「~的狀態」。absolutely意為「完全地、絕對地」,用強調的語氣來修飾後面的no。我之前在線上網站訂購過卻完全沒有什麼呢?從這句話去思考,就知道(C)的trouble(麻煩)是符合整句意思的。incident是指「(附隨的)事件、插曲」,是比accident(意外)更小的事件。

☑ 198

What is the purpose of the second e-mail?

(A) To agree to an item replacement
(B) To confirm a delivery time
(C) To explain an online order form
(D) To promote a sale item

第 2 封電子郵件的目的是什麼?

(A) 同意更換物品
(B) 確認送貨時間
(C) 解釋線上訂購表格
(D) 宣傳促銷品

答案 (A)　[概述]

第1段的We wish..., and will most gladly honor your request.意思是客服中心會依客戶的要求處理。因此,從客戶寫的第1封電子郵件可以看到,第2段最後的I would simply like to have new shelves,表示只想用新的書架來交換破損的書架,所以(A)是正確答案。

☑ 199

What does Mr. Wallace NOT offer to do?

(A) Send Ms. Stevens a new item
(B) Provide a discount coupon
(C) Pick up the damaged item
(D) Set up the new item

華勒斯先生沒有要提供什麼服務?

(A) 送新的物品給史蒂文森女士
(B) 提供折扣券
(C) 取回損壞的物品
(D) 組合新品

答案 (B)　[是非題類型]

請參考第2封電子郵件的第1段來了解華勒斯先生提供了什麼。(A)符合了We wish... will most gladly honor your request.的說法。史蒂文森女士的要求就是用新的來換掉破損的。(B)的說法雖然是有可能,但是這篇郵件並沒有提到,所以是正確答案。至於(C)和(D)都是符合Further, we will have...這句的內容。

☑ 200

What is suggested on the form?

(A) Ms. Stevens has entered incorrect information.
(B) The items will be delivered on October 26.
(C) The shipping charge will be refunded.
(D) Ms. Stevens ordered an additional item.

表格上有什麼資訊?

(A) 史蒂文森女士輸入錯誤的資料。
(B) 10 月 26 日會遞送那些品項。
(C) 將會退還運費。
(D) 史蒂文森女士訂購了額外的商品。

答案 (D)　[何者正確類型]

線上表格(第3篇)是史蒂文森女士接受第2封電子郵件的指示所輸入的。雖然免費換新的書架是Wood Bookshelf(木製書架),但是在下一欄位可看到26.99元的Floor Lamp(落地燈)資料。可想而知是史蒂文森女士訂購額外的商品,因此正確答案是(D)。而希望送貨日是Preferred Delivery Date Mon. 28 October,所以(B)是錯的。

預測成績換算表

各位在完成模擬試題作答後，可參考下表，將答對題數換算為分數，試著算出預測成績吧！
這張表和 TOEIC 實際測驗的計算方式不同，所以請把它當作推算目前實力的一種標準即可。

TEST 1~3 模擬試題

聽力（Listening）

答對題數	預測分數	答對題數	預測分數	答對題數	預測分數
100	495	69	390	38	235
99	495	68	385	37	230
98	495	67	380	36	225
97	495	66	375	35	220
96	495	65	370	34	215
95	490	64	365	33	210
94	490	63	360	32	205
93	485	62	355	31	200
92	485	61	350	30	195
91	480	60	345	29	190
90	480	59	340	28	185
89	475	58	335	27	180
88	475	57	330	26	175
87	470	56	325	25	170
86	470	55	320	24	165
85	465	54	315	23	160
84	460	53	310	22	155
83	460	52	305	21	150
82	455	51	300	20	145
81	450	50	295	19	140
80	445	49	290	18	135
79	440	48	285	17	130
78	435	47	280	16	125
77	430	46	275	15	120
76	425	45	270	14	115
75	420	44	265	13	110
74	415	43	260	12	105
73	410	42	255	11	100
72	405	41	250	～ 10	無法測量
71	400	40	245		
70	395	39	240		

閱讀（Reading）

答對題數	預測分數	答對題數	預測分數	答對題數	預測分數
100	495	69	375	38	220
99	495	68	370	37	215
98	490	67	365	36	210
97	490	66	360	35	205
96	490	65	355	34	200
95	485	64	350	33	195
94	485	63	345	32	190
93	485	62	340	31	185
92	480	61	335	30	180
91	480	60	330	29	175
90	475	59	325	28	170
89	475	58	320	27	165
88	470	57	315	26	160
87	465	56	310	25	155
86	460	55	305	24	150
85	455	54	300	23	145
84	450	53	295	22	140
83	445	52	290	21	135
82	440	51	285	20	130
81	435	50	280	19	125
80	430	49	275	18	120
79	425	48	270	17	115
78	420	47	265	16	110
77	415	46	260	15	105
76	410	45	255	14	100
75	405	44	250	～ 13	無法測量
74	400	43	245		
73	395	42	240		
72	390	41	235		
71	385	40	230		
70	380	39	225		

答對題數 ／分（聽力） ＋ 答對題數 ／分（閱讀） ＝ ／分（預測分數）

國家圖書館出版品預行編目資料

挑戰高分！新制多益NEW TOEIC擬真試題600問＋
超詳解 / 入江泉著; 葉紋芳譯
-- 初版 -- 臺北市：瑞蘭國際, 2018.12
400面；21×29.7公分 --（外語學習；54）
ISBN：978-986-96830-9-8（平裝附光碟片）
1. 多益測驗

805.1895   107018539

外語學習54

挑戰高分！新制多益NEW TOEIC擬真試題600問＋超詳解

監修｜宮野智靖
作者｜入江 泉
譯者｜葉紋芳
責任編輯｜林珊玉、鄧元婷、王愿琦
校對｜林珊玉、鄧元婷、王愿琦

封面設計、內文排版｜陳如琪
錄音室｜采漾錄音製作有限公司

董事長｜張暖彗・社長兼總編輯｜王愿琦
編輯部
副總編輯｜葉仲芸・副主編｜潘治婷・文字編輯｜林珊玉、鄧元婷・特約文字編輯｜楊嘉怡
設計部主任｜余佳憓・美術編輯｜陳如琪
業務部
副理｜楊米琪・組長｜林湲洵・專員｜張毓庭

法律顧問｜海灣國際法律事務所　呂錦峯律師

出版社｜瑞蘭國際有限公司・地址｜台北市大安區安和路一段104號7樓之一
電話｜(02)2700-4625・傳真｜(02)2700-4622
訂購專線｜(02)2700-4625・劃撥帳號｜19914152 瑞蘭國際有限公司
瑞蘭國際網路書城｜www.genki-japan.com.tw

總經銷｜聯合發行股份有限公司・電話｜(02)2917-8022、2917-8042
傳真｜(02)2915-6275、2915-7212・印刷｜科億印刷股份有限公司
出版日期｜2018年12月初版1刷・定價｜650元・ISBN｜978-986-96830-9-8

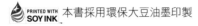